THE TRIBULATIONS OF POOR SAUL

Kevin Shannon

Surrogate Press®

Published in the United States by

Surrogate Press®

an imprint of Faceted Press®

Surrogate Press, LLC

SurrogatePress.com

ISBN: 978-1-947459-16-8

Library of Congress Control Number: 2018942058

Book cover art by: Michelle Rayner, Cosmic Design

Interior design by: Katie Mullaly, Surrogate Press®

Dedicated to my mother and father.
To Carolyn, my love.

And to all authors and readers
who share my love of words.

WHAT PEOPLE ARE SAYING

Kevin Shannon's debut novel takes us on a Machiavellian trek through a dystopian society. We follow ordinary citizen, Saul, as he examines the complexities of life that challenge one's virility, until he finds a spiritual sense of self in a metaphorical avalanche of adventure. Spend some time exploring *The Tribulations of Poor Saul*; you will emerge enlightened. The characters are complex, the vocabulary is prodigious, and the plot stays with you long after you have read the last page.

Katharine Goodman, President of the Red Butte Bards

The Tribulations of Poor Saul is an emotionally taut journey through the twisted recesses of a company man's mind when it breaks. Author Kevin Shannon paints a dark tale with lyrical mastery of his prose.

C.H. Hung, contributing author to
Undercurrents: An Anthology of What Lies Beneath

Few novelists can seduce the reader as well as Kevin Shannon's lush, lyrical prose, and at the same time aim an arrow into our darkest emotions. *The Tribulations of Poor Saul* sets us up with a meek little man who ventures into a side he didn't know he had. The story pulled me from one page to the next page.

*Jef Huntsman, Writer of the Year 2017, League of Utah Writers and author
of the books* Jamaica Rush, Heart Attack, Yak, Yak and Tattered Portrait

THE TRIBULATIONS OF POOR SAUL

Deus me dedit solum toti Mundo,
et totum Mundum mihi soli.

God gave me alone to all the World,
and all the World to me alone.

SENECA

CHAPTER ONE

The welcome early season storm had cleansed the City of its fug of contaminants, and had then continued to drop a heavy load of tainted snow on the alps of Tohu, a fair few miles to the west. Normally, pollution masked the citizens' view of the mountain range, known as *Tohu Va Vohu*, behind a choking curtain, but on this unusual day the peaks stood out clear in the crisp air, and the east facing off-white splendor was blushed with morning alpenglow. For the people, it was a rare glimpse of the heights named for the Hebrew for 'waste and void,' which referred to the world before God created light and sound. The phrase was from the first chapter of the first book of the *Bible* that the enervated public took as their founding document. Tohu was a sight for longing eyes, a tantalizing glimpse of the beyond.

The mountain road that crossed the saddle of the main crest was plowed by giant blade-nosed trucks of grit and gravel, and, eventually, the first vehicles gingerly followed, crawling up and over the pass. But, the snow had fallen on a weak facet of rime that could not hold the unstable drifted weight and an avalanche, triggered by God-knows-what, broke off the pack and billowed down from the highest slopes in a blizzard cascade that carried everything in its path.

A school bus was in the way, with its cargo of children accompanied by their chaperone teachers and an older lady, a caretaker dressed in peasant garb, who was unlucky enough to have been granted a hitched ride down to her cottage in the Upper

Downlands. Her ill luck, which she thought was fortune, was knowing the cursed driver. Her name was Edna and she had just buried her brother.

Large pines were broken like matchsticks before them, and the bus was smashed as a toy by a sledge-hammer. It was pushed so far off the asphalt that it took a full day to locate it in the debris field that stretched for the size of a City block. The death toll was total.

In the City, a few days later, when the people heard of the tragedy, they knew 'for whom' they should pray, but a good many decided that they did not know 'to whom.' This last thought assailed Saul as he made his way to his dreaded appointment.

He breathed deeply the rinsed air of the street as he stepped off the City bus. He had spent a dire journey in the proletarian crush, trying not to inhale the close odor of his fellow citizens, the rain tapping impatiently on the roof. Having been forced to wait for an excruciating half-hour for the vehicle to appear outside his apartment, it had then unduly taken most of an hour to drop him off here, in the heart of the Bureaucratic District. At three grinding miles per hour, it would have been quicker, if wetter, to walk. Every stop seemed to involve a fuss, and every fuss, a stop. There was far more opinion and advice on bus-driving than was necessary. It was a good job he had foreseen the inevitable delay and given himself enough leeway. The Fathers expected punctuality, mainly because they could. The poorer classes were expected to wait, it was part of their poverty. Saul could not afford to keep anyone waiting.

At this moment, though, Saul's uppermost worry was not the disappointment of public transportation, nor the irritation of the weather, nor the tragic accident on Tohu which no *deus ex machina* could fix. He was nervous about the summons he was answering, and its possible consequences. He was worried that he was just about to take a first reluctant step onto a slippery slope where he could easily lose traction. And his tie, his over-thought choice of tie, bothered him.

Saul had sighed at the lurid headline when he had first read it, and given a shrug of resignation, and impotence. He now had the 'AVALANCHE KILLS CHILDREN' newspaper rolled up and held in his armpit, and, as he was expelled by the compression of his fellow passengers from the city bus, he thrust it into the trash can at the bus stop outside the Security Building in a fit of pique. Bad things happen to good people, he knew, but he did not, for the life of him, know why. Good people are not always rewarded, and crime often pays. To an intelligent man, the lack of justice, and its fickleness when it did appear, made no sense. But, his place was not to question it, but to accede to the *status-quo*. Dissent was sacrilegious, heretical.

The rain that had stopped falling a full five minutes beforehand was still dripping from the roofs and the ledges above him. He looked up through the falling drops at the imposing edifice in front of him with a lugubrious shiver of cold foreboding. The Friday downpour had given a greasy aspect to the grey cement exterior of the Security Building and, then, the wind had blown apart the clouds, allowing the sunlight to give a brief sparkle sheen to the wall. With a shake of his lapels, Saul cleared the last droplets from his raincoat and then reached his hand out to touch the damp wall for reassurance. He would dearly have liked to keep the whole thing at arm's length, but now here he was. The moment had arrived and time was out of his hands. He had been bidden to attend the meeting with Father Timon, and this was not a polite invitation he could decline.

Saul sighed in gloom at the thought of the prospect of the interview. 'These things are sent to test us.' He pretended to welcome the opportunity to plead his case, but he could not convince himself of his own unimpeachable motives, and he thought he knew why. The reason lay buried within him, but not deeply. In fact, in a rushed shallow grave, where the ground was clearly turned, as though the soil were tilled. But, he was determined not to let his doubt undermine him. This was the path he would follow, meeting it head on, rather than his default which was delay and ineffectual worry. Prevarication had not been a costly strategy for him in his coming-up-for-many years, but he now needed to be in control, a master of his own destiny. 'Carpe diem,' he muttered, unconvincingly, into his chest, his self-directed pep-talks falling as flat as the puddles he stepped over.

He half-searched his conscience for a trace of guilt, for he did not really want to find any and was scared he might. Saul was beginning to doubt his innocence. He did have a tiny suspicion of why he had been called, and had therefore practiced his casual dismissals and relaxed explanations to deflect any accusations. 'No,' he told himself, 'not accusations, questions!' He had nothing to hide and would not let himself be compromised. But, out of caution, he might as well introduce his case correctly, in order that no mistakes be assumed. 'No, not his case, the facts!' He needed to get his story straight and tell it convincingly. How many had suffered due to a wrong word, an unprepared statement? He did not know, there was too much he did not know.

Saul had spent far more time than usual picking the red tie that morning, trying to give an impression of nonchalance. But, how do you choose something to give the impression you have not chosen it? He hoped the color would offset his natural floridity, but the limp thing hanging from his collar was not helping his mood. It was a poor choice, like so many others he had been reluctantly forced to make, that is if a forced choice can be called a choice. The darned tie that was supposed to impress was, stupidly, making him nervous. He pulled the knot tighter up under his Adam's apple, pretty sure, now, that it made him seem ridiculous.

Saul was not an unpleasant looking man, not unhandsome. Luckily, he was also a man accustomed to being appraised in double negatives. He had always struggled with his appearance, he never felt he looked average enough, but, even if you aspire to be ordinary, self-image can never be objective, it will let you down. He was by no means repulsive, people did not recoil from him nor treat him pitifully. No-one crossed the street to avoid him, but, still, he thought himself a bit of a leper, an outcast. It had not occurred to him that this may be of his own making, for it did not alter him, but it had recently started to irk. Until recently he had not been concerned with his own esteem, it was a self-indulgent concern. He had been happy to bury himself in the collective crowd of Society, but this summons was making him reassess. Perhaps he needed to start looking after his own needs. No-one else seemed to be helping him.

Saul, the dutiful, the rule-follower, who had never welcomed change, was, yet, no stranger to volatility. Every time he saw his reflection he thought he looked different, he could hardly recognize himself, from day to day. It was a changeling quality that belied his countenance. His distinguishing features, a thin, almost aristocratic, aquiline nose, a hang-dog expression in the eyes, the brows falling-down to his round cheekbones, all gave him a characteristic fey look.

And, yet, when he shaved, as he scrutinized his face in the mirror, all he saw was the depressed affect and pinched expression of a tired man staring back at him, asking him 'to get it over quickly.' He wondered if he were to bump into his *doppelganger* on the bus whether he would even recognize himself, or give up a seat to an elderly citizen. And if he did come across his double, he could just imagine himself being ignored, bypassed, snubbed. Such was his self-doubt.

Saul was an interesting-looking man, if that was not being damned by faint praise. But, in his mind's eye, he thought his appearance scrofulous, without knowing exactly what that meant, but it seemed to fit. He was wrong. But he was a haphazard character, diffident, even. Some people suppress their bad attributes, Saul hid his good ones. This did not come across as cloyingly humble, merely gentle, and modesty is attractive, if annoying. It would have shocked him to learn that he had an appeal, but that was, in turn, part of his appeal. He was kind, but liked to hide it as one would a weakness.

Now, he was carrying his uncertainty into the Security Department, the belly of the beast. The State was like the weather, as the joke went, in that everybody complains about it, but nobody does anything about it. The institutions stoic indifference to the everyday plight of the average citizen had resulted in various carping and sniping. The powerless always ridicule their leaders, it is the way of the world. Saul thought of most interactions with the authorities as cardboard adventures, but this time he was not complaining about a gas connection. This time felt larger and, as with his looks, the questions would not stop being asked.

Then, he realized, he was enjoying the strain of cynicism that he found growing through his conceptions like a cerebral tapeworm. His doubts made it easier to digest it all. To swallow the official line required something in the gut, a little sugar cube to make the medicine go down. And, if the State was the be-all-and-end-all, then it had better be perfect or, at least, trying. But, just by looking about, Saul could spot deficiencies. They did not even bother hiding their faults anymore, they just papered over the cracks.

Jonah had accepted living inside the whale as his lot in life, so, up to this point, Saul had assumed his own reality was the truth. His Leviathan was the all-encompassing State. It had raised him, and he had been spoon-fed its truths with his first slobbering mouthfuls of pap. The Government had nourished and kept him, and as a result, he felt thankful but trapped, useful yet compromised. Like all good humans, his nature was rebelling against his nurture.

In some hide-and-seek corner of his mind, Saul yearned for some un-bounding, a decoupling, a taste of freedom. Even though this, as he perceived it, was a curiosity not a compulsion. In fact, freedom was a concept not quite defined by the State and not discussed in polite conversation. An awkward topic of conversation, like toilets. It was an imagining of a different state-of-affairs, with all the concomitant pitfalls as warnings. An adult version of a "what if . . ." game. Imagine if everybody did as they pleased, what a fine mess that would be! Liberty was all around, propagandized, put into practice; freedom was more elusive, like trying to define a color with words. Much, much more than a lack of constraints. A different type of life.

Poor, put-upon Saul was a moderate man, a proudly reasonable member of the Society that had produced him, a willing supplicant. He knew where the power lay and he had gone along with the placating game that needed to be played. However, despite palpable strains in the body politic, the rules showed no signs of slack. They gave like a girdle hugging the distended belly of Society. These mechanisms had worked, so far, for most of the laity, and if enough believed, or were willing to go along, the whole apparatus would continue. The engine lumbered forward, fueled by each member's investment, but at the cost of individual dreams. The strains showed, and whale bones were being tested to their limits. More effort was being spent keeping the whole thing together than in forward progress.

Fissures formed, like crevasses in a glacier, and Saul was finding the cracks more interesting than the safe footholds. He was looking down when he leaped. There was something interesting in those gaps that opened up when the rules were bent or broken. Saul was becoming one of those dissidents he had been taught to blame for the ills of the whole. Still, he did not want to be that scapegoat. And, although he knew the necessity of seasonal pruning for a fruit tree, he hoped he was not to be the limb sacrificed for reaching too far. The Gadarene Swine were goaded over the cliff to kill the evil spirits within, he did not want to be part of that sounder.

As he approached the Security Building he felt a slight frisson, tinged with that familiar ingrained respect for the necessary function of the Department. It was still that rueful admixture within his heart. A middle-aged man whose crisis was an adolescent rebellion. He felt alternatively ridiculous and heroic. Saul's sad, blue eyes betrayed that conflict, the scary and familiar, as he came to the front steps, a short stone flight leading up to the platform that showcased the entrance. As he raised his head he felt an extra droop, a sag, of the face.

He took each step deliberately, giving any interruption as much time to occur as it may require, but nothing intervened. Then, he saw the bas-relief crucifix set in the building's facade, crying, dripping water from its grey bulk. 'There was nothing to fear,' he told himself. He was innocent, but he was not too sure who got to decide how guilty he was. The giant cross was a guillotine blade poised above his neck, a sword of Damocles tenuously dangling. He shivered.

Saul entered the building through the heavy oak doors that the uniformed doormen made no attempt to hold for him. He took off his bowler hat and shook a few drops onto the floor, then regretted doing so, feeling guilty about making the floor slippery. But water could ruin the felt of his hat, and as a fastidious man he naturally harbored his resources, he looked after his things. The guards gave him a sneering glance of condescension and he smiled back politely as he apologetically hurried to the reception desk. There was a malodorous humidity in the heated foyer which he could feel seeping into the wool of his suit. Sweat prickled in the small of his back.

The reception desk stood alone, an island on the marbled floor, manned by two young women attired in that intimidating functionary's uniform he was so used to coming up against. They did not acknowledge his approach, even as he tried to disguise his unease with a forced aplomb and a smile of greeting. 'So that is true to form,' he thought, which put his mind somewhat at ease. He stood none-too-eagerly in front of the desk, fingering the brim of his bowler.

The room was a good ten fathoms long, with the desk sitting like a barrier across the narrow width, allowing a fathom each side for those permitted to pass beyond. The walls above the marble wainscoting were a splattered plaster, the lights hanging from the high ceiling were fluorescent. It was a hard-surfaced echo chamber that demanded a library hush. There was that garish whisper of hushed tones spoken aside. It smelled musty.

The guards stood like bored statues in a museum, looking at each other without communicating. They must have been chosen because of their physical similarity, but their haughty disdain for all around them was probably part of their training. Beyond the desk, behind the receptionists who would not deign to receive, down the other end of the hall were a set of frosted glass doors and, in front, a few rows of leather benches with wooden arms. Around, and on, them a cluster of sheepish men stood or sat, holding their hats in their lowered hands with their heads slightly bowed. A fretting flock of interviewees. Saul had the feeling he would join them soon, and he summoned his humility, composed his look of abject piety.

Suddenly, a trio of black-coated, black-hatted and well-shod men strode in lockstep across the lobby. They were not hiding their presences and the syncopated clicks of their footfalls echoed through the atrium. They seemed to occupy more space than any other three men in that place. As they passed, the guards flinched into attention, but did not salute, nor acknowledge the passing. The guards just lost a little stoop.

A door, that Saul had not noticed before, opened surreptitiously in the side of the room. Doors are normally made of a different material to their surroundings, like frosted glass against marble, to announce themselves as doorways. This one was made of the same materials as the wall, in order to disguise its function as an entry. The milling people parted to accommodate the official party and a slight tinge of intimidation ruled. The door swallowed them up. Saul went to register.

He could not see what preoccupied the attention of the receptionists who ignored him with professional pride. The lip of the wooden counter was at his chest height and their seated gaze was directed down. Perhaps they were both reading the same copy of one of the Histories. Perhaps one of the ones he had worked on before he found his present position in the Distribution Department. 'Should I start a conversation?' There did not seem to be much to attract them so intently below the shelf of the desk. After a minute, the hefty one turned her lifeless blue-grey eyes to him, appraising his suitability for her time. He felt he could emit that slight cough he had been harboring while he waited.

"With whom do you have an appointment?" She raised her painted eyebrows and added, probably out of caution, "Sir."

"I have a ten o'clock Confession with Father Timon," he stated as businesslike and insouciant as he could. The atmosphere gave him a tickle in his throat.

She picked up the Bakelite hand-piece of a hidden telephone. It sat like a small dumb bell in her doughy grasp as she punched three numbers with a lacquered nail. The tumblers clicked the connection, or whatever the electronic equivalent was. She mumbled quickly into the mouthpiece and cradled it back with a practiced boredom.

"Please wait down there with the others until your name is called."

Her attention went back to whatever held it before and he was summarily dismissed from her world. He gave the top of her head a wry smile of understanding and walked around the desk glancing at her slyly from behind. He could see the newspaper unfolded open to a half-filled crossword and a further article, in greater detail, on the lives of the schoolchildren lost in the tragedy in Tohu.

He muttered "God bless," out of civility.

CHAPTER TWO

The metal studs on the soles of Saul's boots, nailed in post-factory to stop the soft rubber soles from wearing out too fast, clicked an advertisement of his presence too loudly. Having already splashed the floor with his injudicious dripping of rainwater, he did not want to doubly offend by scratching the beautiful surface, so he lifted his feet with each step. He tried to look as innocent and inconspicuous as he could while presenting an awkward raised gait like a cumbersome *piaffe*. The guards stared even more balefully across at him.

The sad cluster of other confessors obediently waited for a beckoning sign. Saul sidled up and joined the periphery of the gang, like a penguin joining the colony. Nodding and smiling ingratiatingly, he hoped he did not look as guilty as these others, they looked very shiftless. Under his breath he rehearsed his pleas and excuses, genuinely still believing in the aim of Society, in working for the Good of the Pontificate. He prayed it would not cost him too much if he were convicted. 'God, forbid! I had no idea . . . .'

On the back wall of the hall, double doors of frosted glass acted as a gateway to an inner sanctum. That must be where Father Timon awaited, like Solomon. It was a barrier Saul had no wish to penetrate, like Daniel at the mouth of the lion's den. He was not sure he could pass this test.

As the silent crowd waited, every now and then one door would open and a young girl, about the same age as his daughter, would exit and read a name from a clipboard out loud in a clearly enunciated yell. Rather unnecessary, thought Saul as her audience was already on tenterhooks. He searched his fellows for some sinful secret, as though the Jesuits had a percentage quota to fill, and if he could find the five guilty men, he would then be dismissed. They all looked pathetically penitent, a sure sign of culpability.

As to himself, Saul rehearsed, having been summoned, there was obviously some misunderstanding that needed clearing up. This was the sort of thing you laughed about over beers at some imaginary get-together in the uncertain future. The State had its faults, like any large enterprise it was, by definition, unwieldy and made mistakes, but in the end, it was a benign use of power, even if sometimes a bit heavy-handed. If you cannot trust the Government, you cannot trust anything. He was convincing himself into some confidence.

At ten o'clock, after a ten-minute wait, the fetching young secretary came out and shouted for all to hear.

"Brother Saul? Here to see Father Timon."

He raised himself up holding onto his hat with his coat draped over his arm, in true petitioner fashion. Saul was flattered with the punctuality, knowing he was not too important to be ignored, he felt it was respectful to one of the faithful not to be kept waiting. A few minutes of the Father's valuable time should be enough to put things right. In his mind he metaphorically slapped his hands together, right to left, left to right. Hope springs eternal. 'Make my explanations, apologize for wasting their valuable time, and get back into mainstream, hiding in the masses.'

Time was a negative commodity that, decades before, had replaced the ridiculousness of money. The shekels in circulation were just a useful lubricant, a means of economic exchange, not a sign of wealth. Status was wealth and status brought one to the front of the line. Saul was not rich enough to be late, he could not afford it, or rather, if he could afford it he would be considered well off. There was a subtlety in the nuance of money, of course there was, and worth, even in a society that superficially disparaged materialism. Saul knew his place and tried to keep his timing as impeccable as was possible with the impediments of inefficiency. He hurried toward to the door, prompt and flattered.

The coiffured secretary, who was not his daughter, held the door open for him with the back of a homemade heel and he entered the heart of the Security Building. After crossing what felt like a starting line, he waited for her to move ahead and then meekly followed her down a jaundiced corridor. He fell in step as she strode purposefully with her clipboard clutched to her shapely bosom. Her ample bottom filled out her skirt as if it were inflated and swayed metronomically as she strode on. Then he caught himself, this line of thought was not redeeming him, she was Esther's age and besides his own neck was on the line. 'Do not be distracted with other parts of the anatomy.'

She was also the same height as his daughter and Saul wondered what Esther was doing at that very moment. Probably sitting behind her phone exchange, balancing that heavy headset and using her primmest tone. Doing her job, hopefully. He had early on taught his daughter how to cope in this inflexible world, and he was proud of her willingness to bend to the demands of it. It was, to him, the best life lesson. If you cannot control the elements, then better to bend like a reed so as not to be broken. She fitted in seamlessly and kept her individuality to herself, 'the best place for it.' Esther would never be caught doing a crossword during work hours. There's a lot to be said for conventionality, when there is no other choice. There's a lot to be said for anything, and everything, when there is no alternative.

After about fifty fathoms of sallow passageway, Saul and his young companion arrived at one of the closed, identical numbered doors. They stopped and stood side by side in front of this gateway. Apart from the number it was as featureless as the twenty they had passed on the way. This calmed Saul's fraying nerves, he liked the uniformity, it was all very institutionally familiar to him. The secretary leaned forward and pulled the door open, Saul ushered himself in.

"Father Timon will be in to see you as soon as he is able," she said by rote, with a brief lift of the sides of her lips in a smile, a grimace that was not quite a sneer.

"Bless you, my dear."

Glad to get this thing started, he yet hoped that Father Timon would be a kindhearted soul. The odds were not good, he guessed. It was not a profession that attracted the most sympathetic of characters. Soft, sympathetic interrogators would not last long.

The pale fluorescent light scowled and glowered in a parched space. There was only a mean table, flanked by two metal chairs, which felt temporary. Saul draped his coat over the back of one of them and settled down on the other. He was an accomplished attendant and considered his imperturbable patience a virtue, he could out-wait a saint. His body became unobtrusive and he quieted his mind from a state of mild worry to a calm pessimism. It was a well versed, much relied-upon, meditative technique to deal with the bothersome nuisances of the outside world. Life was frustration and dealing with the annoyance was the key to maintaining a decent attitude, because the irritants were not going away.

After a composed quarter of an hour there was a knock on the door which suddenly burst open allowing The Father to enter at a brisk pace on an easy stride. The door must have been held for him, probably by a factotum acting as a doorman, as it shut dramatically behind him. That was worrisome. 'Why would Timon need a guard?'

Father Timon's woolen suit was tailored compactly over his limbs, accentuating his lithe figure. The tie he wore was standard issue, establishment blue. He carried a stack of files and folders that Saul hoped were a day's worth of cases and not just related to this confession. Surely, he was not worthy of that much official attention. The doubts somewhat unsettled his equilibrium. He was going off kilter. The room was stuffy and cramped, he was discomforted but did not want to loosen his own tie. He hoped the doorman had moved on, the thought of a guard standing outside the door filled Saul with dread. He wanted to dab at his forehead, but he only had his wrong tie.

Timon himself was a tall wiry man of indeterminate middle age and with a fine shaped head of thinning, mousey hair closely cut around a natural tonsure. His face was lean, and his sharp nose made him resemble a heron. His imperious stare was not snapped by any blink and gave the impression he was about to strike out of a studied stillness. It unnerved Saul who felt like prey, an oblivious fish going about his own business. But the Father flustered himself a bit, like a bird ruffles its feathers, as though he had suddenly remembered. Now, Father Timon had a harassed air as though his mind was occupied by more important issues, and the present was merely an intrusion.

Saul wondered whether to grace the Father with a token genuflection, as befitted the authority of his office, but decided that an awkward male curtsey, which it would inevitably become, would only embarrass the both of them. He sat glumly staring at his *provocateur*, 'is that the right word?' trying to exude deference.

Father Timon placed the pile of papers on the table, which immediately made it into a desk, and folded his frame to sit across from his uneasy interviewee. He looked at his adversary with a cold appraisal, and smiled a vapid greeting. His face did not seem comfortable with amicableness and slipped back into official mode. It was obviously an effort for him to smile, the facial muscles having to pull his mouth into a rictus as if by pulley. When his face relaxed a natural frown returned.

Father Timon took a pair of reading glasses from his top pocket and placed them on the end of his beak and then looked over them at Saul. The Father's voice was pitched very, very slightly higher than would be expected from his frame and gravitas, and it had a piping tone with just a shade of nasal resonance. Like a whine, an avian, petulant whine from a demanding bird.

"Good morning, my son, thank you for being on time."

"I just wish to sort this out quickly and get back to work." Saul barely restrained himself from blurting out a complete explanation of his indiscretions. "I do not know why I was required to attend. I can't think of anything I have done wrong that would warrant your valuable time. Is it about someone else, someone I know? Do you need information from me?" 'Shut up,' he scolded himself, all that composure lost! 'What is the point of rehearsal?'

At this point, in thrall to the authority of Father Timon, the hapless Saul was only too willing to aid the weeding out of any undesirable elements that were disrupting the March of Progress. But he decided it was probably not the time to voice this, later he would convince them that he was not an apostate. 'Calm yourself, you have nothing to hide, you just need to persuade them of it.' Saul needed to be told to relax.

"Relax, friend."

Did Father Timon's words aimed to soothe? He glanced down at the bundle of papers he had selected and pulled from a file. Timon seemed erudite.

"I just need to clarify a few points. It is early days, early days, and we need to investigate all angles of the situation. If you co-operate there is nothing to worry about. Just be honest with us and you will find us very fair. I am an agent of the Templars. This is out of the Jesuits hands now, so you know it is serious. I think you have some information that you need to share. We have had reports of another malcontent in our midst. There seems a never-ending stream of them. So, we need to do our jobs and determine how far this alleged, concerted undermining has gone, and where the perpetrators are hiding, and who else they have infected. Time is of the essence, a stitch in time saving nine, and all that. I'm sure you appreciate what we are doing, you seem like an upstanding citizen. We don't want a full-blown Heretic if we can avoid it, or if we can nip it in the bud." Father Timon spoke very slowly and deliberately, in a monotone, he did not wish to repeat himself. He looked up from the sheet and over his glasses, engaging Saul's full iris stare.

Saul relaxed his eyes, unconsciously, or rather, his eyes relaxed, but they did so because of the tide of relief he felt. There was an undetectable sigh at his not being the subject, or object, of the inquiry. He nodded agreeably to Father Timon and bit his tongue until he could learn more. Better play his cards close to his chest until he could see the game developing. He felt a little more in control, of himself, if not of the situation. Father Timon's voice was a high tenor and his speech well-modulated, calculated, soothing enough to make you want to not upset him.

"I have here a photograph I wish to show you. It was taken two weeks ago and shows you and this . . . ." He was going to add 'young,' but turning the photograph back in front of his own sight before doing so, he did not, ". . . lady in an embrace. Our sources place you at Vegetable Market One Four Five. We are interested in your crony. Partner? What can you tell us about her?"

Saul was slightly taken aback, not expecting this line of attack. Was it an attack, did he need to defend himself? Besides, 'she was young!' He felt his cornered heart race as he scanned his past conscience, and future consideration, for suitable answers. His mind convulsed with the acrobatic calculations of compromise. His guilty conscience had alleged him charged with thought crimes, just for being a doubting Thomas and asking awkward questions.

But this was different, this was much more precise, and he needed to scramble to catch up.

Saul had fallen in love, and broken off, with the 'young' lady in question, a matter of months before. The memory of their potent affair still lingered as an echo of a passion he had thought he would not feel again. He had locked most of the emotion into one of his mental compartments, but it was like getting a ferret into a cage, there was a struggle and not all the squirmy creature was contained. The feelings were still raw, the loss still hurt, the worse for being at his insistence. He had broken their collective heart in self-defense. 'Don't ask!' He still felt guilty. Saul nursed a melancholy protectiveness towards her and, narcissistically, towards his own infatuation. Was it love, or was it his love for his own feelings?

The photograph prompted a resurgence of that feeling, the ferret sensed an opening. It was not a prodding reminder, either, not a nudge, but a full welling. An empathy for a previous self, with its character-changing effect, its powerful toxic inundation. Not like a drug, for under the narcotic influence it is possible to re-emerge through a hangover. No, with lost love you are shattered forever. Even if the person is not forever, the feeling lasts. It was still alarming to Saul how damaging something so wonderful can be. Perhaps that was why he had recoiled from the relationship, had stopped seeing her. That power can be frightening.

Saul had loved before, he had adored his daughter's mother, and had lost her to God. He felt punished by that loss, vowing not to let it repeat. Now, he was more experienced, and one thing he had learned was that the hearts of old men do not break the way the hearts of young men do. The heart is born brittle, hard but fragile, it knows what it wants, it is obdurate, and it can turn its attention to another when it has lost. When hearts age they turn mushy, spongy, they do not snap, do not break, they conform. Saul's heart had enveloped and absorbed Leah's, and vice-versa, he had had his heart overtaken.

Leah was a quiet figure laboring inconspicuously in some distant corner of the Distribution Department, where Saul also worked. He had not noticed when she had started there, unsurprisingly, given the thousands of workers discreetly clocking in and out each day. When he did notice her, it was with admiration, because Leah had finessed a strategy of being unobtrusive without seeming shy and retiring. She was one of the legion, her light hidden under a bushel, doing a good job of doing enough. One of the drones in the hive, albeit one of the prettiest, he thought with pride. She was humble without being self-deprecating. But she had poise and bearing and, 'yes, you could tell,' conceit.

In fact, it was her self-possession that Saul first noticed, when he had sat next to her in one of those long drawn-out administrative meetings. That was the quality that first struck him about this demure new member of the Analysis Group. She was assured when called upon to justify some farm production budget numbers, without being arrogant about her grasp of the figures. Her argument against the asinine doubling of quotas, which would have just pushed the inevitable failure onto the farmers, was cleverly thought out and eloquently and persuasively presented. She handled the delicate matter with diplomacy, especially as it was countermanding her bosses. It made an impression on Saul, who appreciated political guile.

In this system, under whose yoke they labored, beating your own drum was never recommended. Unless, that is, you had time to waste and wanted that attention for your own personal advancement. And it was that deft quality of mind in Leah, to be able to defend her corner without deference, that piqued Saul's interest. She seemed self-contained, confident and unabashed. 'Pretty too, had he mentioned that?' But her demeanor was the enticing cover wrapping her beauty. But pretty did not describe the projection she threw, she was stately without being fusty, and handsome in a classical fashion.

He loved her auburn hair when it was tied up to reveal high cheekbones, and frame a delightful *retroussé* nose. Her round face, which carried its age with grace, gave her a deceptively elfin look. But, she was anything but a naive ingenue, she had a superior air that her speech and actions did not belie. Her compact body was completely without uncertainty, but wholly elegant. She was not selling anything, she was unaware of her appeal. Yet, Saul was already bidding up her worth, and he quickly ascertained that admiration was not what he was feeling, it was a lot more. The polished hazelwood eyes shone with an intelligence that she cloaked with quietude. Her skin radiated with that glow of ruddy health, a rare sight in this noxious City, and her clothes spoke of indifference to dress that was not a cultivated insouciance but a genuine bohemianism. She gave the impression of not caring and she did not care about that impression. This appealed to the writer in Saul as much as to the male. It was quite a meeting.

As with most truths, this had been decided in the fillip of one moment in Saul's imagination. It takes only a second to make up a mind, it is the genius of the human brain, but it also makes it the most fickle thing in the universe. It was not a reasoned position, Saul found himself occupying, it was an immediate reaction. You could call it a spark, a flick of chemical reaction.

Leah seemed to pay no heed to any individual in the Analyst group and Saul found even her disdain beguiling. He went to no great lengths to disguise his curiosity and buttonholed her after the meeting with a technical aside. He tried to parlay this follow up into a conversation, which was unlike him. However, Leah did not flirt coquettishly, as Saul would have hoped, but instead gave him her full stare and attention that he found a bit disconcerting, but not off-putting. She wore the perfect amount of cologne.

Saul identified where Leah worked within the Department, the floor, the section and the office and resolved to engineer an excuse to visit her. This he managed the next day and feigned relaxed recognition when he spied her. "Oh, hello. Fancy seeing you again." He asked her out that very night for a casual glass of wine and a garlic wafer. She accepted, but without alacrity, almost as though she would indulge him out of curiosity. He was not insulted. Her haughtiness was part of her charm.

After the first excitement had fueled his persistence so Saul could prove his worthiness by being the pursuer, they became an item. For three, or was it four, months they had seen each other three, or was it four, times a week. Both had been lonely, siblings of the all-encompassing State, alienated for their own good. Both cynical in a sarcastic fashion. Saul, at this point, more scornful of the life they had to live, compared to a more resigned Leah. They propped each other up and called it support. There was that adult giddiness that the promise of an unexpected new start holds out. A life lived in hope and desire, the immersion in another, the loss of self. Then, it was enough to be in the others' presence, next to them at a gallery, a restaurant. And always trying to touch the one within reach. Finding yourself not alone in the world. Then the beauty of the intimacy, the perfect ease of being with one you wish would judge you and find you perfect, even as you hope they love you enough not to judge. To accept and be accepted for who you are, in all your vulnerability. To love and be loved.

Then the doubt, the curse of doubt.

The relationship foundered on their reluctance to take the plunge into deeper waters. Saul was jaded, Leah was curiously secretive. When Saul knew he was in love he knew it had to end. It was a shame, for they were a worthy couple, and he had to admit they were a handsome pair, complementary and stimulating. He finished the emotional affair so that he knew when, and where, it would end. He had to kill it, so it could not kill him. But it did, in a sense, for part of him died. You cannot lose lifeblood and expect the flesh to survive. The gangrene of regret set in.

"I got that wrong," he thought, understatedly. He was looking at Leah's pinched, hurt features in the photograph. She did not look like an elf, the *moue* on her lips made her look supercilious, not playful. She looked like a deprived faun, doe-eyed and scared. The black and white grain did not do her justice as she looked down pensively, 'at the sidewalk?' Maybe what was wrong was that in a hive only the queen mates.

As Saul lingered, for just a little too long, over the photograph that Father Timon had placed in his hands he noticed that he had been wearing the same red tie. That little inward chuckle, that he could not but let loose, broke free as an ironic, exasperated sigh. Gazing at her likeness, he could not suppress a wan smile that Father Timon noted with professional acuity.

"Is there anything you wish to confess, my Son?"

"No, Father. Her name is Leah and she was a work colleague. I know a number of those ladies in that office, Sarah for one, Martha is another. They work on the second floor of the Produce Distribution Department and I have an office on the seventh. I think Leah handled the output of the Upper Downlands. Wheat, some sunflowers. There is some decent wine from the older label Monasteries. Nothing exciting. Or important." He added the last as a protection for her. "What has she done?" This was a distancing, protection for himself. He felt vaguely pleased at his gathering calm, or was it an emptiness?

"Well we have good information that she has been associating with radical groups. In particular with the New Men," then, pointedly added in a lower, more formal, darker tone, "who challenge the validity of everything we stand for." Father Timon glared a textbook glare, but it seemed an affectation, as though it had been practiced for dramatic impact.

"I have never heard of them," promised Saul. "What do they stand for?"

"The destruction of the Church as State. That is all we need to know. They want to deprive you of your freedom to work, to eat, to live in your apartment, to live your life."

"And replace it with what?"

"We don't need to get into details. Suffice it to say that they are a revolutionary group that wishes to destroy that which we have built, that which we hold dear. Have you heard of the Cygnet Committee?"

"No. I have not. Who are they?"

Saul had heard tell of some underground movements that threatened the stability of Society. It seemed a retrograde step, in the inevitable progress of Mankind, to overthrow the hard-won gains achieved so far. Better evolution than revolution was the slogan. But then again, if Leah was willing to associate with these reformists, given her probity and integrity, then perhaps he did not want to judge too precipitously. 'But maybe not here, this is not the place to be revisionist.' The Father was probably not the best person to ask, even if he was undoubtedly well versed in these ideas. Saul's interest was pricked, but then shelved.

"Well, I cannot be of much help." He informed Father Timon, "I only knew her in passing, and mostly professionally." He hoped the white lie held. But it hurt, and Saul wondered if Judas had hurt when he betrayed what he had loved.

"Our research shows you meeting with Leah on at least four occasions. You went to eat at a bistro in the Marmalade District at," here he consulted a typed sheet of paper from the open file, "Butter No Parsnips. Strange place for a romantic rendezvous."

"We went there a couple of times. There's no crime in eating with a friend, is there? They do a wonderful carrot and parsnip *soufflé*. If you are interested in that sort of thing."

"Maybe I will persuade the wife to accompany me there one day. What did you and Leah discuss over the *soufflé*?"

"Probably the *soufflé*. Many other things. The weather in Upper Downland. How irritating the busses are. Architecture. Literature."

"No talk of New Men? Dissident factions? Revolutionaries?" Father Timon was giving him an opportunity to throw in his lot with the authorities, to escape this interview. The dilemma confused Saul's sense for a moment. He wanted to help. Timon, Leah and himself, he wanted to help them all.

"She did talk of a group of friends who circulate some underground literature." As soon as this came out of his mouth he regretted speaking. He knew there was no retracting the moment, that he had opened a door he should have left closed. He had opened the door and then walked through . . . .

"Really?" Father Timon's trimmed eyebrows arched. "Please tell us the complete details." Saul noticed the use of 'us' and the dropping of 'me.' The forces were aligning against him, or 'them,' being Saul and Leah. He could not decide which. He knew this was a seminal point in the interview. Should he save his own skin at this point, or should he defend his innocence, given he had done nothing wrong, and leave Leah to her own devices? That was unthinkable, but it had flashed across his mind, even if only as a possibility, and that constitutes a thought. But that pull, that emotional tug, dragged his mind and it overwhelmed his instinct for self-preservation. It was not an even match, there was no need to weigh it on the scales, it was overwhelming. He could not let her go. My God, he thought, 'do I still love her?' The Father's eyebrows dropped, and his stare hardened from under his interrogatory brow as though he could read Saul's mind as it bargained with itself.

"I'm sorry. Maybe I misheard. She just mentioned something in passing and did not go into any detail. We laughed it off. Perhaps it was a juvenile joke. I can't remember too well. Yes, we were talking about pornography. Lover's stuff. You know the sort."

"I most definitely do not," rebuked his interrogator, "I would never indulge in anything that is illicit. I support the Laws and those who make them and those for whom they are made. If somebody mentioned that they knew of illegal actions being performed, I would report it. I think it is my duty to the general Good. I would hope others would too. Don't you?"

"Of course." Saul felt the heat of the stuffy room prickle his forehead. "It behooves us all to keep the machinery of State running as smoothly as possible. It's hard to see how a bit of titillating writing or a dirty picture would undermine the whole of culture. We are not talking about insurrection here."

"Well, it's the thin edge of the wedge, isn't it? Starts off with flagrantly flouting a minor law. Like eating chicken flesh out of curiosity, or desperation, and ends up with us back in a carnivore society. As disgusting as that sounds, that's the principle. If we give an inch then people take a mile, it is the sadness of the world. We try to look after everyone, give them work, feed and house them and they turn on you. Like ungrateful children, stabbing their parents to death for an inheritance."

"You remember inheritance, don't you, Citizen Saul? When people could pass their chattels down to their children. Before we decided that allowing it only encouraged greed, and that the selfish accumulation of goods was to the detriment of the bigger picture."

Saul nodded, recognizing a rant when he heard one.

"And so, you know," continued the good Father Timon, "that we banned the passing down of money and privilege as it became a symbol of family attachment that weakened the bonds that matter, of the individual to the State. And if someone, anyone, gets in the way of the Good of the people, then it is my job to dispose of that obstacle."

"I think we remove obstacles, not dispose of them," Saul regretted saying.

Father Timon leant forward in his chair, his length pivoting his head past the edge and into the neutral space of the table-top. The gesture menaced Saul, who quivered and retreated back an inch. Then the Father hammered the metal with the soft pudge at the bottom of his fist. The sudden noise worked, Saul retracted another inch.

"And dispose of it I will! You are in big, big trouble my produce-distributing friend if I find out that you have been colluding with obstructive elements. And if you have, you had better come clean and spill some of those beans you distribute. So, tell me, and think slowly here, did you, or did you not, collude with elements wishing to undermine me?"

"Look. I haven't seen her in a couple of months. It did not progress the way I had hoped."

"And what were you hoping for?"

"A bit of companionship with a pretty and intelligent female of the same age and class. I have been alone, living alone, I mean, for over twenty years. A little company is not too much to expect, is it?"

Timon sat back and eyed him scrupulously, up and down, and faintly shook his head, but in assent to the expectation. It was not too much to ask. Saul intuited that he had gained a little sympathy, not that it would last long or do him much good.

"Why this lady? It doesn't ring true. How do we know it is a genuine attraction and she is not trying to recruit you?"

"To what? You know from that," Saul slapped his hand down on the file, "that I'm a good reliable Church-going man. No perversions, no blemishes on my record. A true believer in the cause. It will be in your research. My Curriculum Vitae"

"It does suggest that. But maybe you have fallen off the train. Maybe her sweet nothings hid subliminal messages. Maybe you were blinded by your desires and her female wiles into going over to the dark side. This is a serious position you find yourself in, my dear Saul."

"No! I promise it is a coincidence. I was being foolish," Saul did not, in his heart of hearts, feel he had been foolish, "Kid's stuff. Mid-life crisis. One of the two."

Father Timon decided to institute some tactical silence, a trick straight from his playbook. He sat back in the chair and flicked, slowly but deliberately, through a sheaf of papers as though searching for a reference. Saul leaned forward with his elbows on the table and put his head in his hands. He was desperate for a way to convince his antagonist of his respectability. He had nothing. He felt hot and bothered, and claustrophobic, in the diminishing room.

A lifetime of flying under the radar had left him with no friends in high places, no backup, no strings to pull. The little seed of panic that had started to germinate in his psyche was ready to bloom in the heat. They can do anything and get away with it, they are the Law. The rumors of people involved with the forces of order were legion. A neighbor had simply disappeared. Moses was his name. How could someone with that name lose his way?

Moses had been in the apartment block for years before Saul and Ruth and baby Esther were transferred there, and he liked to let all and sundry share in his jaded outlook. He was the polar-opposite of spreading cheer, his misery craving company. Still, he was a harmless neighbor for all his curmudgeon, he and his wife were quiet and undemanding, but he drank, and, in his cups, he did like to loudly berate all the injustices that plagued him. One day, Saul found him staggering in the corridor outside their apartments, confused, as though he could not find his front door. Moses recognized Saul, who had no chance to avoid the uncomfortable meeting and, breathing his whisky breath over his neighbor, launched into a diatribe. He called out the staff at the Pension Department, the terrible bus drivers, the fact that raincoats were in short supply and the Templars for daring to confront him in the street, for he had the measure of the Jesuits. Saul made his excuses and left as two rather heavy and serious characters, walking side-by-side and taking up the width of the hallway which meant he had to back against the wall, stopped in front of the door he had just directed Moses to go through. There was a loud knock that stopped the shouting from inside Moses' apartment. Saul left, discretion being the better part of valor, and later heard that Moses had been hauled away. His wife, Zipporah, was tight-lipped and it was the time when Ruth had left the family home, with Esther in her arms, and Saul had never found out the consequences of Moses' *in vino veritas* philosophy. It was one of many unmentioned incidents where those who were loud and uncooperative were magicked away. It rankled Saul as he sat opposite Father Timon, who could order such an abduction with the stroke of a pen.

Saul was feeling guilty about looking nervous and *vice-versa*, the atmosphere tightened frighteningly. Saul pulled the noose of his tie down to loosen his collar. Timon's pate glowed faintly under the caged light above and he wiped it with a paisley patterned handkerchief, which Saul thought was an exotic touch for such a strait-laced man.

"There is nothing to explain," Saul had an imploring strain in his tone. "We were just friends. I might have been pushing for more, but she didn't respond. I got the cold shoulder."

"But you spent the night at her apartment. On the . . . ," Timon consulted his notes, "fourteenth, according to my sources. Did you, erh, share a bed? Did you have relations?"

"Well, yes. I did. We did. But just the once and I think it proved to us that it would not work."

"You were not compatible?"

"No. Yes. There was nothing wrong. We enjoyed each other's . . . company. But . . . ."

"You were looking for a stable relationship?"

"Not exactly. I had no expectations. I was not looking for . . . ."

"But you were looking for something. Was it a bit of excitement? Dabbling in a romantic revolution? Heroic overthrow of the oppressors? The fight for justice?"

"No. You can see that is not me. I have kept my nose clean all my life. Done what was expected of me. Followed the rules. You can't pin that sort of thing on me."

"I don't pin things on people. I flush out malcontents and bring them to justice. You seem to have a frivolous attitude to this line of enquiry. My view is that you have something to hide and I believe you need time to stew over your duties and report back to us. We now expect you to tell us about Leah's criminal activities. Can I rely upon you, Citizen? Will you do the right thing?" The tone had changed, but Father Timon did not need to shout. He had that seriousness of voice that showed he knew Saul was in his clutches.

With a theatrical flourish, Father Timon threw the top file closed. Rising suddenly from his chair in one swift move to his full height, he bent forward to pick up his papers. Pleased with his application of the technique, as recommended in the procedural manual, he looked down at Saul who was visibly shrinking and shirking in front of him. Father Timon the technician played the game as prescribed. He observed Saul sag as the weight of the world slowly lowered onto his tired shoulders.

There was a knock at the door and a guard was granted access. He was the same large, rough-hewn man that had escorted Father Timon before. He bent down behind the Father's back and whispered a communique of business into the open ear. Father Timon flinched and spoke one quiet word to the guard and then directed his attention back to Saul.

Father Timon was terse, "I have another confession I have to attend. We will meet again on Monday at the same time. Ten o'clock on the dot. You will tell me everything then. But, and I wish to make it very plain, this is my investigation. I know I am onto something and I do not want to lose the credit for finding your accomplice and her cell. Do not talk to anyone else, no matter their rank. I have done all the leg work on this and it is my baby, but I need results. If you cannot, or will not, lead me to her I will take it out on you. I will make you suffer. I know where you live. I know where you work. I know where your daughter works. Do I make myself clear? Do you understand me?"

"Yes, Father." Saul was bowed and relieved for the reprieve; for the chance to regroup.

Father Timon let the door slam shut as a part of his strident exit. Saul took three long breaths, picked up his coat and bowler and followed him into the empty corridor. He looked up and down and could see nobody. He was leaving under a cloud of suspicion and a threat of retaliation. It was hard to be an innocent man when the authorities wanted to find you guilty.

CHAPTER THREE

S aul had not slept well; his thoughts were un-parked traffic in his brain. His mind had not managed to idle and as his eyes opened it leapt straight to racing speed. Like a boulder that rolls slowly toward a cliff-edge and then plummets off. He met Saturday morning head on in a state of immediate agitation, a terrible buzzing feeling of free-fall.

Gnawing doubts made for uncomfortable bed fellows and, on waking, he found himself letting out groans of anguished frustration. Not the metaphoric ones, but true cries, out loud. Growls of impotence and anger that rattled in his throat like a chuckle forced through gritted teeth. Directed at himself, it was the plaintive grunt of a trapped animal, scared and alone, bewailing its fate, ready to gnaw its leg off.

Toward the end of the nervous evening he had tried to circumvent the inevitable insomnia with a dose of his favorite soporific. Although it was gulped down with a greedy thirst for the oblivion of sleep, the medicinal gin had not really helped, neither the first nor the third. And, now, in the grey morning light, he felt the dehydrating effect of a superficial hangover, and through a muzzy headache cursed his weaknesses. 'The worst of both worlds,' he thought, 'fear and hurt.'

The previous day, after being dismissed by the intimidating Father, Saul had dutifully returned to work in the Produce Distribution Department for the rump of the day. He needed the hubbub of his fellow workers to bring him back to a sense of normality. At his familiar, uncomfortable desk he had calmed himself with some breathing exercises. Sitting upright and imagining a turbulent sea with whitecaps under scudding clouds, the wind pushing waves onto a rocky cliff, Saul then relaxed the weather in his mind and calmed the storm until the sea was glassy and the sun shone over a peaceful scene. He was then the comforted sea and he sat back and reflected, oxygenated, on his predicament, he had regained his equilibrium. The workaday world focused in front of him, and he acknowledged his co-workers with a nonchalance that was his trademark. No-one asked him where he had been. He had missed nothing and had not been missed, apparently.

Saul was on the horns of a dilemma. But, he decided, as there were no alternative paths in front of him, his dilemma did not have two horns, it was just a fateful road stretching ahead. It was less of a bull, and more of a unicorn, of a dilemma, impaling him on his it's one option. He was on the horn of a *lemma,* if such a thing existed, speared like a mushroom on a *kabob.* Maybe a rhinoceros rather than a unicorn, there was nothing *fairy-tale-ish* about his predicament.

The disruptive Leah, 'disruptive?' no longer worked in the building. 'Thank God!' So there was no chance of an awkward encounter at work. If she had not disappeared so suddenly from his life those sadder four months ago, and there was a chance of seeing her at the office, he would have headed straight back to his prison cell of an apartment. Maybe, then, to ask Zipporah, who still lived next door to him, what were the charges leveled against Moses. In fact, 'Where was Moses?'

As it was, he accomplished nothing that Friday afternoon beyond proving a point with his presence and rearranging one of his piles of paper. It was an invidious choice to turn up, but he felt that any decision was devoid of benefit. There was no winning and no correct result, he would have welcomed a dilemma, at least it suggested choice. At home he would be tearing his hair out, yet it was pointless to be sitting here, slouching, on his hard, wooden executive chair, doodling on scraps of paper. The vague, immanent shadow of foreboding stole any chance of concentrating on his writing.

At least he was whiling away his time in public, and had added four hours to his monthly total. 'What was it now? Seventy out of the hundred and fifty?' He was behind, so he needed to bring up his attendance. Even if it meant four hours of unproductive tedium after the trauma of the morning. This was life carrying on, even if it was leaving poor Saul behind. He should have asked for a *carte blanche* at the desk on the way out.

He had held a steady position in the Produce Distribution Department for a long decade. Some two thousand days with his soft ass on this same chair. 'That was a lot of sitting.' During that time, he had kept his nose scrupulously clean, studiously avoiding both responsibility and promotion. He had adequately followed adequate instructions, and had made a concerted effort not to undermine the power structures that supported the, 'frankly,' ridiculous Pontificate. Even when, especially when, they were at their most obstreperous. Saul, generously, put their short-sighted behavior down to incompetence, not malice. But, the authorities were not reciprocating.

He felt victimized by those very forces that should be protecting him, as though his own parents had turned on him. Why was he being compromised? And, it is doubly humiliating when idiots make you feel idiotic. He was being treated like those free-riders the papers loved to write about. After all his compliance and cheerleading. He headed home with a mental gnashing and grinding of teeth, he could find no comfort, even by conjuring up, and calming, seascapes. His evening was desultory, his main accomplishment was delaying the opening of the gin bottle.

Lying there on the Saturday morning, Saul's gamut of emotions reflected their past twenty-four hours. They rode from fear to embarrassment to anger. It was exhausting, and frustrating. So, he pulled himself out of bed minutes after waking, into that shattered-feeling Saturday morning. His normal weekend routine involved indulging himself in an extra hour of lying-in, a warm prevarication in the enjoyment of boredom. Today, it was more tiring in bed than out.

Worry prodded him to the cold kitchen at an unaccustomed hour, which further irritated him. He wiped the condensation from the window above the inadequate sink and stared out into the pattering rain. His view of the Suburb District was obscured by the low clouds, but he knew by routine where the obstacles were situated. The rain drops did not lash the pane of glass as they had last night, but seemed to coalesce on the surface and roll down in tears. He could hardly see out.

Saul filled his kettle with the turbid water from his stiff faucet and lit the stove with a match that exploded a little greeting when it met the mephitic gas. Waiting for the boil, he sat at the plastic table and let his head rest in his hands, a repeat picture of the day before. Murmuring his disbelief over and over, he allowed a forlorn sob to escape. Saul had graduated from groans to sobs, it was an advance.

It was at times like these, alone and worried, that he, usually, mined his teachings for reassurance and motivation. Saul was a well-versed fount of self-help teachings, self-improvement mantras, positive thinking and boot-strapping. Normally, he would castigate his weaker self and then, miraculously, resolve to stop feeling sorry for himself. It was a form of tapping into the austerity of his Calvinistic childhood. Akin to his meditation procedure, which calmed him down, he could also whip himself back into shape.

Customarily, he prided himself on his self-containment and self-possession, and here he was demonstrating the very opposite. Here he was falling to pieces. This time he could feel that wistful sense of ineffectiveness welling up unopposed, like a feckless tide. It was not like him but custom does not always pull its own weight. Clenching his writer's fists, which were used to juggling ideas rather than hammering out conclusions, he made up his mind that he would turn it back, 'like King Cnut couldn't.' The task of making up a mind was overwhelming, but he would get to that later. Self-discipline had got him thus far in life and he was not going to fold at the first sign of stress. 'Hopefully.'

For Saul had worked diligently at achieving and maintaining the modicum of success he enjoyed. He had time to himself, though this morning was a waste, and spent his hours wisely on the betterment of his life. That meant the cultivation of his own internal realities, which gave him a sense of control over his own affairs. If one cannot change the outside world then one can change one's own perception of it. It was a strategy that had served humanity well in its worst days.

Further, Saul liked his job, his standing, the rung on the ladder to which he had climbed, and the respect it brought and, particularly, the small perks it afforded. Within the Department of Distribution Saul had staked out a territory, which he proudly protected, as a writer, a wordsmith, a likable stalwart. He liked working with the expression of ideas in words and the opportunity for mischief it allowed. It was an outlet for his more sardonic moods.

Reports, analyses, memoranda, recommendations, even brochures, Saul was tasked with supplying and arranging the words that conveyed the meaning in the information the Department produced. 'We are supposed to be the people of the Word,' he argued when defending the importance of his role in the grand scheme. 'In the beginning was the Word, and the Word was with God, and the Word was God.' It does not get more fundamental than that, both Word and God are capitalized. So, in the great traditions of bureaucracy, as practiced through millennia, Saul toiled at his typewriter, totting tallies and promulgating policy through the magic of language. Making sense of facts, interpreting and interpolating a constructed reality through a prism, 'a glass darkly.' It was a game of cat and mouse, bait and switch, with the truth whilst he was nurturing his own reality within. He was an accidental existentialist.

In his work, Saul's strength was to be able to put a message plainly, to explain, or, and this was his mainstay, use outmoded orotund grandiloquence to obfuscate. His bosses could take their pick, he could dress things up, or dress them down, to order. The truth was not a commodity, turnips were. Truth was malleable, it depended how you looked at it. His conscience did not balk at this deception, if that is what it was. He felt, anyway, that his work would not be read but filed away just in case some future researcher required some obscure *ex post facto* information. So, Saul spun figures into a web that connected some dots and trapped some flies, but generally just looked pretty. His dewy reports had such recondite titles as;

Riparian to Apiarian, The Marshing of Cross-Pollination and the Effect on Rice Production.

And;

Is Wheat Viable? The Efficiency of Monoculture versus the Dangers of Mass Extinction.

The meaninglessness of that last one particularly pleased him, the text itself holding no relevance to the alarm of the title, being a series of charts showing wheat harvests increasing, due to the eminently sensible use of industrial farming methods. If positivity was required, then downsides were not really part of the consideration. Why ruin a good argument with facts? These attitudes he was paid to assume were supposed to be upbeat, but he did like to have a touch of the dramatic in the headlines. Perhaps, he occasionally thought, he should have worked for a newspaper, writing about serious matters for serious readers. It sounded appealing to be illuminating the benighted masses, although deep down he knew he was ill-suited to endless incendiarism. His natural reticence would make him a poor reporter, and his learned compliance, nurtured in the State Nursery School System, would make him an unsure advocate in a truculent newsroom. He had found his comfort level, churning out vapid publications to the ether. Sending his work out into the great beyond like a child's balloon, 'both full of hot air.' He filled a gap in the mechanist pattern of the economy, and he managed it with a touch of subversive humor. 'And now?' The authorities had decided he could be used to squash some revolutionary gadflies, and they were willing to sacrifice him to achieve it. It was galling, 'That is what it was, galling!'

Saul's production of glib sentences were always checked by some anonymous supervisor for spelling and grammar, then skimmed for political cant and subjectivity. But the utility of his pieces never seemed to be questioned. So, it was somewhat of a game for him, to use his style to write as far away from the given topic as possible without incurring a rewrite. Or, *vice versa*, to title a piece with no reference to its contents so that he could boast of proving that you cannot judge a book by its cover. Of such small internal victories were his personal accomplishments measured. Plus, checking his work gave work to another, the checking of whose work employed another; *etcetera, ad infinitum*. Thus, the great Leviathan continued, swimming through the blind depths of cold oceans. Trawling for the tons of krill needed to keep it swimming. Each blind cell contributing to the higher function of organs, which in turn kept the whole moving, but, *quo vadis*? Heaven knew.

Somewhere, Saul figured, in the recesses of one of those anonymous great, grey warehouses by the Bus Station, there had to lie a burgeoning archive containing his documents. His life's work, 'or his work's life.' The expression of his craft, filed away and forgotten, gathering either dust or mold. If he typed with disappearing ink that dissolved in a month, no-one would be any the wiser, or worse off. There must be libraries of unwanted, untouched analyses out there. It was not as though the subjects were irrelevant, they were just too academic for the muddy business of farm production and distribution. The food industry dealt in terms of tons of turnips, not in calories per ounce, not in nutritional profiles. But the terrestrial God of science had to be appeased, and projections and statistical calculus had to be honored. He wished he would be told to write an article about paper waste in the running of a command economy; his irony would be fully unleashed. 'That would be satisfying.'

So, his job seemed a worthwhile waste of time, but, being a man who cultivated comfort, he enjoyed the plenty of time on his hands, even if he frittered it away. And he was recompensed at a rate sufficient to survive, in this world of enough. He was rich in time, he could spend hours like some of the Clerics spend Shekels. And, to his self-acknowledged credit, he did contribute to the collective, by doing as he was told. He was not along for the ride. Which, he was also told, was a virtue. Anyway, better to write about turnips than try his hand at something truly wasteful, like fiction, although sometimes his fingers twitched over his typewriter keyboard at the thought of Literature, 'with a capital L.' Words put to a higher use, not Church polemics, nor philippics, nor homilies, nor encomiums, nor jeremiads, nor anything propagandistic; but poetry, of which there was little; insufficient to speak to an unruly heart.

Saul was a bibliophile and a collector, or rather a hoarder, of any books he could lay his hands on. His meager shelves contained all the works he could acquire by the sad genius of Gerard Manley Hopkins, those blessed by the Pontificate. Those small pieces were reminders of gems, of gold nuggets in the silt of mountain streams, pearls in the ugly rock carapaces of oysters.

"Glory be to God for dappled things . . ."

or,

"Thou hast bound bones and veins

In me, fastened me flesh . . . ."

These lines were Saul's internal refrains, the aspiration of which he kept alive. The inspiration of which kept him alive. Like a small flame within, a token of the light, whilst his outward appearance was all serious dullness. Instead of fueling this spark, he dutifully fulfilled his undemanding quota of words, as directed, and tried to play with the smokescreen of jargon, and to be witty without being funny, in his production of bumpf.

"To seem the stranger lies my lot, my life

Among strangers . . . ."

The kettle boiled, and its whistle pulled Saul back to his reality, or the intrusion of the world upon his reality. He made his tea in the small metal teapot, another of one of the grim objects that hung around to remind him of his grounded-ness. He turned on his radio and listened to the official news, as was his custom on any given morning. The avalanche on Tohu still occupied the airwaves. There was, of course, no mention of insurrection or revolution, as he knew there would not be. Still, he felt slightly disappointed, as though it would have confirmed his distress. He was more realistic than this, he reminded himself, but the normality was a comfort to him, the familiar voice crackling out from the tinny radio speaker. The tawny color of his tea. One side of him wanted the security of the banality of life, but there was another that was growing, that craved the excitement of creative destruction, whatever that might be.

A sudden rap of knuckles on his plywood front door made him jump to his feet. He did not know the knuckles were arthritic, but he could tell they hit judiciously softly. The noise was a shock, since he did not receive any visitors to his apartment, preferring to keep it as his *sanctum sanctorum.* He let his jolted heartbeat slow to a reasonable level with a few deep breaths. He opened the door to his elderly neighbor, Moses' widow. She was tiny, bent and wrinkled, her drab, worn, wool coat was pulled up to her head scarf. She smelled of boiled beetroots. But she was not to be ignored, or dismissed, she was a survivor.

"Zipporah, how are you? Do you need something?" His manners clicked into service.

"Hello, Saul, how are you? No, I don't need anything, but I wanted to tell you that a couple of rather stern looking gentlemen called on you yesterday afternoon. They banged on your door so loudly I thought they were trying to break it down. When I asked them what they wanted they told me to mind my own business. And I do. As you know. But they had the door open and looked like they were coming in."

"Well. Thank you for letting me know. If you hadn't told me I don't think I would have noticed. There is nothing that has been disturbed inside, that I noticed. I wonder what they were looking for?" The answer to that was beginning to dawn on him as he spoke. "I haven't been having any problems, well no more than usual. And I haven't complained or requested any service or repair. How odd."

"As you know with Moses, things can happen pretty quickly out of thin air. It can be a horrible shock. So, I just wanted to warn you. If warning is in order, let's just say to inform you. It is the neighborly thing to do." Her quavering voice did not seem to get as much practice as her sociability would like. Saul did not feel like obliging her, he was spooked.

Zipporah, without Moses, was one of those countless elderly widows occupying the invisible corners of society. Her voice was as thin as seemed appropriate given her wizened frame. She looked past Saul into his hallway. Saul looked down at the lock to see if there were any signs of forced entry. The door was intact, unscathed. Suddenly his sense of security did not feel the same. His heart rate pushed up again, evoking more deep breaths.

Saul panted his thanks to her and noted to himself that it was the longest conversation he had had with anyone in the building in the last six months. He politely waved Zipporah away down the corridor. He was glad to shut the world out. Now, he needed to be alone with his insecurities, to search for clues as to any intrusion. Burglary was almost unheard of, thanks to the power of the Security forces. God bless the State and the Jesuits and the Templars! The worrisome issue was not that he had no inkling as to what they would be looking for, but that they had obviously called when he was not at home for a purpose. They would know his routine, his comings and goings, because his hours were just like the millions of others.

With his investigator's eyes, he could see that the meagre, standard-issue furnishings were undisturbed, as if it were possible to tell otherwise. Saul kept a neat environment, whether at home or at work, he was tidy if not punctiliously clean, he liked order. There was no evidence of drawers being rifled through, or cupboards being sifted, although maybe that just suggested that they were good at their jobs. After wandering around taking inventory of his belongings, 'as they were,' he decided that nothing had been taken, or nothing that he cared about. He knew there was nothing to be uncovered, nothing incriminating hidden away. His shoulders relaxed a little from under the stress they had been carrying. Surely it was an exoneration; 'they came, they saw, and they did not conquer.' It was evidence of innocence, if such a thing can be.

Then, as his mind turned to the promise of breakfast, for nervousness triggered his hunger, he noticed a new book on his shelf.

When it came to his choice of reading materials, Saul was a man of conventional, yet intellectual, tastes and he made the point of acquiring the most interesting and challenging

works available to him in this censorious, closed market of official publishing. He had the usual Jesuit-sanctioned volumes, Dante, Erasmus, Chesterton, Hopkins, of course, some modern thrillers for diversion, Father Brown et al, and a few more testing and controversial volumes, all sanctioned and published by the Book and Periodical Publishing Department. One perennial favorite of his was *The Book of Disquiet* by the Sage of the Rua dos Dourados, Fernando Pessoa, to whom he would often turn for solace. The well-thumbed cover of this lowly clerk's meditations was a comfort whenever he saw the worn book smiling benignly out at him from the shelf.

With the break-in, Saul was for once glad that there were no black market illegal materials on his commendable shelves. If some had come into his purview, his enquiring mind could have been entranced by some seditious literature. He would not have been able to resist a peek. Luckily that temptation had not raised its head and what was sitting there would not offend a Bishop. The selection tended to the philosophic, maybe suggestive and provocative if one was very unworldly or prudish, but overall his taste was for the academic. Because he lived in a society that prized conformity, his wish for challenging literature was unfulfilled. Unsurprisingly. But, he found his solace where he could, in the officially sanctioned.

His library was graced with some Greene, some Tolkien and any Baron Corvo he could find, for the poor madman was hard to find now that he was out of favor with the censors. All Saul's volumes were ordered alphabetically by author, where applicable, and arranged familiarly and neatly, where not. 'How do you file The *Bible* by author?' He felt he had devoured all the interesting books available, he had even partaken of the pulp published to keep the indiscriminate reader happy. And, he knew his shelves as intimately as any part of his life. Then he saw a new addition, slotted in between Chesterton and Corvo.

The interloper on the book-shelf was a slim volume with no title on the brown, nondescript spine. He took it down and immediately regretted so doing. Now he was implicated in its ownership. Saul cursed a damnation on himself and looked pointlessly over his shoulder, as though the book's owner would appear. He would have to dispose of the thing. His placid temper broke in thinking of the underhandedness of the men who had been in his personal space. They had violated his borders, but worse, they tried to frame him. Tried to set up an innocent citizen with a stupid plant. They needed to be reported. He would tell Father Timon on Monday, until he realized, he would not. There was a game to be played here, in which he did not want to participate. Timon, it had to have been Timon, had drawn him ineluctably in. Curse him, curse them. 'Damn them all.' Timon did not deserve the honorific of Father.

The octavo book was titled *The Oncoming Tide; the Wave of the New Men.* It was published by, or authored by, or credited to the 'Cygnet Committee,' a term he had not heard tell of until yesterday, and so it should have been shelved after Corvo. 'Idiots!'

Saul mulled the title over. He recognized the "New Men" phrase as one repeated in gossip at work, the term used as an insult for ridiculing the inane. 'Who does he think he is, a new man?' His weekly managers meeting was jokingly referred to as the 'Oncoming Tide,' because it was predictable and pompous. Saul flipped through the text, because it was a book in his hand and that is what he did with books. He read a sentence here and there, with his writerly eye, in a critical fashion.

"A creative man is motivated by the desire to achieve not by the desire to beat others."

That seemed rather uncontroversial. Art is made for its own sake not as a means to fame and fortune. Life is not a rat race where the winners survive and the losers perish. That is antediluvian thinking, it went out with the Ark.

"Achieving life is not the equivalent of avoiding death."

Every line appeared to be a quote, in fact it seemed to be a series of aphorisms, not an argued treatise. This line resonated with him, though, because he had spent many years treading water. Like a man waiting in the middle of an ocean for rescue, just staying in place, avoiding death. Whenever he had swam it was because the current threatened to float him away and he needed to work to stay still, so they could find him. It did not make a lot of sense, waiting for the Coast Guard to show up, even to Saul. He did feel a sense of waste at not striking out, at his own talents being squandered. To be honest with himself, the book was right, it was not a life. 'Was that sedition?'

"To achieve, you need thought. You have to know what you are doing and that is real power."

Saul had no wish for power over others, but did feel that he could exercise more control over himself. Maybe then he would experience the liberation he craved, to be captain of his own fate. 'Wait! I thought I was in the water, paddling, not on a ship.' He had been stifled in this overbearing Society, and the idea of breaking out thrilled him. This internal freedom he cultivated through sarcastic asides, was more amusing than fulfilling. It seemed to be playing at life, and there was more to be had, if he could locate it. He would like to have his own life molded by his own choices. Whatever that entailed. However, that looked.

"God, a being whose only definition is that he is beyond man's power to conceive."

This last sentence haunted Saul as he dressed to head out into the rain to visit the market. He felt in two minds about disposing of the book, he would have liked time to peruse the thing, to read whatever he was not allowed. He wanted to know why it was considered so incendiary, although, at the same time, he did not want to be caught 'red-handed with the thing.' This little book could be excuse enough to condemn him. He knew he had to throw it away, but, then, they could plant something worse on him, if they so wished. A *Quran*. So, maybe it was a token, maybe a visiting card to let him know they had come. He had been appraised of their tactics and 'they were not playing fair.'

His raincoat had not dried out in the humid apartment, but he figured that it was going to get wet again anyhow. Living in the City was a constant battle against the encroaching elements. If it wasn't the rain or the winter cold, then it was the summer and the damn heat. Comfort was the reward for hard work, at least for your nearest and dearest, your dependents. Saul figured not having anyone close to you was the easiest solution to that conundrum. He figured that the main part of his job was enduring the annoyances of his life. Or, you could swap those words job and life. 'They should not be in the same sentence anyway!'

Still, it was better than taking responsibility, and raising expectations. The misery and grind shared with his fellow citizens made it easier, 'being all in it together,' but the cold was absolute, not relative, 'and sharing cold does not warm one up.'

Saul walked down the five flights of stairs to the building atrium which housed the grand entrance lobby. His steps echoed on the wood floors and between the plain, plaster walls. The people pulled in the wet on their clothing and shoes for it to be evaporated in the central heating, which made the common areas clammy. Outside, it was trying, quite successfully, to rain. Pulling up his collar to the brim of his bowler hat he set off at a brisk, warming pace, southwards.

One of the few advantages of working in the Produce Distribution Department was having prior knowledge as to which markets were to be provisioned and when. After word got out of a good quality of vegetable, or fruit, at a certain venue, then there was an inevitable rush of eager customers. Generally, the goods would be sold out in hours and those citizens too slow, or out of the loop, would have to fall back on inferior carrots, say, or worse, the tinned. Inside knowledge of food shopping was one of the benefits of his job. Saul was 'thankful for small mercies.'

Saul had heard that Market One Four Five, which was only four blocks, eight short furlongs, away was to receive a shipment of cheddar at eleven o'clock and he wanted to be in line by ten. He intended to drop the book off somewhere along the way, somewhere discreet. Of course, no site readily presented itself, he knew the streets and could think of no disposal possibility. He could imagine discarding the thing to have some good Samaritan pick it up and come after him, shouting and waving it in the air. The pavements were free of any street furniture suitable for his task and he ended up queuing outside Market One Four Five with the offending article still in his possession.

He made a mental list of the other items he needed to acquire once he was inside, cauliflower, oatmeal, some Upper Downland wine, cans of peas and tomatoes, as much sugar as they would allow him, the usual trappings of the single man's pantry. Saul's diet was the bland vegetarian mainstays of most bachelors. After acquiring his pale-yellow brick of cheese, he set out in search of any appurtenances that would make it palatable. Something to go under, over, or in it. The smell of the people and the vegetables on the cold air nauseated him a little. He wished to get back to his refuge.

Milling between the stalls inside the giant cement hangar that housed the market, Saul was suddenly stopped short by the glimpse of a profile. Following the flash of recognition, he pushed through the crowds queuing at the dairy counters and saw the lithe figure of Father Timon. He was bargaining over the price of a bag of what looked like spinach, quite animatedly. His professional guile providing him with less success than yesterday.

Because the distribution system relied more on the merits of self-interested traders the closer the goods came to the customer, and because the stall owner was equally talented in his craft, the greens were not discounted. He would, wisely, not accept less than the stated price so early in the day. Timon could not use the full range of his intimidating methods out in public, at least not on this grocer, and begrudgingly accepted the price. Saul was surprised to see someone with so much clout rubbing shoulders with *hoi polloi.* He imagined Timon would shop in some elite emporium away from the bustle of the common folk. Perhaps Timon was not so highly placed after all, a thought that irritated Saul. He would have liked to be intimidated by someone important, if he was to be bullied at all it should be by someone powerful, at least. He felt slighted.

Saul decided, without thinking, to keep a low profile, and ducked behind a large lady waving a muddy rutabaga in the face of another disinterested trader. Holding his netted shopping bag close to his chest and pulling his head into his coat collar, he tried to shrink. He felt a bit absurd, he was not naturally stealthy. Maybe he should approach Timon, greet him and try to befriend him, to show he had nothing to hide. The first instinct, to hide, set the course. Saul kept his head down.

Timon seemed irritated with his Saturday morning, and so was probably at the end of his excursion. He was obviously a shopper with a thin nerve who could only take so much. The scowl on his pinched face made a pathway open in front of him. The crowd parted to let his long stride through and, surreptitiously, Saul followed in his wake. The thrill of stalking him give Saul a pleasant shiver, he felt strangely drawn to discover more about his tormentor.

Initially it was easy to keep Timon in his sights. The going was slow among the throng, but once outside, Timon's pace was a bit too quick, so that Saul struggled to keep up. Nevertheless, spurred by this chance encounter, and what it may offer, Saul scampered along. The distinction between the interrogator persona and his everyday life made Timon seem imaginary, like an actor, which made the whole pursuit unreal. The snake had swallowed its tail.

Timon's purposeful walk covered the ground very economically. His bag of groceries did not impede his progress by swaying and banging against his leg, as was the case with Saul who had to hug his bag to his chest. Perhaps the bags were designed for the tall, hanging at the right level for them, one size not fitting all. Perhaps Timon was normal, was real, and Saul himself was the misfit. Nobody made bags for Saul's convenience. Timon kept his eyes diligently forward, ignoring whatever was behind him. Saul imagined that he was that way with most things in his life. 'Devil take the hindmost.'

Eventually Timon arrived at the front door of one of the large apartment blocks that made up the Suburban Area. It was not dissimilar to Saul's own block, but a bit better appointed, there was a nicer entrance, a little more ornamentation. Timon wrestled with his bags as he searched his pocket to bring out his key, then he fiddled with the key to find the lock. He then disappeared into the lobby, his gangly frame folded and pivoted through the doorway with a scarcely perceptible shake, like a stork settling on its nest.

Glancing back around a corner he had turned to avoid stopping when his prey had, Saul saw Timon enter the dour grey tenement building he called home. He leant against the cement wall to assess his advantage, and to get his breath back. It was a strange kind of relief he felt, possessing a bit of inside information, the first time he had felt he had a leg up on the towering Father Timon. Seeing him buying vegetables had brought Timon down to earth from being a Father. 'So, Timon, simple Timon.'

And then, Saul was overwhelmed at the pointlessness of the search. Not that it was futile but where was the reward? Each imposing edifice housed about five hundred separate apartments accessed through four giant entrances, one on each side of the block, that lead to cavernous lobbies and corridors like tunnels. It was just more efficient to build on such a massive scale. So, Saul was faced with the difficulty of locating a needle in a haystack, one person out of up to two thousand stacked souls. It seemed daunting and, in his present mood, impossible. 'What would, or could, it avail him?' So, he would know where Timon hung his hat, 'does that help his plight?' The whole affair was useless, best to go home and prepare for the worst. His natural pessimistic sense of victimhood prevailed over the hope this thin slice of luck had afforded. He was just about to turn on his heel, cursing his luck, when the door opened again.

Timon reappeared onto the street, casually hailed another man who had just exited and flapped an envelope toward him. The man walked back and accepted the letter with a wave of thanks. The two exchanged a few friendly words, obviously neighbors who had swapped mail. Saul took his chance and walked toward the front door past the awkwardly social Timon, who plainly felt trapped by the man. At that time on a Saturday there were many residents pushing through a lagging door, and Saul slipped through the opening and waited in the lobby pretending to collect mail from the array of post boxes set in the wall, his back to the hall traffic.

Timon was easily recognized with his reaching step, even behind him, and Saul turned after he had walked past and up the stairs. Saul followed him up a soberly decorated main staircase with a frayed red carpet, an uncommon touch in a much-used public area. This residence block was obviously a cut above Saul's. He padded innocuously, inconspicuously, and when Timon left the main stairwell he managed to follow him into one of those long bland, featureless but ubiquitous corridors. Timon fumbled with his key again as he let himself into one of the numbered front doors that stretched away at least a furlong into the distance. Saul made a mental note of the number on floor three as he walked past Timon closing the front door of apartment fifty-eight.

Back at his own apartment, Saul sat to consider his situation with this newfound information. *Cui Bono?* What did it serve anything that Saul knew his tormentor's address? To put him on a Christmas card list? Things were a bit more pressing than that, December was months away. As part of a master plan? Saul was due to see Timon, 'Father Timon,' again the day after next which left no time for further fact gathering. If there were any further facts that might make a material difference. It seemed a useless detail that Timon lived behind the numbers five and eight.

Monday was likely to be the day of reckoning, when Saul had to either betray Leah or suffer retribution from the authorities. For their God is a jealous God, who does not like his children to go undisciplined. His alternatives were either to lose his soul or have his soul taken from him. A rather stark choice that made him feel that his life was not fundamentally his own. As though the Templars could just foreclose on his very being. It made it feel as though Society owned all the souls out there, and they just leased them out to the people, and then could recall them at will. It was as if everyone belonged to those who had the power. This was not a revelation to Saul, but the injustice, or a sense of unfairness, struck him in a way it had not before. That made for a bleak prospect, so, how to redeem himself? He had to take ownership back of his own self. He had to reclaim, or rebuild, his soul, his very heart. His sarcasm reproached him with, 'Is that all?'

Saul knew by now he was not going to compromise Leah, he was going to protect her. Even to his own detriment, whatever the cost. The cowardice, that he felt as pragmatism, that had made him consider his own skin first, had been renounced. Saul felt heroic, and this revolution in his very depths, was more than a defiant act of love. It was a true act of liberation.

He could not even contemplate the possibility of abandoning her, which left only the certainty of official retaliation. For he would be taught a lesson, that much was clear, he would be the example. 'What would that look like? Like being rejected by a parent? Or like a public humiliation? Worse? Having your soul cancelled?'

It was not just what he felt about Leah, which was flooding through him, it was the extent of the inundation. The surprising strength of his sentiment that could overthrow his inbred, orthodox caution. Leah had been a shadowy figure of exotic allure, a dream figure somewhere out there.

Up until now.

Now, she was being invested with supernatural powers of love and the ability to bestow happiness. Leah was growing into more, perhaps, than any human deserved, or could cope with. The symbol of the new Saul as well as its origin. The cause and effect of his new life. A pagan Goddess of love, an archetype, an Aphrodite. But also, a savior, a messiah. Was this an impossible role for a mere mortal? Or was she now elevated to a higher status? A symbol of his revolution, she was a new world revealed to him, an invitation to regain Eden. It was a Holy Grail to pursue. If he could protect them both would her gratitude know no bounds when she discovered the truth?

What Saul felt for Leah was deeper and more meaningful than his need to detach. His urge to self-preservation was overtaken by a state of love. This was an immense threshold for him to cross, from a sleeping death to a woken state. Enough sacrifice at the altar of the greater good, he needed to choose his own happiness. Leah demanded it.

Saul had not been in this place, not even with his daughter's mother. He had dallied, as he put it, numerous times with various women, until, inevitably, he felt the burden of the commitments unbalancing his life. Then he would bolt, like a bee-stung horse. He had been so much baked in the clay of society, so much part of the machine, that he dared not let a personal matter overshadow his life. He had been, first and foremost, of the Church and its embodiment in the structures that bound the people together. He had been an exemplary citizen. Now he was breaking free. The insinuation that he would not put love above duty was anathema to him.

'What was he thinking?'

He frightened himself.

CHAPTER FOUR

"She is probably safe at work, as it's a Saturday."

Saul mused on his daughter, at her job in Weekend Support. He tried, by deflection, to avoid reflecting on his own predicament, the preoccupation with which loomed over his vexatious afternoon. Esther was his only living relative, and he had tried to raise her as a circumspect member of society. He had determined that it was the best way to protect her, he knew no other. She was a froward recipient of his affections which matched her cautious personality. But the sands had been shifting lately, as Saul could testify. She had started to question, and then began to resent, his endeavors to keep a safe distance between them.

'Love can be a weakness,' he remembered telling her, 'people are unreliable, and you can only be hurt by those close.' Saul now doubted the wisdom of this detachment, which had seemed a good idea at the time. Now, sitting in his own emotional crapulence, he realized that he missed his daughter. He regretted not having her around.

Esther was in her early twenties and settling quite comfortably, *thank you*, into the monotony of her life. Her doubts had not become a bed of nails quite yet. She worked within the larger mindful hive as a happy drone. Functions fulfilled, and expectations met, as had been her father's mantra. Saul's constant exhortations to conform had paid off and she now displayed a resignation that betokened, to him, a promising dispassion. She seemed on the path of righteousness, to fit in and not stand out, well camouflaged against the background.

"Don't show that halo above the parapet," he had said to her. But that was a differently colored time. Or rather, a black and white time before the advent of color.

Esther sat poised at her desk keeping her head down. She was dressed in a blue, gabardine, knee-length dress whose tightness made sitting precarious even as it pleasingly accentuated her embonpoint. Over her ruffled coiffure her headphones sat comfortably in place if, that is, she did not move too quickly. She had to concentrate on neither nodding nor shaking her head as she agreed or disagreed with her distant interlocutors. Attached to her headpiece, the microphone in front of her mouth was the size of a plum and made her look surprised if seen full face. This view was not available to anyone, though, as she sat in front of a dizzying bank of plugs and sockets, her task to direct the one to the other as required. The job was more complicated than she made it seem, particularly as human interaction was involved. The telephone system was for official business only, and outside office hours it was reserved for emergencies, so there was not a great deal of traffic for Esther to cope with. There was some abuse of the system, of course, and the more important members of the Church did use the facility for more mundane reasons. And many more thought themselves important than were. She enjoyed officiously correcting them.

Esther flicked a switch and a voice crackled into her ear. The sound was forced and deliberate, for which she was glad, for normal speech was indecipherable. She listened, after introducing herself, before pulling a rubberized wire by its plug and inserting it into the appropriate outlet. After re-adjusting the headset, she bade the disembodied voice 'farewell' and felt the satisfaction of a task competently handled.

She sat back in a proud haze, happy with her lot and proud of her ability to cope with the demands of the position. Then the shrill high-pitched bell gave a short insistent ring to alert the operator of an incoming call.

"Weekend Telephonic Operative Esther," she correctly identified herself, then waited for the instruction.

A slight pause. "Ah, good. It was you I was interested in talking to," Uttered an obscure man's slow, muffled growl. She had to cock an ear to hear her respondent. It was the first time Esther answered a call for herself, but instead of being flattered, she felt wary. Her answer was automatic.

"How may I connect you, sir?"

"You may not. This message is for you. Listen very carefully, Telephonic Operative Esther, I will not repeat myself. Your father is making enemies of the wrong people. He is not cooperating with those he should be helping. We need him to know that our influence stretches far and wide. You must tell him this. We are powerful and are not afraid to use any means to keep law and order. Mainly order. I hope you get what I mean!"

The line went dead.

Esther's training kicked in as she thanked the emptiness for his courtesy and with a trembling hand signed off. The shock of the statement meant that it took a minute for the scripted message to sink in. For she thought the voice was reading the threat, but she definitely heard the menace. She felt bafflement and agitation, and then a spark of anger at Saul's possible transactions. Just when she had found a solid job, with the prospect of years of easy employment, he had to go and rattle some cage. She liked her role here working with technology and with the bigwigs in charge, it had a touch of glamour, despite the blue uniform. Her comrades were nice enough as well. 'How typical of her father to ruin it somehow.' She would go and see him later that evening when her shift ended and tell him to make it right. 'Whatever it was he had upset, an applecart, a boat, it just needed righting.'

A few humdrum hours after the call, Esther stood outside Saul's apartment door noting that it needed a new coat of off-white paint, wondering if someone had chosen that particular shade of nicotine. It made the corridor linoleum look attractive by comparison, and that was a feat. She breathed a familiar institutional smell, disinfectant and damp neglect. 'God, why is he always so slow!'

She knocked with her customary fervor, knowing that Saul had to be summoned with energy, and she waited with her small, white, plastic handbag held by both hands in front of her blue crotch. It was her normal unobtrusive stance that she practiced in public, a standing-to-attention. After a long few minutes the door opened to the extent of its security chain, not a precaution Saul normally took but one he felt was suitable. Seeing his daughter, he beamed a greeting and closed the door to open it fully and allow her access to his sanctum. A homely breath of warmer, welcome air enveloped her, a domestic hug. The smell of un-emptied laundry baskets and boiled vegetables. Normally, Esther had a poor opinion of her father's living standards but this time she was glad to be inside in the stuffiness. She entered the short, dingy hallway, and kissing his cheek with a slightly less supercilious air than usual, gingerly picked her way to the living room.

"Papa. I need to talk about something that happened at work. Just earlier. I think it concerns you." She pronounced Papa as par-par, in a thin proper tone, a telephonist's articulation.

Saul knew, of course, it had been his preoccupation for over a day now, but it was a surprise that Esther had become involved. The net had naturally been thrown to encompass those around him. And she confirmed it in rather a grandiloquent fashion, as was her way, it came from having a writerly father. Her haughty attitude also let her start to blame him for her difficulties. Saul felt she almost relished reprimanding him, as some sort of payback. She could be rather patronizing, like her mother.

When she had relayed all the scant information, and had got the annoyance off her chest, they settled into the living room to share the ritual of a pot of tea. Saul told Esther of his last thirty hours; the surprise and the concerns, the interview, the shadowing of Timon and the locating of his apartment, the discovery of the planted book.

"And, Papa, what are you going to do?"

"And, darling," he echoed, "I am really not sure, at the moment. It seems as if, because they contacted you, to frighten you, then, obviously, they mean business. Serious business. I do not know how this sort of thing works. This is all new and a bit alarming."

"Maybe I shouldn't have come here. Do you think they are following me? Does this make me look as if I'm involved in something? Papa, do not lie to me. If you are up to your neck in something, you must tell me, you must come clean with them. And with me, don't drag me down. There's no way you can fight them if they have your card marked. You should have heard the man on the telephone, he was scary."

"I can only guess. And I am sorry you are involved. They are trying to bully you into forcing me to come clean. I don't think they want you, you are just collateral."

"Lovely! Maybe I shouldn't have come to rescue you. This feels all wrong now. If you are guilty then so am I. Guilt by association. The Catechism, father, if you look inside you know what is right and wrong."

"Yes. I always had a problem with that one."

Saul felt abandoned to his guilt and, although he did not expect sympathy, would have welcomed a little support. All she displayed here was as she had been taught, so he could not blame her, but still, 'need she be so cautious?' It was a mark of his own perturbation that he questioned his own philosophies in another. He, after all, had been transformed in the last two days, he could not expect everyone else to parallel him. He had not seen Esther for two or three weeks. This was all a shock to her. So, her next comment was as pleasing as it was unforeseen.

"We need to formulate a plan of action."

Saul felt a sob of emotion rise in his throat and he looked down at the arm of the chair, the slowly collapsing old armchair of his, and idly plucked at a loose seam of the canvas cover. He felt surprise at the overwhelm of gratitude for the flesh of his flesh, he masked the second sob with a cough. His lessons had not ruined her love for him. He knew this was not how it was supposed to be, everyone was supposed to put the interests of the whole society before the idolization of one member. But, maybe, love was not dead. God bless him, he forgave the Catechism! He was not used to looking inward for answers, it was a little disquieting, having to rely upon oneself. But doing so made the picture so much clearer.

"Thank you, darling. I cannot tell you how that makes me feel. I needed that support as I'm struggling a bit with the whole house of cards wobbling about. Things feel very uncertain. Not crashing yet, but it does not take too much of a breeze with cards." He had not called her 'darling' for years.

"We are in this together," Esther did not have any solutions to proffer, but reassured her father that he was not alone as an act of love. "We can fight this together and come out the other side together."

"Well, they say togetherness is the ideal."

"So. What are your, our, options. They obviously mean business or they would not have bothered with breaking in here and leaving this," Esther held the *New Men* book rather gingerly between the thumb and index finger of her left, her un-favored hand. "By the way. I don't think I needed to see this and have my fingerprints all over the thing." She tossed the small volume to her father which he dexterously caught and wiped on the arm of his chair.

"Point taken. I'll destroy it tomorrow, absolutely, tomorrow. Burn it probably, that should finish it. I presume they, whoever the thugs were, were meant to hide it so that it could be found during some future search. That's the only explanation. A slice of luck that Zipporah heard them, otherwise I would be unwittingly harboring seditious material. I've heard of people like me on the news. It doesn't end well for them, so I understand. Remember Moses? I've been thinking of him lately. Anyway, I need to get rid of the damn thing fast." This was being belied by the fact of his rifling through the pages and glancing at random phrases. "Tomorrow, first thing. A little fire in the sink and a quick flush down the potty."

Esther looked at him with the condescending face of a child telling a parent the ways of the world. Some small part of her conventional soul was being thrilled by the threat of the situation, and, also, by the forced bonding with her father. It was against the *ex cathedra* preachings and teachings by which the State tried to weaken familial bonds, but she had always wanted a deeper connection to this distant, semi-reclusive figure. Now was the chance, and perhaps it was always going to involve an element of danger.

"Let's do it now," she said in her most imperious tone. "Come on."

Lighting a fire in the sink, the little pile of torn pages curled and blackened under the flame, and they fanned the smoke out of the open kitchen window. Esther saw something in her father's face, handsome in its concentration, as he glanced curiously at each page before destroying it. She saw him in a different light, a man who stands up for himself. He was undergoing a change, there was a different aspect to him. It was hard for Esther to pinpoint, hard for her to describe, he seemed less solid even as he seemed more real.

Adding the ripped book piecemeal to the small fire they had constructed in the kitchen sink, they wiped out the evidence, if evidence it was, in less than five minutes. The powdery crumbs of ash were washed down the drain with the swirl of tap water. There was a sense of relief, but also the feeling of desecration that book burning gives, as they moved from the kitchen. The open windows chilled the damp air on which they closed the door, trapping the smell of smoke.

Esther was still being proprietorial about the proceedings and, as was her wont, wished to summarize the impasse. She liked to reason out loud, she liked the dialectic, it helped her to clarify. "There is the second interview with Father Timon on Monday. Ten o'clock, right? Where you are supposed to spill the beans. The authorities certainly wish to get at Leah, or whoever Leah can lead them to. Right, again? Not knowing where Leah is hiding, they think you are the weak link in the chain and will lead them to the group they are after. They don't know that you know nothing."

Here she looked askance at him, to check for any tell-tale signs of deceit, the shifty glance away, the cough and the hand that covers the mouth. She received none. He was so grateful for her concern, he held no resentment of her suspicion. He nodded for her to continue.

"And we have this useless bit of information about where Timon lives. Oh, and also, that they will, in all likelihood, stop at nothing to pursue this line of inquiry. That is a shocking thought, maybe the scariest part of all this mess, that we don't know what they will stop at. I don't really see any clear path forward. Papa, do you? Do you see where to go? What are you thinking?"

Saul's eyes were cast down onto his fingers, idly picking at the fraying cover of his chair. He was vexed by the conflict, there was a fidget within his breast. He was being stretched thin in opposite directions. He was wondering where the tear in the fabric of his being would appear, if it would rip him in two. That damn dilemma was growing again, sprouting twin horns, the unicorn becoming an ox. There was a fork materializing on the road ahead, he was going to have to take one path or another. But, it was confusing, he was not practiced in making choices and someone had taken down the signposts.

On the one hand, there was the duplicitous nature of the Security Service which had undermined him and used him as a bargaining chip. Hypocrisy and treachery were revealed as the true nature of the Protector of the Good. But, he felt not a betrayal but a deep disappointment, as when one is let down by a trusted colleague. It was depressingly familiar, the tie that binds, only this time it was running out of rope. That way felt like a dead end.

On the other hand, well, he did not know what the other entailed, where that path lead, he just knew he had to pick it. Having ratcheted down his beliefs and expectations so many times in the face of continual debasement, the place he had landed was, curiously, not-foreign. For years, he found it gradually opening to him, a slow-motion drift, the inevitable becoming apparent. It was time to cut the tether, but this time it felt like a leash, not a safety harness, that was being severed.

"Papa? What shall we do? How do we make this right?"

It had only taken this compassionate tone from Esther and his whole mindset had changed, from Socialistic thinker to Individualist. A magic trigger had flipped his world. He knew that overstated the case, it was not as sudden, but he could think of no better way to phrase it. The weighted coin was always going to come down heads.

"By God," he wanted out of this mess. Saul wanted a fresh start, so he could construct another life, to be the author of his own destiny. He had been handed a bottle when he was born, a book when he could read, a tool when he was a young man and, later, a desk as a ball and chain. Someone else was writing his story and he was as trapped as a character in a novel. Don Quixote, Saul thought, for all his oddities and individuality was always Cervantes' fool.

Quiet, retiring Saul had never been known as a man of action, a mover and shaker who got things done. He had hidden his light under a haystack of bushels, scared lest his light attract any heat. He had kept such a low profile that people thought he was flat, two-dimensional, rather a damp squib. But, here he was, feeling a resurgence of something lost, something repressed now being resurrected by a loss of faith. His faith had been a trap, when it was sold as an escape. Well, *caveat emptor*. He was having a liberating moment of doubt, as Jesus had the night before he was caught, when he finally betrayed himself as human.

So, Saul recaptured his quintessence.

The only proof of freedom is action. The lie of religion is that it emancipates the soul. In fact, the opposite is true, it enslaves the soul to doctrine, dogma. Whereas, 'to be is to do,' is the refrain of the untrammeled. The man who commits suicide at the happiest point in his happy life so proves himself by exercising his free-will. Saul, by taking that opportunity to choose, to express his liberty, then freed his soul from its prison. He found being by undoing, by unraveling or uncloaking. He revealed himself in his rejection of convention. And that doing made him.

A dim bulb cast a shadow of an idea, far away in his innermost imagination. There was an alternative. And it involved acting as the human he was, and creating universes, not just possibilities. He was to turn away from the God that governs to be his own god. There was deliverance there.

An excitement welled up inside him, and started to overflow. It was a beautiful, controlled, slow hysteria that coursed through his veins like a drug. An emphatic moment of opiate fix. An alien liquid dispersing in his life-blood.

He imagined a hillside, somewhere, with a thousand springs spontaneously arising on its slope. An upsurge that cannot be tapped and sealed. If one spring is blocked then the water, or the feeling of water, would break out elsewhere. This feeling of his could not be staunched. All that can be done is to step back and let the flow happen, to tend the outpourings into the channel and let it follow its course. As a man transfixed, he said:

"Esther. Let me put something to you. I don't want you to react immediately, give it some time, let us talk it over. This might seem like a radical idea, and radical is the last thing we wish to be seen to be, but I have an idea."

"OK, we need desperate measures. What will break this logjam?"

"I could sugarcoat this, but I want to be blatant. Father Timon seems to be the problem. He gave me the impression that he was the one in charge of this witch hunt. That it was his idea to hunt Leah, to bring her to his justice, which he thinks is the State's laws. I think that he is trying to earn points with his superiors by handing them an unrequested bonus. Leah's head on a plate, like some perverse Salome. So, if I am right, if Timon is acting alone and as a maverick, he is vulnerable to a counter strike. I know I'm being abstruse here but bear me out, I have not really thought this through. I'm thinking out loud."

Saul paused for breath and for a little resolve, then continued. "That would make the good Father the first log in the waterway that has caused the others to jam up behind it. Without that first one the others would just float on by. I think I read that when that happens, when everything gets stuck, one of the solutions is a strategically placed stick of dynamite. Bang! Problem solved. Apart, that is, from the fact that all those built up logs come shooting down the causeway at once. But, the pressure is released, there is a flow, things pass by and are forgotten. Sometimes an emetic is required to clear a poisoned system of its vomitous blockage. So,

I am, and bear me out here, just wanting to suggest that we, or I, or some combination, eliminate Father Timon. There, I've said it."

Saul looked coy at the implication, like a guilty schoolboy, as the consequences dawned on him. He did not know whether just voicing such a scandalous thought was beyond the pale. And, as if he may be shamed into dismissing the solution he had just proposed, he felt a trepidation about Esther's reaction. What would she say? She was in a pause. The delicately painted fingernails on her right hand, a neon pink, fluttered by her mouth.

"Comments?" he asked as a prompt.

The idea had crash landed like a meteor from some high orbit, the original impact was chaotic, but the more the thoughts settled like dust, the more the view improved. Saul did not like the logjam metaphor, dynamiting a river does not sound sensible, but presumably having a lumberjack balancing on jammed logs and prying open the bottleneck is not feasible either. It was not dainty work. The explosion can be at a distance, controlled, or a tossed stick of dynamite and a dash for safety. Sometimes a big bang, an extreme measure, is required, and then escape made under cover of the aftermath. And Saul knew, there should be quite an aftershock.

This formulation had entered his mind almost fully assembled, as the best plans tend to do. It arrived whole and obvious, not pieced together, not built from the ground up, but came complete, full-formed. The problem, the solution and the wherewithal all nicely packaged together, arriving in a flash of inspiration. It involved the crime of pre-meditated murder, but the sensational and audacious nature of the scheme left no trace. The Templars would never suspect a minor character, an upstanding, or at least low-lying, citizen like him. They would assume it was a militant branch of the New Men, insurrectionists, anarchists who were willing to kill. Hardened hit-men with their callous tactics.

Who would think it was Saul? He was not under surveillance, not a suspect, just a witness. His association was minimal, he was peripheral at best. And then, Timon would not be around on Monday to receive Saul's non-news. What was it that Timon had said? That the case was his baby, that he wanted all the credit as he had put in all the leg work? Well maybe it could rest with him! Saul would turn up to the interview on Monday blithely innocent. He was such a small fish he would swim right through their net. The absurdity of the plan was its safeguard.

His moral compass was not spinning. Saul did not feel in a quandary about the possibility of murder. The prospect of killing had not unhinged him. He was happy for the chance to prove himself. He could summon anger and resentment. For if they wanted to play by those rules, us or them, then so be it. He would beat them at their own game. That thought was particularly pleasing, taking the fight to the enemy, standing up for something more than a superior entering the room. Saul's derelict sense of his own virility infused his body, enthused his hopes. He felt his chest swell with pride; manly and radical pride. Perhaps it was that making his pulse race, his breast heave.

The making of the individual, the expression of identity. It was a grand departure from his reasoning of a week ago, but he was versed in the concepts of Damascene conversions. If Saint Paul's *volte-face* was considered a God-send, then why not Saul's? It was an aching silence that this breaking of a taboo had caused. Killing was prohibited, was unmentionable. Even more so in this vegetarian society, where the slaughter of animals was disdained. Or, maybe, the reverse was true. Maybe the lack of animal death made human death less awful.

Esther had kept her unspoken promise not to react immediately, but felt the need to speak and fill the void.

"You are talking," she enunciated each syllable in a slow shock, "of killing Father Timon."

It was a statement, not a question. Having spoken the words, the full enormity of the courage, or madness, to commit such a heinous crime settled upon her. She shuddered at the full weight of the notion as the implications filtered down. The resonance shook her to the core. She balked. "I cannot, I can't, I couldn't . . . ."

She held up a manicured hand, palm toward her father, to preempt any interruption. Esther was in another pause, until,

"Then what? Do you think that if you get rid of Timon then all his co-workers, his colleagues, his superiors and his friends at the Templars, the state police, will just wipe their hands of it? Do you imagine they will turn their backs and walk away, crying shame? No! They will search for whoever killed one of their own with all the means at their disposal, they are the Security Department, the secret intelligence people. They have all the power they need. And when they find you they will come down like the proverbial ton of bricks! Blow up that logjam and all those other damned logs come speeding down the river. You think you are upstream, but you are down below the jam. It is madness! Suicidal! Beyond being just plain wrong. I cannot believe such a thought even entered your head."

And that was when Saul realized he was on his own.

He had not wanted to co-opt Esther against her better judgement, it was never his intention to drag her into his scheme, to force her against her will. It was all about free-will and if she did not want to take this step, then . . . . But he had to go forward, now, he had to follow his fate. No, not follow his fate but create his destiny.

He knew more certainly than the Justice of Socialism that he had to sacrifice himself. That if her objections were true, and they seemed viable, his loss would become meaningful. To reach a renaissance, he needed a self-immolation, as the denials of the true knight tasked with heroic deeds. Convinced that he had to stand up and be counted, he was certain that the Gordian knot could not be untied but needed splitting by one fell swoop of an avenging sword, he embraced the catharsis of action. It was liberating to be an Achilles, an Aeneas, and to make the world in one's image, not have it define you.

So, he needed to 'un-include,' or 'dis-include,' he could not decide the language, his daughter from any heroic feat of derring-do. This was not her bailiwick, this was all his doing. Or un-doing. He was the one who had fallen for Leah, who had made love to her romantic rebellion. Saul waved his hand in the air to wipe away the formulation as an equation on a blackboard. To try to absolve his daughter of his noble folly.

"Forget what I said. It's ridiculous. I'm talking out of my hat. Absurd! Just throwing out ridiculous ideas. What I'll do is explain to Father Timon on Monday what I know and trust to his good offices to understand and let me go. I'm sure he'll be sympathetic. It's fine, my darling. It's just a miscommunication, easily remedied. Honesty is the best policy."

Esther's look of astonishment faded with her father's reassurances. She desperately wanted to believe that, eventually, everything would get back to normal. But she felt battered, crestfallen, and her pale cheeks sagged in sympathy. The enormity of the moment was too much, she was not as precipitous as her father. She needed time and space to regain a sense of trust in the institutions that had raised her. Time to recover the confidence that all her life-long efforts had not been in vain. A willingness to believe was a much-vaunted quality in her upbringing, and conventional Esther displayed it admirably. She was not ready for revolution, personal or societal.

On his side, Saul had misplaced his gullibility, his willingness to believe lay in tatters. His mind raced like a hare chased by a greyhound over a moor. If his reason was the wide-eyed hare then his emotion was the red-eyed dog, panting, snarling. The pressure of the pursuit forced his rationale to flee for its life over acres of ground. His passion was ready to grab it by the throat, to toss it and break its back. It sought out the shelter of the first burrow it could find. Saul thought, 'the truth must win out.' He decided to play the supercilious parent, to placate his daughter, and to see her back to the safety of her life. Then he could wrestle with this radical idea.

This notion that he could act just for his own benefit still split him. His conscience screamed 'selfish,' but his reason retorted, 'I must care for myself, if I do that, then I can look after the world.' Saul's reason darted hither and thither, desperate to avoid the jaws of his conscience. He realized that the way to effect true change starts from the individual deciding to take that path. The first step is to change oneself, and that is within everybody's power, if they choose to exercise it. Then, when all the elements are different the whole will be transformed. All Saul could do was to change Saul.

"Don't worry, darling. I was being crazy. I'll be fine. I love you but I'm feeling so tired, I need to rest. Recuperate and maybe pray a little. Not for guidance, I've decided on the right thing to do, but for a little meditation. Just to settle down."

Saul rather inadvisably clicked his fingers in the air as if he was conducting some mesmerism and was releasing Esther from a hypnotic spell. She found that theatrical gesture a bit patronizing, but he had always been thus. This seemed to signal a return to normality, perhaps the trick had worked?

He stood and conducted his slightly less deflated daughter to the door where she was only too eager to leave. They kissed in parting, not perfunctorily this time, but with warmth. Neither wanted to acknowledge the full import of the preceding few minutes. But they both understood that something significant had passed. Sometimes truth can be known without language, can be perceived through the heart; divined, if you will. He hugged the air out of the body of his, then, grateful daughter. He watched her blue uniform swagger between the narrowing pale-yellow walls, her handbag swinging mechanically on her arm.

Esther paused at the corner, having slowed her prim steps with a deliberation, it seemed to Saul's tired eyes. She turned back to her father and had to talk slightly louder than she would have wished, due to the distance, and slightly slower because of the echo.

"Father. I will miss you. I love you and I will always love you. But I do not know if I can see you again, which tears me in two. You frighten me, this whole thing scares me to death. Call me when you have sorted things out. I know I said I would help but I cannot be part of this madness. I love you, I truly do, but you have to figure this out on your own. It is too much."

Saul could see a glint of the lighting reflected in her welling tears. She turned the corner and was gone. The emptiness of the corridor was profound. He pushed the door back into its latch with as gentle a click as he could manage. Saul went back to his comfortable place on his familiar chair and set about testing his resolve. He could not eat for he felt no hunger, food seemed irrelevant, alcohol inconsequential. Esther was gone and, hopefully, was out of harm's way. He rested as in a taper before a race, preparing himself, body and mind, for the trial ahead.

Tomorrow was Sunday and the one sure thing was Church, compulsory and tedious as all Hell. Father Timon, being of high status, would attend the ten o'clock services. It would be almost compulsory; all the Pontificates would be at the Tens. Any ordinary citizen like Saul had to settle for Nines, and the peons had to turn up for Eights, as if a week of back breaking labor were not tiring enough. There was no rest for those wicked enough to be at the bottom of the heap. It was not deemed necessary that worship reflect the egalitarianism of Christianity. Just that everyone receive the wafer, hear the sermon, pledge allegiance and come out branded. Attendance was the ultimate *auto-da-fé*.

In the teeming City, with everyone crammed in together, discrepancies in circumstances were noticed. So, material differences were downplayed. Money was not the measure of wealth; the difference was time. The rich and powerful had more time. Hierarchies were rewarded with the Sunday morning lie-in, it was one of the currencies of the system. It was how inequality was measured.

Saul seemed blessed with time, his was a rich solitude. He had paid his dues, had been the faithful foot soldier but had received the cold shoulder when he needed help. Then, when he insisted, the authorities turned from him, all he knew was the back of them. And he had accepted it, with the insouciance that came naturally to his temper. He had been taken advantage of, and it rankled. He had believed and they had used his gullibility to their own ends. As he paced agitatedly around his barely adequate apartment he shouted out in a rant of frustration.

"Compromise! Compromise! It is always me who is supposed to adjust, and I am tired of being the one to swallow whatever Commandment is passed down from on high. I mean, I have worked, I have bred, I have lived as they ordered within the boundaries they set. Boundaries that shrank a little tighter each year, a belt cinched in to a disappearing waist. Don't do that, work harder, don't think that, work faster, don't read that, work, work, work, with less, for less. It feels as if life is labor, that we must keep moving just to keep up, like sharks in the water. That we have to change just to fit in. Last year it was food shortages, the year before we had to ration wine. Wine! How can a Christian survive without wine? Now its petrol, bikes, paper and still more people just seem to appear from nowhere, poof! Taking jobs, drinking wine, eating us out of house and home. And where are they coming from? It's as though we are mining them, digging them out of the ground."

"They are not refined, they are the crudest sort, and we all have to bunch up more, we all have to suck it in, and accommodate. Three, four bachelors to an apartment, two families living together, all crowded together, all shoehorned in. Never enough, food or drink or power or books or space, everything at a premium. And it doesn't improve, despite all the hopeful words that turn out to be empty."

"We are all expected to walk on those shards of broken promises, littering the paths. Like sheep we bleat and then tag along with the shepherd, because he has the answers and because we are raised to be followers. Then the shepherd turns out to be wrong, he leads us over a cliff, and those that survive are told to follow the next one because he knows where the cliffs are, but he leaves us out in storms. So another arises from God-knows-where claiming he knows the weather and the cliffs and then . . . . The Pontificate squeezes the people, until all the juice is forced out and all that is left is pulp. Like the stuff they write to keep us all on the straight and narrow, to keep us all subjugated, keep us all in the dark."

He stopped in front of his window and addressed the City or at least the gloom that took up his view. The dark seemed to creep up from street level, from the depths, instead of descending as it was supposed to do. It climbed the concrete walls opposite, bent itself on the windows and inched upwards until it threatened to overtake the world. This night did not fall, it raised itself up and the doughty, yellow streetlights were no match for its ambition, just a distraction.

"I've had enough. I feel like marching over to Timon's lovely door and confronting him right now, knocking the thing down and seeing how he likes it. Fancy accusing me. Me? Who has put up with everything, has taken everything, has let them have their ineffectual way. Threatening Esther, by God! And Heaven knows what they will do if they get their hands on Leah. I need to take a stand, I need to stand up for myself and tell them, enough! I need to stop this madness. This is the faceless leading the faithless and it needs correcting. I am going to start the bloody process tomorrow! Break that damn logjam!"

Saul then sat in a different world, in a liminal state, as a man does who has matured from youth to adulthood and looking back can appreciate knowing both sides, and can say;

"That was the time, that was the moment it all changed, thereafter the world was different, thereafter I was different."

CHAPTER FIVE

Tipping points come in various guises. So no two men will experience the same inflection. For some it is a sudden illumination as if a light bulb had been turned on and all is suddenly unveiled, like a revelation, when a switch has been thrown. For another man, it may be as subtle as the passing of the winter solstice as the days start to lose darkness, instead of losing light. At this gradual pace, there is a deflection when the arc ceases to rise and, cresting, begins to fall. Then it may take time to dawn on the man that the direction has changed, that the projected future looks different. Saul, himself, was somewhere in between, as at a sunrise or a sunset. There was a sea change within him as when the ebbing tide turns, a perceptible difference, but it revealed itself on a human scale, in quotidian time. There was a palpable difference between the before and after, that Saul could only perceive when the change had passed.

The next morning dawned a weak dun through the rain streaked windows of Saul's east facing apartment. Outside, the weather was doing the best it could, but it was not enough, it was still failing, and it seemed to have lost confidence in itself. The sulking day had turned its back on the sun, which could not be seen, nor felt, beyond the hazy clouds, just intuited. Un-welcomed and disappointed, the overcast Sunday morn seemed to echo Saul's mood perfectly. It would have been unseemly to wake to a bright, sunlit start on such a momentous day. Dark as they were, Saul's prospective deeds deserved to be shrouded in gloom. It was much too important a day for clarity.

Despite his apprehension, Saul had slept surprisingly easily, although quite thinly, as one sleeps on a night before a guaranteed verdict. He had vivid dreams, an unsettling experience in retrospect, dreams being considered by common knowledge a symptom of madness. Rejecting that opinion, Saul pandered to those theatrics in his unconscious when they happened and it excited him to spend time thinking on them. What everyone else put down to superstition, he there endeavored to construe a meaning. He noticed that they were at their strongest when he was perturbed and that they often contained his waking concerns. They had become therapeutic to his troubled mind the more turbulent it became, like a pressure valve. Saul could not help but feel that they were trying to convey a message to him.

This particular dream was recurrent, and was an alluring fancy that had haunted him for a long time. On and off, the same sensation had repeated over and over, as though an old man with dementia was retelling stories of his youth. It came with the relentlessness of tides, but it never felt imposed upon his recalcitrant mind, it seemed to well up from within.

Fully asleep, Saul yet somehow knew, if you can know anything when unconscious, that . . . *he was the world (or the size of the world) and the world was him.* The feeling was hard to describe and when awake he was reluctant to recall the feeling. But . . . *And his flesh was the soil; his bones the rocks; his blood the water; his hair the grass; his breath the wind; his eyesight sunlight; and his thoughts, those amorphous unreal things in his head, were the clouds. There is no light for there are no eyes to see. I am the light,* dreamed Saul, *and guide my own way. There is no sound, but there is perception of where noise should be. It whispers calming instructions for me to open further. Then it fades, from nothing to less than nothing, and the touch dies on the ethereal wind. There is no sensa-*

tion, it is a flat line of sameness. I am returning to a reality beyond. I let go of this world, or it lets go of me.

This was all immediately obvious to Saul's hibernating sense, if not to his waking intelligence in the full dullness of daytime. When he later recollected the impressions that had arisen, he felt a curious, and emboldening thrill. And he thought that reaction was telling. He felt he had access to immediate truth, but, of course, dismissed this idea as delusional. Truth was handed down, not out. Yet when he had the dream, or soon thereafter, the timing did not seem to matter, he felt an enlightening of his soul, or the space where his soul should be, the space into which his soul could grow. A light was being cast from somewhere, but of course he could not see the source of illumination, just its effect. As with his biblical counterpart, when the scales fell from his eyes, then Saul was opened to new possibilities.

Prompted by his alarm clock, Saul rose from his disheveled bed at six o'clock, and stood to attention with deliberation, as though on planned maneuvers. He welcomed the signal as a reveille, a bugle call to arms, even though he had lain awake for hours, trying to outstare the ceiling. But, the alarm heralded a time for preparation, for control, not for precipitous action. He needed patience and calm, he would spend his time parsimoniously, until the siren call.

Saul bathed in the usual eight inches of tepid grey water, the color of the inside of the leaden pipes, the metal bathtub retaining its nip. He lathered himself with a sliver of carbolic soap and poured cup after cup of water from between his legs over his head and torso. He cleaned his feet and hands meticulously, gouged under his nails, and vigorously scrubbed his scalp as though ridding himself of hair. Afterward, he wiped his tense body dry with the thin, rough towel that he had been meaning to replace for ages. It was as if he were trying to scrape some repulsive coating off his skin.

He stood on the scrap of rag matting between the toilet, bath and sink; the humidity condensing on the tiled surfaces of his bathroom as the vapor cooled. Facing him in the mirror on the back of the closed door was 'just what you would expect.' He saw the body of a middle-aged man of the milieu. Grey and somewhat paunched, blotched with the scrubbing. A sedentary life and a protein poor diet had left a sallow frame to support the sagging head and anxious face that stared back at him. Would it answer? Saul wanted a warrior there and saw a troglodyte, 'who was judging him!'

He had always imagined his body as solid meat displaying the manifest strength of muscle and sinew. But, he had been flattering himself, his body was more like salad. His arms were asparagus and his legs rhubarb or celery, or some such etiolated vegetable. His shoulders were parsnips, his chest a bag of onions. Saul wanted the exterior to reflect the spirits he had stirred up within, the blood of the Semites, but it would not match.

'It would taste better with dressing.'

Where was the strength of David, the determination of Noah, where was the cupidity and red-bloodedness of Abraham? Surely he was heart and liver and spleen? He had survived all that had been thrown at him. He was the result of success, since the time of Adam and Eve, or whoever the first ones were. And his parents, and their parents, by definition all his ancestors, had managed to survive. The life-force of his millions of antecedents propelled him. They had all made it through to make him, he owed it to them to carry on.

Saul's grandfather's old hunting knife had rested neglected in a box hidden in the back of a closet. Sitting gathering dust with other family artifacts and mementoes, embarrassed, almost, of its function. Since the ban on the killing of animals some fifty years before, not only butchery, but hunting, had been outlawed. The knife was an artifact whose primary purpose was obsolete, like the horse. The latter was replaced by motor vehicles, pets fell into desuetude, animals in the City were vermin. The knife could not adapt to peeling potatoes or chopping cauliflowers. Better tools were developed, techniques were lost. Saul felt a sympathy with his Grandfather's knife as he dug it out of its tomb. His father's father had used this to kill, to skin, to butcher. He cradled the relic in his hands, feeling the history and the link to history in its weight. He could not identify the taste of blood, but thought this must be close. It filled him.

Saul took the knife to the kitchen where, on a whetstone, he meticulously ground a sharpness out of it, or into it. Painstakingly he pulled the knife along the abrasive rock. Tenderly, he was honing his fate. He paid particular attention to the point, trying for the finest he could achieve, without compromising solidity. This, he thought, was the tip that would pierce the skin, would lead the rest of the blade through the flesh to the vital organ whose arrest would cause death. The ultimate goal, the dispatching of another being.

Saul had never before cut meat, nor, beyond licking his own wounds, tasted blood. He had never felt the slicing of tissue, the sawing of tendon, the elasticity of the fascia under a blade. But he knew his Grandfather's knife had torn flesh, when it was 'alive,' and he would trust to its pagan object soul to teach him it's voodoo art. Previously, Saul had believed that only humans deserved souls, that only they had been endowed, but hereafter he would see the world infused with spirits, and he would believe in the meaning that implied. All of creation was animated, there was connection and there was a nexus. As in his dream, everything was part of everything else, everything connected in one, in Saul.

Saul dressed prudently, to look as inconspicuous as possible in the milling Sabbath crowds. He wore his old, red tie and, over his Sunday suit, a raincoat. He thought, morbidly, that any liquid splashing onto him would be more easily removed. And, checking the leaden sky through the window, it did look like rain. He pulled his hat brim low on his brow and exited his apartment. He was also leaving behind his old life, he was shedding a skin. With his right hand he gently toyed with the knife in his pocket, rolling it and nesting it in his palm.

Saul fully expected to return triumphant later that day, later that morning in fact, but not to the same reality. He had tidied the place up, as he normally would, and planned his midday meal, a can of potato and leek soup to which he would add peas and carrots, to be heated and eaten with some aging crackers. It was standard fare for a friendless Sunday. He left the tins out on the counter, but he did not expect the meal to taste familiar. The food would be the same, his sensations would not. A changed man would be opening 'those tins.'

Locking his door with the ugly key that set the bolt, he saw the widow Zipporah come out of her door in a mirror of his action. It was half past eight and Saul was happy to be seen leaving for Church at the prescribed time. He was surprised that his neighbor was heading for Nines, he had assumed she would be attending Eights. 'Still,' he thought, 'all to the good.'

"Good morning, Zipporah, we must stop meeting like this," was the best he could come up with, and that spoken in a nervous, reedy treble. He smiled an unenthusiastic smile that forced the skin around his mouth to crinkle. He really was unpracticed at this social banter.

"Good morning, Brother Saul, I hope you sorted out that fracas from Friday." She wanted to chat. "If they have the wrong address they need to know so that no miscreant is let off."

"I did, thank you! No problems, a misunderstanding. Are you off to Saint Paul's?" This was the nearest Edifice Church, with seating for thousands, and, being conveniently close, the favorite of most of the inhabitants of the building. A lot of forced turnout was about convenience, most compulsory events are attended as economically as possible.

"No. I'm at the Tens, over at Tobias. It takes me over an hour to get there, but I do love the service and the congregation is very well-appointed. Always a sensible consideration, no?"

"Absolutely!" Saul was rather surprised to hear of Zipporah's elevated status and felt a touch embarrassed. He had assumed she was a run-of-the-mill widow, maybe a Nine, if she came from a good family. A Ten was impressive, Saul decided that he would have to be nicer to her.

"Well, have a lovely, blessed Sabbath, Zipporah. I have to rush to Paul's. I'm ushering today." He saluted her with his left hand, the right thrust deep into the pocket to hide any knife-shaped bulges, and headed toward the atrium and down the stairs to the lobby. Zipporah took her sweet time behind, taking the steps seriously and gripping the handrail. Maybe she knew Timon? The knot in his stomach was tightening with each step he took, each stage of the journey he completed. The day was ratcheting up. It would be a coincidence if she knew Timon, nothing more.

"It would be typical to suffer an 'act of God' on a Sunday, wouldn't it?"

Saul tried to slow himself, as his stride covered the slippery sidewalks too quickly. He was stuck in the present, but contemplating the Absolute, consciously planning a crime against both Man and God, against Nature and Society. The ideas inside his head seemed more concrete than the reality outside, more certain, as he headed to confront his Fate. Many of the concepts being juggled back and forth in his mind seemed to start with capital letters; Society, Murder, God, Truth, Collectivism, Dogma, Right, Love. They were the headings of the chapters of his life.

"Get out of my way!" he bellowed to no-one in particular

Walking in a state of solipsistic distress through the ordered and manicured park, his self-absorption blocked any distraction, and created an isolation that hypnotized him. The faithful, out there, were scurrying back and forth, all with an end in sight. The folk were carrying out their duties, just as on work days, both the pleased and the sluggards. The bells tolled solemnly for the hours, and before the strike there was a rush of congregants.

Everybody was using the park as a thoroughfare, Saul seemed to be the only one loitering, dragging laps around the duck pond. It was quite a large body of water and took ten minutes to make a circuit and Saul decided he could make three turns and that would put him on course to intercept Timon at home. He was guessing that Timon, and his wife, would frequent his convenient Church, Zipporah's Saint Tobias. A good career move. It was about four furlongs from Timon's building to the Church, and so Timon would not leave, hopefully, before half past nine. The timing worked, if Saul made three casual laps of the pond.

The pond water was slate grey, the surface was ruffled but not choppy. But no-one noticed as all heads were down, the cruel wind lashed at any exposed flesh. The path was that crunchy crushed gravel that gave a pleasing, grinding sound with the traction of his shoes. An ankle-height fence of consecutive, buried half-hoops formed a barrier to the thin strip of mud and sparse grass that was the shore. A few bemused ducks paddled around the center of the water, not daring to venture to the edge. They seemed to be wondering how they ended up there, bobbing up and down like corks. The stinging gusts brought a tart smell of stagnancy to those downwind.

The first circuit found his mind wandering from threats and grand notions to thoughts of Esther and thence to her mother, Ruth, dead, now, some seventeen years. That was about right. Esther is now the same age as her mother was when she had had her, and Esther was five when the accident happened. He missed the tragic Ruth, the Ruth he had known and had fallen in love with, and the time of their fleeting family-life together. That was a few lives ago. Then, Esther had come to him last night, had wanted to help, had told him that she loved him, but he had to reject her by frightening her, had to push her away. It hurt Saul to find himself causing pain to his daughter in order to save her, and why? Was he sacrificing one love for another? Was there not enough space for both?

Then Leah came into his mind, 'shimmied,' he thought, making an entrance with a swish of a silk skirt and a glimpse of stockinged leg. 'Damn!' She could make him feel his diaphragm had been stolen, that he was hollow, and a beautiful, narcotic, visceral longing filled that void. He remembered her hair, 'reams of golden, no, not reams, bushels, like wheat. Bushels of golden wheat poured over her shoulders, her perfectly rounded shoulders. No! More like a liquid gold flowing down.' His body shivered and shuddered in a clamping way, tensing as if to keep something in, not let it out. 'A staunch of golden hair like a mane of light.' She had always provoked the poetry out of him. Then, 'stay in the moment,' breathe and repeat, 'stay in the moment.' Was he truly a beast if it was she that made him so? Extenuating circumstances? Was Leah his prime mover? The *casus belli*? Had he left Esther for Leah? Even though he had no contact with her?

Saul knew that he wove his memories into stories that he wore like a coat. Like this very raincoat that he hoped would be a protection, even if it could not hope to cover his emptiness. To anyone sporting a coat, it does not occur that they are wearing the constituent parts, a collar, sleeves, pockets, breast and back pieces, only that they are wearing the whole. And, Saul was aware of wearing the garment, he was not parsing his Destiny. If his recollections and memories were the elements, then the course of action on which he was set was the complete thing. Just as his life was more than the collection of days he had spent on this Earth. He looked up into the pewter sky to check that there was no ironic rain about to fall. He told himself that "the threat of rain is sufficient to wear a raincoat." He turned up his collar.

As Saul would have expected, if asked, his doubts fell like blows on his own resolve, his conscience pricked bleeding by those memories. His inner sense of his own identity had lately been crumbling, had been tested and found lacking. It would not answer as a foundation for his life. He felt chagrin at having been convinced to carve out a niche into which he could insert himself, only to find it was like building your own coffin. Then to find yourself unable to settle into that space. It was exhausting, to have to constantly fight to maintain his sense of self. And his only weapon to keep the pressures at bay was his Will, which was existing in emptiness. He was desperate to leave behind his feelings of surrogacy. Saul wanted to find a scapegoat and he was going to visit Father Timon.

The muscles of humans, indeed all mammals, tense and relax and thus pull on the attachments of ligaments and sinew to produce movement through elasticity. And as this act, or acts, strains and thus tires the whole organism, so also with ideas. There is a wearing due to mental and spiritual exercise. As Saul vacillated between the righteousness of a heroic deed and the self-criticism of the same, so his energies were exhausted. It was an enervating process, this back and forth, as two counter revolutionary forces wrung his soul dry. His very self was being put through a mangle. This psychic fatigue was reflected in his body, his muscles ached with tension. Perhaps the stress of the anticipated act is the cost of breaking any taboo.

Saul stood next to the fence at the corner of the park where he had entered, a half hour previously, he was just over four blocks from Father Timon's apartment building. The Nines had dissipated, and the park looked drab. The wrought iron railings showed signs of rust through the layers of paint. It was the glacial time of nine o'clock on a Sunday morning and he was tired already. He would have liked to ask for this cup to pass him by. But, however much he wanted the deliverance, he still had to endure the expectation.

In this way Saul viewed Timon, as a sight that held no substance behind it. Like a supernova in an astronomer's eye, whose light tells of a star long vaporized, the vision of which is just an aftermath. The image of a man as he was, not is. And Saul felt a familiarity because he was, or he had been, that very same man, a man of his time, an Old Man. But, he had now experienced his own catastrophic explosion. Saul was the present, Timon the past. Timon had no substance.

And Timon was, to Saul's eye, a light without warmth, a source without a heart, and this made the possible eradication of this pest easier in the way that killing a bee seems somehow less awful than killing a butterfly. Not from an aesthetic standpoint, but because the hive can produce another member. The butterfly stands alone.

The city blocks passed sequentially, unhurriedly, without incident. Being on the way to the Bureaucratic District, and beyond the park, the large buildings exhibited subtly grander designs. The material was the same ubiquitous cement but there were embellishments, the front or side entrances had patterned etchings in the glass doors. They gave glimpses of higher grade interiors than Saul's building could boast. There were adornments in the pediments above the windows which themselves seemed larger and framed by solid wood, not the slipshod metal casements of the lower end apartments Saul had left behind. Even the sidewalks seemed to be composed of a paving of more impressive flag stones, and the curbs were better aligned and, of course, cleaner and better kept.

Saul scoured the floor with his gaze on this familiar route. He had walked it many times on the way to work, when the weather permitted. Even the back alleyways, the unfrequented service passages that cut through the blocks and split the buildings, seemed a bit better tended. These were the access for the garbage trucks and other back-room vehicles necessary for the relevant residences, and Saul was struck by an idea of enticing Timon into these shadows. He just needed an excuse to lure the Father down.

Saul's finger was poised over the intercom button that would put him in touch with his victim. It was the very word 'victim' that caused the hesitation, and the pause caused the tip of Saul's digit to quiver, almost imperceptibly. He stared at the number next to the button of Timon's apartment, three hundred and fifty-eight, a completely random and insignificant number. Saul hated his squeamishness and muttered. "Forgive me, Lord, for I know not what I do." The finger depressed the small plastic knob and he could hear the trill of the bell, a moment's agonizing break and then the familiar high tones of Timon, familiar from forty-seven-and-a-half hours ago, a voice with enough penetration to come over the wires with the clarity of authority.

"Yes. What is it? I'm in a hurry."

"Father Timon, I need to talk to you. Now. It's very important."

"Can't it wait? I'm on the way to Services. Come and see me at my offices tomorrow."

"No, it can't wait." Saul was wary of his voice being overheard by the passersby.

"Who is this? What is this about?"

"I need to see you now! I have an important confession," Saul hissed his anxiety, trying to disguise his voice. "Can you come down? It won't wait, and I need to get it off my chest right now. I'm going away," he lied with an untruth that had just come to him. "It's now or never. You really need to hear this." He waited for the reply, there was a gap of a few seconds.

"Alright, briefly and immediately. Come up."

Saul assumed that the Confessor's wife would be getting ready, but he needed isolation.

"I'd rather you came down, I don't want to be recognized. I'm in danger. I don't want to meet in the lobby. Meet me out back, by the garbage bins. I'll be waiting."

There was a pause as Father Timon considered his options. None seemed less than irritating, though something in the voice over the intercom led him to think this was relevant. He did not recognize Saul, but he could recognize desperation, and that usually led to results. And, God knows, he needed a result.

"I can give you five minutes. I warn you this had better be worth it. I hate being late. I'm leaving now on the way to Church. I'll just have to tell the wife to meet me there."

"Get down as soon as you can, you won't be disappointed."

Saul pulled his finger away and released the button and nodded to himself at the ease with which that had gone. He had thought it would have required more persuasion and now all he needed was an empty alleyway. He was trembling as he rounded the corner to take his position from the outside of the building. Timon would appear from the internal service doors anytime now. Saul wanted to be in position.

Nobody lingered in the dark and forbidding alleyway, particularly in their Sunday best. The smell was putrid, even with daily emptying, and vermin prospered here. Rats and a few feral cats, who were no match for them. No windows looked down on the putative scene and Saul felt confident, almost calm. This was working out, as though he had Fortune, or Providence, on his side. He slinked into a cranny created by the long array of dumpsters that the householders tried to throw their trash bags into from as far away as possible. He had to scrape some moldy tomato skin from his shoes.

There were ten thousand good reasons not to go through with this, and one bad one to go forward. That bad one will win out, he knew, it was that powerful. Saul was committed to making this thing happen. Later, looking back on this time, it would surprise him that he could not remember more. He seemed to be operating automatically, as though going through a set of rehearsed motions.

In the dark ravine of the alleyway, the road width was narrowed by the line of dozens of containers, each the size of a car and only open at eye level from an aperture facing out. The lidded cans did not do enough to keep the compost smell of rotting refuse from permeating the air. There was the suffocating stench of discarded diapers, mildewed food, stale alcohol. Saul heard the rustle of a rodent then the snap of a trap and he felt the shock of the kill, which was reaction. It was all part of the ambiance of the gutter.

The heavy steel doors that opened from the building swung wide enough for an apartment dweller to hold his breath, take four steps and heave a bag of garbage into the bins before retreating inside and exhaling. The banging of the doors was a given, with so many people living here, dashing in and out. Saul guessed from which door Timon would emerge and hid between the cans. There he was.

Timon grimaced up and down the alley looking for whatever had dared to summon him. He held a paisley handkerchief up to the lower part of his face, but it was him, sure enough. His equanimity did not seem disturbed by his disgust. He looked sartorial, and very out of place. Saul hissed at him in an imitation of air leaking from a tire valve. Timon headed over, heeding the summons.

Saul had picked up a half brick that was used as a wheel stop. This clay rock nestled invitingly in his right hand like the primitive tool it was. Man, and artifact, in harmony. His victim, 'how horrible,' turned the corner of the container with an accusation already forming on his lips. Timon wanted to show this interloper who was boss here. He did not have time to recognize Saul before the brick smashed against his left temple. Timon fell to the ground, Saul knelt over him.

"Forgive me Lord, for I know not what I do."

This mantra, a perversion of Christ's entreaty on the cross, was a common chorus. Saul spoke it to the crumpled figure in front of him rather than to any God in Heaven.

Saul hit Timon again on the same side of the head with a venomous strike. The mess on his temple made a suitable target. And the Confessor, Saul's prosecutor and persecutor, his fall-guy, lay supine in the filth, almost extinguished. Saul made more noise than the pummeled Timon. He panted with the exertion of killing, which is harder work than dying.

Timon felt little, but Saul felt the second hit crunch the thin bone of the side of the skull as the brick embedded. The blow subsided into the mushiness beneath, which absorbed the shock. For Saul, every sensation was heightened and slowed as though blown-up and magnified. Yet, later, he would not recall this callous feeling, he would not let himself.

Timon was inert in the puddle of ooze that spread from under the can. His leaking blood mixing with the sludge that his best woolen suit absorbed. He lay face up, his unseeing eyes open in alarm, a strange pale look of questioning disbelief on his face. His jaw hung to his chest and his mouth gaped. As Saul knelt in the muck over his victim, he could see the pain seep into Timon's eyes. This must be the last glimmer of life, the last beat of the heart squeezing one last thought. Like the light from a black hole. Then the irises were losing rings of blue as the pupils dilated.

"Forgive me Lord, for I know not what I do."

Saul pulled out his grandfather's knife and held it with intent, his thumb along the flat top of the blade. He felt the history of the object, the cold of the steel, the pressure of his hand on the handle. He knew the reason it was in his hand. The wet was soaking through his pants to his knees. Saul opened Timon's jacket as a tailor would, with gentle concern, pushed the tie to the left and exposed his shirted chest. Saul estimated where Timon's nipple sat and pushed the tip of the knife into the fabric just above the point. He increased the weight until he felt the point slip between two ribs.

"Forgive me Lord, for I know not what I do."

Saul levered his own body weight onto the knife and felt the blade break through the cotton, piercing the skin in a subtle tear. After the initial insertion, the knife slid in easily, like a paddle through water. The bones guided the blade down into the body cavity and up against the organs. It ruptured the heart, blessed luck! Only a nick, but enough to spasm the muscle of life into a death spiral. This was Saul's insurance.

The residue tension in Timon released and the body relaxed to a corpse. The animation left and the dead weight material, tissue and bone, remained. Saul withdrew the knife and watched, fascinated, as a red stain gradually spread over Timon's shirt front, like a reverse birthmark. Time moved like a pour of molasses. There was a calm around the scene. Saul wiped the blade on Timon's tie and placed the knife back in his coat pocket and rose, as if from a communion, to his feet. He looked down with contempt, and with a surprise at this feeling of contempt, until his mind snapped back to the reality of the alley. A moment that would last a lifetime had passed.

"Forgive me Lord, for I know not what I do."

But he thought that might not be true anymore.

Not knowing why, even later he could not fathom the reason, Saul reached down to Timon's cuffs, pulling the sleeves of his jacket up to reveal the shirt and Timon's elegant wrists. There was a Saint Paul watch on the same side as Timon suffered his death blow, but Saul ignored this and relieved him of a pair of cheap, common tin cufflinks. He had no use for them and knew they may implicate him, yet he could not help himself. He had to have them as a souvenir. He dropped them into his coat pocket where they rested metallically next to the knife.

Stepping back, Saul checked up and down the alleyway to reassure himself that he was undiscovered. He had no idea what he may have done if he had found an audience watching him in his depravity. But, as much as there was a plan, things had gone according to it.

He felt a welling bolus of vomit come up his gullet which he swallowed down again, his legs felt weak and he propped himself up against the two bins forming their little private chamber, a hand on each bin, spanning the chamber. It felt like an intimate act had taken place and the shame washed over him at the desecration. Bowing over the body he beseeched again,

"Forgive me Lord, for I know not what I do."

Now with haste, Saul hefted Timon's body to a sitting position by pulling on his limp arms. Positioning himself behind, he raised Timon to his full height by pushing him up against the bin. He managed to hoist Timon into the left-hand bin, more by the fearful summoning of his reserves of adrenaline than by a clean and jerk. He worked the body up to head height and tipped the Father into the container with the other refuse. He reached in over Timon and arranged a couple of plastic bags as a disguise for his victim. He had made a victim out of Timon, now. The stink within the can was worse than the alley and acted like a dose of smelling salts to jolt Saul to normality. If anything could be said to be normal again after this offense.

Saul dusted down his raincoat; he had some blood on his hands and grime on his pants and coat, but nothing too egregious. Father Timon's wife, would not raise the alarm for a few hours, he guessed. As he left the alleyway, skulking back onto the road, the garbage trucks came into the alley, belching their diesel fumes, to empty the bins. With luck, the body would be carried up and mixed into the tons of trash in the truck, then taken away and dumped unceremoniously in some wretched landfill.

Saul headed back to his apartment and drew himself a bath. He did not see Zipporah as he entered his estranged home. It was only eleven o'clock, yet he felt hungry.

CHAPTER SIX

Following his bath and a somewhat resuscitating lunch of potato and leek soup, Saul felt strangely confused by the ordinary un-normality of his situation. It was to be expected that it would take some time to fully settle his nerves and to loosen the lump in his stomach, which, he thought, felt like a large bolus of ambergris in a sperm whale's gut. In the short-term Saul knew he could hope for little relief, there would not be an immediate purge of the visceral blockage, and potato and leek soup probably wouldn't cut it. The occurrence in the alleyway was a big thing to swallow, a whole lot to digest.

His strain was overlain with a looming presentiment. The more he concentrated on it, the more he realized it was a peculiar satisfaction in his accomplishment. He had done a remarkable thing, he had pulled it off! That sense of pride, in turn, evoked a shameful feeling, being an affront to his Christian ideal of humility. How could he feel vanity at committing a murder?

His conscience was in as much turmoil as his innards, worry was tightly braided with misgiving and there was little hope for a quick unwinding. He knew that henceforth, there was not to be just a simple strand of emotion in his life, that all was to be plaited together. And that was, partly, but not mainly, why he had embarked on this path, why he had committed this transgression. It is liberating to have complicated feelings, for humans are supposed to be byzantine. Saul had foresworn the meek life of an acolyte, and with it the ease of being a follower, for the ramifications of an ethical life. This came with the acknowledgement that actions had consequences, and, ultimately, that to be human was to own those results. That was free will.

Saul needed something to remind himself of the danger of his own hubris. A *memento mori*, perhaps, or at least a tap on the shoulder, to gain his attention and then a voice to whisper 'beware!' At the same time, he also craved a reassurance, a pat on the back of approbation. But, it was either tap or pat, he could not have both simultaneously. He could not juggle the two. That mental contortion was beyond his abilities.

Patting himself, he thought that, although he was no expert, to do this right, to truly be a professional criminal, one must surely hide out in plain sight. Successfully completing a heist but then having to flee to exile was to make a mockery of the crime. It was not enough to conceal oneself in a Hole in the Wall, one should be able to retreat to a commonplace life where one could wait for the next opportunity to cross the divide. Otherwise, one was living a life of an outlaw, and surely the point is to live a normal life but with an added benefit, extra money, say, or a sense of fulfillment. What was the point of all the gold in the world if one cannot spend that wealth?

Then again, tapping on his shoulder was the little devil that reminded Saul of his iniquity. Father Timon's wife was now a widow, a situation caused by his disgraceful act. He had taken a life, and the full meaning of that could never be understood. It had undoubtedly set off a cascade of consequences. Harm is seldom contained to the recipient. Perhaps she loved her husband? Perhaps she was devoted to him and their life together? The perks of their position may have satisfied her ambitions, or maybe she was above all such inducements and cared only for the well-being of the downtrodden? Maybe she was a good person? Maybe she did not deserve to be hurt even if she was not good? Saul had, in one fell swoop, taken all that humanity away from a woman he had never met. She was an innocent bystander who was negatively affected by his rash and selfish actions.Maybe.

Saul felt the remorse of the moral man, for immoral men are not cursed with thinking of the repercussions of their choices. There was that pride again, having taken a life he congratulated himself on feeling terrible!

Then he patted himself again on the back. It was a necessary thing he had done. Timon had threatened him, had alluded to capturing Leah. He had leered at their affair, that was none of his business, had gloated and ridiculed. And then Saul vacillated to the tap, reminding himself that nothing is necessary. There was always a choice, and that was free will.

Saul felt the spiritual fatigue of the back and forth, that yo-yo-ing, but he knew that, somehow, 'it was the saving of him.' But what was he being saved for? Was there a purpose to this, was he destined for something more? By exercising his spirituality he had resuscitated it, for it had lain dormant for decades, but was that in order to fulfill some manifest outcome?

By one o'clock Saul sat nursing his bruised conscience in his bedraggled chair. The clean knife and the pair of tin cuff-links were on his lap, he was contemplating their roles. It was a mystery that he should steal these two redundant trinkets. Was it stealing, or more like grave robbing? What was he thinking, or, indeed, was he thinking? What had he been thinking? The knife, on the other hand, now that holds meaning. It is lethal; lethal and evil. But the object has no morality, it cannot commit acts of right and wrong, it can only be used by agents. He, Saul, must take responsibility, he must take credit. But cuff-links?

Saul rose from his reveries, still lost in himself. He sidled up to his picture window where he could see far off Tohu over the roofs of the City. The air had been scoured by the wind and rain and the jagged horizon of the mountains created a purple *fata morgana*, a fairy scene that contrasted with the concrete of the nearby buildings. A ribbon of cloud streamed from the peaks of Tohu like a pennant. If he lowered his eye line he could see the opening of the park and then Timon's building and, beyond, the darker grey of the Bureaucratic District, the setting for his lost life. It seemed like a theater stage on which he had just seen a play performed. Then he realized that he was the main actor, but the author was anonymous. It worried him that he may not be the master of his own destiny, that no-one was, that it was all random. Was that worse? Or better?

Saul could not allow himself to consider having done this thing for himself. He had done this for Leah, and for Esther. He had done this thing to Timon and he had done this thing to himself. Leah seemed to be the past, the cause; he was the present, the action; and Esther the ensuing, the effect. There was a balance, here, with himself as pivot. Or rather, a lever, this act the fulcrum upon which the future could be moved. Or flung.

Saul thought, children, offspring, are like shooting arrows into the future, hoping they land somewhere worthwhile, embed in something of value. It is understandable why some parents choose to shoot their arrows into the ground directly in front of them, where they can be looked after, close enough to be tended. But to risk is to aim into the indiscernible, beyond one's line of sight. There is a chance they will not land well but they then have the benefit of distance. Saul had launched a manifestation of himself, on a true parabola, into the beyond, to maximize its range.

He would never know the results of his labors, and probably never could. The consequences branch out like whispers, like gossip. You cannot contain a secret, it is water in the hand. Imagine rushing forward in anticipation, to find your arrow, and finding out that it had landed in water, to pierce nothing. To make hardly a splash and then to bob back to the surface and be rushed away on a current. This was his anticlimax, the uncertainty. Had he committed a sin, undermined everything? Or had he launched the first salvo? Where is his resolution? Had he used it all up in the act itself, leaving himself an empty shell in the aftermath?

Saul thought, 'We were promised strawberries at Christmas.'

And when they came, they arrived hot-house grown and bland. They were strawberries and it was Christmas, but they had lost their taste and texture. Perhaps strawberries needed summer. Are all promises lies, or compromises?

Consider the disillusioned climber who, scaling an unfamiliar peak, achieves a false summit to see his goal up ahead excruciatingly out of reach. Or, the marriage that entails divorce after wooing a shrew, or being wooed by a cad. The twist of fate that results from the twist of the knife. A sheep that knows the wool and mutton are his, yet must bow to the whims of the shepherd. Realities that do not live up to expectations. The disappointments of quotidian life. All these were in Saul's unfettered ruminations. All this was in Saul's juggled mind. Pat, pat, pat.

His fellow citizens had failed him.

Saul reverently held his remote Grandfather's knife. 'This knife,' observed Saul, 'has killed, has pierced a living heart and stopped it beating. It has done my bidding, faithfully, and it knows no ambivalence. It has no authority and no autonomy, it is unthinking and free of blame and shame. But when I touch it, even with a fingertip, it becomes my instrument.'

Saul placed it down and saw it lying on the arm of his chair. The clean blade reflected a little of the thin light, the bronze hilt looked handsome and the rosewood handle sturdy and robust. It had beauty, it had use but it did not have responsibility and so he envied the object. The knife did not care that it broke a man's skin and dived into his heart. That it had pierced a beating heart, and by so doing stopped it. It could not know that it may have saved Saul's soul. If it were used to kill a tyrant or a saint, it would be the same.

Saul knew he had transgressed the laws of the God of his culture. He could break the paltry laws of man, but breaking God's law is rebellion, pure and simple. But, if Saul is his instrument then the evil he has done is in Him who wields the tool. Just as the knife is innocent then so is Saul.

But what a blessed relief!

It is taught that the people live in God's house, but maybe the obverse is true, maybe He abides in the people. Instead of humans created in God's image, maybe He is created in Human image. Instead of being a part of Him, perhaps He is a part of us. Then we have a choice whether to accept or deny. And we can form Him to the shape we need.

We can make Him!

Bend Him to our Will!

Saul needed to comfort his inner chaos with a familiar distraction. He needed a palliative and so, as many times before, he took down from his book shelf, *The Historie of the Valorous and Wittie Knight-Errant Don Quixote of La Mancha*, by Miguel de Cervantes Saavedra. This ancient text was a perennial favorite of his and its escapism a great succor. He loved the fable of the bizarre Hidalgo and his flights of fantasy and of his belief in his instincts. It had always been an inspiration to Saul that the madness of the Don had been absolved by his good heart. That even the efforts of his servants, and the clergy, to bring him back to reality having failed, their instincts were to protect the knight. It was a reassuring tale of the grandness of human kindness and charity, and mercy. Saul needed a sense of forgiveness. It was a parable he believed in. He flipped through his worn copy and read idly from randomly chosen passages.

This led Saul to the ideas of the 'New Men' and 'Cygnet Committee,' thence back to Leah and where she might be hiding. Obviously beyond the wit of the Templars, or they would not have pressured him to reveal what he did not know. The logistics of his plight started to make their nagging interrogations. This was the tap, tap, tap reminder.

Why had the Templars called him in? He was a small cog in the machine, his affair with Leah was short. Sweet, but short. He was not complicit in any subversion, not that Timon would have known that. They could have been trying to flush him out, in which case did he overreact? It seemed a bit strange to call murder an overreaction. If they wanted to find Leah, why wouldn't they follow her path. It was impossible not to leave a trace in the Bureaucracy as you moved through life. You had to fill out forms in triplicate for permission to live in a Hole in the Wall. There was no escape.

So where was Leah? And why did they not follow the paper trail to find her? Why drag Saul into the mess? Not to implicate him, he was valueless when it came to thwarting rebellion, he would admit that. It was unthinkable that the great authorities of the State would not. So, the question was begging, to be asked and to be answered, why Saul?

He needed to find her, to tell her of his act, to seek some reassurance back, to discover what his part was in this un-authored play. He thought he was the lead, he thought he was Othello, perhaps he was Iago. There was a depth to this that he needed to plumb. To get to the bottom. He thought the act of eradicating Timon would bring clarity, but he was as much in the dark as before, now he just knew of his ignorance. This obfuscation, was it a smoke-screen?

Leah could supply the answer, he needed to get to her. Before the Templars, before the New Men. Saul would warn her and then beg her. He wanted some pardon for doubting, pity for leaving. He wanted to know if his new life was to be with the New Men.

Whether the Cygnet Committee could help him now that he had proved his *bona fides*.

He fell asleep in his comfortable chair, the only one in the world molded to his shape. The worn fabric was soothingly rough in its texture against his cheek. The familiar accommodating hug of his chair supported his slumped body. It enveloped him in his own scent. He drooled a little out of the corner of his mouth.

An hour later, panic rudely woke Saul, shaking him out of a welcome torpor. Having done so, it then subsided into an aching anxiety. Perhaps it just needed to check that he was still alive, and the abatement was its relief. The interior of the apartment was warm and humid and the kitchen smell was a pervasive afterthought, a lingering odor of boiled cauliflower.

Outside, the dim grey light softened the workaday city to a pastel portrait. Saul stood for a minute at his evening window, gazing down at the darkening streets, the scurrying citizens. The headlamps of the occasional cars cast white cones into the evening fog, pointing this way and sweeping that as the vehicles turned corners. The street lamps illuminated the atmosphere rather than the sidewalks, they were beacons hanging in the air, their refracted light not hitting the pavements.

Saul prepared his dinner in typical fashion, opening a few cans, peeling a few potatoes, rolling out some once-frozen dough to make a pocket for his filling, that he then baked for most of an hour in his oven that leaked heat. The simmering and baking added to the mild background sauna effect. His mind was distracted and he was mechanical, it was a good job that he could do this in his sleep. His pasty tasted as bland as his cooking ever did.

Saul poured himself a large measure of whisky, gin seemed too frivolous, and added nine drops of tap water, out of habit. The cheap blend was not improved by this addition. This was a mass-produced alcohol with a taste designed to appeal to a teetotaler, that is, repulsive like a medicine. It must have been distilled in a factory for it was redolent of oily metal vats. This stuff could double as a solvent, or an antiseptic. Luckily, Saul had hardened his taste-buds over the years of self-anesthetizing. He drank a good draught of the stuff, it was not for savoring, and he was diverted by the burn in his gullet. Perhaps it was a medicine after all.

Then the suffusion of almost well-being as his senses lovingly unmoored and his thoughts floated unshackled. He was home, and all was well with the world, the alcohol raised his mind out of the realm of the earthly and into a rarefied place free of judgement and emotion. He toasted himself, to his success and his independence. All the while he knew it was the drink talking and this a brief respite from life. Still, it made dinner palatable, and sleep easy.

The next morning, Saul awoke at the start of another work week, except he had an appointment at ten o'clock with Father Timon. He amused himself with the thought of his feigned surprise at Timon's absence. Being in the know afforded him a rare sense of superiority. Then, the guilt weighed on him and he felt bemused. 'A-mused and b-mused, is there a c-mused?' He practiced his facial expression at being told the news as he tied his blue tie in the mirror. Shock, surprise, confusion, they were all within the remit of his plan. He was not out of the woods yet. On the way out he took a mischievous nip of whisky from the bottle, for courage.

The investigation would not die along with the Father, presumably, it would be passed onto another operative, along with the whole dossier of Timon's cases. The Bureaucracy does not grind to a halt due to the loss of one clerk, Saul knew. Dockets have a life of their own and it is hard to kill an unresolved agenda item, even by neglect. Saul would be able to muddy the waters with a new Father, act like the co-operative client he had not wanted to be before, and use Timon's memory as a decoy.

"Poor Timon, we had hit it off last week, I thought we might become friends."

Saul knew how slow the wheels of justice turned and he thought that even if the lumbering department vehicle caught up with him, he would be nimble enough to evade it. And if he couldn't? Well then, he would be run over in slow-motion, crushed bit by bit, and that, he thought, he could bear. He had maybe used a sledge-hammer to crack a walnut, but the nut was well and truly cracked. Humility was the name of Monday's game, a suitably effacing citizen trying to help a functionary do his job. There was nothing to fear today, at least. Nothing to see here, move along, please!

He left the apartment at half past eight, giving himself plenty of time to reach the Security Building on foot, as was his wish. He did not want to prick the bubble surrounding him in the spiky crush of the busses. He could keep his facade up outside, he could not dare risk his vulnerable kernel in contact with his fellows. They would smell what he had done, he must stink of more than whisky.

Saul felt he was playing a game with life, that he had wagered, but was almost confident it would pay off, that he could pull it off. The sheer audacity excited him. He felt in control, as the possession of his secret set him apart. He did not whistle, he kept his head down and would occasionally smirk in complicity, his chin down into the upturned collar of his raincoat. Then the gravitas would hit him like a wave of nausea and shame him. Would wipe the smile off his face.

In the left pocket of his coat, he could feel where the knife had nudged into his hip as he had walked this path the day before. Now, it was sitting cleansed back in its box in the closet, newly abandoned. He had thought about wearing the tin cufflinks.

"What the Hell?"

He circled the pond in the park and regarded the quarantined ducks with a philosophic ease. It is only human to enjoy the afterglow of achievement. Not the celebration whereafter the success passes, but the memory of a plan hatched and completed. Saul winked at the history he had made, a nod to his own self-importance. He did feel special, elevated, and he wallowed in that self-regard. He felt he had earned his leisure, his tourist perspective.

The worm in the apple of his new-found knowledge was the nagging doubt about Timon's new widow. The guilt he felt infected his *sang-froid*, but he did not suffer a fever, he kept his cool. His internal voice was a coach, urging him to stay calm, berating his lack of concentration. It reminded him of his position, his role. Sometimes he felt as if he had fallen off a cliff and was bouncing down the rocks, from pillar to post, back and forth. He deserved this fate because of the pain he had caused. He needed to stay in the moment.

The Father's body should be crushed into pulp by now, hopefully incinerated, or whatever they do with trash. How would they track a body in a mountain of garbage, a needle in a haystack, and a needle that no-one knows is missing? As murder was rare, the methods of detection were not very refined. The Templars were good at catching heretics but not killers. Saul thought he had his own destiny in his own hands, even as he fell, and the ground was speeding to meet him.

His preoccupied pace took him to his appointment at the Security Department with barely enough time to spare. Where had that hour and a half gone? By rushing the last few blocks he managed to arrive without committing the gratuitous insult of tardiness. He entered the large foyer he had visited three days before with all the decorum he could muster. The guards were still disinterested, and thankfully did not grab him as he entered, the dismissive receptionists were still bored by him. But this time was different, today he did not bristle at being treated as though he were inconsequential.

"I have a ten o'clock confession with Father Timon."

"One moment, Sir. I have other business to attend to." One of the hard-coiffured girls raised her gaze and spoke, covering the mouthpiece of an unseen telephone. She rolled her eyes slowly upward under her lids, being careful not to disarrange her lashes. "You are not the only visitor we have to deal with."

Saul was reminded that it was best policy to speak when spoken to when dealing with Government gatekeepers, but he wanted his presence noted. He stepped back, his bowler in his hands, muttering a milquetoast apology. He was on the radar screen as present, and that was worth something, being registered, even negatively. The girl finished her call and enquired as to Saul's name and then assessed his relative unimportance. He merged with the other attendees crowding by the double glass doors that grinned like a mouth ready to devour the waiting, each in turn, like *canapés*.

Eventually, after fifteen minutes of standing as un-imposingly as possible, the same girl he noted on Friday as looking like Esther, called his name. Saul gave her his practiced, strained smile and followed her through. She led him down the uniform passages and corridors to a room so like the last it was indistinguishable. Saul made himself at home, if, that was, he had lived in a prison which, he fervently hoped, was not to be. The chair was still hard, the desk still a table, the walls institutional. There was that sharp disinfectant smell that public arenas held, as if your nostrils were being cleansed. It was time to get this over with. Saul had plans to complete, ambitions to fulfill. Even if he did not know what they were.

After the statutory ten-minute official wait, the door opened to the Sister who had guided him to this room. She seemed very brisk and brusque, very businesslike, efficient, more so than before. Whether it was all flatter and presentation was irrelevant, to appear professional is to be professional. She entered with a perfunctory smile and placed a file onto the table, then smoothed down the tightness from the rear of her skirt as she lowered herself onto the other seat. She did not remind Saul of Esther any more.

"Citizen Saul, I have some news. Your visit, your interview with Father Timon, is cancelled." Saul heard the 'cancelled' that had been chosen over 'postponed,' and felt his abdominal muscles tense. He tried to not look too quizzical. "Father Timon has not turned up for work this morning, and his wife called searching for him which implies that he is missing." She was too forthcoming with information but was probably repeating the message she had been told. Saul nodded blank-faced, expecting a follow up. "But looking at your file," she looked down to the desktop, "there is a note which I have been authorized to share with you. It was written by Father Timon on Friday." She pulled out a sheet of paper and read:

"It is clear that Citizen Saul has no useful knowledge that will enable us to pursue our investigations in the matter of Citizen Leah any further. It is therefore of my opinion that the case be prosecuted along different lines and that Saul be informed his services are no longer required." It was signed by Father Timon, definitively and conclusively. Stamped and sealed. She showed Saul.

The girl placed the paper back in the manila card file and looked at Saul across the metal table with the slightest lean of the head indicating that it was his turn to speak. Her hair hung a fraction longer on one side of her face than the other. Then it did not. Saul stammered the letter 'b' as a precursor of the word 'but.'

"Yes? Do you have a question? If you wish to add something to the record I can bring in an amanuensis from the pool to indite it."

"B . . . b . . . b . . . but, I am a . . . a . . . bit, not shocked, surprised! You are dropping the investigation? In fact, it was dropped on Friday? I needn't have . . . have . . . come in today?"

"Yes, I am sorry about the inconvenience. Father Timon's non-attendance was not planned, we only learned about it this morning. You can tell your supervisors that the Security Department wanted your appearance, and here is your *carte blanche*." This was the printed permission letter that authorized the holder to be held blameless for official business, Saul mechanically took the paper. It was worth a few hours. His mind was disassembling somewhat, and he knew he had this girl's attention for a short time.

"So, Timon? You do not know where he is?" Why ask, why would I care? "So that is it? I do not need to come back? That's the end of it?" He remembered the planting of the book in his apartment. Why would that happen if the case was closed? What did this mean? He was flummoxed. He felt like Don Quixote would have felt if the Priest had managed to bring him back to reality. This was shocking news. Did this take away all justification for his action? Did this nullify his guilt, or double it? Is what happened to Timon worse now?

"You are dismissed, Citizen Saul. Thank you for your time. I wish you the best. Bless you!"

She stood up, the blue of her outfit not suggesting freedom to Saul, because he was stunned, she gestured him to follow her out and led him back to the double glass doors. Her nodding in a shallow bow sent him into the real world. The doors spewed him back into the lobby. His thoughts would not cohere. He found it hard not to act like an imbecile and felt it best not to talk, not that he had the chance. The large oak doors released him out onto the pavement.

"I need to unscramble these eggs."

Down in the bowels of the Security Department, things were not as costive as Saul hoped. You cannot deflect a hurricane by boarding up a window, you only save yourself a pane of glass. In a dim room, three men sat around a table in another of the building's bare rooms. Each of equal stature and position. It was a Buridan's ass of a decision to hold the meeting in one plush office of the attendees rather than another. They were all equal on this committee. This interrogation room, the lowest of the subterranean choices, was the compromise venue. The air was dead in the room.

All three men were almost indistinguishable. They wore the same black suit, they sported the same trim haircut, they sat in the same uncompromising style, they were the same gray color. One of them wore spectacles and the other two thought that choice of eyewear to be insufficiently innocuous, rather *outré*, in fact.

Agent number one said, "We have recovered Father Timon's corpse and now have it in the Department morgue. The autopsy gives the cause of death as trauma to the cranium caused by a blunt instrument, in accordance with a wound that punctured the heart. There was no murder weapon and no clear evidence pointing to a suspect as of this moment in time. We do have a list of possible perpetrators, culled from the Father's enemies, but with the Father being quite assiduous in his prosecutions, it is extensive. He was not popular."

He looked over his sheet at his *confrères*, who nodded in agreement. "Checking on his open cases yesterday, after his widow alerted us to his disappearance and the subsequent discovery of the body in the waste disposal facility, we have a good lead. It is an open case, but not as straightforward as it seems, as none of our issues are."

He looked at his fellows and dutifully received the guffaws he had been expecting. He counted them.

"I expect to have this put to bed relatively easily. There is a willing source of information that has come to our attention and, if it is as productive as it is promising to be, then this may wrap up next week. We have concocted an extension to the ongoing investigation, by means of subterfuge. By that, I mean that we have given the suspect a clean bill so that we may track his whereabouts and thereby see where he leads us. The homing pigeon strategy, as we used to call it. Simple but effective. The hope is that the taint of murder will flush out this cadre of the New Men, who will not want to roost with pigeons. Homing or stool."

The two other Templars did not deign to smile, but considered the first with a loftiness that his smug assumption of chairmanship demanded. It was only that he was on call on Sunday that entailed this succulent file landing on his desk. Availability and scheduling does not a promotion mean, they both thought simultaneously. The second agent decided he needed to speak.

"Father Timon told me he was working on a New Man case, with the Cygnet Committee. Is this the cause of the breach? We have been involved with them for a while now and feel we have them where we need. The lamented Father had set this up rather well, textbook, in fact. We need to give him credit. On a personal note, I have worried for a while about Timon's ambition to join us here and the unorthodox lengths he felt he needed to go to in order to impress and ingratiate himself. It was never quite the done thing. This eventuality resolves that conundrum, anyway."

The third agent was silent, he took off and cleaned his glasses, but the first spoke in reply.

"Agreed. We shall continue monitoring and perhaps intervention may be in order if the case does not break open soon. I propose that we convene again in a week to assess the progress. I now call this meeting to adjournment. All in agreement?"

"Aye."

"Aye."

CHAPTER SEVEN

Saul's first reaction was jubilation, muted by the sheer unlikelihood of the news. At first, he could not believe his luck, then he could not believe the news. Then, as he believed the news, his luck seemed plausible. She had exonerated him, he had waltzed out of the Security Department as free as a bird. He should die, he thought, because with the roll he was on, Saint Peter would wave him right on through those old Pearly Gates. Saul positively glided down the sidewalk, with no sense of direction nor time nor place. After his actions of the day before, the self-accusations, the recriminations, his slate was wiped clean. It took the time it took for Saul to cover a block before the questions arose.

What about that break-in? If Timon had written the note on Friday, as dated, why would they bother to plant the *New Man* book? What could that be about, they had dismissed him and so why leave that calling card? Maybe, just a procedure that was initiated and not rescinded in time? Maybe Timon had written the note later in the day, after ordering the burglary, after learning some new information? But what, 'What could have changed his mind?' Timon had seemed adamant when Saul had left him after the interview. All that stress had been needless, all that worry, the mental torture, pointless. And then Sunday . . . .

Saul had killed Timon because in the aftermath of that first confession the script demanded it. Those were his directions. But, the book he was reading had been closed, without his knowing. What a fallout, guessing an outcome on limited knowledge.

Thinking he was starring in a tragedy, the play had been re-written halfway through as a farce. Unaware of the edit, he had violated the sixth commandment, he had committed the most mortal of sins. Now, he was anathema in the eyes of God. He had thrown his immortal soul into jeopardy on behalf of no good person. And, he was worried about himself? 'Selfish! Selfish!' He had killed an innocent man, and he felt angry that he had been driven to it? That was the injustice? Saul cursed himself, but he could not answer the questions.

His transient joys were drowning in a weighted sack at the bottom of a well. And like a rope following a bucket falling down that well, the dire threat of the universe unspooled him. His fear was flapping and twisting in the air before disappearing out of sight. He grabbed hold and could not let go, if he did he would not be able to regain his grip, and the momentum threatened to pull him into the abyss. The rope burned his palms, rasped his flesh, but he could not let go. It was agony, but any hope to rescue his joys, his sanity, depended on that bucket bringing them back to the surface.

Saul turned the corner of the block, he stopped with his back to the giant edifice of the Security Building and let his legs buckle under him. He squatted down under the weight of his unbearable being, this time his legs allowed his torso to reach his heels. Like Jesus, he wept. It was a relief, a release but also a recognition that his efforts had cost dearly. He cried discreetly into his hands that covered his face, that without his head were held out in supplication. Saul was a beggar, the lowest of the low, unloved and undeserving. He mourned the loss of his past self, the man he could no longer be, the death of hope.

It says a lot about Saul's strength of will that he had an alternative to devastation. Perhaps we all have that power to pull our scattered selves together again, but only some of us are aware of it. He could not, would not, allow himself the indulgence of wretchedness. The crying flushed the emotion from him and the scour inside illuminated an opportunity. For the sake of a passer-by, he made as if he had a stomach cramp, and the realization that other's opinions still mattered brought him up. His blistered hands pulled that rope up, and the bucket was filled.

Saul opened himself up to the possibility of love. And instead of giving himself up to God, and trying to earn His love, he resolved to challenge God to prove Himself. He would seek the love within and nurture that neglected side of himself. If it is true that God is that which makes us think we have a soul, then Saul had found his God, he just did not know its essence, yet.

Ratcheting himself up to standing, he turned on his heel and headed back past the door he had just exited, that, in itself, was brave. He continued onto the Produce Distribution Department, two blocks down, led by a determination he had never experienced before, but one he would need later. He had decided on a mission, that this game was not ending at this pathetic juncture, with him broken in the streets, his spirit drowned. The City looked new and clean to him, he could see into the busy citizen's souls. They all deserved respect and love. He felt his own soul glow.

The three men in black suits who stood on the top step of the Security Building entrance watched him pass. They were unfamiliar to Saul, if he would have noticed them, he would not have recognized them. They knew him, they expected him, they watched him march on with a collective rueful smile split into thirds on their thin lips.

"I did not think he would be coming back this way," said the one with glasses.

Saul gained the familiar entryway of his office building and handed the *carte blanche* over to the unconcerned receptionist to be dutifully filed for posterity's sake. Then he accepted the odd nod of accustom, not needing to show his badge, and climbed the overly long steps in the echoing stairwell. There was an unusual lull in the traffic in the halls, the workers at their mid-morning desk exertions, he supposed. Normally, when he arrived and left the building it was during the rush hour crush, when the corridors were busy. After the first four flights, he found himself dawdling on the landing of the second floor. This was where Leah had been stationed, and where, on occasion, Saul had dropped in to visit her and pick her up when they had met for a furtive date, that was not a date. They had both hated the label. His memory was a tease, both the good and the evil. He was picking at his conscience as one does at a scab, to promote healing. Saul went into Leah's old work space.

Leah's old office contained seven desks, six set out facing the seventh in a classroom style. She had used the furthest one in the back row of three, closest to the grimy window. Her old desk was occupied by a lowered head of grey hair, that concentrated itself on a sheet of paper laid out between her forearms. A pen in her right hand hovered over the margin of a line of figures and she threw quick glances to a file propped open on a desktop easel in front of her. Then she would tick something off and return to the figures. The collection of five female perfumes mixed pleasingly in the warm, studious atmosphere.

Saul composed himself, again, he was looking for Sarah and she was in the desk in front of grey-hair. She had not moved in months, apparently, still holding down the fort. Sarah was not the youngest in the bank of workers here, but not by much. By Saul's judgement, she was young. She and Leah had had a sisterly friendship, supportive and mentoring, Leah the big sister that Sarah always wanted, her own being back at home, intent on breeding, early and often. About a year ago, she had arrived, green and enthusiastic, from the highlands beyond Tohu. A backwoods rube in the big city. Leah had taken her under her wing and good-naturedly chided her in the ways of the office.

Saul had not seen Sarah in the intervening months since his cowardice had pushed Leah away from him, and he had avoided this office. He now approached the desk and, crouching next to her, caused Sarah to break into a wide grin of recognition on her cherubic face.

"Hi," whispered Saul and nodded her out into the corridor. Sarah picked up a sheaf of paper as an excuse to be fraternizing, and followed Saul. Leaning against the whitewashed walls, she smiled and pushed a loose strand of hair behind her ear.

"I haven't seen yer for months. How are yer? Still upstairs?" There was a coquettish element to her voice, her accent still perceptible.

"Yes. I'm fine. I heard about that avalanche last week and thought of you. No-one you know, I hope. Tragic. What was it, fifteen kids? Terrible."

"I didn' know any personally, but their school was a big rival to ahrs. Tha' pass was always an accident waitin' ta happen. I was goin' to head back home next week, if the road opens. I'm finkin of returning permanently. It's a bit overwhelming down here. Its 'ard to make friends, I still miss Leah. I'm not really fittin' in well, even after a year. There's a boy, man, an old friend from high school, he's runnin' the family farm. He asked if I wanted to see about throwing in my lot with his. Not a romantic man, you see!"

Saul was a full head taller than Sarah which made him feel a little paternal, protective, toward her. She was about five years older than Esther, less inured to the vicissitudes of life, had held onto her *naïveté*, although she saw this as a lack of sophistication. Sarah would have admired Esther's cold phlegmatic skepticism, if they had met. She thought her own lack of guile a handicap.

"I hope you find your happiness," wished Saul, adding, "and, as I am in search of mine, I was wondering if you had heard from Leah? Or knew where she was?" He looked at her trying to gauge a reaction, would she be coy? Unforthcoming? Eager? Scared? Her brows knitted, and she looked down to the brown linoleum tiles.

"She sort-ov made me promise that I wouldn' tell anyone where she was goin'. She was feeling so disillusioned with every-fin' around here, she just wan-ed out. The poor fing felt persecuted and then when you left 'er she was like a calf separated from its mother. I know its only months, but it seems like such a long time ago now, like it is history and we can discuss history, right?" Saul thought, aah, to measure history in months. "I don't know if she was more scared uv the Security or 'artbroken over you." Saul felt a little accused by her confession, but it was no more than he had levelled at himself.

"Sarah, I'm sorry if you don't want to be in the middle of anything, I understand." There was a wide gap between understanding and allowing. There was no way Saul was going to permit Sarah to walk away, so it came as a relief when she carried on.

"No. I feel good talking to you. There's no blame. It was just circumstances, she 'ad 'er secrets and you were unavailable, wrapped up in yourself and yer own world. Like two rabbits in your own burrows, you must come up for air sometime, spend some time where it's dangerous. You know, frolic, be those mad march hares. Sorry, I'm blabberin' away here. I am not too sure, Sol, that you knew how much she fell for you, how much she loved ya. She always tried to be above it all, unattached, but she told me it was getting harder. It was you, you lucky man! Then you scarpered. You didn't know what you 'ad and you didn't help the whole thing, always distant, always distracted. But there we are, it's all history. Wa'er under the bridge." She gave an insipid scowl that she pulled up into a pale smirk. Saul realized that she had been hurt by Leah's departure, and blamed him for it without wanting to.

"I think I want to find her again."

"You fink? You wanna find her?" Sarah became suddenly more intrigued in the conversation.

"I have been through a lot. Done things I am not proud of and I need her. Sarah, will you help me? Things are different, I have changed. As much as any person can."

"Of course, but I can't really talk 'ere. The super will come looking for me in a minute. I need to get back to the grindstone. Can I see ya later?"

"I'm just on the way upstairs to my office. I'll call for you at five thirty. Just like I used to do with Leah. See you then and," he reached out and dusted off her shoulder, then stared deeply into her eyes, "thanks. Thank you so much. You don't know how much this means."

He turned back toward the stairs and lumbered up ten flights to the seventh floor. He felt the walk in his heavy legs and it gave him a gratifying moment to not think. Reaching his office, he sank into his wooden chair at his metal desk and found himself faced with a mound of paperwork, demanding to be processed. He found he could ignore it with ease.

The beauty of having everyone work at half capacity was that it was easy to make up for lost time when need be. He should be able to sort through this pile before seeing Sarah in a few hours, particularly if he avoided lunch. It was the work he had had no stomach for on Friday. He set to the task at hand without gusto, but glad for the diversion. It seemed an odd way to celebrate a victory, for he had won a victory, even if he did not feel celebratory. And as the pile of papers diminished so did his self-reproach. He was pleased not to have to write today, copywriting and editing were enough for his sore intellect. Being creative was beyond him. Being anything beyond himself, was beyond him.

That evening, Saul took Sarah to a bar in the Marmalade District where he and Leah had become close to becoming regulars. It was in a cellar under a book store, and retained that signature smell of sour beer and burned cheese. The last time he had smelled that was a few months ago, he was glad not to be recognized. There were no friendly greetings, as there had been, and Saul thought that maybe Sarah was right, it was history.

Sarah had spruced herself up before he had called for her and although her work dress was crumpled and sagged a little, her face was bright with a touch of borrowed make-up. Most attractive was her attention to him, which was solicitude, her face and ears attuned to his needs. Her focus was informational, she had questions, and they traded intelligences. This suited his one request. Over a few fingers of semi-decent whisky for him and a ruby-colored Downland Pinot for her, she spilled the details she knew. He drank too quickly and had ordered another while she was halfway through her first. He needed to exert more control.

It turned out that Leah had left her job abruptly and without looking back, the way Jacob had followed God. This had surprised her contemporaries as they had assumed she was as content as an intelligent person in an undemanding position could expect to be. In fact, for the weeks prior to her resignation, she had seemed positively joyous, blissful even, happy like a skylark in summer. So, it was a shock when on that Monday afternoon she announced that it was her last day and goodbye and wished everyone the best. Sarah had managed to corral Leah into a Pinot after work and Leah had looked like a dirge sounds. She had tried to sympathize with her mentor, and prize out the reasoning behind the decision without attempting to overturn it. As you would expect, the interviewee was unforthcoming, kept her cards close to her chest, and just wanted to reassure Sarah that she would miss her and that nothing Sarah had done had been offensive. The only hint about Leah's future movements, which were completely unconsidered, was the mention of the Upper Downland farmhouse where she had spent an idyllic weekend. Here, Saul nodded sagaciously at Sarah's comments, knowing he was expected to divulge his reasons for being there tonight in a crowded bar with a too young companion.

"So, there was no direct mention of us? Leah and me? She didn't drop any hints as to where she could be found if, say, someone tall, dark and handsome was looking for her?"

Sarah smiled, but out of sympathy rather than amusement. She felt their age difference all of a sudden, not that she had been interested, 'Oh no! Perish the thought!' She liked Saul, though, even if he was a bit too aloof for her. Normally she liked a man who could charm, and she did not know at this point that it was to be a source of great regret to her later self. Saul had an open, honest, trustworthy look, she thought, he must have been handsome ten years ago, but you could never tell with men. Sometimes the most bovine looking youths turned into the most appealing of males when they matured. It was like a test from God as to your vanity. Chose because of character and maybe be rewarded with looks, or just go with a good-looking face and hope there is kindness there. This would remain baffling to Sarah, for the rest of her life.

She did venture, "There must be a record in 'er personnel file in the Downland department stating where she transferred to. She must 'ave put in a request and applied to a new posting, mustn't she? You can't just vanish, can ya? They know where y'arr." She realized that she sounded a touch naive as she spoke, the one thing she was trying not to be. The drink was also bringing out her accent. She thought she might as well try honing her grown-up skills on Saul, practice her suavity. Perched on a bar stool she uncrossed her knees and changed legs. She wondered how it looked. The tight pencil skirt was not helping her look elegant, it was a bind to her strong legs.

"You don't have access to the files, do you?" Saul loomed conspiratorially.

"I could prob'ly sneak a look at lunchtime. If I stayed in the office, the personnel staff always go out togever," there was some implication here that did not interest Saul at all. "Come down tomorrow afternoon. I'll see what I can find."

The rest of the evening was spent in pleasantries, he encouraged her to flirt with the barman and put in a good word with him about her. The barman was a gregarious fellow, eager as a young man should be, and flattered Sarah into a hopeful focus. Saul left, thankful of the distraction, promising to visit her tomorrow and generously tipping the staff. It pays, he thought, to show appreciation for good luck, even when, especially when, unexpected. He needed to get away from the emotions that had hung, drawn and quartered him on this day.

Saul's evening was spent as a penitent. He went to his apartment and drew himself as cold a bath as he could. The immersion was the penance for his soul's sin by way of his body. The cold water constricted his blood flow on a capillary level and tortured his brain into concentrating on the present moment. The bathtub needed scrubbing, the walls were starting to grow mold, the lavatory was unloved. He dunked his head and let the cascade of sobriety wash away anything superfluous. He needed constraint, inner calm and strength, he felt so, so alone in the universe. The universe he had tried to kill. Perhaps this was its revenge. He did not so much sleep as just turn off, he just shut down his brain and rested.

Sarah was tight-lipped when Saul caught up with her after lunch the next day, demure even. He found her hangover wryly amusing but past experiences with his own grown daughter prevented him from teasing her. The older he grew the more natural it became for him to play the role of the father. Not enough compensation for aging, but better than nothing. The real benefit of aging, he knew, was the end of caring what others thought. Sarah had that to look forward to, at this moment she was slightly embarrassed.

"I did manage to hav' a glance at Leah's file. I fink I could have just walked up in the middle of the morning, all brazen-like. I don't think they really care about privacy much." She was stumbling into her vernacular.

"What is private when we all live the same?" asked Saul. "There is the public you, the outside life, and then you sleep, then you die."

Sarah looked askance at Saul, not judgmentally but also not approvingly. She had this romantic idea of being the matchmaker, the bellows on a cinder of passion. But she also had her petty rural attitudes, of which she was immensely proud, her innate conservatism. Her view of Saul was encouragingly benign at this point. He was a slightly heroic figure in her mind.

"It turns ou'," Sarah spun the information out she had. "That Leah did not transfer out of the department, but moved internally. She was reassigned, a' 'er own request, to the field."

Saul digested this snippet slowly. "So, she moved out of the office into the country." He had considered this option many times in the past for himself. Although the work was tedious, and the rural life dull, the housing sub-standard and the pay worse, getting away from the drollery of the City was, sometimes, appealing. The time alone, the fresh food, the salubrious lifestyle of country pursuits seemed alluring to the metropolitan Saul. He had never had the conviction enough to ask for the assignment, it had always seemed retrograde.

"Did you manage to see where she was posted?" he asked in hope rather than expectation. The mechanisms of the bureaucracy were automatic and blind to the subject they processed. The granting of requests was not usual, it was considered lucky to be heard at all, but Leah's move downward, as it would be perceived, was generally allowed. It was beneficial to place competent workers in lower pay scale positions, it was a reverse Peter Principle, people demoted to the level of their competence. There were many possible regions within the Produce Distribution Department, whose bailiwick covered the whole country, and Leah could have been assigned to any of them.

"I did manage to see. I only had a moment, there was a lot of office traffic. People coming back and forth over lunch. Obviously, there is a rift in the Personnel office, I fink that Martha, you know 'er, the large lady, grey hair, she has fallen from grace with the others. I thought it was only a matter of time before they found 'er out. It was Martha who almost caught me with the file, I had to rifle through the cabinet drawer to find the file and didn't get a chance to put it back. It only gave me time for a quick glance. I hope they don't suspect I was up to no good. You know how it is 'round here, with the politics, an' all."

Saul nodded with understanding although inside he had to resist the urge to shake her to divulge the information. And he had to admit he did know that the Personnel people had a reputation as a nest of vipers, if vipers can be said to be back stabbers. They were, after all, his Personnel Department as well, his file was sitting in their cabinet. Still, Sarah was taking a long drawn out time in laying down that last coin, in giving up that last piece of currency.

"Anyway, Martha must have been upset, not to have been invited along wif 'er normal gang and I fink she had bigger fings on her little heathen mind than my little indiscretion. So, she didn't accuse me of anything, I managed to throw the file down on her desk, on the pile there, hopefully to be put away again. I told 'er I was there looking for Tamar, ya know, Martha's best friend, and Martha scowled when I said tha'. There's obviously bad blood between them now. I wonder what happened."

Saul was getting perilously close to the end of his tether, and said, "Sarah did you see any more on where Leah was sent?" He glanced furtively around them as though they were just about to be interrupted and hopefully hinted that time was of the essence. As though Martha was about to ambush them.

"Oh, yes. The file said that Leah had been assigned to the Upper Downland region. I suppose she knew that area well as that was the region she was working on, wasn' it? But, I fink I also saw that she was missing. Hadn' checked in wif 'er supervisor. Not a missin' person, but she 'ad not been seen for a couple of months. That means she could be anywhere."

"Sarah, I think you may have just saved my life."

"My pleasure, Sol. It's not a lot to be getting' on wif. Last sightin' really, from ten weeks ago. She could be back here for all we know.

Anyway, I hope ya find 'er. I hope ya two can make a life together. An' do mention me to 'er, if you catch 'er. Do tell her that I wish 'er nothing but the best. She is a wonderful person. Do mention me."

"Of course, I will. I must go now. I feel a vacation is due, somewhere off toward Tohu. I think I know where to start the search." He grazed a kiss onto Sarah's right cheek, she tasted of powder and smelt of a masking of old perfume. The prospect of progress excited Saul, each step closer to Leah made him happier.

Saul headed back to work, his mind convulsed with unanswered questions. The book, the note, and if there was a mention in Leah's file showing where she had been sent, why did the Security Department not just get access to that to locate her? It did not make perfect sense, maybe it does not have to, God knows there is little perfect in the world, why would this sequence of outlandish events need to make perfect sense?

Martha surreptitiously watched Saul and Sarah, as they pretended to conduct official business. 'Hmm . . . the kiss was rather odd.' Then, when they had finished she felt the need to report the fact that she had almost caught Sarah with Leah's file. In her office, with the door safely closed, she picked up her telephone and punched in the familiar Upper Downland number. The connection was made.

"Hello. This is M. Yes, it all seems to be happening as you said. I don't know where you get your information but it seems reliable. I expect to see you within the week with the mark. The others are appraised and are willing to go ahead. 'A' is in agreement. He sends his love, by the way, as does your mother. Be safe!"

CHAPTER EIGHT

Saul rested his head on the inside of the murky window of the bus that carved a purposeful slice on the roads between the fertile fields of the Upper Downlands. His eyelids were heavy, and a narcotic sleep started to overtake him, as though it were imposed from outside. Then a catch of a wheel in a pothole knocked the edge of his forehead against the dirty glass. He jolted awake and then, a minute later, his head lolled again, the chugging of the diesel engine soothed him. But the seat back was short and, inevitably, his head fell against the window, to repeat the whole process. His head rolled and bumped him awake, over and again, like an insistent reminder. These damn country busses were always shabby and uncomfortable.

The last time he was on a bus was a week before, when he had been fretting about being on time for the confession with Father Timon. The poor straw-man had then borne the brunt of Saul's frustrations, but now, Saul felt no animosity toward the late individual. Was that wrong? Looking back, he was disgusted at himself for committing the flagrant act, but he did not lay the blame on the victim. He felt bigger than that. His magnanimity knew no bounds, he had come a long way.

Now, after a cramped train journey, Saul was having his bones shaken in this bus. He was on the way to revisit the site of last year's idyllic weekend, spent with Leah in this unlikely backwater. Saul's belief in forgiveness was profound, particularly toward himself, but he was looking for more, he was looking for an elusive absolution. A remission from the guilt of pushing away Esther, a pardon for abandoning his love for Leah, and then for denying that love to Father Timon. 'Third, no, fourth, time a charm,' he thought, 'If I can rekindle my love, I will not deny it.'

Saul alighted from the belching vehicle on the road he recognized from the previous summer, at the same stop he used before. He had not eaten a meal all day and a nagging hunger prodded him onwards. The bus left with a sigh of brakes released and a grind of gears. He was alone on the patchy asphalt road with his canvas rucksack. He waved away the diesel fumes that clouded around him as a parting gift and watched the bus disappear grumpily out of sight around the bend. The quiet of the country settled over him, which, he realized, was not a silence, just a different kind of noise. Jackdaws cawed in the treetops.

Saul sighed a genuine breath of contentment at being back in a place that held such treasured memories. The sycamores were brushed by the wind and the sky was infinitely, impossibly far away. A bank of fractured clouds drifted toward Tohu, the sun illuminated the edges of the breaks that gave a glimpse of blue beyond. The scent of the wet earth and the dying grasses and wildflowers tickled his memory, the autumn air was a balm to his lungs. More reclusive birds whistled and warbled in the trees, oblivious of the sanguine man standing below them, gathering it all in. It was the lack of people that struck him most. 'You are alone in all this life,' he thought, 'but let's see if you can beg, steal or borrow a bite to eat and pail of freezing water.'

Grabbing his bag and feeling gloriously liberated from his old self, as though he had left it on the bus, he set off down the road, turning onto the lane that led to the farmhouse. The path was reminiscent of those happy, happy days, the essence of which he ached to recapture. There was the low smell of mint from the verge. The lane was compacted dirt, and due to recent light sprinkles of rain, the ground was soft. Saul noted the lack of footprints and tire tracks and he held out no high hopes as he passed the cedars and saw the copse of spindly oak that clustered around the tired-looking building. As he approached, he saw that the shutters were bolted which made the house look as though it was comatose. His heart fell a little, he cursed his luck, that it had let itself be all used up. His expectations had been realistic, he told himself, yet this was not promising. The trouble with good luck is that you get accustomed to it.

Saul walked around the deserted building. The outhouse was locked, which seemed an unnecessary precaution. There were leaves in the door wells, spider webs in the corners, all the signs of neglect. It was obvious that no-one had been there for weeks. If there had been a ready entrance, he would have forced his way in, but the defiant bolts secured the contents. He sat at the picnic table, under the spindly branches of the towering tree that spread over the garden yard of the property.

He remembered that he and Leah had sat together at that very spot, at that rough-hewn table, still grey with age and growing lichen. Leah had killed a wasp with a spoon, a soup spoon, dealing the death blow with a decisive smack. That moment was still alive for him, he could relive it; the summer warmth, his linen shirt, the feel of the lawn under his bare feet, the radishes in the salad, her sadness when she inspected the squashed insect.

'It had never ended,' he thought. 'It had not finished.'

Saul rubbed the coarse wood of the table top with his fingertips, summoning up a genie. 'Where to next?' No food and no shelter, perhaps he had not thought this through as he should. The breeze was turning cold and nothing seemed to care.

Then Saul remembered the pond they had swam in, back when the weather permitted. It lay a few fields over, and beyond it was hidden a little cottage that Leah had told him was where the caretaker lived. Perhaps she could help, perhaps Leah had contacted her, perhaps she had a bed and bread. It was a few furlongs away through the arcane countryside, but he remembered the direction. And it being the only other habitation of which he was aware in the vicinity, the choice to visit was foregone. Either that or sleep outside, and he was physically and mentally ill-equipped for camping. Saul was feeling every inch the city slicker.

He clambered over two gates and walked in the thick clay mud at the outskirts of the fields. Brown water squelched around his good leather brogues as he picked his way. The hedgerows threatened to pluck his clothes, and he had to take exaggerated evasive moves to avoid the thorns. The going was laborious, and he looked ridiculous, but eventually he came across the cold and sad-looking pond, that made him shiver to think of being in. Then he saw the low thatch roof and, 'thank God,' a smoking chimney.

The cottage itself sat thickset on a small plot with a driveway winding away from Saul, presumably back to the road. Very inconvenient for servicing the farmhouse, he mused, in the rain when the fields are mud. Saul opened a small garden gate in the back fence that formed the curtilage of the property, shouting a greeting as he did so. He felt uncomfortable at not knowing country etiquette, 'Is it acceptable to drop in unannounced?' He did not want to scare, or embarrass, the old lady, in her isolation. He had the qualms of an urbanite, who value their privacy, here, he was not so sure, but he did not want to overstep his bounds.

"Hello! Hello! I was wondering if I could ask you a question?" He yelled at no-one.

There was a faint yellowish hue in the back window of the kitchen. The homely light growing as dusk started to smear the cottage with shadows. 'Night falls quickly around here,' he thought, 'maybe because it is heavier.' Saul shuddered in his woolen jacket and practiced his friendliest smile as he knocked on the old, loose timber door. First a gentle rap and then three good thumps which shook the hinges. There was an echo inside, but no reply came to his searching ear. He started to wonder if he should enter when, around the corner of the building, barely bowing under the low, stick eaves of the thatch, came the spry figure of a woman wrapped in the voluminous draping of a gardener. She had a pair of shears in her right hand and when she raised her eyes to see who this stranger was, she dropped the shears and they stuck in the wet turf. Saul had nothing to drop, his rucksack being worn over his shoulders. There was a stunned silence, an awkward moment of readjustment, on both behalves. They each took off their respective headgear, he scrunched his cap in his nervous fists, her straw hat hung limply in the hand that no longer held the shears.

"Hello, Leah," said Saul, "I really didn't expect to see you." Then, realizing why he had made his way to this lonely cottage, "I came to look for you. I came to find you. I need to see you."

"Well. Congratulations." Her mockery hid her fluster. "It's a bit of a surprise. I didn't hear you. But it's great to see you again. I was just trimming the hedge out front. Err, come in. Come in."

As if she had been a bad host and was just regaining her manners, Leah rearranged her composure. She opened the door and beckoned him to follow her in. He was too nonplussed to even thank his lucky stars that he had found shelter. His heart raced, and his breath quickened to keep up. There was that sink-hole in his stomach. With every little gesture holding immense significance, he noticed that she did not touch him; she did not reach out. He could not take his eyes from her, whereas she barely looked at him. She seemed comfortable in this setting. Saul entered the cottage behind her with trepidation, wary of where this was going, wanting it to go right. With his cap bunched in his hands he felt like an overawed peasant in front of a Lord, if he had had a forelock, he would have tugged it.

She continued in a flurry of efficiency, discarding her scarf, coat and boots in the small entryway in four quick motions. Waiting patiently, for a signal, a clue, anything, Saul was docile, shrugging off his knapsack, hanging up his coat and kicking off his muddy shoes as she gained the kitchen. The room was childishly warm, there was a large, black range on the back wall, a flue thrusting up an inglenook, a fire blazed in a grate which Leah revealed when she opened the iron door with a poker, to add some fuel. She threw in two logs from a stack next to the range and shut the door with a clang as she dusted her hands and turned to her abject guest standing in the middle of the space, his head almost touching the ancient beams that ran the width of the kitchen. There was a smell of baking lingering in the stifle of the stale air. An old and weary pine dining table set was the only furniture and the thick tabletop wore its scars with resignation. On the wall, next to the entryway, was a built-in stone counter and a steel sink large enough to bathe a baby.

Leah filled a large kettle from the faucet and placed it on one of the rings on the range. She pointed for him to seat himself and left the kitchen to tidy herself up, to turn herself into the indoor personage she wanted to be. They had not spoken a word in the kitchen.

After five minutes of Saul warming his feet and searching his soul, she arrived back wearing a simple plaid wool dress and tights, a purple cardigan worn as a jacket and her hair tied up in a rough bun. She looked beautiful, for all the world like a stylish farm-wife. The broad grin that lit her ruddy face, her bright white robust teeth, gave Saul a welcome reason to relax. Leah as earth-mother, he thought. She finally mentioned his name, another detail he had noticed, although he had not noticed that he himself had not reached out to her. She threw a pair of worn men's slippers onto the flagstones in front of him and he obediently slipped them on. Dante was in his head;

"Whoever asks my name, know that I am Leah,

And I apply my lovely hands to fashion

A garland of the flowers I have gathered."

Saul found he could not tell her about Timon, not yet. He was scared that the revelation would spoil this reunion. He wanted, more than he wanted anything in his life, to have an innocent and private few hours with her. Then he would explain himself. He would not lie to her, but he would wait before revealing his depravity, praying she would not judge it so. The thought of her reaction frightened him, the thought of losing her having just found her again. His emotion broke through a logjam of conventions, 'another bloody logjam,' was that the *leitmotif* of his life?

"What do you want, Saul?"

"If I could hole up for a couple of days and rest, that would be enough."

"You can stay, I'm sure we are safe here. I've spent months here. I'm not on anyone's radar. I started off in the farmhouse and the old caretaker lady, who I only saw once, said she had an emergency and had to leave immediately. I think she said it was her brother who lives over Tohu, where Sarah came from. That was four months ago, and I haven't seen hide nor hair of her since. I resigned from the Produce department, actually I didn't officially resign I just disappeared. I stopped turning up and left no information. It is a resignation of sorts. I reckoned that they wouldn't notice a field operative falling off the radar, one of the thousands. I moved in here and have just set up home and looked after the place. I pull her measly wage from the local authority. No-one seems to care up here. I could have murdered her. But, if the house is kept up for the visitors then they hand out a little money to whoever shows up. I don't know what I'll do if she turns up again. I am now posing as Sister Edna."

Leah smiled; finding herself amusing was a good part of her charm. Saul's was to blurt out whatever was on his mind. Leah busied herself lighting candles.

"I have changed, Leah. Not in the last months, in the last week. I have not grown, not had any realizations, no great epiphanies, but I am completely reborn. I mean, everything has changed. Root and branch. I am not the same man. I have the same name and inhabit the same body, but my soul has been transformed. The very meaning of my being has been . . . translated. Not through thinking or reading but through doing."

Leah gazed at him with those slate-grey pupils set like jewels in the olive-green irises, reminding Saul of a peridot ring his mother had treasured. She was so perfect that even the gaps, or hollows, within her could not be black. The bridge of her nose was low between the eyes that were set minutely too far apart. But, that only gave her an aspect of dreaminess. Her upper lip was carved, and hovered slightly over the lower, perfectly over-sculpted, as though conceived by a great artist, and beveled by a round-nosed chisel. To Saul, her face was an epitome, the very personification, of loveliness, of intelligence, of humanity, but mostly of that quiddity of Leah. The most attractive and fantastic quality a person could possess is a proud display of his, or her, own essence. And Leah had Leah-ness in spades. This is love, Saul thought, the effect she has on me, more affecting than hypnotism, more serious than gravity, more important than God. The world was a flood and she was the Ark that could rescue him from drowning. She could murder a thousand men and he would not condemn her.

Saul would tell her everything, he could hide nothing from his love. He wanted her to know him to the depths of his pathetic, brand-new, panting soul. This was a perfect setting because they sat opposite, basking in each other. The ardor in his heart at the sight of her was reflected in the background of the rustic intimacy of the kitchen, a perfect *grisaille* of shadow. The smell of the smoking resin burning off the Tohu pine, greedily consumed in the grate, perfumed the moment in their memories. The range radiated a living heat into the close air of the room pushing their feelings together, melding them in their reminiscences. He would confess his great sin, the last act of his last life, the one for which he could not buy an indulgence. But not yet, he would not confess yet.

The tea was in front of them and Leah had put a pan of vegetable cassoulet on to heat. She had ladled the stew from a pot sitting lidded by the back door, next to the shoes, in true Downland fashion. The smell of the beans and the tomato sauce overcame the cheap, but plentiful, wax candle smoke that guttered from every surface. They relaxed mentally somewhat in the sanctuary of the cottage kitchen, and opened, gradually, to the others' presence.

Saul was more coaxing than her, Leah was more guarded. There was some laughter, polite at first, not forced, but more encouraged than instinctive. Laughter as a tool in social conversation, as a way of putting the other at ease. Jokes would have been inappropriate but sympathetic mention of Sarah's country manners was connective. They both found Sarah sweet and amusing. They found a common sympathy with Martha. A local heavy red wine was dispensed over the fitting dinner.

After the dishes were discarded in the sink and a little blue cheese taken with a *digestif* of abrasive plum brandy, they brought the chairs in front of the fire, now open to the room. Saul threw in a last log and settled back, his feet up on a stool, he wanted to open his heart, but dithered. Instead, he gave her heartfelt thanks for her hospitality. He complimented her cooking without a hint of sarcasm, for he was the cook when they were a couple, and the *cassoulet* had seen better days.

Night had fallen silently and compressed the dusk noises of squabble from the wildlife outside. There were no calls of the love-lorn from the native creatures, rutting was done, offspring hatched and weaned. Any sounds were the calls of those preparing to leave, fatted and unsettled. Their instincts satisfied for the year, they were readying to follow the last paths of escape. They called for company. The cold dark was a dangerous veil to fall. The cottage slumped further into its bed, pulled its thatched cap of a roof down over its yellow glowing kitchen window eyes. It seemed to pull the surrounding trees closer and shake them to stillness, as one would a sheet. There was no romantic moonlight, no warm breeze, the love was inside. Saul was eminently satisfied.

He found his soul was purely magnetic at this juncture; he was the south, she the north, pole. There was a world separating them, but nothing about her could repel him. He was filled with a ravenous need, at this point, the need to regain himself by purging the desire that had cloaked his being. It was Leah's doing, but not her fault. He loved her.

Except.

He could not help dwelling on the fulfillment of his desires. Was he too distant from himself? Were his baser and higher sides too far apart? The athletic curve of the muscled plump of her loins cased in that peach skin teased and compelled him. The musk of her allure, the drive of his hormones, a chemical cascade in his veins. His senses had a predatory heightening, she was the most important object in the universe and he wanted to possess her, as a treasure, as a belonging. Lust filled his majestic chest. There was that animal power! There was the blood rising!

He despised his own arrogant, and covetous, gender at awkward times like this. His baseness was the battle between his longing and his self-esteem, he wanted the former to triumph, so the latter would be taken care of automatically. But he wanted to be better than that and have the latter succeed so that he could feel proud of himself. He needed a moment.

"I have to visit the outhouse," Saul blurted out distastefully, scared of himself, and looked around for a little lantern to take outside. He lit the wick with a spill that he poked into the fire and left the warmth of the kitchen. As the door closed behind him, Leah took a telephone from its cupboard, untied the wire wrapped around it, and plugged it into the socket. Making sure that she heard the old, outdoor lavatory door slam shut before picking up the receiver and dialing the local number, she made a whispered and hurried telephone call.

Five minutes later Saul was still sitting rather languidly on the potty, his trousers and underpants bunched around his ankles, which were spread as far apart as the material would allow. His buttocks were cold on the wooden seat, and getting colder. The winter smell of the outhouse was not as obnoxious as it was in the warmer months: the little respite of solitude and silence were welcome. Abandoning any hope of peristalsis, he dutifully swished a ladle of the water around the bowl and poured down a measured scoop of sawdust, as though he were a baker measuring flour. The night outside was unfriendly, and he coaxed the lantern through the darkness to the embracing mugginess of the cottage. Washing his hands in the great metal sink he also cleaned the bowls, plates and cutlery lying there and left them to drain on the surface. Let no-one say he was not domesticated.

Leah sat in front of the open grate, her unshod feet were up on the lip of the range, her toes wiggling in her wool stockings. The telephone was unplugged and stored away again, sight unseen. With the sleeves of the dress pulled up on her lithe arms, Saul was privileged to have the glance of the curve of a breast down a wide sleeve. It was exquisite, and he could not prevent himself feeling a frisson of excitement, that must be like a junkie with a full syringe in hand. Then Leah's motion, she was pouring another glass of wine for them both, closed the view and he felt a disproportionate sadness at the loss. He was lost and helpless, but at least recognized his plight. As it was, Saul was happy to worship at her feet, and she seemed happy to allow him to do so. He was a fool to allow his conceit to appear, he was nothing compared to her. He was beyond hope, and he knew that that was dangerous territory.

They talked fondly of times past, as old friends catching up will do. Any pain, or blame, from the breakup was dismissed as forgiven, despite what Sarah had said. Leah was accepting, and he was willing, which made him susceptible. For Saul, as he talked himself into an open mind, was starting to realize how much he had to learn. But first how much to unlearn, and that starts with questioning. Saul bided with his guilty secret, and although Leah knew that there was more to his presence than he was letting on, she allowed him to bide with it.

Leah flirted, it seemed required, she played to his interest and started to enjoy the game. Truth be told, she was glad of the friendly, intelligent face for living alone in the caretaker's cottage was intrinsically lonely. Summer was probably not as bad, she expected, she looked forward to it rolling around, but, at this time, there were days when she did not see a soul. And in isolation all friendly souls are the same, not that she did not harbor feelings, oh, no!

With no-one in the farmhouse her chores were limited, and she kept her head down and lived a very circumscribed existence. Saul could appreciate that, surely, she had learned that from him. The old me, said Saul. During the week, she had Edna's rounds to attend to, visiting the local farmers on that bone-rattling old motorbike, remember that? He did. He remembered holding onto her waist as she expertly leaned the vehicle around the curves of the country roads. He remembered hunching behind her and laying his head in the lee of her neck. But that was then, he pointed out, in the warmth, he would not want to try that in this weather. Leah paused a second, and smiled conspiratorially, and then announced that she had a trip she wanted him to accompany her on, tomorrow, Wednesday.

"Where to?"

"I will leave that as a surprise for tomorrow. It is a secret. You shall see. In fact, I need you to promise to keep it quiet. To tell no-one."

Of course, he agreed, he would have cut out his tongue for her if she had demanded, happily cut it out, his only regret being he would not be able then to worship her with words. His longing was on best behavior, but it was still desperate to be allowed off the leash. Maybe that was its plan. Her plan was better concealed.

They talked on, late into the night, the country night which sleeps. They were alone in their own tightly-wound universe. All that existed they knew, all they knew they could see, all they wanted was within easy reach. The flames in the range died to embers, the jug of wine was drunk to its dregs, tiredness was over them, and yet they did not want to break the spell. There were questions about the next step, the subsequent course of events, and demurrals. Eventually, they kissed.

Sitting in their respective chairs they simultaneously leaned across the space between them, as though on cue. As though they could read the other's mind and intentions. Tenderly at first, reaching so only their pouted lips brushed against the other's, they touched. Their lips the only point of contact between them, this almond-shaped oval being the valve through which they were linked. The kiss connected his recently upheaved world, his disconcertion, with her hidden world, shrouded in a beguiling mystery. Then fingers reached out to touch the other's shoulder, leg, hip, head and the kissing became a tasting, an inhaling. Hands that stroked then caressed, and finally grabbed, the desiderata. The mouths opened wider and wider, in order to devour. In this dance the other partner signaling a willingness to be consumed. The gap between them disappeared.

The embrace necessitated standing. Clumsily they clung to each other, one creature learning to stand on its own four legs for the first time. They stumbled like a newborn giraffe, they panted like the mother that had just birthed. The outside world vanished, and the universe grew to encompass them and only them. Clothes became an impediment and were hastily discarded as the quadruped stumbled into the bedroom.

There was a smell of fresh paint from when Leah had started to whitewash the plaster walls just that morning. Paint pots and encrusted brushes in jam-jars sat on a brown canvas sheet splattered with white drips, up against the far end of the room. The bed had been moved to the center and stood majestically like a belvedere adrift in space, like a stage from a theatre in the round. The pink bedsheet and blue blanket were tossed untidily but the lovers did not see the mess, the mess was not in the universe. They climbed into the bed groping their way, led by a force of will. They were lost as they found themselves. The clean scent of drying paint was the most intoxicating perfume imaginable.

A man's muscles are in his shoulders, arms, chest; emblems of his powers to lift. A woman's are grouped in her upper leg, the marble curves of the thigh, the buttocks, twin mounds of stamina function. The female breast's exquisite lines bespoke nourishment. The male leg is speed, not distance. Unwrapped and on display the human form of a loved one is a thing of beauty. Love transforms the ugliness of the clandestine primate flesh.

Desire points beyond the thigh, where the hunger aims. If the mouth could not speak its profundity of poetry, which is located beyond the lips, then it would become this grail. We know instinctively what is hidden there within, we come from there. Then *voluptus* becomes *gaudium*; joy a million furlongs beyond pleasure. The very life force itself reinforced.

Her skin was as smooth as oil as he stroked her nakedness surreptitiously under the covers, the cotton sheet and heavy blanket. They needed that weight to stop them floating away, not to hide themselves. The temperature was irrelevant. Her curves and mounds shifted in response to his play, turned to invite him further, sanctioned his progression. He toyed with her pleasure, exploring the ultimate *terra incognita*, as though he had never visited before. She touched him with a lightness that felt like hammer blows to his heightened sense. He welcomed the hammer blows. Her breasts held up, fulsome, replete, bountiful, her back arched, the muscle pack over her sacrum dimpled, tensed and flexed and the buttocks lifted and heaved as her legs spread in her vulnerability of the most sacred inner temples of her being. Where the edge of life falls off is the power to make a separate one altogether. The two, indivisible, make one, and the name of that one, thought Saul, was the profoundest experience of whatever the Elders call God.

He knew. But she knew better.

CHAPTER NINE

Wednesday dawned unwittingly in the Upper Downlands. The sun was no help at all, its thin light tweaked the dormant world with a feeble heat, it expected life to rouse itself. The sky held that hazy milkiness of high cloud that is a coloration, and the chill in the air seemed a throw-back. There was no wind, the smoke from the blaze in the range ambled and billowed straight heavenwards from the chimney. In the night, there had been a brief foray of guerrilla cloud misting an unnecessary wetness over the countryside. The indisposed fields and pastures waited vainly under the high blue skies for an unbecoming hint of warmth.

Inside the cottage, the kitchen would take at least thirty delicious minutes, from Saul's re-stoking of the fire, before the room was habitable and breakfast could even be contemplated. There was a cozy debriefing to be enjoyed, the body's apology to the heart for its recklessness. Sleep had been deep and restorative, an absolution for them both. Raw spirits had rested and, in the cold of the bedroom, there was a giggling contentment.

When Saul ran naked back to the bed at full streak, dusting his hands on his bare flanks, he could not help but notice the walls of the bedroom in the meager daylight. As he dived for the warmth of Leah's presence he elicited a ribald reaction from her watching him jiggle, oblivious, back from his chore. Then he looked around and saw the art covering the wall.

The pots of whitewash still sat on the drop cloth where Leah had obviously started to obliterate the images from the end wall, but maybe only a quarter, mostly near the floor, had been covered. He looked around, impressed at the skill exhibited in the painting, two full walls still on display. Sitting up he complimented Leah on the work.

"That is some beautiful painting."

"Well whitewashing is not a difficult skill to master."

"I meant the frescoes."

"They are not technically frescoes. Frescoes are painted onto fresh, wet plaster, and the colors seep in. I painted these, this, onto the drywall, I think technically it is a mural. Close to the ceiling, it is a frieze."

"It is surely the right weather for it, then. You have terrific brushwork, I must say. Most people are slapdash, just daub on the whitewash willy-nilly. Why are you covering up the undercoat?"

"It was not meant for anyone's consumption but my own. They are just doodles, really, I was bored. You might be surprised to hear that I don't have many visitors to my boudoir."

"Glad to hear it," he said and added seriously, "You have a real talent, you know."

He gazed around admiringly from the platform of the bed. Saul was used to the sanctioned, institutional, bland artwork that hung everywhere in the City, the inspirational propaganda of the establishment. In those portraits and landscapes, realism was prized, maybe because the depictions of Biblical subjects were so fabulous. These 'doodles' were stylized, not quite to an abstract degree, but they had a very impressionistic look to them. They conveyed more than just a representation and he had never seen their like, they were a different form of art, experimental. It was about the feeling of the image, the sense of time and place. Saul could see how the different parts flowed into one another, to create a harmony, in a full circle.

"What are they about?" Stammered Saul, not having the requisite language to talk about what he was seeing nor how to interpret the sentiments he was feeling. Leah seemed coy about the whole project, looking around the walls with a droll grimace, shrugging her bare shoulders as she sat up in bed. Then she spied something she had drawn over to their left, on the wall with the small recessed window, whose glass dripped with condensation. She climbed down onto the floor not noticing the cold nor her glorious, un-shrouded nudity. Her athletic frame, furled and then unraveled as she pointed to the murals. She was more like an animated conductor than a demure gallery guide. Leah proudly described the technique of producing effects, top to bottom, side to side; all methodology a product of her own imagination. Her very own trial and error. Saul made for a rapt audience, following her indications, her reaching and bowing, as she elegantly traced the representation along its length. She pointed to a cloud wonderfully rendered clinging to a mountain peak.

"I could not get this cloud right, at first, I tried and tried, nothing worked. Then I remembered Apelles, do you know him? He was a Greek artist and was trying to paint a horse. Well, he could not get the foam around the horse's mouth quite right and in frustration threw his sponge at the picture. And *voila*! It turned out. So, being unable to get the cloud, I used a sponge! And it worked! Nobody is going to tell my story, but it worked."

Saul's laughter encouraged Leah the nymph to continue.

"I started off without a plan. Just played it by ear, I had never tried anything like this before. Look. You can see Tohu here." Leah stood on tiptoe and swung her arms wide in a gesture encompassing the mountain. "I started at the door and, as you can see, it progresses through the corner, over there. So, the angle is the saddle between the two peaks where those school kids died last week. The whole thing moves from left to right, although there is no linear story, it is all landscape. Think of it in distance."

Here, Leah performed a delightfully clumsy pirouette as she swept her right arm around the room displaying her accomplishment. Her breasts took on a slight life of their own as they followed her torso, her hair flowed slowly from one shoulder to the other. Saul's attention was on the instructor not the subject and he had to redeploy himself to take in the grandeur of the scene, all of it. Saul gave a self-satisfied smile, as if he were the boastful one in the room, because his self-esteem was restored. He could not, dared not, tell himself how happy he was.

Leah's representation of the mountains was splendid, and would have been admired even by those not smitten. She had showed a deft ability to depict with a brush that which her mind's eye had perceived. The shadows of Tohu's slopes gave that sense of depth that is the true artist's gift, painting a three-dimensional scene on a flat surface. The colors were simplistic, but it appeared she was only working with house paints, mixing and matching by instinct. The foreground of the vision were ochre fields of barley and wheat, interspersed with vineyards, the vines picked out in black lines. These fields grew increasingly ecru, out of the skirting boards, and led across to bottle-green meadows where the room's misted window broke the image. Beyond, further to the right, where Leah had started to whitewash, thin lines of tarmac roads expanded into the near and veered back into a dark depiction of the City. This back wall was three quarters dark, browns and blacks, with the bright yolk-yellow of electric lights glowing from innumerable apartment windows. The buildings were straight, solid, heavy and distinct as though cut from the night by some magical industrial process. The light blue sky above Tohu extended with the flow, as the frieze, to an acrid looking miasma of pollution seething above the City. The whitewash was like a missing piece of a puzzle.

Leah walked past the back wall, sedately and with a dignified equanimity, as though she did not wish to dwell. She conducted the tour with a wonderful naked aplomb and described the use of sponges, stencils, sprays and bleaches. She had stenciled with leaves and brushed with sprigs and bunches of grasses. Whatever was to hand was in her improvisation.

The last wall lightened up again and the painting illustrated trees, forming woods, and then onto a farmhouse. No, Saul realized, this neighboring farmhouse! He complimented her that she must have talent for him to recognize the place. She was not flattered, for she was aware of her achievement, as well as the failures. Again, her level-headedness, which he loved. Apelles all over again.

By this time, he had turned around in the bed, following her traipsing, and sat heavily on his heels, the sheets twisted around his legs. She was a vision to him, a sight of unbridled marvel, her form secure in its healthy plump. As she approached the last scene, a matter of three paces, she opened up to happiness again as though putting the City behind her was a trigger. Saul understood.

The last panel of the triptych depicted their locale, the sky radiant and the farmland generous. With the building, she had managed to hint at the weathered brick and the thatched roof, the picnic table. Saul was not aware of how much his wish to participate in her pride played into the deception of the art. Once he saw the farmhouse, his mind and his eye filled in the blanks in a forgiving fashion, assuming the details she could not portray. He was the most willing of spectators.

Beyond the house was the pond in which they had bathed so naturally last summer. Seeing it as she revealed it to him, for she was master of his attention at this point, he swore he could feel the cool of the water, had to blink at the sun, could smell the scent of the bushes. And there they were, an Adam and an Eve in their Eden, the only two humans alive, drawn simplistically in pencil, colored sympathetically pink, not to stand out but to merge with the naturalness of the setting. He thought again that this is not over, this never ended. When one instant can carry on forever, the thing is not done.

The female figure stood at the side of the pond watching the other. She stood as Leah stood now, in a relaxed manner, arms down, the protrusion of the breasts, the slight sag of the belly and the strong legs bifurcated by a triangle of pubic hair, black against the rose-pink flesh. Leah assessed the image she had made, ruled the proportions with a hand-span, as the image, in turn, judged the male figure. This latter was in flight, off the ground, arms extended above the head, the elbows by the ears. He was shown diving into the water with a competence that flattered Saul. The lines of musculature sleek in the surge of his movement, a suggestion of genitalia because it was true to life. The diver was about to pierce the surface of the water, to shock and disrupt, but in this captured instant, all was grace. All was caught before the splash.

Leah bowed an ironic homage to an invisible audience and slipped back into the bed. There was a hint of goose-bump on her limbs. As she climbed up, she quoted from the *Bible*, Jeremiah two thirteen, "For my people have committed two evils; they have forsaken me the fountains of living waters, and hewed them out cisterns, that can hold no water." Cold water in a desert, cool water in a Downland's summer, both disavowed. Saul reflected.

So Wednesday stretched out before them promising to be a round, comfortable, otiose, devil-may-care type of day. The sort of day that begins when one dreams one is awake and then wakens to find one is still asleep. A slow tortoise of a day, no hare-brained schemes to suffer, no fragments to cement together. It took an age for them to leave the bed in that gallery of a room and it was only done piecemeal and with reluctance. Breakfast was hearty and savored and there were endless cups of muddy tea to wash it down. Perfect, thought Saul, bloody perfect!

Midmorning, sitting outside in the thin glare of the insipid sun on the same two chairs that had supported them the night before, there was a mutual comfortable feeling of domesticity. They sat in a degree of *dishabille* but not enough to count as undressed just enough to soak up any drips of rays that were on offer to skin as white as wash. Facing the low light, they noisily begged Sol out loud for provender in this, his shy time. He was as out of season as foliage, so could not provide. Another second-rate deity, they agreed.

Joking and jesting, teasing and prodding, there was a closeness faster than their proximity. Two lovers at play, the play young animals indulge in as practice for their future adult selves. Saul turned to Leah and, injecting a semi-serious tone to his voice asked,

"Do you want to hear about this recurring dream that has been haunting me?"

"Did you have it last night? God, I was so tired, so drained, that I slept like a baby. Isn't that a stupid expression! From everything I have heard, baby's sleep terribly, awake every two hours for a feed. You know who probably sleeps the soundest? Not the innocent but those without a conscience. A sociopath on death row probably sleeps all day. Untroubled shut eye, don't you think? Untouched by any guilt. Hence, unbothered by life they sleep like babes. Beware the ones who don't care!"

"No-o-o," Saul drew out the vowel syllable for two full beats, "I slept well last night, but not the sleep of the un-conscienced."

"But you have nothing to keep you up at night? I know you, Saul, you are a conventional man, a rule follower. You have kept your nose clean all this time, you told me last summer. Unless something has changed."

"It has. I'll get to that. But let me tell you about this dream." He decided not to pause. "I have had this same dream for six months, it alternates with another, even stranger one. This one is not a dream in the sense of anything happening, it is an image, the same image, over and over. You know what reminded me of it? Your mural. I can understand you painting over the picture as it must be like erasing it from your brain. Seeing that beautiful scene every night before falling asleep, seeing a naked Me, like a Greek Hero. It has to be hard."

"Well, it is a fictionalized account of life, Brother Big Head. And I did not draw you hard, I could have done, but I do not have the small brushes required for such delicate work." She let out that giggle again, the one that made you feel you were in on the joke and that your genius had caused her such joy. The pleasing one.

"Anyway," Saul smiled, pleased, "let me tell you. The dream starts out as a straight image, no motion, no change, just a focus on the subject. It is a picture of a hand, not my hand, a workman's hand, rough and calloused, thick skinned and with dirty nails cracked and split. The hands belong to an old man who has used his hands for righteous labor, they have earned their un-deniability. They cannot be gainsaid, if you know what I mean, they just are! They do not have to justify themselves. In the dream, the image has a pen and ink quality, as though etched. You see! Now you have me talking like an art critic. It is as though somebody has drawn these real hands, hardened and poised. The right hand, and here the picture zooms in on the one, is deliberately reaching out toward something I cannot see, and it does not matter. It does not move but the hand grows in my vision as if my eye is getting closer. The hand is very tactile, very sensitive, the last three fingers are curved in towards the fleshy palm, the thumb and index finger about to pinch the tips together. It is fastidious, precise, as though it is going to pick up a needle. Maybe it is trying too much, trying to surprise a resting housefly, or pick up a will o' the wisp. The rough finger and opposed thumb are held there in place, absolutely stationary but not useless, just still. My attention is only on the flesh, the skin and nail, the shadows and the black ink, I cannot look over to see what it is trying to catch." Saul looked over to a thoughtful Leah who was rubbing a knuckle against her front teeth.

"What do you think it means?" She asked him without removing her hand from her mouth.

"Does it have to mean anything? I'm so glad to hear you say that dreams might mean something. This whole dismissive idea of them as night-time insanity just seems wrong, somehow."

"I think it does. Dreams must come from somewhere inside. You can dream of anything, so the reason it is one thing rather than another, the reason it is a hand and not a foot, is relevant. Therefore, it has meaning, it is trying to say something. Either that, or the image came from outside you, it's hard to say with no indication. And, in that case it definitely needs investigating."

"That's irrefutable," complimented Saul, "So it must mean something. We just don't know what. Where's Joseph when you need him? He was thrown into a cistern, by the way."

"You're a good writer. What would you make up to explain it? If it were in a story."

"Maybe, it means I'm searching. I know when I see the hand that it is about to pick something up. Or is at least trying to. So perhaps deep inside me, lies this wish to grasp something fine, something important. At least, important to me. This may sound strange, but maybe this thing is down a well, a water well I mean, and the dream is the bucket that brings it up. But, one thing I don't understand, is why the dream won't let me see what the object is? Does that mean that the action means more than whatever the action achieves? So, it is a call to arms . . . ."

"Or fingers!" she quickly interjected.

He continued, ". . . and what I need to do to fulfill this yearning is a change, a different tack. It sounds as if it could be right."

"Or that what you want is beyond your ability to get. Or that the hand is pointing you onward. Or is about to slap you unexpectedly." Leah's voice fell off through this last phrase. Maybe she thought that she had punctured his bubble, but if so, with a sincere wish to get to the heart of this matter, not just to bring him down a peg or two. But deep within she heard his loath call for help.

"Saul, I did mean what I said just then. About your writing. I do think you have a talent. I love the way you talk, if you could write a story just as you speak and if you were allowed to publish, I would buy and read it."

"Nothing is stopping me being published, apart from the fact that I cannot write anything that would pass muster. Or, I feel it is not worthwhile compromising myself to see my name in print. I suppose I could come up with a morality tale extolling the virtues of the collective good as evinced in the form of an everyman hero battling the forces of insurrection."

"You see! That last sentence, ten thousand of those and you have the new bestseller. Or *Don Quixote*."

"Ah yes. If only. I do feel," Saul ruminated, "that if a work of literature cannot present life direct and dangerous, warts and all, nature red in tooth and claw, all that good stuff, then it is probably not worth writing. So, then I'd rather stick to the safety of copywriting, a little editing, here and there, and stay out of the limelight. That glare of publicity can burn you up like an ant under a magnifying glass. I don't think I have the fight left in me to suffer that sort of full-frontal attack. And that is the problem, nothing written now, nothing published is worth a damn, because writers are not allowed to address meaningful issues. I do wonder if the world is waiting for my *magnus opus*." He was enjoying himself at this point, talking grandiloquently about himself. He would have been appalled if he had been forced to admit it, of course.

"I hope," said Leah forcing him to admit it, "you are not fishing for compliments. I remember last summer, whenever you talked about Esther you gave the impression of having given up. As though you had leprosy and needed to quarantine yourself for her sake. It seemed ridiculous at the time, how resigned you had become to the whole situation. Society is too big to fail. The Church can never be questioned. You do know that that sort of thinking is the lemming mentality they want to inculcate. If we feel there is no alternative to the powers that be then we will not waste time searching for one. Bread and circuses, the first lesson they teach you in Totalitarian University." Her sarcasm was biting, but sitting on a kitchen chair in a shirt and underwear, with a scarf around her neck giving a political lesson, she was irresistible to Saul. She lifted her feet out of her slip-on canvas shoes and put her heels on her seat, so she sat in a tight ball. It was a younger woman's posture, hugging one's legs, chin on knees. She was still a lissome creature. Saul haphazardly stroked her gathered thigh with the back of his fingers.

Saul said, "That thing I told you had happened to me, well it did change me. It was profound, it was repugnant, it was startling. It was not something, strictly speaking, that happened to me. I was the instigator. I was the one who committed an act. A horrendous act. And yet I still do not know if I should not have done it, even as I know it was wrong. Does that make sense? Does that make me evil? Willfully acting in a way that you know is sinful?"

"You will have to tell me about it, you know."

"I know," confessed Saul, glad of the chance of sharing the secret, if not the burden of guilt, with someone he trusted. His confession was a selfish relief of guilt, he realized, but he needed the unburdening. "Last Friday I was called into the Security Department for a meeting with a Father Timon, who was investigating a shadow group called the New Men and, somehow related, a Cygnet Committee. They had some evidence on you, some photographs of us together from last summer and they think you are involved and wanted to get at you through me. I may have let some information slip, and regret it. Timon dismissed me and told me to come back on Monday. Afterwards, I had time to stew about whose side I was on. Well, on Saturday, I happened to see him at the market, followed him. On Sunday morning, Leah, I went to see Timon, called him down to the trash bins, and I, and I . . . ."

Saul found the words hard to say, voicing the act seemed to cement it in history. It was the first time he had admitted his part out loud and it made it real to him. He was used to keeping his internal world shuffled, this was like being accused of sedition.

"Leah, my darling. I love you. I know that now. When Timon came down I beat him to death with a brick, and then I stabbed him slowly through the heart to make sure he was finished. I killed him, my love, I took his life for you . . . ."

She listened. There was a pause that seemed to Saul to be infinite.

Leah was thinking, about him, about her, about them. She was calmness personified and stoically replied,

"We shall head back down to the City on Friday. There are people I wish you to meet. And I think they need to meet you. Do not crucify yourself. *Alea jacta est!*"

Saul wept.

CHAPTER TEN

Even though Leah had seemingly decided to allow Saul to enter a gate in the walls around her life, the question of whether she were the Trojans or the Greeks was unanswered. She had accepted his laying siege, had acquiesced, indeed; the breach was intended, permitted; but had she accepted a gift or bestowed one? Where was the fifth column? Who was jeopardizing whom?

Regardless, having allowed him access, she wished to give him a tour of her life, on two wheels, no less. So, on the next heathen-named day, with Saul still in the dark about their destination, Leah wheeled from out of the dilapidated toolshed the ancient motorcycle they had used back in the summer to explore the surrounding area. She had to spend a quarter of an hour adjusting the temperamental machine, nursing the old and worn system into balance. She pulled out and blew clean the carburetor and the spark plugs, all with a useless Saul watching on. The engine was on life-support until it engaged and then burst and spurted into paroxysms of life. Then it was straining at the leash to hurtle away.

Leah beamed at the thing with pride, wiping her hands on a rag and signaling to Saul to keep watch, teasing the gas, as she ran into the cottage to put on more appropriate gear for what promised to be a bone chilling ride. She shouted over the roaring chug of the motor.

"I have enough gasoline for now, to get us there and back at least. The stuff they sell up here is awful, silty and diluted. They say the further away from the City you are, the less things are refined."

She was pleased to be retelling this joke, and laughed at herself. Adorably, admitted Saul, glad to have a part at last.

Saul was no handyman, and he was fine with that. He had watched Leah's fiddling with a detachment that was an acknowledgement of his own ineptitude. His admiration was sincere, he was impressed with her capability, and he prided himself that his male sensibility felt not a jot of jealousy. Now if that is not love! Leah knew from a distance that he would manage to make it all about himself. Just like those Trojans, she thought.

He obediently toyed with the throttle, gassing the engine whenever the rocking machine seemed to be dying down to an idle. But then, typically heavy handed and over-compensating, he would send the thing roaring to bursting. Finally, he figured the technique, and he settled into keeping the thing puttering along with occasional flicks of the wrist. Although he had never ridden one of these beasts before, he had clung onto Leah's back for several excursions, and he had heard the machines many times on the streets, and so felt he knew what was required. From a deep gurgling menace to the distant mosquito whine of a more sensibly powered bike, he thought he knew what he was dealing with. He had noticed that bikes were ridden, whereas four-wheel vehicles were driven, but did not really know why. Saul still felt uncomfortable being left in charge of one, even one in neutral, on its kickstand; one he had met before, but to which he had never been formally introduced. He looked it over disapprovingly, its oily, explosive thrusting threatened him a little.

Leah reappeared wearing a thick waxed canvas jacket, buttoned tightly up to her neck, above heavy denim trousers and awkward looking boots, clod-hoppers, his parents used to call them. But, Saul decided, she could make a deep-sea diving suit look sexy. She carried by their straps, what looked like two medicine balls that had had a quarter sectioned from them. First off, she handed Saul a *bandana,* he presumed as an adornment to his city clothing, which comprised too thin trousers and a jacket with the collar turned up and the lapels flattened. He looked at the scrap of linen and went to tie it around his throat.

"It's for your face. I want you blindfolded," said Leah as though this were common practice. "I don't want you to see where we are going."

Saul couldn't decide whether to silently comply or to object on the grounds of safety. He did not feel qualified to complain. Standing next to the grumbling machine, he shrugged and accepted the bandana. His brogues, his whole attire, his inexperience, was a reminder that he was the neophyte here. He blindfolded himself, put on the helmet Leah handed him and waited for her to get on the motorcycle, pull it off the stand and bark for him to climb on behind her. He felt his way on, hands out, wary of the hot exhaust pipe on which he had managed to burn himself last time out.

The suspension sank with the weight of the two. He found the steps for his feet and put his balance, and his life, in her hands. He grabbed her around the waist and felt his helmet bounce against the rubber of hers. Letting his right hand fall he cupped her crotch as a futile gesture of his significance, she elbowed him into behaving.

The driveway leading from the cottage to the road was like the compacted dirt of the farmhouse track. Rutted and potholed, it threw the bike around and they had to creep out to avoid the worst of the pitfalls. Saul adjusted his seat in a fidget to get comfortable and by the time they had made the asphalt he was more at ease as the clinging passenger. Leah gave an encouraging demonstration of a capable steward, she clicked through the building gears in a smooth fashion and leaned the bike through the curves with composure. Saul started to relax and enjoy the security his blind trust allowed, in the same way, he thought, that he could not enjoy the scenery. The blast whistled into his ill-fitting headgear cooling his head until he ducked out of the wind behind Leah's back. By reaching a certain speed the imperfections of the road were ironed out and he settled in to an unknown time reliant upon her prowess. He felt happily shielded behind her, unable to talk, completely at her behest.

The country roads in the Upper Downlands were not well maintained, but did not suffer from the weight of traffic that busier highways endured. They tended to be straight, which Saul appreciated, as there were not many impediments to their engineering. But they were also narrow, which he was spared from seeing. He was not missing much, there were few inconvenient buildings or annoying geographical features. But he would have been able to see an impressive view of the vast range of Tohu arrayed out perpendicular to the distance they were heading.

The snows on the peaks were like an adornment, placed there for effect, to dress the mountains as mountains. Looking infinitely far away to Leah, squinting as she was behind a pair of over large goggles, Tohu did not seem to be swelling as they powered on. They made no dent in the perspective. The road unspooled like a copper wire away from Leah's vision, and to Saul the thud and compression of the engine tapped out a Morse-code repetition of the letter L, dot-dash-dot-dot, dot-dash-dot-dot. Over and over, L for Leah, L for Love, L for leather, Saul even managed a smile of sorts. The thrumming pulled them onwards.

Behind the blindfold, Saul could feel the motion around corners, a braking, a shifting down of gears, a lean and then the force of the pulling away. He had nothing to do but ruminate, and imagined that if his past had been several loops up to now, here he was, finally, on a linear path. He could see in his mind's eye the map of his life; childhood, work, marriage, work, child-rearing, work, church, work, eat, work, sleep, work; all paths set out as though going somewhere only to gradually turn and end up back where they started. If these ways were the outlines of petals, and he could see the tracings behind the bandana, then he had broken free of the return, he was now hurtling down the length of the stem. It was a pattern that was clear within him, he needed to leave the circularity of time behind and to move on. The floral pattern was copied on his retinas and he was happy to be blessed with, at least, a feeling of the gift of oversight. Leah actually saw the road spooling under the front wheel, she anticipated the way ahead.

Eventually, after the best part of an hour, Leah turned the motorcycle onto another dirt drive, Saul felt the slow bumpiness and could hear the telltale sound of loose gravel under the wheel he was astride. For all he knew they could be back at the cottage. Leah parked and the deafening adrenaline rush of the trip subsided. He wrested the helmet from his head and pulled down the bandana, blinking at the sunlight and the surroundings. Saul was surprised to find himself on a concrete courtyard that sat as an apron in front of a large barn structure. The looming roof above them was a dull, green metal, and the solid walls were practical breeze block. There were the industrial leavings to the side, stacks of pallets, rusting metal sheets, scrappy piles of paper waste. A backwoods factory, when he had been hoping for a sylvan glade, some country Arcadia, with a stream running through, a romantic spot, somewhere.

A man was walking purposefully toward them, waving to Leah in a friendly gesture of reacquaintance, she waved back. She introduced him, and Saul shook his ink stained hand with alacrity and not without a degree of curiosity.

"Any friend of Leah's . . . ," he *cliché*-d.

Ham was a tall, statuesque character, about Saul's age but better preserved. He was trim and lithe, with a beak of a nose that, along with his mane of dark hair and olive skin, gave him a corvine look. He was wearing the traditional tweed jacket and demure tie of the successful merchant class. Although familiar with Leah, he was somewhat circumspect around Saul, wanting to know his provenance and questioning him more than a host should.

"I called, Ham, did you not get the message? I told Mary that I was bringing a friend. I can vouch for him. He is trustworthy. And he could be valuable." Ham opened the large sliding doors and Leah led them through into a wall of sound, that felt almost physical. They pushed past the cushion of heat waves released, generated by the exertions of the machines working in the poorly ventilated factory, on which the noise rode. A distant smell of oil and ink made up the full-scale assault on the senses. It was disorientating, factories are slices of hell to the uninitiated. Ham and Leah adjusted, Saul scanned all around him, it seemed like Inferno to his office sensibility, maybe 'violence,' the seventh circle.

Leah and Ham were deep in shouted conversation and at ease enough in the tumult. Ham pulled Saul to one side, pointlessly as the oppressive noise was everywhere, and told him that one of the supervisors, a certain Abel, would conduct him on a quick tour before meeting them in the office. Saul nodded, assuming conversation to be impossible, shook hands with the young white coated Abel, and followed him into the belly of the beast.

At the center of the space was a giant machine, running steadily at full pelt, with a lethargic bass drum backbeat. Single sheets of paper were lifted from a stack and then fed singly into a press at the rate of about two a second. A few workers, intent on ministering to the machine, finessed dials and delicately gradated knobs, then pulled tons of blank paper from a giant guillotine by means of a trolley. They fanned the sheets to separate them and fed them onto a moving conveyor that inched them to the printer, in a continuous operation. Paper was guided through rollers that looked like giant mangles and that were being drip fed copious amounts of black ink. The large sheets were swallowed, pressed and then ejected into another neat pile, duly printed on top and bottom. The finished piled sheets were carted away to another part of the factory. Abel pointed out that each of these larger sheets contained sixteen finished size pages and took Saul to the bindery where the books were finished. Saul relished the fresh ink smell, it reminded him of new books, fresh newspapers, words made flesh.

The printing press required some climate control that the other processes did not, which was why the building was divided. The smell of ink here gave way to the dryness of paper dust. The printed sheets were folded on massive custom machines that made precise little booklets which in turn were collated together and then run through a binder that glued the spines into the covers. Handfuls of these books were then trimmed by large guillotines, operated by hydraulics, and the end product parceled up in boxes, two dozen in each. The whole sequence was intricate, but logical, from plain paper to book. As a large industrial procedure, the difficulty was in the details, especially when the operation had to be conducted in secret. For the material produced was subversive, at least in some eyes.

Abel concluded the tour within a half hour, from start to end, from the messy plates to the waste paper extraction and storage. There was plenty of shouting into ears and gesticulation, but that difficulty made the information more valuable, it seemed. At the guillotine, Saul picked up one copy of the ten-thousand run of books and recognized it immediately. It was a copy of *New Men*, the self-same book that had appeared on his shelf, and which he knew, from experience, burned so well.

Saul understood the subterfuge, he was appreciative of any well-organized enterprise and was in turn complimentary. Abel seemed rather proud of the process, the magic of industry. But, Saul wondered why he was being treated thus. Leah had taken a chance on him to invite him into this aspect of her involvement, to show off her connections. Or was he the one being shown off, after his confession of the murder, had he crossed a Rubicon? Was it an initiation rite he had passed unwittingly? Saul was quite gushing on both counts. 'It was those damn Greeks and Trojans, again.'

The small office had only one dusty window that looked out onto the courtyard where Leah's motorbike was leaning on itself with distinct languor. There was, unexpectedly, no other traffic, or parked vehicles, as one would assume attendant upon a normal vibrant enterprise. Indeed, from the outside the factory was very incognito, no signage, no activity. It was doing nothing to draw attention to itself which was unusual for a commercial enterprise. They were isolated, as Saul could just discern, behind a series of farm buildings. It was hidden away, as perhaps the printer of the banned *New Men* should be. Not prone to flights of gangster fancy, Saul felt secure in the collective guilt of those around him, all tarred with the same brush. His act of anarchism a badge of honor amongst these thieves. He felt he was closing in on his new home and he nodded knowingly.

Ham sat behind an expansive desk that was a mess of office stationery and supplies: staplers, files, pens in cups, rulers, ruined copies of books, loose papers, all in glorious disarray. Behind him a stacked credenza looked anything but organized, creaking as it was under the weight of previous jobs, samples, invoices, magazines; the accumulated clutter of a busy man running a complicated organization. Leah sat opposite him, across the clutter of desk, and when Saul entered they both dropped the topic of conversation and looked intently at him.

"Thank you for the guided tour," said Saul. "It's one of those things that you never think about, how paper becomes material. Seditious material."

"Yes," replied Ham, assuming the role of the proprietor, "we like to run a tight ship here. A discreet and secret ship, at that, we do not encourage tourists. What we do is an important part of the association, not only to supply the literature, but when not engaged on this sort of material." He pointed a pencil at the door that muffled the noise of the machinery. "We are the biggest source of income for the Committee."

"You can see why we don't like people snooping around," added Leah. "I told Ham and the others that we can trust you. Just as you trusted me with that information last night. Saul, sit down. We have been discussing the situation, and your place in it. We want to have you join us. Become part of the movement. We need competent, level headed men. Young volatile hot-heads are plentiful. We figure you could really help us to overcome. What do you say? We think you have proved your commitment."

"I see. You don't apply to join, then, you and Ham select who you want, and go and recruit them?"

"Not really. There has to be some sort of application, the possible members must express a clear wish to be a part of this. Then they do have to be of use, this is a movement we are running as a business. We need able people, who can be of use, and you demonstrated that amply last night."

Leah smiled conspiratorially at Ham. Obviously, the previous evening had been a subject of discussion. Saul felt a slight sense of embarrassment at this most personal of details being out in public. He reached across to Leah, perhaps to hold her hand. She was unresponsive, probably due to being in the presence of her boss, thought Saul. He reverted to best work behavior, questioning the two of them about this new horizon.

"So. If you are inviting me in, and I have proved my bona fides, will you spill some beans? What are the New Men? Who are the Cygnet Committee? Or should that be the other way around?"

Ham spoke first, and Leah acquiesced to him without demur. It seemed a well-rehearsed exposition.

"We are a group of like-minded individuals who all believe that the Christian stranglehold on Society is harmful to the members of that society. That harm manifests itself in the suppression of the personal expression of the soul to benefit those in positions of authority. It is willing to sacrifice the minority, those with different ideas, those not wedded to the utilitarian cause, for the benefit of the majority. We consider that immoral. The 'New Men' are a loose collection of various disillusioned people. People from all walks of life, men and women, all souls are equal under the system we propose, the one we are fighting to achieve. A Christian soul is no better than the soul of an alcoholic heathen, it just has different needs. We strive for our voices to be heard by subversive means. You cannot accuse us of being violent revolutionaries, although we would like to overthrow the current government by offering a clear alternative and allowing the citizens to decide. To us it is common sense."

"If you know your history," Leah challenged Saul, "it is to go from a Hebrew to a Greek concept of human society."

"I think I get what you are alluding to. Away from patriarchy and back to democracy, I think they called it. Quite a leap. Most of the people I have met are not up to the task of choosing a leader. I think most would want the Devil they know, they are not an enlightened bunch."

"Leah and I both agree. It is not just a case of removing the Pontificate, for who would replace the necessary machinations of governing. It would be like bringing farmers into the factory and putting them in charge of the presses. They would ruin everything. But the farmers can be trained to operate the machinery, printers are not there through divine right. To enable the realignment of society will take generations, of re-education and gradual change. Hence our philosophy is not of sudden revolution, but careful evolution. If you read that copy of *New Men* that we smuggled into your apartment last week, you would get the idea. Caution not chaos."

"I flipped through it before burning it. I thought it had been planted by the Security henchmen. My neighbor, Zipporah, told me a couple of thugs broke in when they could not find me."

Leah laughed, "I would not call Aaron and Daniel, intimidating. More like a four-hundred-year old Abraham and a rather disappointed Isaac. If you are agreeable, Saul, you'll get to meet them tomorrow night. We arranged a meeting of the Committee at your apartment in the City, eight o'clock Friday evening. I presume you don't have any standing arrangements? You and I are heading down tomorrow. There is a lot you need to learn."

Saul sat, pensive, there was a lot to learn. He was having greatness thrust upon him, and was not confident he could shoulder that weight. He did not seem to have a choice any longer.

"I'm in," he said, perfunctorily.

On the motorcycle trip back to the cottage, Saul gripped Leah as if for dear life. The uncomfortably tight blindfold did not stop his sarcasm shining through. He was struck by the irony of the policing done by those complaining of the policing by the authorities. The wind whipping over Leah's shoulder and into his open mouth made him gasp and gulp. He felt chagrined, somehow, disheartened. Was he ridiculous for thinking this group of petty bourgeoisies could hope to destroy the system from within? If he was one of them, then why the damn bandana?

The ride was uneventful, Leah gunning the machine with a nonchalant control through the country roads. Saul hung on behind, still slightly amazed at the magic of gyroscopic motion, and the centripetal effect, and thankful for that physics as he felt the ground rearing up at them when they listed. Eventually, with relief, he heard the dirt road under the motorcycle wheel and sensed the jolt and slowing to rest. Pulling off his helmet and uncovering his eyes, he kneaded his compressed skull and handed the items to Leah before she even had a chance to doff her own.

They stood across from each other in the shed where Leah had parked the bike, there was a lingering sulphur of exhaust and their ears still rang with the din of the engine dying in the confined space. Saul was still sulking a little, he felt a little patronized, as though he had been undervalued. They had talked about him, behind his back and had shown no great enthusiasm at bringing him on board. But then Leah gave him a windblown smile as she ruffled her hair, she looked satisfied at the ride, the meeting, and he succumbed to his desire.

"What shall we do with the rest of the day?" asked Saul. It was late afternoon, a few hours only of sunlight left, the air was temperate for the lateness of the season.

"We could head to the pond. If the water's not too cold, we could risk a quick dip. Let me go and change into something a bit more comfortable. Something not designed to counteract road rash."

Fifteen minutes later they were plodding through the drying mud of the environs of the field on the way to the swimming hole. Leah in a brave summer dress with a cotton throw, carrying a hessian bag of towels, books, matzo and cider. Saul was still in his city livery, which was looking disheveled and crumpled after the last few days, but his heart was as neat and orderly as a soldier on parade. They had not discussed Ham nor the New Men.

"Where do you think we are heading?"

"Just the other side of that hedgerow," she joked, "so we can re-enact the mural."

"But when we get back to the City, what becomes of us then? Do I get to see you? Are you going to stay up here? Should I try and transfer somewhere close?"

"You are thinking way too much. Relax and enjoy the moment. You will meet three very important comrades tomorrow. Let us see how this all pans out, then make plans."

There was a stillness hanging over the scene, a reverent hush as in a church. A collective agreement of bated breath. No birds sang and there was no whistle of wind in the treetops. Without waiting for a signal from the other they stripped off their clothes, hanging them on a low branch and they tiptoed tentatively into the raw-umber pond. Mud squelched underfoot, parting coldly between the toes. They had to push away a film of debris buoyed on the surface tension as they lowered their pallid bodies into the shock of water. Swimming gently around, breast stroking, without splashing, they laughed at the audacity of a middle-aged couple frolicking. They paddled cautiously, circling the pond, trying to avoid encountering any unforeseen obstacle lurking in the mire. It was impossible to see their own limbs under the surface, the thought of what shared the murk made them shiver. When they had tired of the action and with heads still dry, they crawled back onto land and scampered to their clothes.

They toweled themselves down and dressed and Saul built a token fire from the twigs the early winter storms had left scattered. Sitting on a fallen log and squeezing the heat from the tepid flame, they ate the crisp flatbread, with a little soft cheese, and drank the vinegary cider whose sweet first impression gave way to a sour aftertaste.

Dusk descended as the shy sun ran for cover and an astringent chill blew in on the evening breeze. It was a subconscious reminder of Tohu's looming presence in this low land, the cold warning breath of the mountains. Crows started to circle the trees and cawed a greeting to each other as they arrived home. Then a cackling chorus broke out and Saul and Leah decided that it was a valedictory gesture, that they were being ushered home to the cottage.

Wearily, ponderously, they doused the fire with the cloudy dregs of the bottle of cider, wrapped themselves up and sauntered back to the cottage, over the stile and through the cloying mud.

Later that evening, back in the warmth of the cottage, Leah ladled out a thick aubergine *ragu* onto a bed of sticky pasta and handed the bowls to Saul. They sat at the table, a bottle of a heavy tannin-rich Cabernet standing between them as a challenge. It was to be no contest, Saul announced, the affront of the wine will be overcome. 'Maybe,' he thought, 'the bitterness they had subjected themselves to had made this reunion that much sweeter.' Maybe you need to know the bottom before you can appreciate the heights. Maybe the pasta was that good.

Leah told Saul of the Cygnet Committee, about their role as a distinct coterie, although she declined to use that term, within the looser group of the New Men. She told him that five of them comprised this organizing committee, herself and Ham, a long-time associate called Aaron, a young and eager agitator named Daniel and Martha, the latter had recruited Leah when she worked in the City.

"Is Martha the large lady, runs the personnel office in your old place?"

"Yes, that's her. She has been a Heretic for as long as anyone we know of, apart from Aaron. Of course, you should remember that the Committee is a disorganized bunch, we are just a grouping within the New Men. We don't control the whole movement, no-one does, there is no hierarchy. There could be other factions operating independently that we have no contact with. So, the less you know about your fellows the better, the less harm you can do. The Cygnets concentrate on materials, printing and distribution. And having Ham and the presses resources means we are in better shape than most New Men. You are lucky to be a part of such an exclusive clique. You must have friends in high places."

"I feel like the proverbial mushroom, kept in the dark *etcetera*. I had no idea you citizens were out there. Why did you not tell me last summer?"

"I was only interested in you as a new man for me, back then! When we met and started to get to know each other, I remember you saying that you liked to keep a low profile, head below the parapet, and all that. I was just acceding to your request. I thought you would have thanked me if you had found out."

"I think I might. Talking of that, how do you think Timon managed to find out about you? Do you think there might be an informer?"

"That we have not managed to figure out. In fact, tomorrow, after the introductions, that is the first item for discussion between us five."

"Five?"

"Ham cannot make it down to the City. He has the most responsible position out of all of us, in a way, running the printing shop. Keeping the business turning over and the money flowing to the cause. He would be quite well off, definitely a Ten with plenty of time off, if he didn't spend it on the team."

"So, does the money keep the group afloat. Salaries, expenses as well as the literature?"

"It does. Martha works, of course. I am not even part-time, at the moment. Aaron is on the payroll of the Committee, Daniel works but won't tell anyone where, he is very secretive. We coordinate with the wider group of New Men, but the money in the Committee gives us a clout that can cause friction with some others. Talking of logistics, I did want to put a proposal to you. You are on board. I assume?"

"Yes!"

"A warning, though, it's not all as glamorous as this, you know! Anyway, my offer is that you throw in your lot with us and become a sort of staff writer. We have the printing setup as you saw, we could knock out brochures, pamphlets, jeremiads, all the stuff you have been fact checking and editing these years. Currently we have the means of production and no product, you would be that missing link. I was talking it over with Ham earlier and he thought it a splendid idea. At first you would stay at the Produce Distribution Department, stay in the same apartment, and gradually become a full-time writer for the Committee. Then you could drop out, and then we would put you on the staff at the factory, as a rep or something. How does that sound?"

"Very intriguing. It could be just what I need, to dedicate myself to something bigger than the everyday. I do believe in the cause, although if you made me swear to every covenant, I doubt I would be comfortable taking that oath. But give me a few months of writing it out, fleshing out the bones of a philosophy, and I think I will be there. I'm flattered, Leah, and I'm also feeling the start of some literate project. This could be my big break. I could write my happy ending. I can just picture it, my first bestseller. So popular that the Pontificates have to tempt me out of anonymity in order to shower me with plaudits. Awards, grand prizes, acknowledgements, glittering prizes land in my lap. Am I getting ahead of myself?"

"Somewhat. Let's start with a pamphlet on how the Government lies in the statistics they put out. There are no artichokes and yet there is supposed to be a record harvest being picked, that sort of tub-thumping, 'why-oh-why' piece. Then maybe graduate onto the iniquity of the suppression of the individual soul. The political stuff. Let's start small, test the waters and then plan on making waves."

"I see what you did there, waters and waves. Very clever, you are not muscling in on my patch, are you? You really should leave the allegorical metaphors to the professionals. It's a tricky business, and we would hate to see you hurt."

"I can look after myself. Don't you worry. You concentrate on getting the right words in the right order. I'll look after the rest."

"Finally! A kept man at last."

They arose early the next morning as there were several duties to perform to put the cottage into recess for the next few days. The farmhouse was unoccupied, so she felt her unannounced absence until Monday could be excused. There was still the shuttering of the cottage, the securing of the entrance, the cleaning of all perishable provisions, for Leah had learned that you cannot leave food lying around.

Saul quoted to her, "*Naturam expellas furca tamen usque recurret,*" to which he added in response to her blank stare, "you can throw nature out with a pitchfork, but she always turns up again."

'He has no idea,' she thought to herself, sweeping the kitchen flagstones.

Leah decided to take the motorbike instead of the bus to the provincial town, the regional center, where they were to catch the train to the City. Saul, whose punctuality was prompted by a deep-seated anxiety of missing a step, allowed himself the luxury of being in Leah's capable hands. Without the blindfold he would have enjoyed the three-quarter hour journey to the station, except a lack of eyewear meant he had to keep his gaze strictly averted from the wind. Still, he was starting to feel like an old hand at balancing on the back of the hammering machine as it plowed its way through the fall air and its musty perfumes. They parked up close to the train station and secured the helmets with a chain that had held their baggage on the rear rack of the bike. Scurrying, due to Leah's timing, with Saul deep breathing to keep his anxiety at bay, they made their carriage with ten minutes to spare. Far too close for Saul's comfort, a waste of time according to Leah.

They settled in, books acting as plates for a picnic lunch of apple and cheese, with crackers and a plum pickle. Leah had even managed a bottle of frothy stout that washed the lunch down like the flushing toilet they were both eager to be reacquainted with.

The train set off with that slow pace of strenuous pull that eased as the inertia was overcome. At first the coupling was strained as the backsliders were forced into motion, but by the time the chain of cars had reached the edge of the town the locomotive chugged along merrily maintaining velocity, with the following lazy wagons shrieking and grinding on the iron rails. Out the obscuring windows, the brown countryside passed sedately, like a rolling film to be admired at a distance. Saul imagined a future, fantasized a world from an atom. He looked fondly across to Leah who travelled backwards, viewing what she was leaving behind.

Three hours later the first hints of the City appeared in the landscape. There was a buildup of urbanization as the occasional farmsteads gave way to town centers. The suburbs multiplied, spilling over the ground in a testament to civilization. Between the spread of small, boxy, semi-detached houses there were pretty parks and noble schools, linked by strips of shops. Then ersatz countryside deteriorated into a disease of factories which sprawled malevolently next to the rail tracks, with their intimidating messes. As back up, of power plants spewed their effluence defiantly through chimney stacks that were never tall enough. Any spare space was filled with rows of terraced housing, that rippled over the benighted land. And in this spread of urban blight Churches and Hospitals sat billeted as bastions of control. All was brick, black with soot, the people, a greater presence than in the verdant Downlands, were bowed, weighed down with their lots, going about their businesses.

Traffic became an imperative on the roads that paralleled the railway and crisscrossed the outskirt. Lorries heaving, trucks hauling and tramcars plying a trade, the insect drone of a passenger car, all belching out fumes. Then the buildings seemed to grow as the train fathomed its way closer to the center of the City. The architectural pressure of being unable to spread outwards resulted in a reach upwards, like the geological process that had grown Tohu. The train itself stopped, as if it had decreased in importance, and a tableau of human progress now unwound outside the window. Eventually the cityscape seemed less chaotic, the layout better ordered and the structures more impressive, as they moved into the order that lay at the center of the State.

Saul felt a return to normalcy as he approached his home, his familiar environment. Leah, on the other hand, felt the weight of all that had suppressed and repressed her over her conscious life. She felt a resurgence of the reason she fought against the system, the stifling atmosphere and her scramble for air.

Saul mulled over the word "bathos."

A reference came to Leah's mind, that people are "common with singularity," that is the masses are monotonously diverse, like the scree field she had painted in her bedroom, all one color, all one brush stroke. The train started to squeal on its brakes as it settled next to the covered platform with a hiss of relief. The passengers poured out, tumbling politely over one another in the rush to get away.

Saul said, "It reminds me of that first passage from Lamentations, 'How deserted lies the city, once so full of people, how like a widow is she.' Of course, that's Jerusalem after the destruction of the Temple. But look how bland everything is, how indistinguishable the citizens are, one from the other, like birds, or sheep, in a flock. It feels like the Babylonians have laid bare the place, enslaved the people."

Leah was even more disaffected and was intent on joining the melee outside the carriage. She translated her upset into action as they gathered their bags and shouldered their way to the station entrance and out into the dull, dense air of the crowded City. They picked up a taxi from the anticipation of cabs lined up along the curb and headed through the unlikely throng to Saul's apartment. When they arrived, Saul, displeased that the Cygnet Committee had not picked up the fare through Leah's expenses, jostled his key in the worn lock and entered to find three huddled comrades waiting silently for them in the cool damp of his home.

Meanwhile, elsewhere in the awful City, in the bowels of the Security Department, the small cabal of black suited *apparatchiks* were huddled over papers. They were crossing t's and dotting i's and connecting the dots and planning the next step with cross referencing and general collegiate hegemony. The telephone information was proving useful, but they had to wait for events to progress. They were used to waiting. You did not get to where they were by being impatient.

The one with glasses, who was wishing to push back on the *ersatz* chair's authority questioned the next move, to prove his use to the two without spectacles.

"I think, Gentlemen, that we should reconsider our course of action. This desperate bargain may be a last gasp of the group. We could exploit our advantage further, to delve deeper, in order to cast the net wider. Their obvious weakness is to our benefit when it comes to negotiation, no?"

They disagreed with him, and took delight in over-ruling. It did not even have to go to a two-to-one vote. The mechanism was in place, the trap was set, and it was deemed pragmatic to allow the agreed course of action to proceed.

"Let us not get greedy," said the one on whom the success would most redound. He thought he was being generous.

CHAPTER ELEVEN

Aaron sat in Saul's favorite armchair, staring ahead through the thick lenses of his round black-framed spectacles into Saul's jejune apartment. Unoccupied with his surroundings, he seemed to register nothing; he exhibited an imperturbable air. A homburg was still perched on his chubby head; the flesh of his neck spilled over his stiff collar. He did not look at Saul and Leah as they entered the main room, as if he were blind, or completely disinterested. His focus was elsewhere, he was preoccupied with larger issues, as though making some grand bargain.

Martha and Daniel rose, embarrassed and awkward at welcoming the householder into his own house. Not thinking it their place to receive the couple, they were effusive in their concern for the journey, the comfort, the timing. Saul exaggerated a display of warmth to mask his fluster at seeing Martha in the anomalous surroundings of his own apartment. The presence of two other strangers did not disturb him as much. The awkwardness was emphasized by the unusual, but not unpleasant, smell of tobacco smoke wafting around. Then, whilst assessing a gushing Daniel, and deciding to get to him later, he found his attention drawn to the taciturn Aaron, sitting and staring like an armchair *grandee* turned *philosophe*. Luckily, it was Leah who was garnering most of the attention from the garrulous ones, which relieved Saul.

Aaron had a briarwood pipe clamped between his stained teeth and was gently inhaling and expelling smoke from a smoldering plug of tobacco buried deep within the bowl. It was a rare sight to see a smoker still pursuing his relaxation, as the herb was, if not illegal, at least not officially available. That discouragement, of course, only deterred the *dilettantes*, not the true addicts, who always find a way. Not only are they unrelenting in their pursuit, they also resent those who stand between them and their pleasures. The demonization of tobacco had only increased Aaron's abhorrence of the Pontificate and made him redouble his efforts toward their overthrow. The sweet smell of the cloud emanating from the obstinate man struck an old chord that resonated with the others. They all had fond memories of older relatives who had indulged, back when the guilty pleasure was permitted by the State, which had, of course, cultivated and distributed the crop. Now it was a reminiscence, embodied by the avuncular figure of Aaron, sitting comfortably *in situ*, intractable and hatted. The tolerance of the fumes was as much a sympathy of the young for their elders as it was for the habit itself. The forbearance of Aaron's habit was also a bond that the lesser members of the Committee shared.

Aaron's fleshy face was lined yet fluid, motile, as though it were made of heated toffee. He acted like he owned the place, thought Saul, but reverentially, he did not resent the old man. He looked harmless in his preoccupation and Saul would have to learn to tolerate the smoking. In fact, it was Aaron's myopia that had created the benign patriarch persona Saul saw before him. The one that could not see him back as fully. As a youth, some fifty years before, Aaron's weak eyesight had condemned him to a bookish existence. His dim view of the outside world translated through his reading of literature, then through a pursuit of science, until a philosophy cobbled by *legerdemain* had given him a cause to promulgate. Finally, he had found his *métier*. He had cultivated these principles in private, over years, until he had found himself the intellectual basis of the resistance movement. Not through political machinations, but by osmosis and endurance, by outlasting. He quite liked being the elder statesman, and his patience when waiting in the wings had paid off, much to his gratification. It tickled him that he was considered a revolutionary, he thought of himself as staid and boring. And here he was lauded as the torchbearer of the Cygnet Committee, the justifier in chief.

Being held in esteem had enabled him, over decades of quiet engagement, to develop what he called a professional sonar. This meant that he occupied his vocation the way a bat does the night. He navigated the world by sending out messages, sometimes insults, sometimes queries. Always provocative and telling, he then gauged his standing and position by the replies he received. He also learned a lot about those in front of him by the style of their replies, by their wit and candor. If Aaron engaged you, in a Socratic fashion, he acknowledged your existence, that you were worth prodding, then your reaction spoke volumes. He might dimly see you, like a ghost, but he was the one-eyed man in the country of the blind.

Daniel, of the undisclosed occupation, was the polar opposite of Aaron. He was a young firebrand, an idealist who was unafraid of spreading the gospel of the New Men, wherever and whenever the opportunity arose. He was passionate and energetic, tired of old nostrums and frustrated by the glacial progress of the movement. Physically, Daniel was rake thin, and his head of dark hair made him look like a disheveled mop that had been used on an ink spill. Below his flowing fringe, which fell over his eyes and necessitated a continual flicking back, a long, pale forehead betokened a quick and un-restive intelligence, which his beady eyes turned into an impatience. Time would not pass quickly enough for this young man and his schemes; his iron was always hot.

Daniel cultivated a patchy beard, an attempt to create a serious mien on a youthful face. But it could not mask his over-eagerness which, in turn, also belied his age. He envied Aaron his *gravitas* and, what would prove fatal, his ability to smoke, a habit Daniel tried to cultivate over the objection of his lungs. He was stuck with a fidgety flightiness that ruined the calm impression he was keen to make.

Daniel flittered around the seated Aaron, fingering ornaments, picking up and opening books, moving from one window to the next, and overall making the group skittish. He liked to hover over Aaron, to hang on his words, and he was ignored like a lion ignores a fly. Daniel was a useful acolyte to his leader, though, even if on more of a domestic, than political, level.

Between these two, when Daniel allowed some space on his peregrinations, sat the solid, and phlegmatic, figure of Martha. She of the personnel department, who knew Saul professionally. This role in the proceedings made her pivotal in the group, as she was known from as many angles as Leah herself. She was a devotee of Aaron and an ill-humored big sister to Daniel. So, it was up to her, she knew, to make the connections and break the ice. Martha was the first to properly address the arriving couple after the initial flurry of inquiries, with an enthusiasm of barely hidden relief.

"Well, fancy seeing you two here. And together, what a nice surprise."

"Thank you, Martha. Good to see you," replied Saul, "I do hope you all made yourself at home. It is tea time, if anyone is interested?" Saul hated the catering aspect of entertaining, he did not even know if he had enough cups to go around if all assented, but he felt he needed to offer. He wondered whether it was more appropriate to offer alcohol, but judged it too early, too frivolous; tea goes better with business.

Saul adjourned to the kitchen to boil the water and rustle up some rusks, leaving the old hands to form a quorum, if they desired. He banged around, to demonstrate his location, letting the cupboard doors slam and rattling the cutlery, but always with a reaching ear attuned to the whispers from the next room. He caught nothing of value, just some small talk and then a susurration of lowered voices. Doggedly going about his galley task, he felt a doubt about the outcome of all this. He was not alone in that thought.

Back in the living room there was a quick confab of the Cygnet Committee, it was the first time they had congregated in a while. Leah filled the rest in on the condition of the printing business, and Ham's health and wishes. She had a very thick and formal envelope that she took from her travel bag and handed to Aaron who poked it directly into his inside jacket pocket, where it jutted out tellingly. As she handed it over, she fondly squeezed his shoulder, and then leaning in, gave him a familial kiss on the cheek that Saul did not see.

"Your family has missed you," croaked Aaron, his emphysema making him a man of fewer words than he would have liked.

"I will make up for lost time. I have missed them too. Business first, as you always preach!"

Daniel was concerned about the trustworthiness of the man in the kitchen and did not hesitate to cast aspersions. "Who is he? Can you vouch for him? Has he proven himself? Have we checked his story, his background?" He was a suspicious young man, always looking over his shoulder and always thinking the worst. This questioning was very tiresome to Aaron's nerves, even though Daniel served a useful and complaisant role. Leah allayed, or rather overrode, the queries with a dismissive disregard that her position allowed her to get away with. Martha listened attentively to the conversation, leaning her bulk into the circle they had formed around the seated Aaron. Leah was adamant,

"Ham really insisted that he be welcomed in. He can play a very useful role in the group and, in the end, could be a highly valuable asset for us. So, we want everyone to be welcoming and accommodating. Let's show him our typical hospitality, our usual camaraderie. Don't be suspicious as though he were a stranger. Let's treat him like a friend. It will only be for a short time. Until he proves his worth." Aaron nodded in support.

There was a tremendous crash from the kitchen as a tray that Saul had loaded with the refreshments overbalanced from the counter onto the tarnished linoleum floor, tarnishing it further. A crockery roll of debris followed as the items settled into their new positions where they could fall no further. Then a heartfelt bellow of consternation proceeded from the offended Saul.

"By the Piles of Jesus!"

There was a pause and a synchronicity of attention toward the kitchen by the huddled conspirators. Then a giggle from Leah and a chuckle from Martha. Daniel was irritated by the amateurish nature of the accident, the incompetence. Aaron broke his customary scowl in favor of an involuntary snigger, his hearing was fine.

"Sorry! Don't worry. I've got it!"

Saul was mortified at his *faux pas* and cursed his clumsiness. He gingerly picked up the sharp pieces of a shattered saucer. Piles, indeed! Probably from all that donkey riding. Maybe if Satan had offered to cure Jesus' hemorrhoids, instead of tempting him with riches, the whole of history could be different. He set about reconstructing the tea tray.

Eventually, Saul appeared sheepishly in the cramped living room, now as full as it had ever been. Five people, and their cups and mugs of tea and plates of various hard-tack biscuits, were as many as had ever been gathered there. Once the refreshments were dispensed and a little extra desultory small talk as to milk and sugar choices was out of the way, Aaron convened the meeting. Saul found the clandestine proceeding a little thrilling and he knuckled down to the protocol.

"Ladies and Gentlemen." Aaron's timbre was sonorous and came from deep within his barrel chest and out through a nicotine tarred throat. It carried the weight of a voice used to being obeyed when it did not quite know why. Even Daniel settled down to listen and calmed his twitching. "I hereby convene a special meeting of the Committee as called by Ham, according to regulation, in order to discuss the introduction of a prospective, new Cygnet. Let us call him a gosling." There was a consensual murmur of laughter, although Saul thought the joke rather tame. "Leah has known Saul for six months," Aaron looked quizzically over to Leah who confirmed the assumption with a deadpan nod, "and he has been under consideration for most of that time as a suitable candidate for inclusion. We have been as prudently cautious as we should be and that has served us well. Recently, though, certain information has become common knowledge to the group regarding Saul's eligibility. As you are all aware, normally a test is set for a prospective candidate to perform, the success of which proves his, or her, mettle and not only their worth to the group but also their commitment to the cause. After all, what is a committee without commitment?" It occurred to Saul how unusual it was for him to be sitting in on the discussion of his application, the one he had not made.

"I have known of Saul for longer than that, if only at a distance." Martha smiled deprecatingly at Saul, she enjoyed this *hauteur*. If he had treated the well-endowed lady with condescension in the past he was unaware of it, but he felt some power balance shifting as she spoke. "He was not known as a revolutionary in the Department, and that is a good thing. Conversely, although I can vouch for his occupation for some years, he seems to have done little to warrant election to the group." She drank from her cooling tea to soothe a bothersome throat and before she could continue. Daniel piped in, as though it were his turn.

"I agree. I don't know him from Adam. He looks rather unassuming, but that could be a virtue, or it could be cover. How do we know what he wants? What he wants from us?"

"Yes," Martha reclaimed the floor before Daniel could draw breath, "it is unprecedented to allow a novitiate in without any vetting, or with just the hearsay of the leaders, by *diktat*. We are supposed to be a democracy. Further, we need to be on high alert, not that we ever let our guard down. We know the Templars are delving further into our business, I mean not just the usual chasing us to keep us on our toes, but genuine harassment. I think they want to disband us, which means we all suffer individually. I have seen it in the office, the Security Department agents are sniffing around a lot more these days. Asking for files on all sorts of innocuous characters you would not think were worthy of attention."

"Do you supervise Saul's office?" Daniel asked.

"Not directly, but our sister office does, and I may be able to find out if the Templars have been asking."

'No need,' thought Saul, and, 'This Committee is rather sloppy.'

"I handle the personnel issues so requests for information come through me. But, I do know that they have set their sights on Sarah, who Leah and Saul know, and who could not be any more unlikely a subversive. And of course, Leah, before I tipped her the wink. We were close on that one." Leah nodded in assent, and Saul felt the stage curtains open another inch or two.

"All that being noted," having regained his breath, Aaron took control of the agenda again, "we are here to welcome Saul in, not to assess his acceptability. No, strike that, we are discussing his eligibility. Last weekend, it has come to our notice, with his back to the wall when the authorities were closing in on him, he took the sort of direct action we could do with a lot more of in our ranks." He paused for breath and looked at his pusillanimous band of warriors with a disdain not born of conviction, more as a tool of management. Aaron was constantly berating the group for their inaction and timidity, even Daniel, who spoke a good fight but was a perpetual disappointment. He did not want to play the overbearing father, but felt that they left him with no choice. "Maybe we need some fresh blood, a man who will grab the metaphoric bull by the allegorical horns," Saul winced at this attempt at humor even as he enjoyed the compliment of being described as a man of action. "If the Jesuits or Templars are coming to get us I want to bow out in a blaze of glory." This defiant sentence finished despite a rasping cough emanating from Aaron's chest. An attempt to dislodge something immoveable, by the appalling sounds of its impotence. It was not a fitting end to an inspiring speech. The hovering Martha slapped his back as he lurched forward in the armchair and she sent Saul off for a glass of water with one flinching look. Daniel saw his opportunity to grab the limelight, and he raised his voice to be heard over the choking.

"Well. I for one would like to see a more dynamic thrust. I think the establishment is there for the taking if we would dare to risk. We should be fomenting riots in the streets, barricades at the crossroads, whipping up frenzies. We are never going to get anything done by all this talking and planning just to . . . what? Undermine the confidence of the authorities until they capitulate? I don't think so." Aaron had soothed his smoke ravaged throat with the water and the group had turned to Daniel with a collective petulance.

"No surprise there, then," stated Leah, voicing the room's weariness with the young firebrand. "Let's put you down as a yes vote for Saul's joining."

"Anyway." Aaron felt calmer after the wracking, settled enough to pull another plug of tobacco and stuff it in the bowl of his pipe. "The secret that was revealed just yesterday, or Wednesday, was that Saul had el-im-in-a-ted . . . ." He drew out the offending verb into its full length, giving each member present a syllable and having one left over for himself. ". . . a notorious inquisitor. I think we have discussed Father Timon enough, over the years, he has been a thorn in our side for years now. Well, now no more. He is gone. Disappeared. And we know this because the magician himself is in our midst."

"Do you mean . . . murdered?" Martha filled the shocked silence that had fallen even though she and Daniel were the only ones in the dark. "That is very, very serious. I mean, that changes things a lot. We had never thought of crossing that line. Do they know that Saul did it? Are they looking for him? That puts us all in a very compromising position . . . ."

"Finally!" shouted a jubilant Daniel.

"Careful what you wish for, for it may be granted." Martha cautioned. Then expounded to the group, "I think it's dangerous to have Saul here. In fact, given that we are in his apartment, it probably makes us conspirators. This is too much! I don't think we should be associating with him. Sorry." This last was addressed politely to Saul who deflected the apology with a raised palm, a civilized display of manners about the implication of murder.

"We will not have a vote today," decided the chairman, "as I am a Yea, as is Leah and Daniel. So, Martha, unfortunately if you vote Nay you are overruled and, so, we shall call you a Yea for unanimity. Agreed?" This unusual convention confused Saul. Martha consented and the motion to accept the group's newest member passed officiously without dissent. Leah, who was taking notes, put it into the transcript. Martha wondered if her objection should be registered in case the minutes fell into the Templar's hands.

Saul was disappointed there was no ceremony attached to his acceptance, in fact there was just a mumbled welcome from those present and no more, no initiation. No secret handshakes nor codes revealed, no hiding places and definitely no spoils of war to share in. He was just in, just one of them. And they got onto other business. At least now Saul could listen without feeling as though he were eavesdropping, although he did not feel qualified enough to contribute to the discussion. On the other hand, he did realize that he had lost plausible deniability about the Cygnet Committee or the New Men if uncovered, but that came with the territory. The reliance was on loyalty. If everyone is bound together then you sink or swim with your fellows. He was tarred with the brush of insurrection, or at least sedition, like the planks on a clinker-built boat that were tarred to keep the whole afloat.

It was the first time in decades he had felt a belonging, rather than being a bystander to life, a participant not a passive recipient. But the epiphany, the heralds of trumpet-blowing angels, the sense of victory, they were conspicuously absent. Even Leah just gave him a cursory pat on the shoulder blade as though he had cooked a nice dinner, rather than entered a secretive cabal.

"I need to be somewhere. I have an appointment in an hour," Aaron informed his disciples, "and need to leave." He started to heave his unpliable frame up out of the armchair, whose cushions wanted to go with him, and pocketing his pipe paraphernalia, he levered his bulk to standing. He nodded to Saul, to encourage him to accompany him the ten steps to the front door. Saul felt obliged to help him on with his gabardine raincoat, Aaron leaned his hatted head into a conspiratorial distance and told Saul to meet him in the park at the west side of the duck pond tomorrow morning at ten o'clock. Aaron's breath at close quarters held a smoker's repulsive tang. Saul hissed a short "Yes," for he did not want to inhale, and held the door for Aaron to waddle out into the grey corridor

Friday dawned reluctantly, as a gradual palliation of the haze that the City wore as a cloak for its more embarrassing functions. Smoke and fog swirled together in an interchangeable mixture of pollution and flatus, the water vapor mixing the soup of atmosphere in a slow tumble that gave the appearance of weather. The miasma fumed with disgust over the desecration of the air, but could bring no alleviation of the cloud that hung like a bad conscience over the City. It was a worse day than usual, the pollution seemed eager, a beige rhetoric scolding the citizens left coughing below. This is as bad as it gets, thought Saul, it makes me long for the Upper Downlands.

Dump trucks grinded and belched their ways around, shouldering the other traffic aside in their dutifulness to pick up any refused and rejected items. Street sweepers pushed their shameful carts along the littered pavements and through the crunch of the park's gravel paths. Workers woke and yawned at the repetitive day, at the tedious demands of their labors. They stretched their limbs, trying to grasp beyond reach some motivation beyond routine. It was the last day before the weekend, the advent of which at least heralded a different kind of chore, for one's own benefit, not the grind for some impersonal organization. Laundry and cleaning were on the to-do list, not meetings and reports, not check and trim. But time was precious. There was never enough time. No-one ever had enough time.

Saul and Leah woke shoulder to shoulder, cramped in Saul's sagging bachelor bed. Leah wriggled until Saul turned onto his side to give her space, ceding the old mattress concavity. He then decided, gallantly, to jump start the day in the cold and clammy apartment, and abandon the warmth of the bed to her squirming.

The commonplace disappointment of the initiation of the last evening had dampened Saul's morning expectation. His stock of tea had been decimated thanks to the thirsty mob from last night, but he had some ersatz coffee, chicory mostly, that, warmed and sugared, made for a decoction of some sort. There was also enough fare for a breakfast of beans and crisp-bread. A meager meal, but enough to signal the body that effort was going to be required. It would allow the couple enough time to rouse themselves, before Saul had to meet Aaron, and Leah had to do whatever Leah had to do.

Turning the unreliable heating up to maximum, they still had to keep the oven on, and open, for extra heat. It was not the luxurious log-fueled range from the cottage, yet they could pretend. They ate breakfast naked over the small kitchen table, with coats over their shoulders, the flesh of their nether regions sticky against the plastic seats. The symbolic nudity should be a bonding between them as well as, Saul commented, between their buttocks and the furniture. They slouched around like long-marrieds, pottering in their own rituals, politely ignoring the other. She read while he dressed. They independently decided that nakedness should be a preserve of more natural surroundings.

Leah was tired and disinterested as she had no role in the City anymore. She moped around the apartment listlessly. She told him she was going to visit an old friend, with the emphasis on friend, not old. Saul thought it might be code, but did not press the issue. She snapped at him a few times, regarding his insistence on not wearing clothes at breakfast, which was, now, admittedly, a stupid idea. Leah was very distracted for someone with no work duties in the City. Perhaps his telling her that she was under government suspicion had spooked her a little. He wondered if the Cygnet Committee always had this effect on her. He could sympathize.

Saul wondered what he had to be told by Aaron that could not be said in front of the group, but did not bring his concerns up with the irritable Leah. He left the apartment at a quarter to ten, a jog to his memory of a poignant anniversary. Was it just a week? Leah saw Saul off from his own front door with a kiss, her lipstick left a cerise smear on his cheek.

Last Sunday, he had circumambulated the duck pond with dread and fear, yet he could hardly recall that day. It seemed so far from where he found himself. Three times he had walked around the park, like Peter denying Christ three times the night before the crucifixion, or Jesus praying three times for reprieve, or the three hours of darkness after the crucifixion, or the three days before the resurrection. Jesus' death was hung up on Threes. And these days? The bureaucracy celebrated it by making every form in triplicate. Saul hoped he was on the right side of history now that he was part of the solution, that this third time was a charm.

The well-trod path to the park seemed part of a fading memory for Saul. In fact, the whole City, the soaring blocks of buildings, apartments and offices and markets, the acrid rush of importunate traffic, seemed as if from a separate history. From a past that had been left behind and was, now, only a dim oneiric vision. His acquaintance with the surrounding world was distant. He crossed the last street in a daze of disconnection and entered the calm order of the park through the ornate gates set in the railings of cast iron spears. The metal ormolu tips were ornamentally lashed together by a wrought iron tracery of twisted rope. It was all very solid, very impressive. In the arch over the open gate was an enameled plate on which the image of an ancient oil-press was fired, beneath the picture was, in gothic script, the name of the park, Gethsemane.

Saul saw Aaron sitting on one of the weather-beaten wooden benches that were placed on the outer perimeter of the gravel path that circled the western edge of the pond. The pale morning light seemed lost on him, as though it could not pick him out. Like last night, Aaron was wrapped up in what looked like a profound introversion, swaddled in a cloud of tobacco smoke. Cloaked like the City itself, in the side-effects of addictions. Under his chins, his wattle shook as he drew on the pipe. Aaron did not see Saul until he had sat next to him and Saul had involuntarily choked when he breathed the smoke. Aaron turned to Saul as though he recognized the cough, and pulled the teat of the pipe from between his clamped teeth to say, in his slow, deliberate and hectoring way,

"Thank you for coming, Comrade Saul. Thank you for your punctuality. I personally value that sort of dedication, it speaks of an ordered outlook. The serious minded are few and far between these days, the people are befuddled. They are a wooly minded bunch who follow anyone with a staff and a title. It is going to be an uphill struggle to convince them that there is a better way, to convince them, indeed, that there is an alternative. The wool is well and truly pulled over their eyes. We have set ourselves a mighty task to open their eyes."

He pulled on his pipe, but the wetness had dampened his cinder of tobacco. Still, he gave it three hopeful and wheezy sucks. Then he looked into the bowl and knocked the ash onto the gravel.

Saul was feeling a bit on edge, he did not know where this interview was going.

"Since I have been in charge, the Committee has struggled to make any headway. Well, to be honest it has never had the impact we really wanted or, maybe over-optimistically, expected. Heaven knows we have tried, pushed for a platform that we could disseminate, at one point we even tried some low-key terrorism. It turned out just to worry people, not to frighten them. Our hearts weren't into hurting anyone, we were trying to help them. Do you remember our campaign of graffiti, giant warnings springing up on walls all over the City, telling people not to take the busses, or suffer the consequences? Well, each night the City Maintenance Department took the opportunity to spruce the whole damn place up with a new coat of paint. Everyone loved the new look, the effort at making the City pretty. And, I must admit, some of those murals were an improvement over concrete walls. But we were hoping for more of an effect than civil beautification."

This lecture was a bit long-winded for Saul, but he felt it impolite to interrupt.

"It was when Ham and the printers came on board that we found our niche. Publishing subversive material instead of rabble rousing. Plus, the finances improved, which was a relief and meant we could do more, but it made us lazy. We started arguing about fonts and cover art and paper stock rather than how to bring the Pontificate to the table. That was quite recently. The group impetus, what do we call it? Yes, the group dynamic was lacking. Ham is too busy running the business. Martha is a hangover from her youth, she has been around almost as long as I have. We brought Daniel along to inject a bit of youthful vigor, but we all grew a little weary at his enthusiasm and hot-headedness. Then there is Leah, who of course has been there from birth."

"From birth? How do you mean? Sir."

"Oh, did no one tell you. She is my daughter. She was born into it. Had no choice, really. Straight after her Christening, we took her to a Committee meeting. A babe in arms. She was a very cute little baby. Then when I finally made the Chair, when was that? Fifteen years ago, she was of course at my right hand. It is not nepotism, oh no, she is not there because she is my daughter. She is there on merit. Plus, it is very useful to have her around."

Saul was dumbfounded by this. He thought that it would have been mentioned before this time. But, what difference does it make? An oversight, maybe, just a mistake?

"Am I there because of Leah?" asked Saul. "To keep it all in the family?"

"Family? No! You have your own place, but I will get to that in a moment. I enjoy these little debriefings, so do indulge me."

They fell silent as a couple of young mothers pushed their prams past the bench. The wheels were sticking in the gravel, but they were determined to show off their motherliness in the park, by making the full circle. It would be easier to pull, rather than push, the prams, but that was not done, that was not how this thing worked. Saul and Aaron watched them pass with a coordinated turn of their heads. Then Aaron continued.

"I don't know if you are getting the gist of what I am saying. The Cygnet Committee has become rather redundant, we have run out of steam. There is no momentum left, no wish to man the barricades, or set fire to the Treasury, or incite an armed uprising, even if we had the means and the backing. The thing has run its course, I fear. Time to wrap it up. Our motto used to be, 'We split the ruptured structure built of age . . . .'"

"'. . . Our weapons were the tongues of crying rage.'"

"Precisely, well done. We could have done with having you around five years ago, young man. You could have carried the torch. Unfortunately, as I say, it is extinguished, now, due to a lack of fuel."

"So, why did you bring me on board last night. Just to tell me we are disbanding the next day? This is sounding a bit absurd."

"I could see how you might think that, Brother Saul. In fact, your presence is the denouement, as we say. Because you are here we can all go off in our own directions. Really, I wanted to thank you for your service. Without you it would have been much more problematic, how to wrap up this silly resistance nonsense."

Aaron gave Saul a sideways stare, it was a strangely contemptuous look where Saul thought he was in on the secret. It was given with a gimlet eye, surprising from such a soft face. It pierced Saul's frail carapace of confidence, his shell of assurance had been gradually cracking for a while. A curious veil of anxiety fell over him, when it should have been lifting, it was an ensnaring net of impending peril. Aaron looked away, out over the crushed gravel path along which the vagrant underemployed were sauntering. The two professional mothers had not made it very far, having to force their offspring along. He scanned across the pond, out over the water to a lone gull sitting nonchalantly, like a decoy. He looked up past the iron railings on the far side of the park to the robust buildings of the Bureaucratic District, solidly occupying the view in the distance. Saul twiddled his tin cuff links and felt the world shrink.

Then Aaron did the most unexpected thing that Saul could have imagined. Later Saul remembered how stymied he had been by the act. He had never been taken aback before, never been petrified. Aaron pulled from his jacket pocket, the one into which he dropped his cold pipe, a small cylinder which he put to his pallid lips and blew with the lungs of a dedicated smoker. A shrill, piercing whistle stopped everyone within sight and turned them around to see the source of such an importunate sound. Even the mothers heard it.

Then, a couple of very serious, determined men, besuited but with the physiques of laborers, strode the three fathoms in six paces over to Saul. Unfamiliar men in suits who make a beeline for you are never good news, thought Saul. They looked almost comical, their bulks bulging out of their jackets, their sure movements bunching the material. Are they going to protect me from Aaron's confession? Instead, they grabbed a surprised Saul from either side, one each, before he could react, and then he could not react. Saul finally became outraged at the breach of etiquette, it was such a bizarre turn of events, and he decided to try to resist. But before he could struggle to gain leverage, their combined strength and weights had pinned him to the seat. His arms were pressed down, his legs prevented from kicking by the knees of the two assaulters, he could but shout out in angry disbelief as to who they were, what did they want, what did they think they were doing, did they know who they were dealing with, and other inadequate execrations in a similar vein. But, it was only to blow off steam.

As his captors tightened their suppression, Aaron was catapulted from the bench as if he was on the other end of a see-saw from them, and then backed away from the ruckus. His sprightliness was a result of his disdain, and fear, of physical violence. He put the tin whistle back in his pocket, what else would he do with it? Saul looked over, imploring some help from his prospective protector, but saw Aaron satisfied, not distraught, not in the least distraught. Then, to Saul's stunned reaction, to top it all, Leah emerged from somewhere in the background, to stand shoulder to shoulder with the leader. Behind them, three black suited officials looked on dispassionately, pleased but not too much. It was all in a day's work. One of them nonchalantly adjusted his glasses.

"What? Who?" Was all Saul could mouth, so many things physically and mentally overwhelming his body and mind. He was quizzical, and in pain, and dazed, and thinking of fleeing if an opportunity arose. It did not.

"I'm sorry, son, that you find yourself as collateral damage in the Committee's machinations, but it had to be done. We told you that you were valuable to us, that you had a vital role to play in the plans, and we were not lying. We could not have done it without you. I suppose we owe you a vote of thanks. I do, though, find it hard to believe you are so gullible, so naive as not to see what is right in front of your nose."

Aaron felt emboldened enough to approach the trussed and restrained Saul as the men turned him around to place a shiny pair of official handcuffs on his trembling wrists. When we are disloyal to people, we always denigrate them, as if to make the crime their own fault, for betrayal is a heinous crime against morality. Aaron felt the need to explain to Saul a little more, to ridicule him a bit, to make him see that this was his own doing, in order to exonerate himself. He even managed to generate some righteous indignation to justify the scene. And he could not but elaborate.

"They have been tracking you for Timon's murder, you know. It is not a ticket for jay-walking or insufficient hours worked. It is a bloody serious crime, it is there in the commandments, for Christ's sake. I don't know what drove you, or what you were hoping to achieve, but thank you for letting us be the ones to turn you in. The Templars are very pleased with the Committee, it is a big break for us. Plenty of Government contracts for Ham, retirement for me, and Leah. Well, Leah."

Words failed on all accounts at this point. Saul had not looked away from a defiant Leah, how could she look angry, what did she have to be angry about? She should be abashed. She should be ashamed. Saul was the one being humiliated. He was forced to kneel on the path, the gravel cutting into his knees through the fabric of his cheap suit. The men were roughly pulling the tin cufflinks from Saul's shirt sleeves, tearing the cotton. He mouthed the 'why?' question to his erstwhile lover. Why had she betrayed him? A plaintive whimper escaped his tortured face. Had she not loved him, had they not felt the same, was this revenge? Leah stood detached and alone, steely-eyed, impassive, almost as if she were trying to be reproachful. Was she teaching him a lesson? A lesson in love?

Leah turned her head, but not seemingly in distress, more in distaste at the disgrace of a man she had once known. He was anything but that now, not known and not a man. He was face down in the dirt, an abject trapped animal, not bothering to struggle, ready to face its fate. Trussed up ready for the sacrifice. Saul was almost deformed in his contortions, his clothing in disarray, his red tie over his neck like a slit throat. The cheek she had planted a blood red kiss on less than an hour before, was ground into the path by the way his hands were compromised behind his back. He was a sad and sorry hostage to fortune and to the bargains of a fish-eyed self-server. Aaron stood over Saul as a tradesman stands over his stock, proprietorially and at a distance. Saul was an item to be bargained over. One of the suited men walked up and shook Aaron's hand and told the guards to take Saul away with a backhand wave.

Leah felt slightly nauseated, she had never liked the business side of life. Everybody seemed to turn away from Saul at the same time, as if they were embarrassed. They hauled him away. He did not resist. He could not argue.

CHAPTER TWELVE

Saul woke early on a stuffy late-summer morning to the muffled strained groans of a pained Gadd, tossing and turning in the upper bunk, an arm's length above his own face. Gadd was a poor sleeper who suffered greatly with the cumulative aches that had been gathered over a lifetime of beatings. He seemed to acquire thrashings the way the other prisoners did contraband. The latest had been happily delivered the day before, for insubordination. Whichever way Gadd lay was only a short reprieve, until the contusions and swellings forced him again to rearrange his damaged body into another temporary relief. He was an annoying bunkmate to have to sleep under, but in here choices were limited, usually to obeying or suffering. And Gadd still seemed to think he had the pick of the two. He did not, he was still trying to work it out, unlike his bunk-mate.

Saul himself had managed to avoid the physical abuse, but the unrelenting anguish kept him from any true sense of peace. His compliance did not bring relief, just respite, exactly as on the outside. True peace was not to be hoped for in this penitentiary, where one was expected to be a penitent; the punishment here was the life lived. Sleeping under Gadd was an extra insult.

The stifling barrack room was under ventilated, and fetid with the smells of a dozen sleeping men. The recently risen sun had started to fall on the corrugated metal roof and bake the wooden box of a billet. Gadd was always the first to wake, rousing himself with his traumas to a day of re-injuring them. Saul gently greeted him to the new day, Gadd grunted back, suspicious, but glad of any affection. The cabin would be unbearable in an hour, and the gong was sounding for the first parade, so the twelve discontented men organized themselves according to peevishness for the start of the day. They all thought themselves innocent, all bar Saul, and their sense of injustice fueled a lot of the culture, and thus most of the routine, in the prison.

It was four months to the day since Saul's arrest in the park. Sad and sadder were those months, as his writer's aphorism had it. If it was miserable before, it was worse now. It had been eleven weeks since the trial, a public five-ring circus where the publicity gave a platform for all his friends and colleagues to disavow him. The Pontificate also saw the opportunity to showcase the presence of revolutionary forces and to demonstrate their efficiency at handling security. The press coverage had finally wiped the news of the avalanche off the headlines, to everyone's satisfaction, as explaining tragic 'acts of God' was a tricky business no one wanted to conduct. Far easier to blame a few rogue, evil people for the problems and injustices in the world. The 'New Men' had been exposed and destroyed, a brazen murderer brought to justice and Law and Order restored. All by the reliable folks who ran the show, and brought you bread. You are welcome! It was a win-win for all involved, except Saul, who had to take the blame, and even he could not complain that he was wrongly convicted. He felt like the Gadarene swine, sacrificed as a vehicle for someone else's salvation. He was the only one in the barracks who admitted his guilt, but that did not make the other eleven innocent. In fact, it showed them up, and they resented elitist Saul for that.

After a dreadful breakfast of stale bread and lukewarm tea, with a spoonful of jam per inmate, the men presented themselves for the second parade of the young day. Sticky with the residue of yesterday's sweat and still in patched canvas clothing that had a further three days before the weekly wash, they aligned themselves military style under a heartless sun. It was nine o'clock and the men just wanted to receive their work instructions and get on with their day. Saul's status as one of only five murderers in the three-hundred-man maximum security camp ensured he would be shackled to the other four, and sent out under armed guard for laboring duties. Part of his punishment was to be constrained with his own kind, as a reminder of his iniquity. He accepted the companionship of the chain gang, and took his marching orders.

As with the last two weeks, he had been assigned to the felling crew. He would be chained to other men with whom he would not exchange a word, until out in the forest they would be released to their own set of leg irons, the fetters heavy and sharp around the ankles. He would work under the beady eyes of the suspicious guards looking down at him, often through a gun sight. There would be the minimum amount of freedom commensurate with being able to wield an axe and chop the thick pine trunks. At least he was outside, and out of the camp, for ten hours at a time, and it was better than the Brig where he had spent his first month up here, not being broken so much as melted down, before being poured into the mold of a model prisoner. Unlike Gadd, Saul had decided that resistance was pointless, and he had cooperated, but had managed to keep a nugget of hope alive within.

The prison camp itself sat isolated from any human settlement, on a large flat clearing in the ancient primeval-feeling forest on the foothills of Tohu. They were leagues from the mountaintop beyond which lay the City, which had metaphorically turned its back on their suffering. It felt to them as if Tohu only had eyes for its favorite, the dirty and perfidious City, and that they, the prisoners, were on the ass-end of its attentions.

The compound was composed of twenty-five low, ugly and mean barrack houses, hastily and shoddily constructed. The ramshackle housing promised a sweltering summer and then a brutal winter to the reluctant habitants. There was the larger mess hall, the guards camp within the camp, the infirmary and the administrative headquarters, where things were left to tick over, and the workshop which included the under-used laundry and the over-used Brig. The whole had a sense of impermanence that the next morning consistently disproved. It was uncomfortable and inconvenient for all concerned, but there were no high priorities here demanding proper treatment, just voices in the wilderness.

Saul was issued with his adze and shuffled into line to be bound to his fellows and then dragged by an uncoordinated crowd to an idling lorry. They climbed onto the benches in the back and sat shoulder to slumped shoulder waiting for the half hour ride to be over. Any interaction, in this forced intimacy, was spent grumbling and fantasizing, goading and belittling. There was no friendly banter, as there were no friends here.

At the work site they were told to clear a path through, and of, the forest. This meant cutting down the majestic trees, some of them six rods tall, the trunks four arm-spans around at the base. They were ordered to appreciate the ennobling effort of manual labor, but it was hard to do so through the exertion. Toppling the giants was work enough, but each destructive felling had the reward of a dramatic ending. The rushing of the drop, the collective yell of "Timber!" as the soaring branches swept to the ground, the tree cut down in its prime, the destruction. Pulling up the stumps took the band of men most of a day. Logging and then dragging the wood away was exhausting. It was backbreaking and grueling work, taming the forest for arable land so in a few years it could grow half a ton of feeble cabbages, each acre, each painstaking year.

Saul was silent on the commute, staring down at his heavy hemp boots that were threatening to disintegrate, twirling the adze by its handle. His mind was empty for most of the hours he was awake, he seemed to live more these days when asleep. That was when his imagination, and his memories, thrived unconstrained. In the daytime, he would not allow himself to dwell on his own mistakes, or his betrayal, or the life he had nurtured so carefully just to see it frittered away for no end. But he could not rid his memory of his daughter, nor avoid the reproach of his absence. He still felt there was uncompleted business left over from his past. And, his present circumstances frustrated him, as much as angered him, because he had no opportunity to finish it. It was a driving force, this ambition to write an ending. He kept his own counsel for those twenty-three and a half hours out of the day that he was with the other prisoners, and he prayed under his breath for a chance at redemption.

Apart from Gadd, with whom he would confide the trivialities of his routine, he projected a facade that made him unapproachable. This taciturnity kept the undesirables at bay, for he still had the supercilious conceit that he was above his fellow inmates. His reputation for having killed raised his notoriety, and his status, in the camp and, in turn, meant that they left him to his own devices. This introverted self-exclusion served him well, for he did not want to have to explain his guilt and, at the same time, his conviction that he should not be there. That contradiction was not culturally acceptable.

What was acceptable was the aggressive and combative nature of intimidation, not just from the authorities, but between prisoners. There were always squabbles. Fights became violent at the misinterpretation of a wrong look. And, the guards were constantly trying to break up the latest factions before they formed into gangs. Men were transferred without rhyme or reason, or alert, to keep an uncertain disruption. It was a successful strategy, the only deaths in the last year had been work related.

There was only one road bisecting this old growth forest, it was unused and in disrepair, and down a gravel road spur, the work site had been painstakingly enlarged to a few square furlongs. The humpback of Tohu loomed above the ever-receding treetop horizon, like a reminder of the eternal, out of reach, but enticingly in view. The endlessness was as distressing to those boxed-in as the ocean to a landlubber, as a starry night sky to a city dweller. The prisoners tended not to raise the level of their eye-sight beyond the clearing. When they disembarked, the work gang waited to be unattached from each other and then lolled around the decimated swath awaiting instructions, although they all knew the procedure. There was a great deal of time-wasting, the men wanted to relax, and the guards just wanted to get back to camp as soon as possible, having fulfilled the quotas.

The sentries formed a perimeter around the men and the head guard walked through them, barking commands, asserting authority. The guards, with their backs to the woods, kept their rifles cocked and ready to lift to the shoulder for a shot, if need be. If one relaxed the others took up the slack in rotation. Three gun barrels bore down on the fifteen men at all times, but no-one could tell which three were the targets. Probably the loudest and the boldest, and the ones who wanted attention. Saul was not one of those. As the day progressed, as the sun rose, and the high mountain air seemed to magnify the sun's power, the guards would slacken their vigilance. They would sit and joke among themselves, would relieve one another for breaks, but always keeping a safe killing distance to the prisoners, dismissively watching the work from afar.

The task was to fell the pines, trim the trunks and stack the logs. The lumber would be picked up by enormous, muscular diesel lorries, with further trailers extending their articulated lengths. These would creep onto the prepared dirt roads the men would level as they slowly progressed into the forest, and transport the valuable resource to some distant saw mill. The prisoners would then have to hack out the stumps with axe and adze, with pick and shovel, with rope and brute strength. The work was arduous and punishing. The dog days of summer boiled any activity, and most of the men stripped down to the waist to wield their tools. As a result, they were bronzed and fit and strong, healthier than any had been in the City. They worked in teams, not enthusiastically, but with enough concentration to keep the foremen off their broadening backs. To the steady beat of the chopping of the harvested wood, the cicadas added a gospel beat. The birds were silenced at this time of year, nesting done, they were intent on fattening themselves, harboring instincts of massing and leaving. The men carried on slicing and parsing the work, moving further into the scented wood, inching away from prison life. Heads down, they labored on.

When the sun hits its zenith, the prisoners were afforded an hour break for a much-coveted lunch comprised sparingly of flat bread and either a tapenade or, more often, the reviled clabber. A trustee, who had been institutionalized into subservience, generally one of the older, more decrepit men, who could not handle the physical workload, was tasked with supplying water fetched from a nearby stream by means of a bucket. Even the water carrier would be overseen by a guard, standing on a hillside aiming down into the gully with his rifle. The drink was rationed and considered precious in the heat, so any spillage was punished and any wastage scorned. Not because the water was limited, there was plenty, even if the water-boy was slow, but as an act of authoritarianism. Power has to be exercised or it shrivels up.

The men perked up after eating and supping and the usual tetchy silence of work gave way to a sardonic ribaldry, a relief of guffaws and wary banter among the deadness of the forest floor. For under the pine canopy the brown needles lay acidifying the ground on which a lack of sunlight fell and no underbrush grew. Saul loved the proximity to the stark harmony of nature that this work detail gave, there was no jungle confusion here. The background was sterile, the life brazen, it was black and white. In the hot breath of middle-aged summer, he was glad for the escape from the confusion of prison. And the alternative? He could be working in the kitchens, the laundry, the sewing room. Perhaps at Christmas, when winter gripped the forest in its iron fist, he would relish the closeness and heat of the indoors, but that was not in his plans.

Gadd, the bruised, worked in the kitchens, with the attitude with which he approached nearly everything, half-heartedly. After proving himself incompetent as a cook he had been sidelined to quartermaster, it was not the kitchen head's finest management decision. But Gadd liked the new role, he thought he could prosper and so dedicated slightly more than half his heart to his job. He was adequate, which for him was success. This put him, eventually, in charge of the goods the kitchen required, the vegetables and the dry goods, the precious dairy and the sacks of rice and grain, the cans of preserves. It was putting the fox in charge of the hen house, but it kept Gadd occupied and everyone wanted to be as able as possible to ignore poor Gadd.

All the raw materials for the men's sustenance passed through his hands and opportunistic light fingers. And Saul had quickly exploited his acquaintance with his feckless bunkmate for his own ends. In return for any protection his friendship could bring, Saul had asked and received cans and small bags of misappropriated foodstuffs. Gadd had assumed that Saul supplemented his diet with these bland treats, but Saul's interest was in the long shelf life, his plan was longer term than snacking.

Saul would hide these rations about his person and take them on work duty to the clearing. He had found an abandoned rabbit burrow close to the latrine and every time he had to make use of the disgusting facility he secreted away another small meal in his illicit larder. He had not worked out the logistics of exploiting this store, of how he would ever get to use it, but it reassured him to know it was there, waiting like a nest-egg. It calmed him to think that he had a secret from the insular world of the prison, that institution that occupied its inmates like a foreign colonizer. Gadd had also procured a few items of cutlery, and even a paring knife, for Saul. All gratefully accepted and hidden, all covered and disguised, in the ground under the pine needles littering the soft earth. All Saul had to do was tolerate Gadd for longer than his forbearance would usually permit. It was a small price, but excruciating.

One time, Gadd approached Saul curious as to his desire for these goods, and maybe to see if there were some extra service he could demand. Gadd had a natural belief in economic inflation. He spoke in the local accent, but heavily, with the same drawl that Sarah, Leah's erstwhile work colleague, had succeeded in losing. The vowels were elongated, Saul noted, and the glottal stop was pronounced. To most City dwellers it was a lazy way to talk, it was ugly, a mark of ignorance.

"So, Sol," Gadd addressed his lower bed partner one night, just after lights out, "wha' 'ave you bin doin' wif thos bits and pieces I've been pinchin' for ya? It str'ies me th' I neffer see you eatin' any of it. You ain' passin' it on, are ya? I wouldn't li'e tha'. These otha scumbags don't deserf any extras. If you ge' wha' I mean."

Saul did not want to converse with this vulgar man, he disliked him and his grasping attitude. But, conversely, he genuinely did not want to be snobbish about Gadd's provinciality. He prided himself on his egalitarianism, which was daily tested, though he did not feel the need to practice his magnanimity. And, as much as a conscience, a superior air was frowned upon in prison as much as it was encouraged back in the City. So, Saul winced to himself. If only Gadd had a likable bone in his body, it would be so much easier.

"Don't worry, Gadd, nobody else knows about your generosity. I do appreciate your kindness and I promise I won't tell anyone else about it. I know it embarrasses you. The secret of how nice you are rests with me."

"I di'n mean tha'. I juss fough' you maybe wass benefidin' from my risks. That would'n be fair, now would it?"

"No. Not at all. It's all for my benefit, my friend. And I thank you, and my stomach thanks you and . . . ." Here Saul could think of no other person that would fit on that list. Not Leah, no friends, just, "Esther, my daughter. If I ever get to see her again. Jesus! You and she are the only people I've got in the world!"

Gadd leant over the edge of his bunk but could only see a shadow of the recumbent Saul.

"Nonsense. You muss 'ave loads ov people araand you, all the time. Popular guy like you. Reglar popla, you would be, I reckon."

"I wish someone cared, Gadd, the girl I did my deed for turned me in. That sends a stark message. It was a hell of a break-up. I had burnt a lot of bridges for her, as well. All my family is dead, apart from Esther, my daughter, and we don't know each other. It was starting to turn around when the shit hit the fan." Gadd giggled at this ridiculous turn of phrase. "Hey, Gadd, you're from round here, right?"

"Well, sort ov. Abaa' twenny miles norf. I remember this place from the a'tside when I was a nippa', we wuss allus scared of it. Told to keep away. When we'ed pass it on the way to To'u, or to the cidy, we'ed be told how dangerous the men were, are, and to avoid it like the plague."

"So, what's the lay of the land? Is it just trees for as far as you can see?"

Saul thought, 'Turtles all the way down!'

"Pre'ee much. As many bloody trees as you could wan'. When you live 'ere you sort ov pray for a fire to burn it all down, just so you can see more than a furlong. It's like be'in in a cage that moves aroun' wif you."

"And toward Tohu? How far is that on foot?"

"On Shank's Pony? You godda be kiddin." It was Saul's turn to giggle, he had not heard that idiom, and would not have called it an idiom out loud, but he could guess what it meant.

"Yes. As the crow flies. What would it take to get from here to the City, say?"

"Abaht a lifetime, I would guess. A flippin' lifetime." But he did the calculation, "Abaht two days to the moun'ins, a cuppla days gettin' over 'em and then anovver two down to the Ci'y. Wha's tha' then? Err, juss over a week. Good luck over tha' terrain, though, tha's sum pre'ee tough land. An' the wevver, it can turn on ya' li'e tha'. No food to be 'ad, eiver, wa'er would be fine, but, Jeez!"

"I think I'd like to try it," confided Saul. And just as he had started this whole damn situation in motion by an offhand comment to Father Timon, so he wished he could take the comment back. He tried to cover his tracks by explaining how impossible he recognized the idea to be and how impractical, being an inmate, shackled more than not. Gadd's lizard intelligence caught the fly but seemed not to savor it. But it set a little spark in both minds, the spark that imagination fans to a flame, which fire warms a selfish heart.

As Saul made as if to sleep, he started to fantasize about escaping, not just imagining himself elsewhere. He felt he could not start planning until he had more resources, and besides there was the small matter of the guards whose jobs it was to stop him. And, as Saul plotted, so the sly button in Gadd's concern for his own advancement was pushed. Gadd heard the implication and wondered how his ostensible friend's slip could advantage him. His vainglory, always concealed under a blanket of false humility, smoldered.

Gadd was silent, and Saul had no illusions as to his bunk mate's native wit. Saul did not panic, there was no need. He was not a man given over to rashness or impulse, he tended to side more with regret and remorse. He realized as he lay on the thin straw mattress that did not quite cover the boards, that time was now of the essence, that a countdown had started with Gadd's calculations. He needed to act promptly and the borborygmus of his belly, the daily squelch of his gut, suggested how. There was a rampant dysentery that was sweeping the camp, as always, and that would be his meal ticket. These thoughts were not conducive to his queasiness, but they soothed his mind.

At the clearing the next morning, having smuggled as many personal items as he could surreptitiously manage, wearing two vests, two pairs of socks and with a stub of a pencil and as many loose pages from the *Book of Disquiet* as he could hide in his underwear, Saul decided that he might as well get a head start. He had such a long journey to undertake and every thousand-mile voyage starts with a first step. The next step was always clear, as was the first and by logic the whole path should make sense, but the last step, that was always somewhere far down the road. That was the unknown.

The detail had only just started into the morning's work. He called to his least favorite guard, an unpleasant, sadistic and resentful petty tyrant who stood scowling on the outskirts of the group. Saul made as if he had an embarrassing personal matter to discuss and the guard came to within spitting distance to hear his complaint.

"Look," pleaded Saul, "I have a touch of the cramps, I think I have diarrhea, I need to go to the latrine. Could I ask you to take off my shackles so that I don't shit all over the chain?"

Saul's nervousness gave him the proper shiftless look of a man pale with suffering. The guard, normally so stern, must have felt a rare stirring of compassion, and agreed that Saul could have one leg freed. Saul made sure it was the tighter ankle, out of comfort. He limped and stumbled toward the relief of the ditch, the right fetter still on, the length of chain over his right forearm, the pretense of doubling over with stomach pain, well sold. The disgusted guard stalked behind a respectful distance, his bouncing rifle sight leveled at Saul's spine at heart height. He could not help but sniff the air for any offending odor, a deep wish to be revolted.

Saul turned as he approached the thicket that hid the pit and pushing his hands together like a praying angel, begged for a little privacy, for both of their sakes. The guard waved him on and leaned his rifle up against a tree trunk, then searched his pockets for one of his thin, black-market cigarettes. He tidied up the shreds leaking out the paper, and drew deep on the lit tobacco in hope that the smoke would act as incense against the animal smell of the latrine.

As Saul prepared himself, he made suitable noises that the guard tried to ignore. He groaned for effect, stamped around and shook his chain. He then padded softly around past the boards that lay over the noxious trench and, grabbing the shit-shovel with which users were supposed to cover their leavings, rounded the tree and threw the trowel. As the guard spun, surprised by the dull, dim sound of the trowel hitting the spongy needle humus, Saul swung the short length of chain and fetter and caught him squarely between the eyes with a fearsome blow. The guard crumpled to the ground, his open mouth seeming to take a bite of the soil, his lit cigarette hissing in the saliva at the back of his throat. Saul panted deeply and rapidly and waited for all the energy of the scene to dissipate. He kept an ear out for any outside reaction, and hearing none, congratulated himself, "I must be getting good at this."

Saul bowed his head and genuflected, as though in penance, in front of his stricken victim, dropping the chain of the shackle into the soft ground as he did so. Time slowed down to a dripping tick of moments. Fight left his mind on foot and flight entered on wings to replace it. He scanned around for heaven knows what. The only noise was his breathing easing, from a shallow pant to a slower sigh. The cicadas had not been interrupted.

Saul pushed the slumped figure to a sitting position up against the tree, knocking over the rifle as he did so. There was no crack of gunshot, no summoning alarm, no surprise. As though briefed and prepared, although acting instinctively, Saul pried off the man's jacket, and put it over his own shoulders. Finding the mean little key, he unlocked his fetter and left it where it fell. He undid the laces and pulled the boots off the guard's inert feet, tying the laces back together and placing them round his neck. There was nothing else to loot from his victim apart from his military cap, and so he left the man to die, if his injuries decided, alone with his God.

Saul strode back to the latrine and over to his cache, his hidden store of goods. Fashioning a makeshift bag from the extra jacket, by buttoning the front and tying a bind around the waist, he emptied the burrow's contents into the bag and tying the cuffs together and slinging the thing onto his back, he left. He set off into the darkness of the wood that he hoped would envelop him. He wanted to be swallowed by the immensity of the forest. Away from another murder, away from the inevitable baying pursuit, away from servitude and incarceration.

At first, he scampered, thoughtlessly, or rather, inattentively, up banks and down gullies, looking behind as much as forward, choosing thickets as cover. For an hour he fled, realizing that the guard would have been discovered and anticipating a search party, wishing he had been more purposeful in covering his tracks. But, after a hard half hour, stopping to listen over his strained breath and thumping heart, he heard nothing, just the workaday sounds of the trees, the wistful birds and the pacifying wind. He decided he could afford to be more circumspect, the boots banging against his chest, the jacket bag gently punching him in the kidneys with the weight of cans and rice, he needed to stop and re-gather his thoughts.

Then he came across a water course, he heard the splashing further over from his roughshod path, and headed toward it. A brook fell over itself rolling down a rocky ravine, that was not quite deserving of that name, the water was more playful than riled. Saul stepped into the ankle-deep water whose coolness soothed the abrasions the fetters had left on his lower leg, chilled his hot-bloodedness and, most importantly, gave him a sense of direction. I could have been running in circles, he berated himself, following my own adrenaline-soaked sense of flight. Now he could head up, away from the road which traversed the petty gradients here, away from the work site and the yokels with rifles and away from the camp, toward the mountains. The mountains of Tohu, of escape, of peace, of solitude, of 'waste and void,' the place without form.

Saul drank and threw cupped handfuls of water up into his screwed up face. But he did not dally, he had one ear cocked for the snap of a twig, one eye for the flurry of pursuit. He thought he caught a glimpse of some movement, but it was ahead of him and he decided that it must be his imagination. Walking in the stream bed for another fifteen minutes, until the land leveled off and opened out, he then paralleled the stream on some animal trails. He felt he had a head start over whatever came after, and as he became lost, he relaxed.

He maintained a brisk but manageable pace and he realized that the sprint had turned into an endurance event. This was a tortoise and hare chase, now. So, they would have to discover the body, perhaps raise an alarm, he had heard no whistles, 'but would he?' They would make a cursory search nearby, but would then run back to the main camp and tell the warden. 'Boy,' he would like to see that reaction. Then they would send some of the more professional, fitter guards, a *posse*. With some proper equipment, guns and tents, an expedition! They would need it, for he intended to lead them a merry dance, 'a merry dance indeed!' Or maybe they would just sit back and hope the wolves or bears got him, or the frozen nights, or the lack of gear, or any of the many hurdles he was faced with. Either way, he would progress until halted. He plowed on, resolute, fired by a manufactured indignation at some assumed slight.

After three hours of marching, of picking out the most difficult terrain to pass over, of avoiding any ground that would give a clue as to his route, Saul felt more and more sanguine about his prospects. The day was warm, and he was hot, he had filled the flask he had secreted away some weeks before for this very moment, and was feeling pleased with himself. He sat in the shade of a grove of hickory trees and rested, his senses still alert to any unusual noise or disturbance, still mainly aware of the danger from his own species. The vast woodland was a refuge to him, a place to hide, a protection. He felt safer lost in the wilderness than he had for a year in the company of his fellows. Then the doubts rolled in.

Saul took stock of his provisions, laying them out in front of him as a reprimand to his arrogance at thinking he could achieve this feat. What was he thinking? Two or three weeks alone in the wilderness, a mountain range to cross, no support and precious little food and no shelter? That is not a madcap adventure, that is an intimidating task. The rifle, 'he had not grabbed the rifle,' and the trowel, that would have been of use. In the rush of his leaving he had been negligent. He would need to be more thoughtful, to up his game. He needed to get a grip on the situation, take charge. And, if he could evade capture or death and arrive back in the City, he had nothing to look forward to, no friends nor allies. Abandoned by all, save his daughter, and that might be only because he had pushed her away. But now, the Templars would be watching her, the bait in a trap to catch him. If they don't get me out here, then they will definitely snare me if I show up at home again. Home! An impossible concept!

All his possessions, everything he had worked for, was gone, the apartment, his job, his standing, his love, his acquaintances. To be honest, all was lost fifteen weeks ago, but he had kept a little promise alive in the back of his romantic skull, of the prodigal son returning to acclaim. It was foolish to think that he could get back to how it was, as though it was a nightmare from which he was going to wake, but he could not stop himself. Saul knew it was ridiculous to wish so, but he had needed to keep hope alive when hope was more valuable than time. And now, he was trying to evade himself, he did not want to have to give truthful answers, even to himself. He had lost everything, and now was trying to lose himself.

Saul wept. Silently. As befits a refugee. Not as a manifestation of his despair, but to manumit his emotion. It was a release that would allow him to continue. It hardened his resolve to survive, even if he did not know how, why or for what end. He would see this through and then decide. One hour at a time until one day at a time until one week until the lengths of time stretched to an extent that he could rest within them. Where he could find peace in the pauses between the necessities. Saul shed tears not for himself but for the world that would test him so, and not out of pity, or for any revenge he would have to wreak, but for the fact that the indifferent world cared not for one of its own. He finally realized the solitude of the enlightened. His community had enslaved him, he had escaped.

Saul had now stepped outside his life. The old certainties were firmly rejected, the old rules rescinded, the material world of work and sacrifice as though men were ants, not creatures made in God's image, was consigned to the regrettable past. He would commence a pilgrimage, but one without an objective, no sacred grotto or church as destination, no established route of the saints to follow. This would be a heuristic mission, the physical course undetermined, except for 'away,' for this would take freedom to accomplish. He was seeking liberation, the way for him to exist in freedom and he needed to be alone for that quest. Wolves and bears permitting.

Saul's complete worldly possessions were arrayed in front of him. To the materialistic world it may have looked woeful, but to a man in extremis, it was a bounty. Nothing he owned was frivolous, all were tools to aid him on his journey, nothing was extraneous. He had besides the prison issue work clothes he was wearing, another pair of socks and boots and another cap and the jacket that made a surprisingly effective sack, courtesy of the poor guard. Inside the jacket pockets Saul was pleased to discover two books of matches, which reproved him, for he had not thought of a fire source. The bad habit of the guard was turning out to be a blessing in disguise for Saul. And there was a half-smoked packet of cigarettes, to justify the matches.

An absolute boon, and one that truly elevated his spirits, was the discovery of a hip flask the crafty man had hidden in his jacket lining, to get him through the day. Inside was a half pint of liquor, and Saul celebrated with a quick swig. It tasted of that plum brandy Leah had once served, the astringent sting of the crude alcohol detonated explosive memories in his tired brain. Leah had called it her local poison, and she had remained loyal to that atavism. She had peasant tastes, really, 'He should have known better!' He raised the flask to thank the unlucky guard, to toast his fight against the hurtful memories of Leah, then to wish Esther his benediction. There was a lightheadedness he had grown unused to, and he did not drink any more of his precious liquid cargo. He would have swapped it for a rifle and a trowel, though.

The other items were mainly foodstuffs. He had two tin cans of tomato paste, one of peaches and one, incongruently, of *marron glacé*. He was not too sure how the kitchen would have intended to use that chestnut paste, but was pleased to have the thing with him. He had an empty glass bottle, that he had scavenged one wet day a few weeks prior, that he had filled at the stream, and a smaller bottle full of rice. In fact, he had a couple of pounds of flour and sugar in various small bundles and sachets and the bottle of rice, plus about a pound of dried beans. It was no buffet picnic, but he reckoned the calorific value could last up to a week, if he rationed himself. But he would need to supplement these provisions if he were to succeed beyond that.

There was in addition a dinner knife and fork, and, very usefully, a sharpened paring knife, not suitable for defense but 'if he needed to peel a potato, then . . . .' He also had a pilfered salt shaker that despite nestling underground for a week was full and dry. Rounding off his supplies were eighteen pages of the *Book of*

Disquiet and half a pencil which he would have to use sparingly. At least he had the means of sharpening it.

It was not worth contemplating what he did not have, the test was to survive with what he did have. Saul cut the laces on the boots in half, and tied up the eyelets alternately as effectively as he could, with the view to preserving some twine for later. The boots were a size too large for him, and so he pulled the spare socks over his own and eased his un-calloused feet into the rubber and oilcloth. He could foresee a tortuous journey of blister and pain until they adapted. The hemp boots went back into the makeshift sack. He wore all the clothes, bar the jacket.

He had no delusions about the enormity of the undertaking. Every time he caught a glimpse of the *bossu* of Tohu, his north star, he was reminded of his insignificance. He was but an insect in this landscape, a locust alone in the desert, and hopefully as hard to find. Concentrate on the present was his mantra, the thought of what lay ahead was too daunting, he had to focus on the next step, always the next step. With his meagre belongings packed into his improvised pack, the heavy boots loose around his feet, if tight above the ankle, the cap jauntily back on his head, he took that next step.

Having had time to strategize, he thought he had the measure of his *poursuivants*. As he maintained his easy consistent pace he decided to throw any trackers off his scent by means of a sudden change of direction. He therefore abruptly turned hard left off the natural incline he had been gently ascending and hopping from boulder to boulder until he reached a rocky outcrop, inched his way laterally along a small cliff until he made the neighboring drainage. He climbed again, this time through a steeper terrain, fending off and grabbing as handholds, low bushes and undergrowth. The trees could not gain purchase on this channel and he exited left again in order to confuse anyone who assumed he would take the fastest route. Finding a more benign route on animal tracks, he proceeded up the slope, realizing that all the gullies would meet eventually, like the spines of a hand fan closing in on the handle. All the paths were heading to the same high point, he wanted to choose the one that met the latest. Saul spent a good hour attaining the next drainage, hoping to find the next section over, so that by the time he would meet the junction with his original path, way ahead, he would be so many fan-segments away, that he would be beyond capture.

Knowing he had to face deprivation if he was to have a chance of surviving, he chose to practice self-denial, by allowing his hunger full rein. Much better to suffer now and spread it out over, what was that Gadd said? 'A week?' Rather than eat heartily at the beginning and have no supplies left, and always mindful of his rather unreliable digestive system, he entertained the thought that self-immolation could be healthy. So, he walked mindfully through the time when his erstwhile fellow inmates would be trying to enjoy lunch, and manfully through the pangs that assailed him, until he could feel his body shudder with the lack of fuel. Then he stopped, exhausted but exhilarated, and rested like a pilgrim, virtuous and blessed, on a fallen trunk that was in the slow process of turning to sawdust. The work of termites, he supposed. He wondered if they were edible.

He had learned a lesson by pushing on until near collapse as he had no strength to prepare for the night, and he knew he needed to take precautions. Commanding his reluctant limbs to one last effort he dragged dry tree limbs to the fallen trunk and laid the collected branches over the dry and soft bed of sawdust, forming a shelter of sorts. He prayed that the termites would sleep as well as he intended to. Then, as the light was dimming enough that any smoke would not be visible, he made a ring of larger rocks around a shallow pit he scraped with his hands and laid a fire that he lit with one of the beautiful, magical matches with which he had been blessed. He opened the can of chestnut puree and, carefully scooping the contents aside for a while, he boiled water he had stored in the wine bottle with some rice and beans and salt. Adding a little *marron* and a spoonful of tomato paste made the meal colorful, his appetite made it palatable. Night was upon him, a forest silence fell.

After he had eaten, he cleaned up, putting the paste back in its blackened tin, and sat back to commune with the diminishing fire. For now, he was happy, it had been a momentous day, as too many of his had been in the last year. A year ago, he had been settled, and if anyone had cared to ask, content, but he was a hypocrite. He was bored and agitated, he just didn't show it, and he assumed everyone felt that *angst* that had infected him. Now, here, he was alone, depleted, homeless, lovelorn, or at least loveless, with one, maybe two, murders under his belt. Yet he did not consider himself a violent man, in fact, he thought of himself as a decent citizen, not a boat-rocker or an up-setter of apple carts. How it had all come to this he would have to try to fathom in the next week of make or break. Saul allowed himself a temporary wallow in victimhood, knowing it was pernicious. Although enticing, he would treat the indulgence sparingly, with the same reverence as for plum brandy. 'A lovely swig of self-pity.'

As he entombed himself in his shelter for the night, the journey that had brought him to this desolate spot, and the irony of his situation, was not lost on him. The feeling that he had let build up in his chest was a nugget of humanity he would always treasure, he knew, and was the last worthwhile idea in his life. He hoped it was a flame, or spark, that could warm him, for he could feel the chill descending from above, the altitude having a marked effect upon the temperature. He had started to conflate the mental and physical. If he felt that he had evolved spiritually into adulthood over the past half year, this physical test would be his rite of passage into being a full man. Survival against the odds, the combat to preserve life when God wants you dead, when Nature throws her worst indifference at you, and you emerge victorious because you still stand. That was the mark of a man, to pass the test presented, the one of self-examination.

Saul could smell the last smoke of the dying embers burning his urine, it was to be the smell of his home from herein. His pillow was his pack, he was as swaddled in clothing as much as possible. His boots, for they had become his once he had walked a mile in them, were beyond his feet, airing in the cool breeze that gently swept this little plateau. The hemp boots covered his blisters. He was tired, as tired as he could remember ever being and it was delicious. He was replete, satisfied with his mark and his condition, whilst realizing that he was only at the beginning of something, and he would not let himself contemplate the future. Like Anthony of Antioch, he would live in the moment in the desert.

Saul could see the bright half disk of the moon through the boughs that formed his sloping ceiling, an owl hooted a distance away, recalling the regret of a better time with Leah. Clouds edged their silhouettes in front of the moonlight, 'The moon that speaks of bats,' and he fell asleep with one ear pricked for possible ambush from out the coolth. Saul was as comfortable as he could hope, the sense of adventure creating a small furnace within. And he thought, that even if he had been captured, here and now, he would have blessed the fifteen hours of liberty with which he had walked away.

CHAPTER THIRTEEN

Saul awoke before dawn and waited, sheltered but vigilant, until the sun pried the edge of the night into spreading color. It was as though the day was gently lifting a lid off the world, trying not to disturb it, but perhaps to see if it were done yet. He had his head propped on a dead tree branch, his jaw slacked against his chest to open the ear canals to any un-dawn-like noise. But all was merciful peace. The birds announced, the trees seemed to sigh, the slow unfurl of the heat of the new day was a seepage of deep reds and jubilant yellows.

As the light hinted itself onto the jagged horizon of pine treetops, he stirred, like a man emerging from a grave, pushing foliage away from his body and his miserly pile of foodstuff. Saul stretched his frame that had been forced into compaction to retain heat in his nest. He was keen for the adventure of the day, the early bird, and desirous of keeping his advantage, the worm.

It felt like a foot race now, no vehicles could penetrate this terrain and horses, some of which grazed around the perimeter of the prison, would only get you so far. He knew time was of the essence, but relit his fire anyway to boil some water and oatmeal, to give his body some fuel for the day ahead. It was not a scramble, now, better he can feed his stamina and get a good day's tramp in. At the next stop, over the next impending crest, through the next stretch of forest, he could forage, when he had leisure to reorganize. After his porridge, he dismantled his bed and placed the branches over the buried ashes. It was a token covering of his tracks, but he felt better for having made an effort.

Saul set off uphill again, his improvised bag on his back, the merest hint of night still in the northern sky. He had no concept of distance on this terrain, but figured he had covered at least three leagues, he was hoping to strike off the next three before camping again. At times the steepness was slowing him down to a crawl, each step meticulous. Occasionally, he was forced to walk with his hands pushing down onto his knees, looking straight ahead against the gradient of the route in front of his eyes. That was painfully slow progress, but if anyone was following, well, their curses would be praise enough for his efforts. Tonight, hopefully, he would be twenty miles from the road, the worksite, the prison, the rising number was a measure of success. He would earn that distance, that safety.

At noon, Saul sat to rest, three hours of exertion behind him, if he had had a schedule he would be ahead of it. He sat with his back against the massive trunk of a sycamore, a tree whose broad canopy claimed one of the last deciduous refuges on the slope. He was exhausted in the way that the exercise of unused muscles, that then grow into their use, makes a man empty. Saul was proficient in wielding an adze, a spade, an axe and had developed strength in his torso and upper body in the last few months. Now his legs were undergoing the same treatment, and it hurt, his hamstrings and calves could not rid themselves of the lactic acid he was forcing them to produce. Building muscle and growing flesh is debilitating work, made worse under starvation rations. 'I must concentrate outside,' he told himself, 'I must not linger on the pain.'

Around Saul, there was now a preponderance of pines, where a mixture of trees had previously made up the forest. Even the firs had conceded the struggle to survive at this altitude, and there was plenty more to come, the summits were rising ever upward. The mountains climbed on the backs of lower mountains like a scramble of visionaries, immobilized in bedrock, standing on the shoulders of giants. The oaks and sycamores gave way to the maples, skinny and hesitant trees; there were soft needled junipers, and the eventuality of aspens. Scatterings of evergreens started to connect in the hills above him, copses became woods which merged into the vast forest spilling from the mountain apron toward him. Beyond the carpet of dark olive, that gave the hillsides a soft, almost furry suggestion, the conifers prospered until a tide mark set the tree line and the bare, bare rock and loose boulder slope acceded.

That was un-euphemistically called the kill zone.

For it looked forbidding and treacherous, as it puckered Tohu up to the pinnacles. A last run of lingering snow, brilliant white in the summer sun, was set against a surround of ancient washed distant granite and the enamel blue of a polished sky. It was not the scenery that stole Saul's breath, though, it was the labored climb, even his lungs were adapting, and paining him in so doing.

Saul ate a mealy cake of cooked rice that he had wrapped the night before, it was wonderfully starchy, but not enough. He knew he could eat most of the food in his pack in one sitting, and he was having no luck in identifying new sources of food. 'How do those damn bears do it?' He was beginning to think about meals he had enjoyed, his favorite tastes, that breakfast of doughnuts, that roast cauliflower curry, that *caprese* salad sandwich, those olives. He found a bush that advertised its red berries against its greenery. If there is food he would not be the first to find it, so the berries being untouched must be a sign they are poisonous. There were many other competitors, much more successful than he, scratching a hardscrabble living in this magnificent desert. Best to avoid the obvious.

He kept his bottle filled from the frequent brooks he negotiated, the water was crisp and refreshing in the stifling afternoon.

But even the sun could not flay his spirits, he was feeling elated, perhaps prematurely, but it made his job easier. His small victories, over his hunger, his fatigue, his capture, they all alleviated his way. Fear may have provoked more initial speed, but the positivity of outlook simplified the ongoing climb. And he felt he was learning; not mastering, but familiarizing.

As the heat increased, Saul noticed great rolling clouds that materialized behind him and then threatened to encompass him, but without yet reaching him. When he turned around, the ground he had covered the day before lay darkened in their encroaching shadow. He resumed his climb but when he looked back again, they had amassed further and crept farther, as though stalking him. The clouds were black bottomed, giant wells of menace expanding overhead. 'Like giant cartoon brains, dipped in cinders,' was all he could come up with. There was a manifest menace looming, and that did not need learning.

Then came the wind as though the nearing clouds were pushing the air ahead of them in their thrust up the hill. The impetus helped Saul in his climb, a gentle hand pushed on his back. The breeze cooled him down, and he felt the impending force. He knew that he would need to find protection. He could smell the rain and it made him pick up the hurry in his suffering legs.

The lightning behind his back lit up his way, an angry, derisive flash of immense power, a warning light. A bellowing echo of thunder followed close on its heels, he could feel the percussion on his back. That was a shove, not just a gentle reminder. Saul looked around ready to bolt for cover; whatever was coming was not in a mood to argue. He saw a small cliff of rock on the side of the ravine up which he was funneling, it folded back in on itself, back toward the ground. It was not ideal, but it did face away from the direction of the storm. There was an overhang that formed an upper lip over a thin depression of a mouth. It was a sanctuary that was not worthy to be called a cave, but it was a shelter. Saul scoped out the resting place and seeing it suitable for one prone body threw his pack in to claim his place, and set off to gather kindling. In two hurried minutes he had an armful of twigs, branches, moss, leaves and bark; he also had two hands worth of scratches and punctures. The gale was racing up in pursuit of him in the way that none of the guards were, he could literally feel it breathing down his neck. The urgency felt familiar.

The winds whipped, and the first large drops of rain splashed languidly down. The precursor was almost playful, like the count-down in hide-and-seek, ready or not here it comes! Then the first hail pitted like flick-knives of ice flecks bouncing off his scalp. Crawling into the sullen lair on all fours, he rolled against the back wall and pulled his small haystack of tree limbs in front of his chest, over his pack. He tried to wedge himself into the space as best he could, hoping the brush would keep some of the worst of the weather away. Saul summoned his patience and waited for the maelstrom.

There was no earthquake, nor any explosions, no toppling of the giant trees, despite Saul's worst City fears of the dangers of the mountains. But the deluge on the steep slopes was Scriptural in its ferocity. Where he had been walking a half hour before went from mud, to trickle, to brook, to stream, to torrent in the same span he had taken to get out of there. 'This is unearthly,' he thought, when, in fact, it was the complete opposite. The wind drove the rain through his faggot of a hurdle, as though he was being hosed. In its vicious spitting, it wetted his jacket but did not drench him to the skin. He shivered, but half out of intimidation, and he prayed to whichever God may be left up there, to hear him, not to spare him but to give him strength. He wished he could have bottled his earlier elation to drink, now he needed it, and then he remembered the brandy. As he felt the fumbled bottle press against his lip and as he shook a drop of the precious nectar onto his tongue and swallowed, searing his throat, he muttered, 'This too shall pass.'

Saul struggled to sleep, and having achieved that state held onto it with the will of a parent protecting its child. No dreams could take root in his disequilibrium. The wind gusted higher and longer, always in spurts, then a subsidence brought relief before the next wailing assault. His little pocket of refuge, tucked into the alcove of the bare rock kept the worst at bay, the bundle of sticks pushed into him then sucked out by the wind. He had to brace himself and hold on to the guard, to keep it from being snatched away.

As he tried to ignore the End of Days, outside, the storm grew more furious. He thanked God that there was an outside for that meant, by extension, there was an inside. Raging and railing at the geology and geography of the mountain's solidity that had incited it by resisting its winds, the storm vented its wrath futilely. Between the turbulent air and the unmovable rock, the organic skin of vegetation and soil took the brunt. The tempest grabbed the surrounding trees like a bully grabs the lapels of his victim, and shakes him into submission. But Tohu was impassive, impervious, uncaring and obdurate. If it lost some cover then it was of no consequence, like a boy scraping his knee, it will regrow. And, secure in the crevice, Saul slept the providential semi-sleep of the prey that had escaped the hunters.

Now, he 'almost' dreamed of Anchorites, but he was too disturbed and uncomfortable to allow his consciousness to retire and fully appreciate the repose. Saul half remembered, and half imagined, reading of those fanatics whose self-inflicted plights were perturbing and fascinating in equal measure. The thoughts of their boredoms were suitable to his predicament of turmoil. These hermits, choosing to withdraw from the world, would undergo a funeral rite whilst alive, and then be entombed in a cell built into the wall of a church. They would be able to receive sacrament and hear services through an internal window to the nave. And externally through another, receive sustenance and, presumably, pass their waste. They were officially dead to the world and lived and died in such a state as would drive one of weak faith mad. Perhaps they were the sacred insane that all religions venerate, and were thus not allowed to change their minds.

These Anchorites would embrace *The Cloude of Unknowyng*, with the fervor of their certainty, secure in the belief of the life beyond. Perhaps Saul felt as trapped in his decisions as those devotees and the thought of their safest of safe worlds, however impossible, was a comfort. In his stupor, maybe in a dream state, he imagined in his slumbering mind that he had been walled up, satisfied, dead to the rest of the world but able to observe little slices of goings-on through a small hole in a wall. He saw Leah dancing an introduction to her mural, the *ragout* in that crockpot in the cottage, Esther in her blue uniform, Timon's sagging body in the alleyway, his threadbare armchair with a copy of Hopkins saddled over the arm. These were worlds away. He imagined that he was forced to lead a life of constant meditation, in an attempt to make the life he had been condemned to live bearable. He had made himself a voluntary convict. For many prisoners, even those just escaped, the idea of being immured is anathema, for Saul the prospect was a purgation. His liberal mind dreamed of the indemnity of belief. At least he had an out, an escape, once the storm had passed.

Saul came to in a claustrophobic darkness, surprised at the silence, he was held like a written prayer stuffed into its niche in the Wailing Wall. A supplication for salvation, that had been answered. The storm had abated and died in the upper reaches of the mountain. 'Tohu, the cloud-splitter, will have rent the tempest in twain and stolen its power.' As he pushed the bundle of sticks aside, he pulled his starched limbs into the open, and he cautiously sniffed the clean and scoured air. There was a freshness that only a rumble can deliver, a blowing away of fust. To Saul's mind sprung a quote, "In dreams begin responsibilities," he knew not from whence it came. It gave him something to chew on.

As dawn was penetrating the eastern rim of his inky world, it started to reveal the destruction of last night. Branches were down, large pine brooms with needles for bristles, dead tortured branches that would not lie flat, the weak and old, culled from the trees. No trees had succumbed, probably because they undergo a regular shaking and only the adaptable would sustain. Only survivors would reproduce and give their flexibility to their offspring the better to withstand the next test in this precarious world.

The torrent, that had been Saul's trail, had subsided into a stream, although its path was everywhere present. There was still a corrosive flow, the water flinging itself over itself and over anything in its path in its eagerness to disappear down its own gullet, a rush to dispel its entropy. Saul tried to think sympathetically of any pursuers caught out in that force, but could not. If they had not been as lucky as he in finding shelter, they would have been swept down in an avalanche of debris. He stood at the edge of the rocky shelf and peered down the cliff into the grim dark depth, the dim light just starting to show the mayhem. He was like Moses staring back at Pharaoh as the Red Sea healed itself. Moses would not have felt merciful, either.

Saul gathered his bag that he had had no time to unpack, nor the space to do so. He had cuddled it like a child against his chest all night, as he remembered doing with an infant Esther, a comfort in the circumstance. There was a stillness, now, in the filtered atmosphere that allowed a restful humidity to fill the vacancy the storm had created. The hunkered world of life, the cowered children of Earth and Sky, were beginning to emerge. They would exert their rights and privileges again, until the next time that Mother Nature's tantrum was again unleashed on the passivity of Tohu. Saul, unbeknownst, was one of them now.

He readjusted his prison issue summer dress and tightened his boots, and as he did so he spotted a perfect stick, straight and unknotted, that would act as a staff. It felt like a gift, as an apology for the fight last night, and he accepted it. Then, turning his back on the past, he carefully picked his dim-sighted way upward, following the storm track. He would make his way to a flatter, drier, less exposed spot to spend some time foraging for some additions to his supplies and to scrape together a decent breakfast to reward his endurance and fuel its continuation. He had probably bought a lot of time. 'The devil take the hindmost!'

Succeeding beyond the first steep pitch of climb, vaulting himself from one slippery foothold of rock to one of mud, Saul came to a plateau. As he crested the last thin notch of the ravine he took his first full encompassing view of the land before him. There was a stillness that storms leave behind, but he saw ahead a glimpse of movement, some distance away among the trees. Whatever it was dived out of sight, it was obvious it did not want to be caught. Saul had the impression of a slash of brown, which he took for animal hide, but it was thin, and quick. He called out, instinctively, but saw no other trace and dismissed it as a deer, probably scared out of it's wits by last night. 'The poor thing!'

In the ballooning light he could see that the ground stretched a half league, or so, in thick forest to the next slope. The pine trees crowded this conifer idyll, emaciating their neighbors, forcing the growth upward in a race to height, a grab of sunlight. There was a lessening gloom below, where Saul, glad of the smooth passage over soft beds of needle, strolled as though through parkland. The density of tree canopy had kept the ground mostly dry, but he was more pleased with its flatness. He came across a clearing, a rock field where huge boulders were strewn around like jacks, and the wooden roots could get no purchase, and there he chanced upon a beneficence. A gift of God lay in Saul's path, illuminated by the new day, an offering from above.

The sodden land was grass covered and toward the edge of the wood, Saul found a dead rabbit, 'no, a hare!' The poor creature's limp body half floated out of a water-logged burrow. It's wet fur glistened jewel-like, a radiant brown he had never encountered before, and he squatted down and gave the thing a cautionary but loving stroke. It felt smooth and cold, as soft yet lifeless as a pillow. It must have drowned at home after an inundation trapped the hapless beast in a storm drainage of its own undoing. A victim of poor planning, where an egress had siphoned a sudden wall of fatal water.

Here it lay, an unrequested donation, giving of itself to another. Its unresponsive eye, still beady, like the black marbles of Saul's youth, unafraid and undemanding. There was no reproach there. Saul stood and picked it up by the ears as he had seen in pictures was the correct way to do so. He twirled it round to examine the opportunity, it dangled from his grasp, as heavy as his manacles had been, he guessed. It was just another object, fresh from life, a reward. Saul's reverence turned to curiosity and he carried the thing, at arm's length, into the forest to find a dry place to rest, to recuperate and to butcher. Of course, he had read about such archaic practices, 'and how hard could they be?' Desperate times call for desperate measures.

It turned out to be quite hard, mainly due to a dull paring knife. Saul found a suitable site and built a fire, all the while staring sporadically at the dead hare lying prone over a fallen trunk, front feet in the air, back legs akimbo, the floppy body formed over the cylinder of the log. With the smoke spreading rather than rising, the whole scene was shrouded in a white stifling cloud as Saul approached the sacrifice. He had read, maybe in Don Quixote, the concept and practice of turning dead flesh to edible meat, but it was all so alien.

He pushed the knife through the skin at the top of the long belly just underneath the protruding sternum, he then pulled down toward the tail but the blade would not slice and he had to saw. There was a minimum of blood, Saul had expected it would gush like Timon's, but the silent heart was not pumping. Saul then plunged both hands into the body cavity and cupped the viscera, pulling the soft gelatinous mess away, ripping its attachment to the animal it once served. He threw this sensual handful of guts and organs onto the fire which responded with a hiss and spit and a further cloud of pungent smoke. Saul smelt his dirtied hands, trying to tap into a long-lost instinct for his actions. There was a slight odor of compost and flatus, that was all. It felt like surgery rather than the sin of butchery.

Deciding that he would need another way to cut the meat, he carefully emptied his smaller bottle of the rice left inside, and hit the glass with a rock as gently as he could, to shatter it without scattering the shards. He found a suitable razor-sharp edge that when held in and through his cap, he could use to cut. Knowing that he had to remove the skin, and wishing to preserve it as intact as he could manage, he made surprisingly quick and light work of stripping the carcass up to the head which he detached in an act of nullifying, and flung onto the fire that had started to give off a tantalizing scent of cooking flesh. Saul felt saliva gathering in his mouth, which shocked and surprised a lifelong herbivore. He thought it was going to be repellant and that he was going to have to choke down the meat, but it was becoming appealing, in a disappointingly primal way.

Laying the pelt aside, he cut off the legs at the joints, the hips and shoulders, and threw a hind leg into the flames. It spluttered as the fat caught and he reached in with a stick to pull it to one side and then, covered in ash and pine needle he put the meat into his mouth and gingerly bit down.

It was the strongest flavor he had ever encountered, a taste more stunning that chili-peppers or curry powder or alcohol or . . . even cod liver oil had not been so shocking, and that was disgusting. The taste was interesting, a difference of kind, not of sort, than he had experienced before. As the first mouthful went down he could feel his system respond, at first with a paroxysm and then with, what he could only describe as, a loving embrace. That sounded so wrong, but there it was, he had no-one to judge him and no-one to take any cues from, it seemed to fit.

It suffused his body with a form of energy, what he thought may be the magic of the animal life-force giving its power to its consumer, as though the soul of the hare animated his own. It was an almost spiritual moment of rejuvenation, of infusion and embracing of external strength. Saul had to sit back, off his heels where he had been tending the fire, onto the log, next to the array of flesh displayed as meat. In this posture, he finished off the leg, still with trepidation, deciding that bones were not to be consumed. But the possibilities before him were wonderful, this resource was a Godsend, he thanked the dismembered corpse.

Guessing, rather than knowing, he fashioned a spit out of twigs and half roasted, half grilled the remaining cuts above the flames. He reasoned that searing the meat would help preserve the food, and that he would be able to eat the remains over the next few days. The fat was still dripping into the fire causing outbursts of flames, flares that sizzled invitingly, and Saul sat proudly, in a daze of bewilderment, surveying his deed.

Then he suddenly jumped up, and grabbing a leaf of paper from his store, he pulled the skewered meat and dripped the fat onto the page. He had flour but no fat and there was no reason to let that perfectly good rendering go to waste. He was going to preserve it by letting it soak into the paper and then roll up the sheet and let it cool. Excellent, just like that! The grease soaked into the paper, obscuring the page number fifty-one with a drip, and then the text which Saul could read was gradually splattered illegible.

"A landscape for hunters and anxieties, with rushes growing along rivers whose jagged banks jut like miniature muddy . . . ." The rest obliterated, 'ob-literature-ated,' Saul punned to himself, and the printing on the obverse was made visible. "When Christianity passed over souls like a storm that rages all night until morning, the havoc it had invisibly wreaked could be felt, but only after it had passed did the actual damage become clear." Strange, thought Saul, that that passage passed muster, and now all that beautiful knowledge is to be held in congealed fat and eaten by me at a later date. Fernando Pessoa would have enjoyed the irony and the appropriate justice of that.

Then, while the meat of the hare cooled and the page from the *Book of Disquiet* emulsified, Saul played with handicrafts. He laid out the fur he had stripped and stretched the pelt by hand as much as his strength would permit, and then stretched it more by winding it around a bough, he was trying to rid it of its last elasticity, the quality of its muscular life. Saul then cut five thin ribbons around the edge, to give as much length as possible to the strips, and with the paring knife tried to create a crude needle from a small femur. He sharpened one end and created a hole adequate for the strip of skin in the other. He dried these ribbons by the fire, unsure of when they would come in useful, but absolutely certain they will.

Saul made a hand hold for the larger shard of glass he had used to butcher, inserting the back edge into a small handle of bark, he ended up with a sharp, if unsteady, scraper. Pleased with his ingenuity, he looked around for another project. The neck of the bottle was still intact, and Saul shaved the top of his staff, although he had had it only since that morning, and jammed it on as hard as he could without cutting himself. The result was a pike with a crown that, from full on, looked like a lamprey's angry mouth. Then another idea struck him, another trick he had picked up from what was turning out to be his useful file of useless reading.

He fixed the jagged head in place with copious amounts of resin from the damaged pines, where they had lost limbs in the storm they gave of their sap. He tenderly scraped the sticky suppuration up with a twig and spread it into the lamprey's mouth and under its gills, it would have to dry before he could tell whether it would glue. He harvested the seeping resin that oozed from the cuts the trees suffered, he stored it in linen, bound with a strip of hare's skin. But in the interim, the staff became a spear and a defense against the dangers of this clean-swept, brand-new world he was bequeathed. It was the ceremonial scepter of his forest coronation, the meat was his mass, the storm his ceremonial robes.

Saul felt the need to give thanks, for the generosity of the earth. The hare, the fire, the resin, this knowledge that had appeared from the library of his mind, his shelter during the storm. He undertook a ritual that he had practiced many times in his life, always in shame, generally under cover. He would take himself in hand, and leave something of his own fertility in recompense for the abundance afforded him. It was a payment. This time was not a pleasuring, it was an extirpation, an un-damming of a blockage and an expiation. The compulsion he felt was not overpowering, it was a conscious choice to indulge himself. He could have ignored it but wanted to express something, even if it was just the persistence of his baser nature. There was no disgust involved, before or after, it was an act of pure physicality and animality. It was the act of a Satyr who had been played for a scapegoat.

And when it was completed, for the uncovered Saul allowed the culmination, he was surprised at the result. He observed it as if from afar. He was squatting on his heels, laboring at the fulfillment, and the gurgitation brought him down on all fours, his breath fast, his pulse racing and a beautiful well-being coursing through him. What had felt so vital inside him, so necessary to allow, became just a gouted spurt of cream, pooling in the soil and the disinterested pine needles. 'Why?' he asked.

The wrong seed in the wrong place, no fecund bed here for creation. He covered the evidence and threw a handful of dirt into the dying embers of the fire. He dressed, packed his new stores and, brandishing his walking stick, headed off in a tranquil daze leaving a dead fire in the noon hour. He headed upwards, over the plateau, the sun shone in a scoured sky, replete. The shame of Onan was replaced by the pride of Odin.

Saul whistled through the itch of his beard at the delight of being a man alive, so alive. And as he left the scene of his triumph and debasement he thought he saw again that fleeting movement, a shadow crossed. It was so isolated and definite, it was not a gust of wind, it must be a creature in the wild. It was ahead, in the direction he was traveling, and perhaps his reaction to the flit of a purely natural animal was because of his shame. A shame is hard to lose, so ingrained is it in the urban mind, the one that calls itself civilized. But, Saul would walk it out, you bet he would!

CHAPTER FOURTEEN

Saul marched onwards, with a ragged nobility that declared his sovereignty. He felt like the king of all he surveyed, and even if the thick forest limited his scope, the crowded trees were his subjects in wooden awe of their lord. If he were a latter-day Quixote, then he was content in his delusions. Even the land acquiesced to his prerogative. The flatter terrain allowed him to make up time the climbing of the previous day had stolen. So, he was in a sanguine mood, semi-euphoric to be the master of his own destiny. The path ahead seemed clear, at least as far as he could see.

The day was surpassing itself. It had started out promising a dividend, and then delivered a windfall. Truly an unexpected bonus. Saul wended his way between the bulky trunks of ancient pines that outreached each other, like schoolmates clamoring for a teacher's attention. The red, scabby bark masses on ground level would have taken three men to circumference, and the branches blotting out the sunlight far above shaded him from the heat of the day. The work party would have struggled to fell these monsters. In this forest twilight, Saul slalomed through mile after mile, keeping the falling sun to his right, where he could. He felt as though he were traipsing through some giant organic chamber, the trees as pillars, the roof a pine canopy, that seemed to stretch infinitely onwards. Under the boots which were adapting to his feet, if not *vice-versa*, was a carpet of needles, with a very fitting pine-cone pattern motif. There was a pleasing crunch from the desiccated jetsam lying around, which had fallen like slow-motion rain from the trees onto the brown sterile ground. The bone-dry air seemed to vacillate from hot to cold, according to the shade, and Saul even found that variation pleasant. The storm seemed to have overshot this paradise.

A pine scent was all pervasive, the sheltered place smelled penetratingly fresh. Over the course of the afternoon, a gentle breeze developed high up and brushed the fascicles, the fistfuls of needles, causing the blown branches to sway in waves. Saul felt as unperturbed as a crab on the ocean floor that, when the surface roils, stays safe beneath all the tumult. In fact, the wind sounded like an ocean, piped by currents, the swish in the canopy like waves above were his accompaniment. Down below he glided through the respectful, clean silence, watching the end of his staff dimple the ground where it fell.

Along his way, Saul noticed little seed pods that had been loosened and scattered by the storm. He saw at a distance the busy, chattering squirrels collecting their due. They were gathering the nuts as quickly as they could, stuffing their pliable cheeks. Saul thought he should join in, if the squirrels eat them then they should be *kosher*. He spent ten laborious minutes on his hands and knees scouring the floor for the casings, picking and pocketing handfuls. He tasted the first one he picked up and recognized the powdery taste of the pine nut, reminding him of his recruitment into his mother's pesto production, the mashing and grinding by mortar and pestle. It reminded him of the smell of the basil and garlic, the delicious slime of the olive oil, his mother's hair falling and his being told to push it back up. When all his pockets were full he continued, his pack over his shoulder his crowned staff tucked under his arm, shucking the nuts and gnawing the tiny kernels. He would shell the remainder when he camped. He left a little of his childhood in that spot, but he had plenty left over.

After five hours of pleasant trek, Saul came across the course of one of the numerous streams. There the cold mountain snow-melt ran down to a coalescence where the collected waters danced over a pile of conglomerate in their eagerness to leave. They dived in a fissiparous delight, burbling and gurgling, unwilling to wait. It was a Sylvan scene, as still as a painting, aside from the flow of the creek, as quiet as a graveyard, aside from the water's splash. Saul could not walk on and bypass this site. He made camp, in anticipation of delicious rest, on a flat area under the protection of the forest giants.

Later, after an hour of as deep a nap as it is possible to enjoy by oneself in a strange environment, Saul shivered and stretched himself into preparation. A feather had fallen and landed on his chest, as if placed there, he rolled its lightness between his fingers. This was now his new life, for as long as it would last, scavenging an existence in the woods, traipsing during the day, evading capture. Being blessed by nature.

Saul could expect to be always on the hoof, without a terminus, with no end-point. But, there was a goal, or, at least he felt that, deep down, the meaning of his life was being revealed to him, and that revelation would direct him. He had left his old self behind, he had bludgeoned that Saul, had rejected his truths and now was open to a new reality. His privations were a test of his suitability, and his travails were a foundation of the 'New Man.' For he felt he had crossed a Rubicon, and his future was in the towering peaks of Tohu that lay ahead, confronting and daring him, as glimpsed through the thicket of his present. He could see the runnels of snow clinging valiantly to the northern facing slopes and packed into cracks and clefts in the walls, the germs of glaciers forming a dirty white lace network against the rock context.

There was a clearing over the creek allowing Saul access to this view, and sprayed in there, among the grasses, was a constellation of tiny yellow specks; stars that Saul recognized. He emptied his pack, unceremoniously, and forded over to collect a pound, at least, of dandelion greens, maybe two pounds. On his knees again, scrambling for food, plucking and tearing the offering of Nature, delighting that this new God did not demand sacrifice, but gave gifts, as a loving God should. Dandelion, he thought, from the French *dent-de-lion*.

"I will eat the jagged leaf of the tooth of the lion, how noble."

He took the harvest back to his camp site and deposited the armful of greenery and, wanting to ride his luck, set out for further exploration. A fortuitous thirty minutes found him returning exultant, carrying sage leaves and some wild mint, and chancing upon, as he crossed the creek to return, packages of watercress thriving in the swift flow. His *al fresco* kitchen would test his culinary talents, but it was rewarding to concentrate his efforts on his own well-being. To work on being well.

Saul first made a tea of sage and mint, a fragrant combination, not unpleasant when sweetened with a generous amount of sugar. It made him feel a degree of civilization to be sipping from a blackened tin can, and he complemented his beverage with the remains of a can of peaches. He scarfed the syrupy fruit as if it was Christmas. Left, then with an empty can, Saul cut through the bottom of the cylinder with his paring knife, leaving the base attached as a handle, and he rolled out the tube, pressing up the edges, to form a small frying pan. He greased the pan with a small tear of infused paper, and mixing some flour, water and the little nubbin of rabbit fat, he formed a patty, which he proceeded to cook over the spluttering fire. It was hard to keep the temperature constant and harder to persuade the patty to not stick to the tin, but as beggars cannot be choosers, so those who eat 'forest bread,' as Saul christened the delicacy, cannot expect a perfect bake.

The result was a thin bun of chewy, half-cooked dough that tasted to its creator like a product of the finest Royal Patisserie. He nibbled the delicacy staring at his regal stave and wondering if he was becoming unhinged? Was he turning into a delusional hermit who imagines himself a king? He decided that it did not matter, in fact, he decreed that it was of no concern. It was good to be the king!

Saul boiled some dandelion leaves in the other can, the one that he had used as a teapot and teacup, until they were a warm mulch and spread them on the bread with some pine nuts, rabbit meat and watercress and with much salt, he managed to fashion a proper meal. He had then to dispel the lingering aftertaste with a sip of plum brandy. A meal fit for the ruler of this idyllic glade. Even the washing up, a task he normally avoided, he undertook with relish, because it was so mundane, so reassuringly mundane. *Noblesse oblige.*

In front of his fire, with rocks banked at the rear to retain the heat, Saul sat with his back against one of the pines, his knees up supporting his forearms. His head sagged and with his full stomach and its demand for the body's blood, he felt himself drifting off despite the nap of a few hours ago. Dusk was filtering into the forest, and where the sky could be seen between the spread of branch, the color was leeching out and the powder blue in the West was turning cerulean and then descending to black.

There was a tremolo hoot of owl, fading to vibrato, that reminded Saul of wine-kissed days in Upper Downland, a longing settled in the back of his mind. Then a cawing of some type of crow that was nesting; if it is a singleton then it is a crow and not a rook, he noted. The smoke from the fire, with its food smell, was held in place like a drape under the skirts of the trees, Saul gave no thought as to how, or whether, the scent may attract scavengers, he was learning as he went along. So, he sat content, a tramp in his prison clothing, contemplating his vagabond kingdom.

He assayed a little light repair work on some seams that were coming apart, using the short ribbons of rabbit skin as a thick thread, and using some of the collected resin, mixed with ash from the fire as a glue to plug some other gaps. The light from the fire was too unsteady, flickering as it was, to perform any delicate operations, but he was a clumsy darner in the best of circumstances, and so he sewed as if repairing a sail. A chill began to settle over the site in the gloaming in the primeval forest. A bat flitted like a nagging doubt you can't quite identify, and far, far off a canine yowl grabbed Saul's attention. A shiver of primal apprehension trembled him. It was the first time since his escape that he had felt threatened by anything living, even though the storm was as animated as anything he had seen out there. Something buried deep within his instinctive self, below language and emotion, was triggered by the awareness of a predator who might view him unfavorably, a challenge or a meal. He settled down for the night, the fire his only friend, the cloaking darkness a disguise for those nefarious, nocturnal prowlers who may, or may not, wish him ill. Let's assume they do.

By the time Saul woke, to the dawn twitter chorus as a celestial alarm, the ashes were tired in their pit and the charcoal had all become powder. Stirring himself, he brought the flame back to life and started the preparation of oatmeal and tea that constituted his breakfast. The new food dispelled the old and he was glad of the traffic in his gut, he was not used to stretches of privation and was glad to ease his body into it, gently.

Then, blowing onto his sage and mint and pine needle tea to cool the boil to a palatable level, his sleeve a glove against the tin, his costive mind, perhaps in envy of his digestion, began to tick over more esoteric matters than life or death. An idea popped into Saul's head, and looking it up and down, appraising it, he found himself attracted to it. He flirted with the idea, and, as one does with something attractive, he courted it. He entertained it, would have bought it dinner if possible. He gave it flowers, and eventually was seduced by it. Then he proposed, or it proposed, at least marriage was mooted. Not being a possessive man, but also, not being able to share it with others, he found himself wed to it. The idea was his, now, to have and to hold. 'Til death do us part?'

When you do not have the framework that the company of other people gives, when you lack, that is, the collective buttressing of explanations, then you have to make it up as you go along. If there is no-one to go along with you, then you go along with yourself. The solitary figure does not have the ability to spin a thread of yarn into a tapestry. That takes two, or a loom, at least. But the individual can follow a thread, from one end to the other, quite easily.

'This line of thought is not very precise,' Saul admitted, 'but it has enough substance to be taken seriously. Maybe I did leap into this with both eyes closed, but I have made my bed and so must lie in it.'

So, if one cannot build a reality alone, because of a dearth of feedback and fact-checking and affirmation, then one must fall back on one's own resources. If there are no reinforcements, then one has to go it alone. One, whoever that 'one' may be, must resort to words, to one's own literate world.

'And here,' thought Saul, 'are a couple more apostrophes to go around that last one. While I retreat to the grandiosity of solitude. For 'one' is never alone with words, they lend a separate voice in one's head. Hence, words as the vessels of ideas, are as important as the building blocks of philosophy. The discrete units that can be added, subtracted, stacked and discarded, and thus built up into a system. Just as this 'one' has chosen to resign from being.'

So, 'here is Saul,' reasoned Saul using the third person, 'he is alone and bemused,' and having had his old-world idea snatched from him, he has to create a grand idea in order to carry on. Therefore, he, 'meaning me,' can become a 'New Man,' absolved of the sins of the past and free to 'think and act as he,' as the measure of all things, 'sees fit.' And how can these words, these elements, be pieced together into molecules, how can little inert atoms become the fundaments of life? Simply, or so it seemed to Saul who had no-one but the trees to bounce the idea off, by constructing phrases, sentences, paragraphs into a stream of ideas that would confluence into a broad river and so travel naturally, to the wide, wise sea, an ocean of thought in which every question could be drowned. 'There,' Saul thought, 'there it is, to write, unabashed, untethered, if not with style at least with abandon, and in there to make good.' All he knew, all he had learned, would be weighed in the balance and some things unlearned, if deemed unsupportable, some retained, if meeting the criteria that he would elucidate. 'Well, let's start now.' Being reasonableness, clarity and applicability.

Saul had made that leap that terrified him, that had intimidated him for all his City life. From wordsmith, a filler of crosswords, an editor of information, a compiler of reports, a composer of briefs, to that most isolated of stereotypes, the writer! Like many things, it took no qualification beyond the definition, the identification. Saul had named himself, and outed himself as an author. It was a heavy burden and he hoped he was not biting off more than he could chew, and that in turn reminded him . . . .

Gadd, the illiterate bumpkin, had given him a tip to survive out here, in the deep, dark woods, and he would try it out and then leave for Tohu. And so, he thanklessly cut a strip of thick bark from the tree that had sheltered him, and beneath the skin he gouged out the white inner bark that Gadd, in his wisdom, had said was edible, and even nutritious.

"I's gud fur ya, Sol, tas'es li'e crap, but I's gud."

Saul seemed to remember it being called the "cambium layer," and, indeed, Gadd was right, it was a stringy texture and like *nougat* without the sugary sweetness, it had a faint taste of nuts and pine, 'of course it would taste of pine, how could it not.' So, he gathered the pith and, chewing with gusto, carrying his mean belongings, stepped out, a page of paper in his left hand. He could read out loud when he did not have to look after his step, and could study when he had the uninterrupted leisure. Pessoa again, his balm, his therapy, he would use Pessoa as a conversational tool with himself, for Pessoa was always correct.

"The higher a man rises, the more things he must do without. There's no room on the pinnacle except for the man himself. The more perfect he is, the more complete; and the more complete, the less other."

And, so, Saul advanced, albeit slowly through the difficult terrain, but, meaningfully in his defiance. 'Onwards and upwards.' Over the succeeding days, he became further accustomed to the world of the forest as he adapted to his predicament. The night-time howls of the wolves did not panic him as much, he had developed a practicality when assessing threats.

He thought he saw that deer, or elk, 'It was definitely a large animal,' elusive and quick. He heard the occasional twig broken, but put it down to the elements. It seemed to be ahead of him, but never within reach, as though it were leading him. Then, maybe, behind him? Circling? Saul realized that he may not be the top of this food-chain, that humility may be a survival technique. Then he knew he was not in the position of superiority that his species usually claimed as a birthright.

And it was a different world to any he had known, in all senses. He was getting used to the chiaroscuro the trees cast, the play of light and shade, that he had not seen in the City. There he had been faced with rectangular shapes, edges and perpendiculars, the constant grey of cement, pewter of sky, the ash of asphalt. In the City he knew the dangers, where and when to face them, where and when to hide, it was the environment he was born into. The forest was no more perilous, it was just that the threats were hidden. Or, he had not learned them yet. And he did not know where to conceal himself, where to shelter. He felt there was no hiding and that may be why it was liberating. At least it was less treacherous being outside the society of men. At least now he had the primary colors of nature, at first blinding to his tarnished vision. Now he had the world unblemished, the graceful organic curve of life. It was beautiful compared to the manufactured City, but it was the great unknown.

It was all so new. The pressures of freedom, the need for improvisation, the lack of company; all these novel, distressing demands. And, the reliance on self when the self is cracking. He had left the camp, the shackles and humiliations, and the slumped figure of the guard, not having an idea of his end-point. Saul was fleeing, and reaching the starting line was the goal. He had made that, and needed to reiterate that he was, now, in a process, of strengthening, of growth, the building up of a new man. He was not in a test of his mettle, this was no rehearsal, and he had no idea of the travails he would have to endure. He had somewhat planned his provisions and his route, 'if 'up' is a course any more than 'out of here," but could not foresee the strangeness of absconding. The choice of not belonging.

In his first days, Saul had talked to himself for comfort, weathering the storm with prayers, reassuring his irrational fears and reasoning with himself about the preparation of the hare. After less than a week by himself, his mind had calmed, had settled, once it had realized that hysteria was not a strategy. Now, he did not feel the need for a separate voice inside his head, bargaining and coaching him onwards. He had become a part of the environment, not an interloper or trespasser, and his worries settled into a focus on his external condition, not his internal state. He realized the truth of his place, accepted the dangers, and he felt complete. He was not a consciousness being carried around on a litter, he was not just along for the ride, but he was a whole thing. The voices were not missed when they were silenced, for he then had no use for guarantee.

Saul was used to everyday distances, furlongs and leagues, but there was a different scale of large out in the wilderness which was disorienting. The trees were Goliaths, Tohu unfathomably huge, but dwarfing all were the skies which did not seem to come to an end.

At night, looking up into the vast overturned cauldron of the heavens, spotted with moons and planets, the blur of the milky way and beyond that, the other galaxies, Saul felt miniscule. He had never seen so far before and the enormity was profound and intimidating. Saul felt, even lying on his back with the whole world supporting his weight, he could fall into the heavens. He was convinced that he was not looking up but staring down into depths, the great endless deep. It was a *vertigo*, and gravity was just a trick to make you stay in place. At night, each star seemed further away than the one you looked away from in order to pick it out. In sunlight, the blue was infinite, the clouds seemed neighborly.

This must be what God would feel, except He would not be overwhelmed by the size of the universe. Saul was still learning to embrace the confidence of accepting that which lay outside him, God would never have to face that doubt. Saul found the liberty around him, and therefore within him, to be unsettling. "By thinking so much I became echo and abyss." That was Pessoa, written on one of Saul's scraps of Disquiet, he read it a lot. Even when he had the nine simple words memorized, he still read it out loud.

Like a whisper magnified through a megaphone, his imagination expanded, and as it did, it allowed the prospect that by watching the stars and not feeling belittled, he was letting himself be completed. Beyond his boundaries, where the not-him lay, there was as good, as worthy a 'stuff' as that within. He learned not to differentiate himself, and that was when the voices left him. He trusted that the part of himself he sent out northwards as a feeler would come full circle back to find his south. Then he would encircle his existence, he could contain it, or, alternatively, accept the unbounded nature of his-self. That he could conceive infinity, even as an algorithm, meant that he was an end in himself not a means to another's end. That he could accept being part of it was a God-send.

Those nights were cold. Saul would build a nightly coffin, corpse-sized lean-tos covered as thickly as practical with pine boughs. He would nestle on the ground, but, having no bedding, his hungry body could not escape the penetrating cold. He rationed his fires and counted each burned match from his total as he soaked in the warmth from their use. It became a religious ritual to preserve his dwindling stock and to nurse the fires, kindling, twigs and logs, into lasting as long as possible. Fuel was not a scarcity, but sleep was, even a cold sleep.

Saul would boil his tea, fry his unleavened patties and cook soups of the foraged greens and tubers, supplementing this diet with tentative nibbles of cold meat. He could not separate the image of the hare from the grey and slimy meat his teeth tore into, the taste he knew his stomach liked. He had seen other hares in the open spaces the mountain kept, between the darkness of the forests. They were quick-silver, bounding muscled bullets in flight, stumble-bums when nibbling the thin grasses. They had a beauty in life that he found hard to reconcile with the corpse, and then the meat, that stringy protein gift, how could the one be the other? In contemplation, he would deplete his body on long uninterrupted walks, covering leagues at a measured pace, leaning into his staff, dragging his feet, hauling his carcass. It suited his constitution to cover the ground in relays, with longer and longer rests between bouts. Or, perhaps, his body was adapting to his will, evolving as they both were.

The atmosphere was tinder dry, the wind pulled any humidity from the air, swallowed it and blew it away. The lower streams had not made it this far up the mountain, but Saul managed to find enough to drink in storm puddles that acted as dew ponds. He saw his reflection as he bent over them to drink and he did not recognize the face staring up out of the water. It was not the beard, nor the scruffiness, it was the wisdom in the lines on the cheek, the look in the eyes. He liked the transformation.

The quiet in the higher forests, which he found disconcerting at first, when it felt like a prelude to an ambush, became a peacefulness in its docility. As the character of the terrain changed, the trees seemed sparser and smaller, but 'wiser' and more resilient. There were few insects, up here, the sporadic chirrup of a lonely cricket, the bustle of a kingdom of ants, a confused fly. Sometime at night the choral howl of a band of coyotes chilled him, or he heard the haphazard bellow of elk, rutting at a distance, only leaving scat and hoof prints to reveal their ghostly presence. The intentional absence of bigger predators, those playing a zero-sum game, made him wary. He felt an accompanying presence of some beast, observing him, not 'out there,' but by his side. The fear subsided and became less oppressive and he began to feel less alone.

He started to mimic the subtle movements of the animals who left little trace of their presence, and no evidence of their goings. Saul still had not dismissed the idea that there were hunters out to chase him down, and tried to be as unobtrusive as his forward progress would permit. His fires would not be lit until the smoke could not be seen at dusk, and the light would be carefully shielded. He would cover his camps, bury his waste and try to stay on rocks and dry ground to minimize his tracks. Saul knew, though, that all these paths he was taking were leading to a central crux, all his drainage hopping might be effort wasted if his pursuers did not give up. The increasingly massive bulk of Tohu, revealing more of itself with each pitch he climbed, every step closer, was the prize, and the mountain pass that straddled the peaks was the pinch point. And he would rather die out there, in nature, than live back in prison, or even as a free man. He felt that 'a day out here was worth a year back there,' it was riches beyond the dreams of greedy ambition.

Thus, Saul suffered his privations willingly, savoring his time as a gift. He remembered that punishment was supposed to be the cancellation of evil, and so his struggle, his fears and wants, became his atonement. His sufferings were leading to his redemption, just as the gradient of the slopes and the nod of the haphazard trees were directing him to an escape. The stoic trees stood blindly urging him uphill, leaning into the hillsides and pointing him to the summit.

The forest thinned out and the bark of the older trees displayed a black veining against the usual ruddy color of the trunks. This camouflage gave the outward impression of red marble, a pine porphyry. Inspecting closer. Saul saw that a devastating fire must have swept through, decades before, decimating the trees. There were blackened stumps, and burnt lower branches on the older survivors. The staining on the older trees was a singeing. There was a reforestation of young, fit trees, achingly green, miniatures of their ancient cousins in whose shade they unfurled. Saul saw a little way ahead, in the middle of a small, steep meadow, a black skeleton of a tall denuded pine. Its charred corpse still standing aloof, a memorial to that conflagration, and a testament to the destruction it could not avoid.

Seeing this polished frame, outreaching the adolescent forest surrounding it, Saul spied a younger tree that the storm of a few nights before must have toppled against the skeleton. Its root-ball was chthonic soil and exposed fiber, not yet dead, yawning above the pit it used to occupy. Maybe pines at the edge of a clearing are more prone to suffer the brunt of the elements, like the stragglers in a herd are picked off. The felled tree was hanging up on the dead rigor-mortised lower limbs of its ancestor which held it up from the ground as if it had swooned into the arms of its neighbor. It made a suitable ramp for Saul to reach the climbable ribs of the skeleton tree, that looked like a reverse ladder with the rungs outside a central tapering axle, or like a fish skeleton planted in the ground. Saul felt singularly blessed at this sight, he had no idea why, and was filled with the thrill of a boy's chance to play, to ascend above the myopia of ground level.

Propping his staff against the base of the incline and unburdening himself of his pack, like a *bedouin* at an oasis ready to dive in the water, he forgot any resentment of giddiness. He knew automatically that the dried weather-beaten wood would easily support his weight. Saul even rubbed some resin from his lamprey's gills on his hands, for grip. He knew they would sweat, for had no head for heights and could feel the nervousness already growing in the pit of his empty stomach. 'It was a welcome change,' he thought. So, he picked his way to the skeleton and stood and pushed and pinioned and pulleyed and levered his way almost to the brittle top where the sway arrested him. He held the dead branches at their thickest and, twisting out into the air, he turned his body away from the trunk, so he was pinioned, connected by his four extremities. With his chest opened to the view, he was like a topgallant sail catching an upper breeze, or a high-diver an instant before the launch. He could see out over the vast expanse of land he had covered in the last few days, the soft treetops, the spines of the promontories that sat like fins between the canyons, the plains below. He felt six wings of bliss!

Perched in his aerie, his feet together now, and his arms stretched out, he felt like a second-rate crucified messiah. He could see from where he had escaped, he could see the wrongs of the world. He could see the iniquities that he could not correct, and the corruption that he could bring to attention. The breeze rustled his hair and patted the shell of his beard, for he had scratched resin into his itchy jaw. His journey to this point was laid out before him, he could not see every step he had taken, but could appreciate the sweep of the travels. The landscape seemed to wave to him, it was probably the wind in the grasses and the canopies of the forests, but it was as if the land was wishing him well, was wishing him Godspeed. And he realized, unlike a Stylite, fasting and meditating on his pillar, that he had accepted Nature in all her multeity, her forgiveness and acceptance. And as he had done so, he had rejected the God of Virility, with his insistence on strength and subjection, just as he had rejected Society's God having seen the world from

His perspective. He was a ship's figurehead as the prow parted the heaving sea, the proud blade of a sword that was wielded to vanquish the infidel.

Saul felt an ichor ran through him, invigorating his flesh, a strength born of the mountains coursed from his feet and hands. Where he touched the hardened, desiccated wood there was a flow of a life-force, as though a vitality were being conducted via him to the universe. He relished the sense of numinous rebirth, the butterfly of his new being shedding the chrysalis of his old life and taking wing. Saul's mind ran as clear as one of the streams pouring from Tohu, like tears down an orphan's cheek. For Saul knew that if Satan had tempted him, as he tried to do with Christ in the desert, then he would have rejected the emoluments. No bread from stones, 'he had planned and foraged his food out here.' No demonstration of power, 'he was as comfortable as a welcome refugee and had no need for hubris.' And there he stood looking over the extent of creation, knowing he did not want to own it, or have power over it, but wanted to be a constituent, a part of the beauty of that world. This was his destiny and his achievement as a man. Now, he needed to continue his journey, not running from anything but to see where the road ended. Saul lowered himself to the ground in a baptized state.

CHAPTER FIFTEEN

Even if he had looked up, Gadd's eyesight was not clear enough to allow him to see the eccentric figure clinging to the branches of the enormous tree up ahead, a league away. The dead one, with its deracinated twin, that stood out against the living forest and that had become a sort of Jacob's ladder to Saul. And, in turn, Gadd could not be seen, even from Saul's elevated viewpoint, as he slinked along, muttering imprecations on the very ground he covered. They were as oblivious of each other as they were motivated by the possible presence of the other.

The bedraggled Gadd knew he was on the right track, because he had guessed that his quarry was headed to civilization. His hunches were 'always correct,' and even when they were wrong it was always someone else's fault, it was well nigh impossible not to pin the failure somewhere else. Saul had as good as told him, anyway, letting slip his intentions when mining for information, back in the camp, in the warm bunkhouse. It made sense to Gadd, the City was the font of all wealth and power, a natural destination for anyone looking to get lost.

And Gadd was good at this tracking business, he had spent many years exacting revenges and running down fugitives in return for favors. Generally, it had involved him in finding bad criminals for good criminals and performing criminal acts upon them. Back then, before the slammer, that had been more like detective work, and this felt more like trapping an animal, but, in most ways, it was all the same to the rebarbative Gadd. On the outside of goal, his clients were dealers and loan sharks, slum landlords and the vengeful. His present mission just had him starting on the right side of the law, but he had no qualms about overstepping those bounds. This time his bosses were legitimate, as far as he knew. For what that was worth.

Gadd carried a rifle, the same one Saul had declined to take from the guard, and a large pack of supplies. He labored under his backpack, his mean but lithe frame tilted by the weight, and he also labored under a misapprehension, that the warden would keep his promise. For Gadd thought he had a contract, that if he could stop the escapee then he would earn his remission, he would be free and clear. One of the main drawbacks to his metaphysics was the trust he placed in his betters, and the contempt with which he held those loathsome hordes below him. He accepted none as his equal, but what was important was that there were more under him, than over. The warden was one of the minority, and his power over Gadd put him slightly above Saul, who only spoke well, but had no benefits to lavish. It was a strict hierarchy in that sly mind, a shuffling precedent that took attention to maintain. And plenty of resentment, it was fueled by rancor. Gadd thought he had a commission, but he did not, and he did not know enough to be indignant.

Both men were pursuing liberty and mercy, both were searching for a way out, but on markedly different levels. Gadd's advantage was that he operated in a simple material sphere, and Saul's disadvantage was that he had no idea his erstwhile companion was hunting him. Ironically, the gap between them was never closer than now, even when they slept three feet apart. Now they were interlinked.

Gadd was a poor specimen, both physically and morally, and what particularly condemned him to the ash-heap of humanity was his short-term memory. Along with a self-serving urge and an automatic respect for wealth, he possessed an uncanny inability to learn from even recent mistakes. This, of course, ensured their repetition. He could not help himself, and would never accept the aid of well-wishers. So, just as soon as the pain from the last beating had been consigned to history, with the welts most times still evident, the next was being prepared. Like a man who cannot feel hunger and forgets to eat, however much he enjoys food, so, Gadd could not stop fomenting the next insult. It was not even a matter of indiscipline, it was a woeful helplessness. If he were not so detestable, he would be deserving of pity.

Gadd found it hard to break the cycles that repressed him, the short ones and the long ones. The poverty of his youth begat his lack of schooling, and thus his lack of discipline, these in turn led to a laziness and a wish for quick gratification that led, in turn, to a life of petty crime. The pettiness of his criminality led to a rejection of societal norms, children out of wedlock, indebtedness to violent money lenders that entailed, in turn, to more serious transgressions of the law. The Templars knew of him, the ones who had lent him those last Shekels to keep the wolf from the door knew where to find him, his children knew him not at all. And, so, the wheels turned, as the days and the seasons, and poor Gadd was always heading back to where he started, an unwitting victim of a noose around his neck. The other end of that rope was tied to a post, so as he moved he was pulled in a circle, it did not let him follow the straight and narrow. It was a repetitive rut.

Gadd sulked covertly through the commonplace woods tracking and trailing Saul, a hope of release and vindication in his unexercised mind. He was a small man, sinewy, with a canine awareness, abrupt in his movements. And that jerkiness gave an impression of a beast straining at a leash, but maybe it was only that noose. The whites of his eyes were jaundiced, the pale blue irises swimming in the bile. The pupils did not seem to receive outside light so much as to project malice, as though the darkness within Gadd was being excised, exported, as a weapon, a lance made to puncture those on whom their gaze fell. And, as his eyes darted and then alighted, so his head swiveled to catch up, his eyes never led. This air of wariness gave him the jittery air of a lizard. And, in a similar fashion, he seemed to taste the air. The large, diaphanous ears that hugged his triangular shaped face were alert to any noise, or disruption of normality, just as in prison he was alert to any slight or disrespect.

His features were pinched, his nose thin, the sallow skin sunk in over the concavity of his large temples, his hairline a smudge where his dishwater blond hair sat greasily on his insipid scalp, not quite hiding a palm-sized puce birthmark that leaked onto his forehead. His body was frighteningly strong, as a whippet, it subsisted on anger and bile, but was never put to good use, it was only in the service of his own appetites. He had no plan as to what he would do if he caught Saul, forethought was not a Gadd quality, but he knew that if he did not catch him then he would not return to report his failure to the warden. He was not going back without reporting success.

"Bleedin' 'ell fire! You wooden fink a pansy could move so bluddy fast. I'll teach 'im a lesson when I catches up. Ee's gunna be surprised to see me. When I pops out ov the woods, all "ello Sol, wot av you bin up to? 'aving a nice stroll in the trees? Luverly day for it, innit? Mind if I join you? Shall we 'ave sum tea, tha'ud be nice, eh?' I 'ope he's found sum grub on the way, I'm sick an' tired ov this crap they gave me to keep me goin'. Biscuits an' cheese, you get sick ov that pre'ee fast. I can tell you."

Gadd had set off on Saul's trail, only after the storm, and it was a testimony to his dogged perseverance, his terrier determination, that he was within hailing distance of his prey after four days. The battered guard had been found, still alive, although concussed enough that when he did wake, he did not remember that he was a smoker. And, after a panicked search of the environs of the work site, the group of jovial prisoners and stern guards, rushed back to the main camp. They had to hear the vented spleen of the warden, whose blood-pressure reached dangerous levels as a result of the cowardice and incompetence of his people. The prisoners had the rest of the day off, lounging and lazing about, annoying the kitchen staff, telling Gadd about the state of the guard and that Saul had high-tailed-it. The warden was incensed that his leadership would be compromised, and that he could be personally humiliated in the process. He denounced the worth of his men and, only then, swore vengeance. Saul meant nothing to the warden, but his value as an example to those who sought to undermine his authority suddenly shot up.

Saul was suddenly a valuable commodity and Gadd's devious intelligence saw an opportunity to profit. He wormed his way into the warden's office and offered the little information he had, Saul's bunk talk of Tohu, in return for some good graces and a bit of time off. The warden was disgusted by Gadd's obsequious proposal, in the way he was revolted by Gadd's persona, and, more out of desperation than careful planning, made his own counter offer.

"Prisoner Gadd. You are from around these parts, are you not?"

Gadd did not know how to answer a question posed in that form and stammered.

"Yezz, I am from 'rahnd 'ere. Yez, Zir. I am."

"Listen to me. I cannot afford to have this lapse be broadcast to the authorities, it is embarrassing, and might be the final straw that sees me relieved of duty. So, I have to keep this *schtum*. Am I clear?" Realizing he was not, he continued, "What I mean is that not a word is to be spoken. Complete hush-hush. Do you fancy a secret mission? I can't trust my men to go after Citizen Saul, they are too stupid and lazy. But, you know the lay of the land, you know the climate, would you consider going after him, by yourself? No questions asked, no duties, no orders but to find Saul and stop him. And when I say stop him . . . ."

"Say no more, Guv. I unnerstan, but whas innit for me? Thas a risky ask, dangerous out there, alone. Should be wurf a pre'ee wage, I reggon."

"Dammit, Man! If you get rid of this problem for me," the warden stood up behind his desk and paced up and down the length of the small office. He could smell the kitchens on Gadd's dirty white overalls, onions and grease, over the usual smell of boot polish. "I promise you your freedom. I will give you an exoneration, it is within my powers, while I still have them, a full pardon signed by me. You'll be as free as a bird, no parole, no Templars harassing you, you can even get Welfare. And if you don't, if you refuse me, then you can look at a good long time beyond your sentence. I mean if you chose not to be co-operative. I know that you were secretly supplying Saul with foodstuffs from the kitchen. I think you may be in this deeper than you are letting on. You probably came to see me to try to hide your guilt. Well, I'm not buying it! I think this stinks, and the smell is all over you. Now, I'm not threatening, you here, just pointing out consequences."

Gadd could see the writing on the wall, he was compromised. He thought to maximize his return by getting the best deal he could negotiate. That bloody Saul had landed him in it. He knew he shouldn't have been so nice to him. Those posh ones always screw you. His anger was finding the absent Saul a proper target.

"An' munny. I wan' a," he plucked a large number from out of thin air, "fowsan Shekels when I come back wif his head . . . ."

"No! Discretion, discretion! This is a clandestine agreement, don't come back with anything. No, strike that! Bring me that idiot guard's boot, just the one, that will be proof enough. Bring that back as evidence and I'll grant you your freedom and the money. But no telling anyone, do I make myself clear? No one! You will be gone for, what? A week? I'll cover up on this end, I just need you to tell me that he won't turn up somewhere, sometime and come back to haunt me. He needs to be eradicated. Do you understand?"

"I do. I do unnerstan tha'. Okay, I'll do it. Five undred up front." No mention of 'sir,' or even 'zir!'

"No! I'll have it here for when you get back and tell me that the job is done. Now, you probably don't hear this much, but I'm trusting you. If you come back successful then we are both in the clear, and you are a lot better off. If you don't come back, then the guards will visit your family to find out where you are. You know Shadrach from the Brig? The arsonist? I will send him on a visit to your home, see if he can find you. Your family will pay if you abscond. I know your village, close to here isn't it? You have a wife and child? It would be a shame if their house went up in flames! Wouldn't it? And, they could do with the money, I suppose."

Gadd's eyes flashed with that red mist that, descending like a fog over his reason, had lead him blinded to many unfortunate situations. This fury at being threatened was his automatic defense. His feelings for his family were obligatory at best, but not inconsiderate for that. Those of his ilk were a conventional crowd, the warden knew, their loyalties not unsound for being misplaced.

Gadd's sense of injustice was finely honed, attuned to any grievance, and he felt abandoned by Saul who had used him and then absconded. Now, he needed revenge, out of duty, as much as anything, for to not exact any punishment would be a tacit admittance of weakness. And he had been taught that the greatest insult he could suffer was to have his strength questioned. He wanted Saul to pay for the warden being able to compromise him and his family.

Gadd could cheat on his wife, neglect his children but woe betide anyone else who defamed them. They had better look out! He would find Saul and teach him a lesson, and maybe even come back to claim his money. He choked down his anger for his own advantage. It hurt him, it was not easy. He was battling generations of grudge bearing.

"Orl right. But I will need a gun an' ammo and supplies. Food an' a tent."

"I will arrange those now. I want you to set off a-sap. I mean, as soon as possible."

"Tha'll be tomorrer, there's a big storm comin'," the first heavy drops of rain patted onto the tin roof as he said that, the warden took it as a sign of Gadd's fitness. "If'n I go nah, I'll ony hav ter wait it out stuck unner a bluddy tree. I'll go fresh in the mornin.' Nah, I need to sleep the rest of the day, make sure I haf my energy. I need a bo'ole 'o booze, now, for me pains."

The warden, feeling boxed in, complied. He felt he had struck a bargain with a devil, and accepting that Faustian deal, realized that he did not have any idea of the chance of this operation's success. But, he also felt he had no alternative, he was in Gadd's hands now, until either Saul was gone, or Gadd himself. He had no idea which was more likely and, in the interim, had better issue a lock-down, suspend the evening meal and impose an early curfew. They had to learn who was in charge. They shook hands with misgivings on both sides.

Gadd went to bed drunk and pleased with himself, he had been entrusted by management, that was a vote of confidence for him, a source of pride. And, in his own way, because he was like everyone else, Gadd did love his family, the kid was cheeky and a handful and the wife petty and a nag, but they stuck with him. The threats had literally hit home. Gadd admired that in a perverse way. He decided that to bring a boot back from Tohu could earn him a great deal. And, there was a great chance of pulling a fast one, somehow. But to get him out of the prison, put money in his pocket and get in with some elite, or other? That was a golden opportunity. This could be a nice break for sorry, put-upon Gadd. And if he didn't manage it, if he died up there, well then it didn't matter what happened to anyone then, did it?

That was the last decent night's sleep Gadd had enjoyed. Up on the mountain, he was hating the hiking, the relentless uphill, under that big pack. He had despised this sort of stuff since he was a boy, when all his friends went camping, he had preferred to drink. But here he was, a big payday in prospect, the closest he had come to a job. Gadd sniffed the still air that was trapped around the base of the trees, he could smell Saul's last fire. He was getting close, that was the first sniff he had had. He was not to be thwarted.

"You're gunna be sorry, my lad. When I gets ahold ov ya, I'm gunna av ya guts for garters. An' ol' Gadd is gunna be in the clover. Free as a bird, an' wiv' sum Shekels in me pocket. You ain' comin' back wiv me, my son, There's no way I'm spendin' a minit more tha ni av to up here is this Godforsaken wood. Bang, bang, you're dead an' I'm out ov 'ere. Quick as you can say Jack Robinson. Straight back to claim my money ov the worden and then off to the tavern. Drinks all 'round, all on good ol' Gadd. Evr'yone'll be glad to set eyes on me, all me ol' mates. Nuffin' like free booze to bring them out of the woodwork. Parasites! Wood work, that's what this is, wood work. Harhar."

With that snigger, Gadd commentated himself along, the hurried patter of his steps a pent up nervous tension. He dreamed of the good life that would see him stoned for a week and then tempt him back to prison in a month, he deluded himself again that this time it would be different. The hounding of Saul is the most solid objective, the most certain goal, he had had in his vapid life. He detested being told what to do, but he always did it. And, he relished the thought of being out the camp, and cutting someone down to size. He decided that he enjoyed the job, but that he hated the work. Gadd looked forward to taking revenge on the snob who was causing him this trouble. He was irritated, but it was nothing personal. In a way, he wanted to thank Saul, then kill him. It was not easy being Gadd, as he kept reminding the forest. It wasn't easy being "gud ol' Gadd."

The forest ended abruptly, first for Saul and then some two hours later for Gadd. Saul was glad to get out of the containment of trees and onto the precarious animal trails that wended steeply up the rocky terrain. The pines had given way to a landscape of scattered dwarf bush. A feature of this higher terrain, it survived with little competition, he could see for miles over the stunted vegetation. It was a real fighter of a shrub, with its roots in the thin and unsteady soil and, yet, it persisted through being buried in snow for almost half the year. It was the herbal equivalent of Gadd. But Saul was not to know that, as he strode majestically along, his pursuer following far behind, like a tardy retainer playing catch-up.

After the draping effect of the forest, the vistas spread out to reveal, like a maid opening curtains to greet her Lady in the morning, magnificent views down from these higher slopes. They were velvet with pines, all the way to the woolen-looking deciduous level that transitioned the mountains to the blanket quilt of the valley. With one sweep of his sight he took in the spectacle and Saul guessed that he could see more trees in that look than there were people in the City. 'Apples and oranges,' he thought, 'souls versus vegetation.' But these sprites, the Dryad spirits of the trees, even trapped in their woodenness, being out here, seemed freer than the poor shackled masses back 'home.' You can be imprisoned in your own essence, 'that which should make you free' can also be your trap. Just as, the very humanness of man means never being able to feel the openness of flight that birds take for granted. And the immobility of that giant pine consumed by fire, it had no chance to flee, it could not escape because of its nature.

That morning Saul had changed his *modus operandi*, by not making the satchel out of his jacket as per normal, but wearing all his clothing. This had entailed him leaving behind some provisions, the empty brandy flask and some implements, those he could not cram into his bulging pockets or down his craw. Gadd had, then, come across Saul's small pile of jetsam, the tin fashioned into crude pot and pan, the small, crusty, empty bags and thick shards of glass. In contempt, he kicked the neatness out of the leavings, scattered the remains in anger because there was no use to be had there. He cursed the empty hip flask, after he had sniffed the mouth and tasted nothing tipped out down his open throat.

Out in the barren rock fields, that were the wreckage of landslides, Saul had to pick his way over rubble where nimbler footed creatures had passed for years. He balanced on his staff, a prop and a vault when needed, the guard's sturdy boots, 'no, mine,' unsteady platforms in the scree underfoot. He slipped and slid, his footing unsure, on the shingle of the bone-dry trail. The whipping wind slapped his exposed skin, the sun shriveled the moisture from his face. It was exposed out there, everything laid bare to the rudiments. He closed himself up to the elements to protect his well-being, he drew up the lapels of his jacket and cowered into his clothing. Saul feared the cold weather and had no idea that the biggest threat to him was shuffling along now half-a-league behind. If he had turned and studied his wake he might have been able to make out a speck on the same bare path where he had trod not an hour before. But, his sight was cast down to his next footfall, as was Gadd's and the two carried on their slow-motion chase, an attenuated conga-line.

To Saul, the magnificence of the mountains was as a background in a painting hung in a gallery, against which a curious spectator picks out the subject. The openness of the terrain had pushed him back into himself, that sense in the forest of expansion of his consciousness was a genie being forced back into a lamp. There was so much outside, here, that his inside compensated by hardening and by setting limits, it became his foreground.

The constant breeze whistled up its rigidity to stiff, and his internal monologue started up again, a plaintive, nagging confidence building. It was his way of keeping himself detached from the awful vastness, so he did not fall into solipsism or grandeur. A reminder of the balance he needed when the volume of the mountaintops threatened to drown him out. He had to exert himself through his mumbles and muttering.

The cirrus veil was being shredded by stratospheric winds. The monstrousness of the landscape gave a glimpse into the chaos of the upper atmosphere. The wind had a deadening effect on the pursuer and pursued, the air was cold in the covered ear-canals of the men. It pinched cheeks, dried eyeballs, chilblained fingers. A change was threatening, the weather being as fickle as Gadd's appetites, his low-concentration desires. Saul shivered in his pilgrim's sackcloth, knowing his journey was likely never to end.

A shadow tracked across Saul's path, it distorted, grew and morphed before shrinking, as if pulled on invisible wires and stretched over rocks and boulders. Two others joined it and they sidled and waxed and waned through the landscape and yanked Saul's attention outside his wandering world. Looking up, he caught a glimpse of three giant rooks gliding through the air with consummate ease, like fish in water, like anything in its element. The great birds, in formation, a full fathom from stretched fingered wingtip to splayed feathered wingtip, tipped their aerodynamic heads, one after the other, in succession. They were as black as good coal, as obsidian, they seemed to absorb all the light that fell on them. Except for the one on the right, who had a tiny streak of white in the plumage around his eyes, which set him minutely apart. Then, with a quick adjustment of ebony stub beak, the ultimate tool for not being a tool at all, Saul was evaluated. Three glassy pitch marble eyes took in the unusual sight of the stationary man up-tilted, now, undignified as he gawped with a hand shading his eyes in a perfunctory salute the birds did not feel inclined to answer. He was triangulated and found wanting. Saul was adrift in this realm, where vast distances need be covered with the haste that mountain weather necessitated. He was dismissed as beneath concern. The rooks rode gravity like an opening, sliding under the skies, three holes crossing the heavens. Black, black windows of judgement and portent. They glided on the wind and all men below were made ponderous, hardly moving. It was a mockery.

"De profundis clamavi ad te, Domine!" Bellowed Saul to the world, and those words drowned in the wind like a drop of rain in an ocean.

The evanescent, funerary birds gasped full-throated cries, in echo, that was not a valediction, nor a warning even, not language at all. It was a declaration, 'we live,' said the first, 'we will,' said the second, 'we believe,' said the one with the flecks. The beasts were gone as quickly as they appeared, on the endless quest for carrion. Gadd heard the caws as they bounced around cliff and gorge, they merged and sounded like 'fight for the right to be right.' But it cannot have been and Gadd set his pace toward it, he recognized that beckoning.

"Ooh, there's gunna be a price to pay for dragging me up this 'ere 'ill. When 'e slows dahn I'm gunna catch 'im an' giv' 'im my tuppny-'apenny's wurf, makin' me work like this, when I could be sittin' aroun' wif me feet up."

Saul advanced, poling himself up the trail which did not wend back and forth in a serpentine pattern but attacked the slope with perpendicularity. He headed straight uphill, 'as the crow flies.' The stones shuffled underfoot, and he kicked them aside as he implanted the toes of his boots into the crevices afforded. Every furlong, or so, he found a bird feather in his path, they were piebald, brown and white, and silky smooth, perfectly preserved as though the bird itself had proudly given them up. They were similar to the one that he had woken to find on his chest. It was only after the third one that he realized they had been placed between rocks, poked into little crevices and cracks or just prodded into the thin layer of dusty soil. They had obviously been deliberately put there, they were secured, and Saul, just as deliberately, collected them. When he had ten he was another portion of a league further advanced and held a lovely little bouquet of feathers daintily in his left hand. When he came across the subsequent one, he had to put down the staff to pick up the new one in his right hand, place it with the others and then resume his trudge. He grew grateful for the trail marking as the path petered out, here and there, there was precious little of it at times. He scoured his way for the feathers, anticipating the next, puzzled over how they came to be there, who had taken the pains to decorate the mountain so delicately. And when, for there were no footprints, no disturbance to suggest the trail had been used by anything aside from goats, all year. Their little black pelleted leavings were set in piles here and there. Was a trail laid for his benefit, how could it be? It was impossible, and yet it wasn't because there was another. Was it connected to the rooks? How?

The ground around his feet felt ancient, it laughed at the ephemera of living things. It was beyond and above all that. This world he traversed was eroded over unknown millennia into a crumbling desert, not grown from the ground up. It was gradually exposing itself over geologic time. The two men were a blink of inconsequence. The life in the woods was organic, the world compost, growing from seed and root, reaching upward. Whereas here was hard and unfeeling, unforgiving and dangerous. All would be revealed, but they would not be around to understand.

Saul found he missed the intimacy of the trees, the chirrup chorus of the small, darting birds, the crows had overawed him. This place, the upper reaches of Tohu, was unsettlingly stark and forbidding. The sun was a spotlight cast upon his insignificant solitary figure. In the forest, there were so many shadows, 'the dreams of leaves and twigs.' In the City, the shadows had been sharp-edged, straight lines that cut light from dark, a Manichean world, but at least you knew where you stood. In the wood the shadows were amorphous, flittering, ever-changing, spreading and withdrawing. They made the solid tree trunks and branches dance with life, breathe with light. Here, above the tree-line was 'Do or Die.' The forest was the indistinct place where stories mattered, Saul felt above storytelling, this was harsh nature. The light up here shone through a man, like an electro-magnetic ray that only recognizes bone and nail, beak and claw. Flesh was out of place, a couture style that was out of fashion, 'how could you be seen in that thing?' Rock was the building block, anything else was too weak to be considered. Saul found the next feather.

Saul's handful of plumes somehow reminded him of the dawn chorus he would wake to with Leah, in the cottage. The warming greeting of blackbirds, thrush, and wren, heralding a new prospect, and the refrain was not an alarm. In fact, it was a settling, a reassurance that the ticking-over of the days was on schedule, and that the sun had risen again. The sun as provider not as punisher, as source not as commodity. What noise would the birds make if they awoke on Armageddon? Would they sing their same refrains? The ones their ancestors have sung for hundreds of millions of years? The ones they sung in a swamp-land before the idea of the City, and when the mountain tops were pristine? Or would they sing a different verse, the next one, the secret one they were holding back for just such a moment? That song would be the one to raise the dead not to greet the living. To warn and not to comfort. Saul prayed that there was that power there for the birds to keep conjuring up the world, for he did not want it to die, nor his part in it to end. He prayed that the birds could force the sun to rise and the Earth to turn. He picked up the next feather.

He did not want to be in a world made for the imperious raven, in its entirety and its singularity. He yearned for the complexity of the billions of interactions that made up a moment of the richness of life. The raven searches for disaster, feeds off death, he is an omen looking to draw Saul into his sinister existence. He looks as if he hates the word "enemy," that the future he heralds has no place for dissent. That the planet would, and should, and could, be made in his image is a perversion of the Good. A world where all is potential carrion, which values scavenging, killing, survival of the fittest, 'nature red in tooth and claw.' Which does not hope to overcome the baser laws of nature.

In short, the world of the metronomic Gadd, marching up the slope, bringing in his devilish self, a corvine justice.

CHAPTER SIXTEEN

The next day at noon found Saul still climbing, even as he felt the ground easing off its slope. He had spent a disrupted night cold and hunched in a thicket of the hardy, thorny bush. There was no fuel for a fire, and he ate pinches of the dry 'forest-bread' that had milled in his pocket, picking the crumbs from the seams. He drank the last of his water and discarded the bottle, he was without sustenance now. He had not slept, at least he was not aware of sleeping, he may have dozed off, he had shivered a great deal. The woody vegetation gave no cover from the night weather, the wind carried the cold into his refuge and poured it down his neck. It was a symbolic hide, for he would have fared as well in the open, he futilely attempted to cover himself with leaf litter. Each time he had moved, his cold body came into contact with an even colder piece of his clothing. It was a thoroughly miserable night and it was, also, as much as he thought he deserved. He was a willing sufferer, but suffer he did.

Gadd rested for the equivalent amount of time, during the darkest hours, unlit by the lambent, milky moonlight. He laid down on the path, feeling no transgression for blocking a thoroughfare. Although he covered himself with all the available material haphazardly stuffed into his pack, still he was cold, still he whimpered. But, Gadd did not consider himself deserving of suffering. He complained, and he accused, and he wanted someone to pay. He cursed the ground and the sky, he blamed the warden, he vituperated the very idea of Saul.

Now the sun was at its pathetic zenith, and with each step Saul tucked under him, he lowered his leading foot an infinitesimal length more than he had lowered it the step before. He hoped, as he lifted his ancient foot from the stability of the past and kicked it through the enemy air, that the future was going to be solid enough to hold him. Slowly, the rock and dust in front, at eye level, began to fall away and the horizon, just above, peeled back. A rather lunar landscape was revealed, as he picked his way over the saddle of a pass. This, he assumed, was the high point of his venture. He could feel the altitude, he had to work at his breath in a way that was alien to his chest, he was aware of the vascular muscles around his lungs bellowing, in and out, and still he felt short of oxygen. The thinness of the air weakened his system, but it concentrated his mind on the economy of his actions. Saul slowly crossed the high bald plateau, where even the gnarly shrub could find no purchase, which left just the wispy grasses. He had to pick his way through the fields of boulders growing lichen on their northern faces.

He then started to descend the other side which put him past the divide where the drainages then coursed down to the City, not back to the prison. This was a boundary crossed, but it was a hollow homecoming, empty of any deep sentiment. His speed increased with the change in terrain, gravity pulling him. It was a relief after a week of climbing, but it did not seem to be a climaxing, a summiting. It was just another milestone on his trip, albeit a metaphoric halfway point. The Upper Downlands were below him, he was heading in their direction, the intimation of the familiar enticed him on. Memories reeled him back and empty promises that needed to be fulfilled. An hour later, Gadd felt the opposite, as though he was crossing into hostile territory, leaving home, and it heightened his resentment.

"Bluddy 'ell. If'n I don' catch 'im soon, I'm gunna 'ave to climb back up. Sod that for a game of soldiers! I'll be buggered if that arse drags me too far. 'Ere goes."

With that, he moved up a gear and into a loping jog, except his stride was so truncated it was more of a shuffle. As it flopped about, the backpack slapped him and geed him on, like a jockey riding a horse on the home stretch. His speed increased and, as he crossed the saddle, an hour after Saul, he started to cut markedly into the latter's advantage. He had an instinctive sense of flight and fight, of track and trap.

Saul trekked onwards, unperturbed and oblivious, as serious and blinkered as a philosopher wrestling with obscure questions of ontology. A *flâneur* who feels the answer is within reach but is not to be rushed, and not one who is trying to outrun ignorance, or put distance between himself and nescience. There was an imperceptible jauntiness to his walk as though he were about to cry out, *eureka!* Or maybe it was a looseness, as the tired hamstrings handed the workload over to the unsuspecting quadriceps. His faithful staff now reached out in front of him, and searched the path for suitable landing spots that were prodded then gained. In the same way his curiosity reached out in front of him, tested the foothold and let him proceed. Another feather!

"What bears no weight can be used to explore." The tip of the pole hovered in the air before being shaken into the forward position, a backstop no more, but a vanguard.

"Zu sein es zu tun. Zu sein es zu tun. Zu sein es zu tun . . . ."

Saul had to negotiate a few awkward descents on the way. At first, slip became slide as the loose gravel, between the tufts of dead grasses that were sparse carpet-knots in the soil, gave way underfoot. Then the land plummeted over the near horizon, following the debris he kicked loose. Dry rivulets became gullies, that split into ravines, rent into the hillside. The providential feathers still confirmed his way, like Hansel and Gretel's trail of breadcrumbs. They led him on a plumed treasure hunt. His curiosity as to their provenance had passed by him, he collected them as one harvests fruit in the proper season, for later.

Gravity flowed between the sheer walls that, at another time, funneled spring snow-melt into waterfalls. Periodically, Saul had to turn around to face the rock, and then ladder himself from shelf to shelf, to keep all four limbs securing his body. Then, the staff was an encumbrance that he would throw ahead and collect, like a game of self-fetch.

Occasionally, the ground would level off, then Saul could brake with his heels, a severe test of his balance. 'Nice and slow,' he told himself. It was a strain on his joints, which were much older than his ambitions. He could only advance with deliberation, he had to think about his next step, the consequences mattered. Weakened as he was, his cautious movement gained a grace almost royal in its restraint, 'but it was slow.' Gadd was built better for covering this terrain, his shorter physique allowing for a safer scramble, he would leap down from ledges, hope he could get purchase. And, he would trust his luck as he trusted little else in this vindictive world. Even if the pack slowed his progress, as its bulk rode him, even then Gadd closed inexorably in on Saul, for he was the one who knew he was in a race. Saul flounced without caution.

Then Saul started to see the forest appear again before him, but not the same forest, or rather a different part of the same one he had left the previous morning, that had skirted the peaks he had crossed, a vast blanket punctured by Tohu in the center. The forest was the hair on the tonsured head of the mountain, Saul was a flea. To him, the crossing had been a step into a different dimension and now he was returning to his own. The crest was a tipping point, and he knew about those, he had experienced so many that he felt nauseous, and this side of the forest was a new Eden. One that was worthy of being inscribed on a picturesque bedroom wall. One that contained the innocence that he had moved through, and that by coming full circle, *via* a short-cut, he could have a second chance to attain. It was his Elysian Fields, where his soul could find its concord, and *requiescat in pace.*

After meandering through the familiar stands of trees, interspersed with brush, in the lee of the mountains, the forest suddenly erupted again. It appeared like a wall in front of him, but one that held an endless number of open doors, welcoming Saul into its dark embraces. It still felt as if a distinct forest boundary was breached, 'as though a 'no tree' sign was suddenly ignored,' and once inside, Saul felt protected and hidden. It was safer because he was decidedly less exposed. He had felt glad to leave the forest back on the windward side of the mountain, and felt as glad to enter its other arm. He had crossed the desert, that fractured and desiccated land, and had made it back. There was a fecundity he could take part in, a chance to forage for food, to find shelter after the windswept vulnerability of the high plateau. The pine scent hovered in the stiller air, there was bird song. He plunged deeper into the heart of the forest, following the natural trails that veined the floor, that drained the woods.

After about an hour, he came to a flat meadow, green with late summer grasses. In the middle of the open space he could see a structure, but it was not big enough to qualify as a building. As he approached with a vagabond's suspicion, he could see that, 'no, it was more of a cairn,' cemented into permanence. There was a peaceful hush around the space, almost reverential, spectral but not frightening. The warm air was not bestirred by any intrusive wind, the trees seemed to be staring down at him to see what he was going to do.

Saul pushed on to inspect the rock pile, the first thing constructed by the hand of man he had encountered for a week.

From the back, he saw it was made from mortar and granite. About chest high, it stood alone, a gravel bed surrounding the wider base like a stone moat. Saul heard the curious crunch of his step, as he edged around to the front, as the noise of civilization, an unnatural sound he had not heard in a while. The short pile was a monument, so a slightly tarnished brass plaque attested. A testament to a tragedy that had occurred on this very spot, a year and a half ago. Saul remembered the event, it had happened that fateful day before he had been summoned to address the Security Service, with 'what's-his-name,' that Confessor, the Father . . . 'Timon, that was it,' Saul's first victim. How could he forget that? He couldn't.

Saul's memory spilled like the grubs, and stink of infection, from a split in the bloated carcass of a long dead past. He recalled the barriers, the damned-if you-do moments, the compromises and the resentments, the last straws, the end-of-the-tethers, the cul-de-sacs of his own life. In short, what had brought him here. He remembered the schoolchildren, here he squinted at the plaque to see how many, fifteen, 'terrible,' then the avalanche, the headlines in the newspapers, the tut-tutting of the faithful faced with undeniable hypocrisy yet again. The splintering of Timon's head with that brickbat, the feeling of the death blow, his Grandfather's old hunting knife. Leah, 'where is she?' Esther, also? It was all such a long time ago, 'all so far, far away.' Saul turned and noticed the familiar asphalt of a road at the end of the gravel path. He saw the steep hillsides with the fallen timber, that must have been the path of the avalanche, the new growth starting to hide the old destruction. There was no traffic on the road, no vehicles had passed since his arrival, no reason for him to hide anymore! Saul turned back toward the memorial, overwhelmed by the emotion the memory had dredged up. And talking of maggots . . . .

He saw Gadd on the other side of the structure, leering at him down the barrel of a rifle, which was impolitely pointed at Saul's head, at that little spot right between the eyes. He could only see the firearm at first, not the man aiming it, who seemed to be hiding behind the thing. It was an innocent metal tube, Saul could even see a little way down the barrel. It looked benign, really, as though water could start to trickle out of the spout, or a smoke-ring comically appear.

Saul thought he recognized the gun, although they all look the same from the sharp end, and then felt the fear he ought. He could not imagine the violence of the contained explosion, the projectile splattering his brains. He could only visualize the outcome, and he was not in that future, his body was, but he was not a part of it. Saul dropped his staff, and as Gadd's eyes followed the stick as it settled in the grasses, Saul's attention focused on Gadd's face as he lowered his sights.

There was a lop-sided smirk forming a bristled dimple on the left cheek, the right was distorted by being pushed into the stock of the rifle, even as it relaxed. The beady eyes were piercing and, because they were not darting around, searching, Gadd had a different look. He did not look like a cornered animal, but he had a penetration that Saul had not seen before. Gadd seemed serene, a man with a mission who was just about to execute a plan, and Saul had a hunch that he was that plan, yet he felt no panic. He thought he had the measure of his bunk-mate, he always had, and so he smiled in greeting, he even bowed slightly. This was the hubris that snobbishness throws up. Gadd spoke first, as befits the man with the upper hand.

"'Ello, Sol, 'ow are ya? Fancy bumping into you out 'ere. Bet I'm a bit of a shock, ain't I? Well, I've been sent to teach you a lesson. Jus' fink of me as your teacher. That's a turn up for the books, eh? Used ta be you lernin' me, now the tide has turned. Now, you godda lissen to me. I'm the boss. You bedder do what I say. First off, step back, keep your distance."

Gadd signaled Saul to head toward the road with a wave of the muzzle. Saul complied, turning his back on his hijacker, so he did not have to walk backwards. 'No, not hijacker, guard!' He also thought it showed an ease with the situation, he wanted to appear calm, and at least as collected as Gadd was. Saul could not decide whether to hold his arms up, that stance of surrender, but Gadd was not demanding it and, so, he held his arms out. He felt hot in the afternoon sun, which stared out with fascination on the scene, and so he signaled to Gadd and slowly shrugged off his jacket. It was a calculated move and ordinary enough not to be threatening. Yet now, because it was unsolicited, it showed a shift in authority. Saul did not raise his hands back up after letting his jacket fall to the ground, but let his arms hang by his sides.

"Wha' are ya doin'? Don' do anyfink 'til I tells ya, OK?"

"Sorry, Gadd. I didn't mean to upset you." Saul turned around to face him, managing a thin smile of acknowledgement and complicity. "Should I put my hands up?"

Gadd's expression was hard, but Saul saw a small glint of famil-iarity in his rat-stare. He let his smile spread to a grin of greeting. "How are you Gadd? You look well." He lied. Gadd visibly relaxed, his shoulders dropped a notch.

"What do you want? Are you going to take me back in? I don't think I want to allow that to happen."

"Did ya know that tha' guard did'n die? No, course ya don't. Well, he's a nidiot, but 'e's alive. But you ran, tha's bad, Sol, tha's baaad. I'm the one with the gun 'ere. But, don' worry. I'm not here to take you back in. Not sure how I'd do it anyway. I fink it all ends 'ere."

Gadd pressed his cheek into the rifle, lovingly, and tensed his whole body, as though in preparation. Saul felt a frisson of fear shudder his instincts. 'Was this it? So quick, so meaningless?' He had walked a million miles, had endured the tortured twists that a vicious fate could contrive, all to bring him to his knees, and still he had walked on. The betrayals and humiliations that seemed designed to make him crawl had not been effective. Still, he walked on. The deprivations that should stop a man in his tracks had not stopped him, still he had walked on. He was a living testament to the resilience of human nature, that basic instinct of preservation. And still he walked on. He had walked from being a slave to a Man into the freedom of the forest, from a means to another end to an end in himself, from a part to a whole. It should be celebrated, not terminated, not expunged. It was a victory, being here, by this monument to a feckless God worshipped by those with scales on their eyes, not a defeat by a mangy cur of a man. A man with no finer feelings, no insight, no clue, yet a man with a gun. *Homo Ballisticus.* The endpoint of human evolution, human development, the ultimate weapon that allows, finally, might to rule, might to receive its rightful place. The pen is not mightier than the sword when the sword cuts off the scribe's hands. Desperation rose from dejection.

"Now, Gadd, be careful. Do not act in haste. Do not do anything that cannot be undone. I have never harmed you. I was your friend. I listened to you. I understood you. I cared for you." But there was a strange transformation in Gadd's clenched features, a light in his eyes that normally presented blank, a furrow in his dirt colored brow, weather beaten and dusty. There was a pursing of the lips in a hint of intelligence, which was quite becoming. But all this was obscured by the pointed rifle, its barrel a single indifferent eye judging Saul. It was hard to see past this last hole. The weapon was no more the tool than the shooter. Saul balked.

"Sol. Sol. Sol. You always looked dahn on me, din't you?"

Gadd's thick accent was ameliorated. He spoke slower, more assured, as though his speech were worthwhile. Saul wondered if the moment of death always had this transmogrifying effect on the executioner. Hell, it would be nice if some good came out of all this farce.

"I had it all planned out, how this would go down. I'm smarter than ya know. You think I'm stupid, but I put on a show for you. I bow and scape and say 'yes zir and no zir' and you all fink, 'gud 'ol' Gadd' only half a brain but he respects his bedders. He knows where his bread is buddered, where the munney is. Well, me ol' mate, looks like I'm the one with the budder an' you are the one who should respect his bedders because they 'as a gun aimed directly at your noggin. An' this fing will make mincemeat of your educaded brains, like an 'ammer on a melon. Are you ready?"

"Now, Gadd. Old friend. Don't be hasty. You know you can't trust them. Whoever put you up to this. Was it the warden? Think about it. He has always lied to us, you can't trust him further than you can spit. You know, when you get back, he'll just shove you in the Brig. Accuse you of escaping, probably shoot you in the back and tell the superintendent that they caught you red handed, in the act. You know there won't be money and freedom, just more humiliation and anger. More locks and kowtowing."

"As I said, I'm not as green as I am cabbage-looking. Now, take off your boots. Don' ask, just take 'em off. OK, I'll take 'em off for ya after. I'm still doing stuff for ya, even now. I can't win wiv you lot. Even with the gun I can't have the upper hand. So. I'm not relyin' on you to 'elp me, I'm takin' wha' I can. The warden is a bastard, but 'e's my bastard because he can make or break me. You, you aren't worf tuppence now. You can't do anyfing for me. Your yuseless. I've made up me mind. I'm not taking you back. I've got a job to do, this is it. I can't afford to be stuck out 'ere in the back 'a beyond, like you seem to want to do. This is bluddy 'orrible 'ere. 'N where would I go, if I don' go back? I don't 'ave anywhere that wants me, don' 'ave any friends, they know where my fam'ly live. 'N I'm not going to live like a scumbag beggin' in the cidy, tha' ain' me. This is a fing for me, you don't realize wha' a chance this is. I could be an 'ero if I get back with yer boots. I could 'ave a nuvver chance. 'N I ain't be given many of them up to now. Your doin' me a favor 'ere, an' I wanna fank you for that. Consider it a payback for all that stuff I got for ya. You know, all tha' food an' then you drop me in it by runnin' away. That ain' wha' friends do for each over is it? Now, I'm tired ov talkin', its not doin' any ov us any good. 'N me arms ache. Do you want to turn aroun' Sol? So you don't see when it 'appens?"

Saul was about to decide whether it was worth turning. He was Gadd's property here, Gadd called the shots, and he was at this scatological peasant's beck and call. He could not lunge at him, Gadd kept his distance, and Saul was weak and did not know if he had the beating of him. Running would be fruitless, Gadd could pick him off anywhere within three rods, besides which, bolting would just invite the shot. Saul's best bet was to keep him talking, negotiating if possible, but there was nothing Saul had that Gadd would want. A few pages of Pessoa? The staff, he could just take. Then . . . .

"I have the guard's cigarettes, if you want them?" 'Buy time, buy time.'

"Well I figure everything you have is mine at this point. But, hey, fanks." Gadd hesitated, thinking, much to Saul's hope. "I do have one thought, one question I want you to answer."

"Absolutely, my friend. Shoot. No! Don't! Just an expression." 'Keep talking.'

There was, again, a slight grimace of humor on Gadd's dogged face. But deep down, he knew that however Saul had reacted to being caught the outcome would be the same. Gadd was not susceptible to charm, for he was charmless himself. If he fell for a soft sell occasionally it was because it was good enough, that was all. If it did dawn upon him that he was being manipulated then he would react with violence, it was automatic. Gadd said that he liked integrity in people, he expected it, and when it was not in evidence he was insulted. But, having none himself, he could not recognize it. He constantly mistook loyalty for integrity. It was a strange brew of expectation and disappointment to find in an ostensibly simple man. And it was not, by any means he could see, to Saul's benefit.

Gadd liked Saul, that was a shame to him, he did not want to kill him, but he must. Needs must. It had to be done and Gadd was the one there with his finger on the trigger. If it had not been him, they both would agree it would be somebody else. The end seemed to be here as there was a lack of reasons for it not to be. Saul could see a difference in his antagonist, he was calmer than he had been in the camp, and he himself was also less distracted, but having a gun trained on you will do that.

Saul had nothing that Gadd wanted. That much was plain, and it was hard to think what would have swayed the executioner, a kind word, a note of sympathy, friendship, wealth and celebrity? Nothing that Saul could provide, or wanted to, given all he had gone through. It would be a betrayal of his life to grovel now for a life diminished by that very method of salvation. The main point he had learned, at great pains, was to be true to himself and his heart. Buying off Gadd for a few more years of breathing was the opposite of that. The point here was to die with dignity, that was the lesson. To go out with integrity, even if Gadd would never spot it. It made no difference.

The seconds ticked silently as the wind rustled a few higher boughs. Dusty pine scent stuck to them both. Gadd decided he was getting bored and that he should finish this task and get on with the next, hopefully to one that would yield more pleasure, for there was scant joy to be had in this forest clearing. Saul coughed in embarrassment and resigned himself to his fate. He was tired of answering questions and did not pursue that last one.

"Oh, well. Sol. Nice knowin' ya. I fink you answered that question."

There was a thudding noise like a heavy, apoplectic bird falling to the ground from the skies. It did not seem in keeping with the program, here, it was out of place even in this grim scenario. Then Gadd's eyes widened to their fullest extent, in a paralysis of surprise, and he looked confused, utterly baffled, as though his world had suddenly been turned upside down and shaken. His mind seemed to grope for meaning, and he looked as if he were just about to ask Saul what had happened, for some explanation.

Saul stood there, unable to seize the opportunity, suffering a contagion of shock. The rifle fell heavily from Gadd's grasp and bounced on the gravel. Saul stared at this change of heart, he wanted to thank Gadd, but he saw his executioner stiffen and lean forward like a toppled tree, stiff as a board. Gadd was dead before he hit the gravel, and the fall revealed the shaft of an arrow embedded in his back. It stuck out of his jacket where the backpack had rubbed the color from the fabric, between the third and fourth ribs, at a slight angle to the plane of the back. Saul rather stupidly wondered if it had been there all along. Then, he decided it must have been the arrow that made that thud. It was a good shot, delivered by an expert. Saul looked over to the edge of the wood from where it must have been shot and saw an impassive man very, very slowly, with a minimum of effort, lowering a bow. 'A savior? A savior!'

The man turned and left the scene with a calmness and surety that made Saul wonder if this was commonplace. Perhaps it was, and that intrigued the unbidden Saul to where he could not but follow the receding figure that merged into the shadows of the forest. At least, that was his explanation when later, to himself, he tried to make sense of his rescue. The man started walking with a phlegmatic indifference to the corpse he had created, and also to the soul he had spared. That spared soul seemed to intuit that his benefactor would not wait for him, and so Saul grabbed Gadd's pack that was resting up against the structure and threw it onto his back. He pulled the arrow from the lifeless body, so he could roll Gadd over to get a last look at his face. He did not know why he felt the need to confront, but, gazing into the serene face, bade his onetime associate a final farewell. 'Although I doubt he can fare at all in his state.' Saul was glad to leave Gadd looking peaceful at last. It was the least he could do, he thought.

He then threw the bloody arrow away and scuttled off in a crouched run after the mysterious figure. For the second time, Saul elected not to take up the rifle for out of everything, truth be told, it scared him the most. Gadd's assailant had no need of it, so why would Saul? The man did not stop to pick it up, or roll Gadd over to say goodbye, and he was obviously to be followed. It was clear to the overburdened and harried Saul that the elegant stranger knew where he was headed. The man would not respond to any attempts to hail him, nor reply to any questions, and he did not try to dissuade Saul from accompanying. Unless, thought the straining pursuer, 'his pace was designed to throw me off.' Saul tried to settle into the expedition. He was thankful for this, what seemed like extra, time, although he was not being given a chance to enjoy this new lease on life. The uncomfortable pack bit tightly into his shoulders as he struggled to keep up.

He caught the stranger and grabbing his attention, which seemed in short supply, said:

"Thank you."

Saul received no reply and thought, 'this is going to be interesting.' He berated himself that having been thrown a lifeline, having been granted the grace to meet a savior, he could only comment on how entertained he was at the outcome. But, there was little alternative for him, he had come this far with no set plan, it seemed perfectly natural to tag along. Even if just for the ride.

"My name is Saul. Yours is . . . ?"

Nothing.

"Are you going far?"

Perhaps there was an alternative for Saul, to not treat the taciturn stranger as benevolent because he had saved him once. But that would show no appreciation for Saul's weariness. Having been raised in a society where faith in the *status quo* had been compulsorily enforced, and then having had his faith shattered, his wish to believe needed to be exercised. Having been reliant upon his own resources since being expelled from the proper company of others, his soul craved a little solace of fraternization. This stranger's presence seemed to be a gift, or a message, or both. It could not be ignored, this quest for truth and meaning and, maybe, he had found a prophet, or rather he had been found by one. But he did not know what that message was, or even if it was the right one. It was not as easy now, as it had been before, when he was told what to believe. It was not as easy as when he could be the reactionary. The deed could have been that of a man with a bow seeing an injustice and righting it, not wanting to stand on the sideline. And, certainly, if that was the fillip that shot an arrow through Gadd's black heart, then Saul needed to listen, that was a prompt he had been waiting for.

"Do you live out here?"

The man continued on, deadpan, but with a stately mien, the noble and practiced confidence of a being in his natural setting. Saul jogged behind, having to break into runs to keep from dropping away, puffing and tripping as he went. The retreating back of his deliverer did not tilt or lurch, pitch or yaw, but the shoulders, broad and muscled, seemed to glide on an even glide plane. The moving body below absorbed the unevenness of the forest floor, the shapely head above rolled, in order, it seemed, to pinpoint the senses. His grace showed up Saul's clumsiness, made him ungainly by comparison, although, truthfully, he was awkward in the absolute, just as the man was grace personified.

"Where are your people?"

He wore only a skirt of deer hide, a material that was unfamiliar to Saul, who knew only it was some form of leather. It formed a living flow of casing that almost perfectly matched his skin in its golden coloration. His limbs moved with a practiced ease, there was a perfect equilibrium in the movement of his body, all his efforts appeared almost choreographed. He was shod in a moccasin, but they were mere coverings as his feet, naturally splayed, which did not stomp on the ground, but seemed to grasp it with prehensile toes. They seemed to grab a loving embrace of the earth, and then pull the solidity they encountered up the strong legs and into the skirt. There was a quiver slung over his back, containing five delicately fletched arrows, works of art in themselves, fashioned out of cedar. The willow bow was over the other shoulder and the shaft kept the pouch steady. This left his hands free to balance and counter balance his stride as he would vault logs, leap ditches and pick his footfalls in a way that left poor Saul feeling rather inadequate.

When there was a pause in the progress, after a succession of Saul's pleadings for rest, the man turned his full face to his follower and stood waiting, as though counting out a precise allotment of time. He cut an inscrutable figure, his composure unruffled and probably imperturbable; 'definitely imperturbable.' He would not venture any information, let alone an explanation, yet Saul had the feeling that his questions were understood, they were just not deemed worthy of response. He chose to cease his hectoring and soliciting, if there were details to be forthcoming, he would be patient. He was accomplished at waiting.

It was as though this savior was built out of a separate substance to Saul, not only to a different plan but out of another material entirely. A difference of sort not just of kind. The man, if such he was, took from his waist band a feather, the same as made the flights of his arrows, and, ignoring Saul's reach to accept a gift, placed it in a log that had fallen across the trail, so it stood up and proud and visible. Saul took his collection of the same from his pocket and handed them to his guide, who received them with no acknowledgement, and Saul did not feel rebuffed, although he did not want to part with them.

The man reached into a pouch in the front of his loincloth and brought forth a crystal, clear and translucent. It shone against the man's brown, lined palm as he offered it to Saul. In return for the feathers? Saul took the knuckle-sized gem, its facet's glinting in the low forest light as though illuminated from within. He delicately held it up to his face to study the compelling object, and could see the man turn away. Saul hastily, but carefully, placed it in his shirt pocket, next to his heart, and hurried in pursuit.

Saul felt an awe he had not experienced in another's presence before, as though he were standing in front of an alien from another planet. A being not human at all, just made to look like one so as not to frighten the natives. He stared into Saul's eyes, an unnerving piercing that Saul wished to avoid but found he could not, it would have been unthinkable to do so. His stare was so open it seemed to emanate from inside his skull and the eyes acted as prisms to distort the real man inside, who was too potent to be comprehended directly. Like looking at the sun. Yet, the man was absolutely present, there was no dissemblance, the man was completely there. The crystal was like a piece of this essence that had been offered to a lesser being.

The warrior's long, night-black hair was plaited on the hemispheres of his skull, and the ropes hung down, behind his ears, to brush his shoulders. The manes framed his rugged, strong-featured face. The nose was long, and almost preternaturally straight, firm as a beak, that could savor every breath. There was a wisp of beard on the chin, and, more noticeably, on the upper lip, either side of the carved philtrum under the identical nostrils. The hair having been cut, and the jaw never shaved, there was no unkempt beard, unlike on Saul's scraped and ravaged face. He wore soft down, just long enough to follow the natural lines of the face. His skin, exposed to the elements, was of a uniform color and smoothness, a consistency that mocked Saul's patchiness, just as his steadfastness contrasted with Saul's fickle character. His irises were brown, a bronzed nut shell brown, like polished hazelnuts against the clear whites of his eyes.

The man's cheekbones stood very high on his face, as Saul noted, causing an almost flat platform under the eyes. Two stripes of white clay were smeared there, leading from the bridge to each ear, the effect enhancing the natural symmetry of the face. Against this specimen, Saul felt unformed, ill-bred, but this was purely his own comparison. He felt no judgement from the other side, there was no resentment. Saul knew this was a lesson to be learned and he was eager for the truth. Not just any truth, not just some truth, but something lasting and pure. He felt privileged to be in the presence of this commanding serenity. It was a long time since Saul had felt this secure.

Saul wondered how he had arrived here, in this place at this time, and guessed that he was not quite in charge of this situation. It was a stark revelation for Saul, whose journey over Tohu had reinforced his sense of his own destiny. He had achieved this pinnacle, 'Liberty' he called it, and then Gadd had tried to rob him of it, at gunpoint. It was an attempted mugging, an extortion with menaces, from which he had been rescued by this mystical ghost and he felt compelled to follow. Having risked his life for freedom, Saul was prepared to throw in his lot with a stranger and become an acolyte.

In thrall, whatever this man was selling Saul wanted to double his order. He just wished the man would spill a few words, give some hint of his being, his thoughts, tell Saul what he was buying. He wanted to be given a sense as to why, as his heart commanded, following this Actaeon was the right thing. There was still a residue of his past life attached to him. We cannot ever leave the past behind.

Saul felt stuck, like a lonely wanderer caught in quicksand, whose struggle only hastens the drowning. What to do? Nothing, but relax and wait to see what is underneath the surface. To hope against hope that it is not an ending, that, miraculously, there is another life down there. Then Saul, when his silent deliverer started off again, deeper into the towering woods, followed like a dog who cannot fathom the reason for his actions, or a bird, in the autumn months, that has to obey an irrepressible urge to fly south.

They had been making their way around the nape of Tohu, along a gradient, ascending and descending as the terrain dictated, all the time in the bosom of the forest. The two of them, not always a pair, forged onwards for hours. Saul would lag and lose sight of the man and would redouble his efforts to bring him back in view. They would stop, and the man would magically hand Saul some fruit, or berries, or nuts, and water from a wooden ladle. He could make these provisions appear from nowhere. It was twilight by the time the they reached the crag, which seemed a gateway of sorts. It was a high notch in a fin of granite that stood out from the mountainside, visible from quite a distance. They saw it from four furlongs away, where it looked like a gunsight. The primitive trail they were on, tramped by the animals that spent productive summers up here, led right up to the opening and they passed through. Now they entered another realm. The man did not pause, nor alter the pace of the progress, he was implacable.

A profound tiredness, that was more than fatigue, it was a vacuum of energy within him, an empty space, overcame Saul. He lay down and fell into a sleep that was like drowning. He woke after a few hours to the man tending a fire, roasting a spitting leg of meat, the hoof still discernible sticking out the fire. The smell of food in the smoky air had roused him with a watering mouth and after a satisfying gorge of the food offered by the man, he fell delightfully back into the depths of rest.

Saul was not aware of the man covering him with the blanket from the backpack, nor of the man resupplying the diminished stores therein. He was unaware that the man left him thereafter, and that he would never see him again. He did not know that he would not have an opportunity to ask questions about his predicament, his state. Saul would have to teach himself based on his own experience. That sounded very easy, trite even, but was more than he had managed up to date.

When he woke, alone, Saul did not feel abandoned, but was thankful for the encounter, for the lead. The new morning was a blessing. He remembered the crystal he had exchanged for the handful of feathers, and patted his shirtfront. It was still there, but when he pulled it out it turned out to be dull nub of quartz, the type found in abundance in granite, the product of volcanism, not magic. It was a dull milky cream, not the brilliant diamond he thought he had put in there. Still, he kept it, close to his heart, and found that it was a totem, more than a symbol, of the being he would seek to be.

Then, refreshed and curious, Saul packed up his few belongings in his inherited baggage and set off along the trail he had left the night before. He surprised himself that he was not upset that he had been left. He relished the challenge of living, and thought he deserved the chance to make his own way. The first step he took on the path he saw a feather, stuck in the tramped dirt. He left it there, it was a reassurance.

Saul started to compose, in his head at first, tasting the words in his mouth, chewing them. The words seeped up from heaven knows where, then bubbled and boiled into a stew in his hungry consciousness. And, then he would stop and write down lines, before setting off again, following feathers, leaving feathers.

Those pages of Pessoa and that stub of pencil were his tools, the beautiful, aphoristic, printed prose was becoming hidden by Saul's scratched musings. He wrote:

"I have lost many fellow travelers

In the thickets of memory that crowd

This forest of blind pines we navigate."

His pace of walking gave it's cadence to his words. He realized that he was waxing poetic. The lines were composing themselves, he was just the screen onto which something was being projected. After the sclerotic years of scrivening, some blockage had been removed, he was writing from his heart, or, his heart was writing, at last! It was a conduit for his feelings, for his experiences as a human to be made manifest, and that made it all the more real, and therefore meaningful. And that was all he had been striving for, meaning; truth and meaning being the same. And, at least, it made the time go quicker. In fact it gave meaning to time, which passed un-noticed, for that which we understand we can accept, and let pass.

"Many a sojourn has been disrupted

By a disbanding of friends and lovers,

Whose chosen paths seem random."

Amen to that. He wondered how poor his poetry was, and then forgave the self-criticism. Doubt was to be seen for the pretender it was, it could never fulfill the role it wanted. He could dictate beauty, define it. If his words affected him, then they were worthy, and therefore beautiful. Art was the supreme, and its essence was beauty. That was what he would worship.

And that was not to decry the God of his people, whose essence is love. But the corruption of that idea that was practiced down below, had not served Saul well. They had started from 'God,' not from 'Love' and Saul resolved to start from 'Beauty' and arrive at 'Art.' However tortuous that path. He would learn from past mistakes as much as he could. He would allow himself to be wrong!

Saul, the pilgrim, was searching for the 'new man' within. Writing was to be his balm, and his salve, and his method. The search for meaning in words. This was not like writing those puff pieces whilst chained to a metal desk. This was moving through a forest, writing about moving through a forest. Which was most inconvenient for writing, but wonderfully conducive to composing. The man had left him, but not alone, and his muse glided onwards. So perfect, so absolute; to find an end in endeavoring; "and if thine eye offends thee pluck it out, and cast it from thee." There must be an Eden we can achieve, a Heaven on earth, where Justice and Love can prevail.

"Some of the lost have set up camps
Along the way, or carved farms from
Hectares of resilient wood, some
Have climbed beyond tree-lines
To orientate themselves in the maze
Of trunks that baffle direction below."

His stub of pencil was wearing down and Saul had to rest and scrape a point with the paring knife. It was his last sharp edge against the forces arrayed, his last weapon, and he used it to fashion a tool for his words. He was at last in his element. If he had ink, he would fashion a quill. He would write with charcoal, scratch words into dirt, graffiti into bark.

"They have all abandoned the search

In favor of a settlement right here
That they may become bourgeois."

Saul had been taught from an early age that he was not a suitable topic for discussion, that to talk about himself was *infra dig*. Biographies were discouraged as an entertainment, autobiographies were beyond the pale. For Saul to interject his own persona in his writing was a remarkable step. His soul flinched at the attention he afforded himself. But, to see himself as an individual was not, he realized, an act of weakness. It was an act of courage, if one was to step up to being human, having been assured that to be human was a step down.

"And I? I intend to delve
Into the underbrush whence
The dark gradient drains the forest."

Let no man tell me different, he said, let no man try to command me to strictures that bind. I am a Free man in a world of Beauty and the lauding of that Will justifies my own place here. Just look at those marvelous capital letters! The space I occupy is not a waiting in line, it needs to be worthwhile. I need to feel that none other would be more valuable in my shoes. I wish to be of help.

"I will hack at an entanglement of willows
And wishes, the spider's web entrapment,
That needs must I destroy to escape."

This he felt; that he was freeing himself from the tendrils of vines that he had let grow around him securing him in place. His feet had sprouted roots, his arms had become branches and he had become that fabled 'Greenman.' Like these red-barked giants, he had been immobilized, not by a rootedness or belonging, but by a tradition that preached stolidity. He was flexing his muscles, moving through new groves in his mind, and when he could, dragging his spirit behind like a child pulling on a kite-string, trying to keep it aloft.

"I choose to follow the impetuous flow
Of the incontrovertible River Sophus,
Her torrent plunder from wooded slope
To languid meander in delta fan."

No more superstition, no more learning by rote, no more blind faith, no more being told not to question. 'Let the human measure be my guide,' he thought, and the man-to-follow, the Everyman, strode on unabashed, unwavering, as the truth is supposed to do. Determined, set in conviction, in lockstep with nature.

"To her communion with the fate
That gravity and kinesis decree
Where the implacable sea sips the
Accumulation of every drop of
Time experienced. Raindrop to teardrop."

Saul had never seen the sea. He had never had the opportunity to breathe the ozone of the coast, to see the crashing of the breakers as they hurled themselves endlessly on the rocks, to feel the sand of a beach or see the whole world move as the tide heaved in and out. He had read a romantic, idealized impression of the composition of the majority of the ill-named Earth, but he had not swum in its enormity, never felt as small as the sea can make you. He had never been so far out of his element, even in the wilderness, for gravity was still dominant. Pessoa had lived by the mighty Atlantic and had mentioned that reality just in passing, the smells of the docks, the harvest of the seas, the cries of gulls. Saul longed to know, or dared to indulge himself in imagining, the oneness of having every drop of brine linked through its neighbor to the furthest of its brethren sitting in its antipodal sea. The watery girth of the planet. It was not the same with the air, it was hard to think of the pollution of the City connecting one with the top of Tohu. But, it seemed to Saul the very epitome of sanctuary, losing oneself in infinity, realizing that this creek is a tributary of that ocean.

"Banks can barely contain the spate
Until they cannot, then are washed away
In the revered Nilotic fecund flood."

So, with us. As the River Sophus inundates the plains that the puny humans try to harness, then wisdom spills and encompasses the world. Then we wake up to the unknowable essence of reality and realize that we have to be borne on the current, where it will. Then we are powerless, and our sense of our frailty is enabling, allowing us to drift with the flow of events.

"Until a new run course carves a rill
Of un-silted channel and opens up
To margins of vistas. The coastal end.
All the river's forks are upended
Two into one coalescing, pointing the
Direction to a wisdom of understanding.
And on that beach, I hope, sight-lines
Stretch forever and the unhindered
Wide arc-view is worth having, at last."

Saul broke his pencil lead gouging out the two last words. "At last. At last." His 'grand climacteric' had passed, and all the pain of his life was dissolved in the promise of the future. He felt that he was to be made whole, in a way that the threats and promises of the others could never deliver. As though he were the world, and the land masses on his surface had come full circle to recreate Pangaea, and all the differences and the separations of life were to be healed. In Eden.

FIN

ACKNOWLEDGMENTS

To Carolyn for her patience and support. To Lauren and Tom, Emily and Ollie for encouragement. To Stephen, Martin and Simon for minding my affairs, with a particular thank you to Annie. To all my scattered family whom I hope take pride in this accomplishment. To the Salt Lake City Scribes for their help and advice, in particular Cindy, Jef, Kathy, Gene, Heidi, Nolan, Tate, Olivia, and Jae. To Martin and Dee for their love and hospitality. To Stacy Dymalski, an editor *par excellence*, Katie Mullaly at Surrogate press, and Michelle Raynor at Cosmic Design. Finally to Sputnik, Cho, Mary, Sophie and Michael for companionship and wonder.

ABOUT THE AUTHOR

Kevin Shannon was born in England almost six decades ago, and has spent half his life in Utah. When not writing, or thinking about writing, or trying (or not) to write, he sleeps, eats and enjoys the great outdoors of the American West, the place he considers his true home.

www.ingramcontent.com/pod-product-compliance
Lightning Source LLC
Chambersburg PA
CBHW071735190726
48292CB00003B/758